Into THE OUT OF

ALAN DEAN FOSTER

WARNER BOOKS

A Warner Communications Company

Warner Books, Inc., 666 Fifth Avenue, New York, NY 10103

W A Warner Communications Company

Printed in the United States of America

First Printing: October 1986

10 9 8 7 6 5 4 3 2 1

Library of Congress Cataloging-in-Publication Data

Foster, Alan Dean, 1946–
    Into the out of.

    I. Title.
PS3556.O756I5   1986   813'.54   85-40914
ISBN 0-446-51337-7

To Bill and Sally Smythe,

Who took us to the edge of the Out
Of and made it fun despite the
sweat, the lack of sleep, and
the tsetse flies,
This book is dedicated with friend-
ship and affection.

Into THE OUT OF

1

Tombigbee National Forest, Mississippi—9 June

"**M**an, look at that mother burn!"

"Sure is a pretty sight." Luther Vandorm's eyes were shining.

"Hey, BJ!" Walter Conroy called over to the stocky, vacant-looking man who stood close by. "Do me a favor, will you?"

"Sure, Walter. Anything."

Conroy strode toward him, fumbling in the pockets of his ballooning white robe. He had to steady the conical white hat that perched uneasily atop his head. Finding what he'd been digging for, he handed the compact 35mm camera to the other man.

"Get a shot of Luther and me, will you?" He showed his friend the camera, knowing that he had to keep any explanations simple. "See, it's one of those new Jap all-automatic jobbies." He flipped a switch, the camera beeped once, and a small built-in flash popped up. "Just wait till the little red light comes on in the viewfinder. That means the flash is powered up and all set to go."

The other man eyed the camera uncertainly. "I dunno, Walter. I dunno anything much about cameras."

Conroy tried not to sound too exasperated. "I told you." He spoke slowly, forming the words carefully and leaving BJ time to catch up. Everyone knew BJ was a little slow, but he was willing enough to help with anything and was much stronger than he looked. "Here—it's set now. Just point the lens at Luther and me and press this here button

1

and the camera will do the rest. Just make sure you can see both of us through the viewfinder, okay?"

"Well, okay." BJ accepted the camera with obvious reluctance. He was solidly built, deceptively muscular, with an undistinguished face and a hairline that was beginning to recede. Currently he wore the expression of a tenth-grader trying to cope with a Cray computer.

"Hold on just a minute," Walter urged him as he ran to stand next to his buddy. "Wait till I give the word." Then he was standing next to Vandorm, who managed to cram his wife and kids into the picture as well. Conroy put his arm around his companion's skinny shoulders and they all forced smiles into the camera.

They were not alone. Plenty of their friends were standing in a circle behind them, hooting and hollering as the huge burning cross threw glowing embers up into the night sky. Some of them were laughing a little too much. A definite boundary had been created around the cross. It was composed of discarded beer cans and shredded cigarettes.

BJ squinted into the flames, listening to the crackle of the burning cross, and waited while Vandorm pulled his wife close to him. She was holding Vandorm Junior in her arms. He wore a miniature white sheet outfit she'd sewed for him herself. Twelve-year-old Mike stood restlessly in front of his mom and dad. He looked like he wished he were somewhere else.

They stood grinning back at BJ until the corners of their mouths began to cramp. Finally Vandorm's wife whispered to her husband. "If you don't tell that idiot to shoot we're going to have our rear ends toasted. I can't hang around here all night, Luther. The clothes in the washer are going to start to mildew if I don't get 'em in the dryer pretty soon."

"Hush up, woman. He'll hear you."

A short, sharp laugh. "So what? He don't understand a tenth of what he do hear."

"Don't be afraid of it," Vandorm told BJ. "Just look through the little window and push the button."

"Sure thing, Luther!" BJ waved cheerfully, then raised the camera and aimed. He hesitated. "I forgot which button, Luther."

"Shit," Vandorm snapped. "The one on the right-hand side. Just push it once!"

"Okay." BJ carefully followed the instructions and the Vandorms heard the click as the shutter snapped.

"Praise the Lord," Mrs. Vandorm murmured, "he did it. Oh, damn, the baby's wet again. Mike, you stay here with your father." Trying to juggle both the infant and the awkward conical hat, she strode away

from the blaze toward the line of pickup trucks and station wagons
parked nearby, chiding the baby gently as she walked.

Walter Conroy took back his camera. "Thanks, BJ." Meanwhile
Luther Vandorm was clapping his older son affectionately on the
shoulder. In his sheets and pointed hat, the twelve-year-old looked like
an uncomfortable downsized version of his old man.

"What d'you think of all this, son? Your first cross burning, I
mean."

"I dunno, dad. I mean," he hastened to correct himself, "it's neat,
really neat."

"Thataboy." Vandorm looked proud. "Ain't he somethin'?"

"Sure is," BJ agreed.

Vandorm leaned over to look into his son's face. "And what is it
you want to do when you grow up?"

The boy took a deep breath and turned away so he wouldn't have
to confront his father's eyes. He would much rather have been home
playing basketball with his friends. You could do that at ten o'clock at
night in Mississippi in June. Even reruns on TV would've been better
than this. But his parents had insisted and he knew better than to argue.

So he recited with as much false enthusiasm as he could muster.
"I want to save America by ridding it of all the kikes, niggers, and wops
who've taken control of the government."

"That's my boy." Vandorm would have ruffled his son's sandy
brown hair except that it would have knocked off the white hat. There
was a dark stain down the front of his own sheet where he'd spilled
the Coke float they'd bought at the Dairy Queen. His wife hadn't let
up on him about that until they'd reached the site.

As Mike Vandorm was gazing at the fire a mischievous grin spread
over his face. "It would've been better if we could've brought some hot
dogs and marshmallows."

Vandorm gripped the boy's shoulder hard. "Now listen, son, this
is serious business your daddy's involved in here. Ain't nuthin' to joke
about. I don't ever want to hear you say anything like that again,
understand? Not unless you want a taste of my belt."

"Sure, dad. I was only kidding. Hey, can we go soon?"

Vandorm straightened. "I know it's a little late for you to still be
up, son, but this is more important than anything they're teachin' you
in that damn school. This is an important moment in your life and I
wanted this to be a big night for you. You don't know how proud it
makes me to have you here with me."

"Yeah, sure, dad." Mike's voice fell to a whisper.

"Anyway, your mom'll take you and Junior home soon. Me and BJ
and Walter and Mr. Sutherlin got an important meeting at the Suther-

lins' house tonight. Real important." Vandorm puffed himself up like a toad frog, trying to make himself look bigger than he really was, not only in his son's eyes but in BJ's as well.

As he thought about the meeting the air of paternal affection vanished. His expression twisted into something blind and unintelligent and nasty, the sort of look an australopithecine might once have favored an enemy with. It was prompted by a mixture of uncertainty, fear, and grim determination, all wrapped up in a basket of bigotry nurtured by twenty years of menial jobs and hard times.

"Gonna be *some* meeting. Ain't it, BJ? We finally gonna do something besides talk."

"Sure are," agreed the simple man who'd taken the photograph. Instead of evil or viciousness, BJ's face displayed nothing more complex than stolid anticipation.

Poor ol' BJ Tree. He worked nights as a janitor at the Junior College in nearby Tupelo and when you got right down to it, he didn't appear to have the brains God gave a crawfish. But he was of similar mind and feelings as the rest of them, a lot stronger than you would think, and most important of all, he was ready and willing to do what he was told.

The organization Vandorm and Conroy and Sutherlin had formed had plenty of use for a man like that. The three of them had enough brains for four anyway, Vandorm thought with pride. None of the chapter members suspected that there was a more committed subchapter operating in their midst.

"Can I go now, dad?"

"Sure, go on, git over to your mama." Vandorm shook his head dolefully as he watched his son scamper off toward the old Ford wagon parked at the far end of the line. "I dunno, BJ. Maybe he's still too young. But I had to bring him. Got to do somethin' to counteract all that crap they keep fillin' his mind with at that school. All that garbage about ecology and equality when they ought to be teachin' the kids the basics—reading and writing and good old American educational values. Got to look out for your own kids these days. Commies and homosexuals running half the schools."

"Don't I know it," said BJ. That was BJ. Always agreeable. A crash sounded behind them and both men turned to look. One of the arms of the cross had finally burned through and fallen, sending up a spray of embers which nearly set Warren Kennour's sheets on fire. He and Jeremy Davis and a couple of the other boys were so drunk they could hardly stand. Vandorm chuckled.

"This secrecy's been pretty tough on Cecelia, BJ, but she hasn't complained. No sir, not a bit. She's been supportive right down the line. It's just that tryin' to get the tuition together to send Mike to

that private patriot's school is damn near about to break us. But I'll
teach him myself before I see him play football with a bunch of
pickaninnies. Now I hear tell they got a couple of Vietnamese goin' to
school there too. I tell you, BJ," he said seriously, "somebody's got to
start doin' something to wake up the people of this country or we ain't
gonna be no better in twenty years than the dogs at the pound, just a
bunch of mongrels and mutts nobody respects anymore."

BJ nodded enthusiastically. "You said a mouthful there, Luther.
Hey, you want a beer? I got a six-pack in the car."

"That's mighty fine of you, BJ." Luther never offered the other
man a drink. For one thing, there was no point in spending the money
to keep the big dummy in suds when he couldn't remember from
whence the largess originated and, for another, BJ always seemed to
have plenty of beer on hand. They headed back toward the line of
vehicles. A few were parked on the far side of the old fence, away from
the others.

They were five yards from BJ's battered Chevy pickup when two
men stepped out of the darkness into the flickering light cast by the
slowly dying blaze.

"Luther Vandorm?" The man had a heavy five o'clock shadow and
was clad in jeans, short-sleeved shirt, and boots. His companion wore a
suit. The speaker's eyes flicked to his left. "BJ Tree?"

Vandorm's gaze narrowed as he studied the intruders. He was more
upset than concerned. Sure, cross burning was illegal, but in rural
Mississippi that still meant no more than a small fine and maybe a
tongue-lashing from some county judge.

"Who the fuck wants to know?" He didn't recognize either of
them. They didn't look like Sheriff Kingman's boys, who would look
the other way so long as there was no damage to public property. Nor
did he care for the accent of the speaker. Not from around here, that
was for sure.

The man removed a small billfold from a back pocket. When he
held it up to the light the bottom half dropped down. "Federal Bureau
of Investigation. You're all under arrest."

"Hey, what is this? Who the hell do you people think you are?"
Inside, Vandorm was trembling. Not because he feared being arrested
for a little harmless cross burning, but because of what was concealed
in the pickup next to BJ's. It was brand-new, boasted four high-intensity
lights on top, halogen fog lamps in front, a chrome roll bar, and
displayed a bright Confederate flag on the flanks. It was Walter Conroy's truck.

In the glove compartment was a small folder. Inside the folder
were the plans that he and Conroy and BJ and Sutherlin had worked
on for the past three months. The plans that described in detail exactly

how the four of them planned to blow up the office of the American Civil Liberties Union in downtown Jackson.

In addition to the pair of hunting rifles mounted on the back window rack, the pickup held a secret compartment behind the seats. Vandorm had installed it himself, working nights when the garage was deserted. The compartment contained two Uzi submachine guns that Conroy had bought in New Orleans. Considered together, the machine guns and the plans were likely to bring more than a tongue-lashing down on all of them in any court in the country.

He took a step backward and stumbled. His white hat fell off and he stumbled again, stepping on it. "Just let me get my ID." He turned and pointed toward the other cars. "It's in my wagon over there."

"Just hold it right there, friend." The man in the suit produced a small blue snub-nosed pistol. He held it loosely in his right hand—but not that loosely.

"But my ID," Vandorm whined. He'd never had a gun pointed at him before and it shook him pretty bad. He felt a warm trickle start crawling down his right thigh and saw the disgust in the eyes of the man who'd spoken first.

There was no way out. More men in suits had appeared and were rounding up the rest of the celebrants. The station wagon was gone and he thanked God Cecelia and the boys had gotten away before the bust had come down.

Two new vehicles drove in on the dirt access road and pulled up in the parking area. The big vans had little bars over the windows, just like on TV.

He could see what was coming as clearly as he'd seen the porno film that had unspooled at Sutherlin's last weekend. All their planning and careful preparation was going to go down the drain. The dynamite and blasting caps and expensive Uzis would be confiscated. Just when they were ready to do something and wake the country up a little, this had to happen.

How had they found out? Who'd given them away? He slumped. Maybe no one had given them away. Most likely this was just a routine roundup. The government men probably knew nothing of the plans or guns. But they'd sure as hell find out when they searched the truck. And they would search the truck, Vandorm had no doubt of that. Of all the dumb, stinking, rotten luck!

Across the way he could see two of them going through Sutherlin's Cadillac already. Sutherlin stood nearby looking stiff and uncomfortable in his neatly pressed whites. Probably wondering what this would do to his lucrative accounting practice when the word got out, Vandorm mused. The Cadillac contained a duplicate set of plans. About the best he and Conroy could hope for was that, having found one set of plans, they wouldn't search the pickup and find the guns. His spirits lifted slightly. There was a chance the rest of them might get off light unless Sutherlin talked. He didn't know if they could count on the accountant's silence.

"You fellers are making a big mistake," he told the pair of agents who'd confronted him. "We weren't doing anyone any harm. Just exercising our Constitutional right of assembly." It seemed as though hundreds of agents were prowling through the woods, though in reality there were fewer than two dozen. Men in whites, his friends and drinking buddies, the neighbors he shot pool with, were being hustled into the waiting vans. Some of them were too far gone to know what was happening to them. Soon he and BJ were being marched across the clearing to join them.

"Don't you people have anything better to do?" BJ said angrily.

Vandorm was surprised. BJ didn't volunteer much in the way of conversation. He reacted instead of initiating. Apparently the actual arrest had triggered something within him. Vandorm was glad because it took the agent's eyes off him; those accusing, disgusted-looking eyes.

BJ wasn't finished. "Why ain't you out bustin' the Mafia or runnin' down burglars instead of harassin' regular folks who ain't doin' anyone any harm."

"Just keep moving," said the man in the jeans. His companion no longer held the pistol pointed at Vandorm. Luther gazed longingly at the shielding darkness of the woods nearby, but he didn't feel his legs were in shape for anything longer than a ten-yard sprint. What would've been the point? They had his name, had identified him at the beginning. Running would solve nothing.

It occurred to him suddenly that their chapter must have been under surveillance for some time. In addition to being embarrassed, he now felt like a fool.

The rear doors of the van gaped wide. BJ was still talking.

"It's damn wrong, that's what it is. Y'all ought to be out doin' some decent work instead of troublin' honest folks."

"Just get in, BJ," Luther told him. "You don't have to say anything to these people. Wait till Sutherlin's lawyer talks to you." He was starting to regain a smidgen of his former self-confidence. A backward glance revealed the big pickup squatting alone and uninspected on the far side of the clearing. Maybe they'd even miss the papers in Sutherlin's Caddy. They might get out of this yet!

"You guys are making a big mistake, you'll see. What did you go to all this trouble for? So you could stick us with a drunk and disorderly? A little cross burning on National Forest land? It's our damn forest! What's that gonna get us, a warning and a fifty-dollar fine? Damn waste of taxpayers' money is what it is."

"Just find a seat," said the man in the jeans. His companion gestured casually with the pistol.

"Come on, hurry it up."

BJ stopped, turned, and took a step toward him. He was smiling that silly, sappy grin Vandorm and the others had come to know so well these past several months.

"I don't 'preciate being rushed, mister—especially by ugly people. And you're just about the ugliest people I ever did see."

The agent's gun whipped up fast to crack BJ across the face and send him staggering backward. He sat down hard near the right rear tires. The first agent stepped between BJ and his colleague and grabbed the latter's arm. The agent was breathing hard, glaring down at the man on the ground. A thin stream of blood dripped from the corner of BJ's mouth.

"Jesus, Bill, take it easy!" the first agent muttered. The other agent made a visible effort to calm himself. His reply was low, barely under control.

"Easy. Yeah, right. Look, you take care of these two."

"Sure. Go and help Dave with the paperwork."

The agent nodded, staring at BJ as Luther helped his friend to his feet. The hatred between the two men poisoned what little fresh air remained in the clearing.

"You listen to me, cracker," growled the agent. "You better hope I never meet you on the street when I'm off duty, man."

"That'll be up to me," BJ replied easily, "because I'll be able to smell you comin', nigger."

Vandorm's eyes got as big as light bulbs. "Holy—Get in the damn van, BJ, come on, get in the van!" He was pushing and shoving at his friend.

"Yeah, get in," said the first agent. "Look, we're all highly trained here but we're human, too. You better get your friend inside," he told Luther sharply, "before he opens his mouth one time too many and we have a serious situation on our hands."

"Right, yeah, sure." Vandorm practically dragged the grimacing BJ into the vehicle, making sure they got seats away from the doors.

"Christ, BJ! I always knew you were slow, but I didn't think you were crazy. That guy could've killed you."

"Hell, I ain't afraid of him." BJ's brows drew together. "Are you afraid of him, Luther? You once told me you weren't afraid o' no gov'mint men." Another brace of celebrants was shoved in before the doors were closed and locked from the outside.

One trailing the other, the two vans rumbled off into the night, following the access road that led out of the forest. After a while other vehicles began to follow, emerging from concealing brush. Most of them were four-wheel drives.

Eventually only two remained. Their occupants began a thorough examination of the cars the cross burners had left behind. A couple of them started spraying the collapsing fire with extinguishers to make sure the blaze wouldn't spread to the nearby woods. They would all be there long into the morning hours and then they too would drive off, leaving the clearing ringed with a ghostly semicircle of abandoned vehicles, all facing a pile of smoldering ashes.

2

Seattle, Washington—
9 June

Merry Sharrow was taking her final order of the morning and almost enjoying it. Almost enjoying it because Mrs. Gustafson the supervisor wasn't peering over her shoulder to make sure every little box and line were properly filled out. Their shift ended simultaneously, but Gustafson had enough seniority to depart nine minutes early. Merry and her co-workers were left to carry on alone until Fred Travers and the rest of the day shift punched in.

So she was able to relax as she took the order from the young man from Missoula. He was buying his first real sleeping bag and was full of questions about loft and rip-stop nylon and the technical differences between goose and duck down. She was happy to supply the information (that was part of her job) but not to the point of staying one second beyond quitting time.

She didn't try to hurry his decision. Never rush a customer, she'd been told while training for the job. A rushed customer is an irritated customer, and an irritated customer is one lost forever.

At two minutes to eight he finally made up his mind and bought a pair of Himalayan goose down bags, comfort level forty below, five-year guarantee. He put it on his VISA card and bid her a pleasant farewell, explaining that he was already late for work. The refrain was familiar to Merry. The majority of the country was on its way to work just as she was getting off.

Merry worked the graveyard shift at Eddie Bauer. Midnight to eight in the morning. For her the rising sun signified the arrival of early evening. It wasn't as bad as people usually thought. She'd trained herself to sleep from six in the evening until eleven at night. She was free every day of her life. All pretty backwards, but her friends understood. Because of necessity most of her friends were the women she worked with. They shared the same problems, the same time-shifted lifestyles.

She totalled the night's calls and receipts, made sure all the orders had been entered into the central computer, and prepared to check out. There was no hurry. You didn't hit a lot of rush hour traffic going east out of Seattle at eight in the morning. What traffic there was was coming into the city, not going out.

Yes, she had most of her life free, even if she didn't do anything with it. Shop and sleep and watch soap operas and take it easy and if she wanted a semblance of a normal social life, there was always the weekends.

Her social life pretty much consisted of her relationship with Donald. He was a junior designer with Boeing. They'd been going together (a convenient euphemism for sleeping together) for four years. Merry was twenty-eight and getting edgy. Admittedly, it was difficult to sustain anything like a normal relationship with another human being when you only saw him on weekends. Or in the evening, when he was lively and full of energy and all she wanted to do was go to bed. Correction: go to sleep.

They managed somehow. Donald was bright, cheerful, attractive, all-in-all a nice catch. There was just one drawback. She was beginning to suspect he didn't want to be caught.

All her life she'd done what she was told, been the good girl, the complaisant woman. Maybe it was time to make some changes. No—no *maybe* about it. Twenty-eight. Nobody was going to change things for her. Her friend Amy was always telling her that. She was going to have to take charge of her life herself, going to have to force any changes herself.

Easy to say. Change a life. Take charge. Change your world. How? Where do you start?

Maybe by going home. Eddie Bauer's phone lines were open twenty-four hours a day, seven days a week. There were sixteen operator stations designed to take incoming orders. During the graveyard shift only three were occupied. By Merry, her friend Amy, and Nikki the Cat, as the part-time dancer preferred to be called. After 1:30 business usually dropped off, picking up again at 5:00 when it turned 8:00 on the East Coast. That's when people in places like New York and Boston and Washington, D.C., began waking up and spending money.

Washington, D.C. Here she'd lived most of her life in Washington state and had never seen the other. Well, why not? She had a vacation coming, they *owed* her a vacation. For some reason the nation's capital felt like the right place to visit. By God, why not? Do it, do something for yourself for a change. Don't even ask Donald if he wants to go.

She felt better than she had in months. She'd made a decision.

"You okay?" Amy was eyeing her fellow operator uncertainly. "You look funny."

"Just preoccupied." She reached under her table, recovered her purse. "Ready?"

"Sure." Amy rose. "You're *sure* you're okay?"

Merry joined her and the two women headed for the exit. "Fine. I just had a great idea."

"Going to tell me about it?"

"Later." They were in the cloakroom now, checking out their raincoats and umbrellas preparatory to making the usual mad dash through the rain to their cars. This close to the parking lot you could hear the water drumming on the asphalt. It was coming down hard and steady outside and had been doing so off and on for over a week, with no clearing in sight. The delights of living in Seattle.

Amy popped her umbrella open. "Maybe it's let up a little." She opened the back door.

Sky full of lightning, night full of thunder: black steady rain falling straight down. No wind, no nonsense, no surprises: just water.

"Terrific," Amy groused. "You know, I worry about you living so far out of town and having to drive through stuff like this all the time. You ought to move into the city. Matt and I could put you up until you found a place."

"The rain doesn't bother me since I got the Wagoneer. I just throw it into four-wheel drive, set the cruise control, and mosey on home. Besides, all the traffic's going the other way and I've got both eastbound lanes to myself. Now what you guys ought to do is move out next to me. I spend my free time with deer and birds and squirrels instead of junkies and bums."

"That's it, put me in my place, no quarter given." Amy assumed a fencer's pose and jabbed the sky with her umbrella. "And as she ends the refrain—thrust home!" She charged out into the storm with Merry close on her heels.

"You haven't got the nose for that line."

"Thank God. See ya tomorrow." Amy veered off toward a solitary Subaru while Merry struggled to unlock her Jeep. Once inside the dry steel cocoon she was able to relax. The pungent odor of spruce filled the car. The back end was full of firewood.

It started up instantly. She put it into four-wheel drive, honked twice at Amy, and turned right out of the parking lot. Thanks to the dense cloud cover it was black as midnight. She cruised up empty Stockton Road, heading for the I-90 onramp. Despite what she'd told Amy, she was tired and not looking forward to the long drive ahead.

But she loved her little house in the forest. The privacy and greenery made the commute well worth while. The house was just big enough for her, and for Donald when he could make the time to come out for a visit. She had two acres instead of two bedrooms and liked it that way. She didn't see how Matt and Amy managed to sleep in the city in the early evening and late afternoon. Peace and quiet was worth a little driving.

The muscles surrounding her left eye itched and she rubbed at it with her left hand. Have to wash it out when I get home, she told herself. The wipers threw water left and right, keeping the road ahead halfway visible. The fog lights stayed off. Because of the dearth of traffic in the oncoming lanes due to the storm she could make the drive with her high beams on.

After pushing the Wagoneer up to fifty-five she set the cruise control and crossed her legs. The all-weather tires and four-wheel drive would keep her going straight. The lights of metropolitan Seattle vanished from the rear-view mirror.

Busy night. She thought back to her last order on which she'd spent nearly fifteen minutes of phone time. Perhaps she could have closed the sale sooner, been a little more formal and less chatty with the nice man from Missoula, but she'd enjoyed talking to him. Merry appreciated nice voices. The sleeping bag buyer's had been particularly rich and resonant.

Wonder how old he was? You could never tell just from the sound of someone's voice. He could've been anything from eighteen to fifty. If she'd had to hazard a guess, she would've bet he was in his thirties. Early thirties, close to her age. She wondered what he looked like. A voice was no key. Someone could sound like Burt Reynolds over the phone and look like W.C. Fields in person. Same thing held true for women.

She knew she had a fine speaking voice or she wouldn't have been hired. Was the man from Missoula on his way to work wondering what she looked like? She glanced up at her reflection in the rear-view mirror. Amy had called her pretty, but Amy was prejudiced in favor of anything that would help to hype her best friend's self-confidence.

Her skin was white, chinalike, and she hated that. Nothing she could do about it except curse her ancestors. "Tan" was not a word that existed in the Sharrow family vocabulary, though "sunburn" loomed prominently. Pale-blue eyes and white-gold hair so fine the frayed ends tended to vanish under a bright light. A very few lingering, fading freckles marring an unlined face that was narrow without being gaunt. Small mouth, lips that seemed to double in size with the addition of lipstick, no dimples. All right, not beautiful but pretty, yes. Definitely pretty. She could live with that opinion.

Now Amy—Amy with her long red hair and electric smile—Amy was beautiful. That's what Donald called Merry. As far as he was concerned she was the most beautiful woman in the Northwest. Even though she never believed him, she never tired of hearing it. Donald's middle name should have been Charmer. Smooth, sharp, intelligent, quick-witted, he was a young man on his way up.

Trouble was, Merry wasn't sure he wanted to take someone like herself up with him. If Amy was right, someday Merry would find herself left by the wayside while Donald—good old affectionate, loving, handsome Donald—decided to give someone else a lift up life's ladder. She thought about that a lot, far more than she let on to Amy. Because in spite of the fact that she was pretty and owned her own home and had a good job and was moderately well educated and could handle herself in general conversation without taking charge of it, in spite of all that she was terrified of losing Donald. She was all of those things, but one thing she was not was confident. Donald was the only long-term relationship she'd ever had and she was terrified of losing that emotional anchor. She was much better at establishing relationships with people over the phone than she was in person.

It was one reason she liked the graveyard shift at work. She loved the night. There was none of the intensity and crowding a daytime position would have forced her to deal with.

Donald hadn't even asked her to move in with him.

So what? How much longer was she going to let other people pull her strings, push her buttons? Maybe it was time she started making some of the important decisions. Like taking her overdue vacation and going to Washington. She sat up a little straighter in the seat. Funny how just taking charge, even in your mind, can make you feel better. The feeling of exhilaration that raced through her was utterly unexpected. It was as though she'd crossed some unsuspected, invisible threshold. All that merely by deciding to take some time off. This decision-making was *fun*. And she hadn't even had to buy one of those interchangeable $4.95 self-help paperbacks to tell her how to do it. She'd done it on her own.

She was feeling so good she almost missed her exit. Be home soon. The mental planning, the thought of taking a trip that she'd planned and not Donald, had completely preoccupied her. She headed down the offramp, the Wagoneer's wheels hugging the road despite the rain.

Something darted out in front of the car.

She hit the brakes and swerved to the right, not nearly fast enough.

Something went *thunk* against the front bumper, a dull wet noise that echoed through the Wagoneer. The brakes squealed as she slid to a halt just inches from the edge of the offramp. Below the high beams struggling with the rain was a fifteen-foot hole that hadn't been there when she'd left for work the evening before.

She sat there in the car, gulping air, and leaned forward to study the drop–off. The damn highway department had been at work. She could see where the guardrail had been removed. Putting in culverts or something, she thought. Thank God she'd had the brakes relined two weeks ago. Otherwise the road crew would have arrived in the morning to excavate her. She could see herself going over the sharp drop, a split second of realization, her face slamming into the steering column, the unyielding plastic smashing her nose flat, driving through her face into her skull . . .

She gagged, felt the gorge rise in her throat but didn't vomit. All to avoid hitting somebody's dog. And she hadn't even managed to spare it. Swallowing, she put the car in reverse and slowly backed away from the pit she'd nearly plunged into. She dreaded what her headlights would illuminate on the pavement, but though she backed up several yards there was nothing to be seen but rain-swept asphalt. No large furry lump like a hunk of discarded carpet lay in the road in front of her wheels. The discovery made her feel worse, not better. She hadn't killed the animal, had merely shattered its hip or something.

Ignoring the rain, she lowered the window on the passenger side and stared at the pit which separated the roadbed from the forest beyond. It was almost nine o'clock and starting to get light out despite the dense cloud cover. There was no sign of whatever she'd struck.

It was hard to believe it had survived the collision. She'd been going at least forty down the offramp and struck it solidly. She couldn't get the sound of the impact out of her head. It hadn't been flung out in front of her and she hadn't run over it, but not even a big dog could live through a collision like that.

It came through the open window straight for her eyes, claws and black blood accompanied by a guttural growl that froze the breath in her throat and caused her insides to constrict convulsively. She let out a single primordial scream and flung herself back on the seat. The paw dug furiously, frustratedly at the air inside the car. The power window controls were set in the center console, near the gear shift, and she flailed wildly at all of them. By extreme good fortune and pure coincidence she struck the control the right way and the window purred as it closed. If she'd slapped down on the switch it would have lowered the window instead, allowing the thing outside in the rain enough room to get inside the car.

With a furious howl it pulled its arm free, leaving her lying on the seat, hyperventilating, her face full of rain. She forced herself to sit up, to stare out the window.

There it was, racing back toward the tree line. She stared after it until it had vanished back into the woods. After a while she realized another car might come along, hit her from behind, and knock her into the pit she'd barely avoided. Her arms wouldn't work. She willed them forward, willed her hands to grasp the steering wheel. The engine refused to turn over.

Please, she whispered silently to it, *please start. Don't leave me stuck out here. It might—come back.* Start, *damn you!*

The engine growled, came smoothly to life. She put it in gear and rolled down the rest of the offramp until she reached the stop sign at the bottom. There she hesitated. She had to make a right turn and she didn't want to make a right turn. Cedar Falls, home, lay to the right. But that was also the direction the visitor from hell had taken, and she didn't want to go that way because she might come upon it again.

"Don't be an idiot!" she said aloud, and that frightened her because she wasn't in the habit of talking to herself.

You're just tired. Tired, and it's raining. It was just a dog. You broke its back, you couldn't help it, you didn't see it in time. It's gone off to die somewhere deep in the woods. Probably a stray, maybe it didn't belong to some kid. The rain made you see the other things.

As she cruised down the familiar country road she found herself eyeing the blacktop ahead with unusual intensity. Her gaze kept darting unwillingly from the road to left and right as she tried to penetrate the damp darkness that still cloaked the drainage ditches and primeval woods. The storm turned the forest into a solemn, threatening wall that might hide anything.

Crazy. It was already dead or dying somewhere far behind her, back in the trees, not close to the road. There were no angry, burning eyes following the Wagoneer's progress, no vengeful, crippled wraith stalking her parallel to the pavement. *Get ahold of yourself.*

She talked to herself like that for another ten minutes before she finally started to relax. She had to relax because she was coming into Cedar Falls and the Wagoneer was doing an uneasy, dangerous seventy miles an hour. Not sensible on the narrow road. At that speed she'd finish what the animal had tried to do.

What? That was crazier still. It hadn't been trying to hurt her. It had been trying to get out of her way, and had only gone after her when she'd hit it.

Almost home. Sunlight was finally beginning to add substance to the shadows dogging her progress, chewing at her thoughts. The dark shapes haunting her imagination faded under its influence. She would take a long, hot bath and then climb into bed. First she'd make sure all the doors and windows were locked.

In Cedar Falls? Who needed to lock their doors in Cedar Falls? Yes, she would make sure everything was locked and that the fireplace flue was shut and then maybe, just maybe, she'd be able to fall asleep. When she awoke again it would be mid-morning or afternoon. The sun would be shining and the memory of the incident would have faded. Maybe it had been a mad dog, she told herself. Maybe she'd done it and the rest of the county a favor by hitting it. You couldn't tell in the dark. Certainly the way it had tried to come through the window after her suggested something beyond normal animal behavior.

The trouble was, it had only looked like a dog when she'd looked at it out of her right eye. When she'd turned away at that desperate moment and fallen back on the seat, she'd seen something else out of her left eye. Something black as night and maybe two feet high at the shoulder. Without tail or fur, smooth-skinned as a baby rat, and with bizarre triangular ears that went off in different directions.

And those claws, stuck on the ends of what surely had to be hands and not feet.

It had been looking straight at her, and that had been worse than the claws and the horrible sound it had made. Because the eyes had been a pair of fiery smears against the face. They'd illuminated a skull made of molten rubber. The lower jaw had hung loose, like a toothed tail attached to the wrong end of the body. She thought she must have broken it when she'd struck it with the car. Except it didn't look broken. It looked grotesquely natural, slobbering against the rain-slicked window, trying to rasp its way through the glass. It was not the face of anything that had ever been as wholesome as a dog, not any dog that had ever lived. It was not the face of an animal or a person but of something evil and unnatural that was less than either.

Then she'd started to sit up and had looked at it out of her right eye and had seen a dog again. None of which made any sense, no sense at all.

She shivered and the sensation ran down her back like ice water. It was just a poor damned dog, ugly and misshapen and abandoned, and now it was dying slowly somewhere out in the woods because she'd hit it. Bad judgment, darting out in front of the only car for miles around like that. Almost as if it had done so deliberately. But why? To make her swerve toward the gaping pit by the side of the offramp? Her imagination was running away with her.

On the far side of town she turned left up the dirt road that led to her house. A flickering, steadily weakening memory of those glowing eyes clung to her. Eyes that looked as if they'd been gouged out of their sockets and could tumble to the ground at any moment. They couldn't have been dog eyes. They couldn't have been people eyes. They hadn't really looked like eyes at all. But she'd seen them.

She tried half a dozen times before her shaking fingers finally slipped the key into the lock. The worst thing of all was that the thing had made a noise as it had run off into the woods. Not a sound like a child or a dog would make. She felt a little better. That proved she'd hallucinated what she'd seen out of her left eye. She had to have hallucinated it anyway, but the sound she'd heard confirmed it. Surely anything that had been run over by a car wouldn't have run off into the woods laughing.

The bathroom was just ahead, and inviting thoughts of a hot, steaming bath helped to relax her. A wild thought made her giggle. Why, if she'd slid off into that excavation and killed herself, she wouldn't have been able to take her trip to Washington.

3

Near the Olijoro Wells, Northern Tanzania— 10 June

There was no telling how old the tree was, but with a base thirty feet in diameter it surely was a grandfather among baobabs. It was a suitable place for a council of elders to meet. The gray bark had been shredded to three times the height of a man by hungry elephants and still the tree thrived. Like a gray mountain the tree was home to hundreds of creatures who flew and crawled and slithered among its bare branches. The rapidly narrowing leafless limbs caused tourists to call it the Upside-Down Tree.

To the Bantu peoples like the Chagga and Kikuyu who dominated the governments of East Africa, the branches of the baobab resembled the graceful arms and hands of dancers, dozens of dancers frozen in mid-leap.

The Maasai knew better. To them this land was simply Maasailand, a country in fact if not in boundary. They had taken it to themselves centuries ago by force and they retained control of it through their persistence and determination. They knew the truth of the baobab: that it was an old witch woman planted deep in the earth. The branches were the wild strands of her hair. So they walked carefully in the baobab's shadow lest they anger her.

The tree would have provided protection from the north wind save that there was no wind this time of year. The rainy season was not long over and it was hot but not yet brutally so. Around the base of the great tree the grass of the African savanna still clung to its brief flush

19

of green, though the yellow-brown of dormancy was already beginning to spread across the veldt.

Other baobabs dotted the landscape, spaced well apart from one another (the witch women did not like to be crowded, the Maasai knew). Acacia trees spread their leafy, flat-topped umbrellas over selected patches of earth. Close by the wells themselves grew a multitude of trees not commonly found on the open plains. Off to the west, vast herds of zebra and hartebeest, Thompson's gazelle and wildebeest dared the ill-defined boundary of a national park. Infrequently visited by foreigners, barely patrolled, it would have been a haven for poachers save for one thing: the Maasai. No poacher would run the risk of encountering a band of Maasai, for the Maasai might think he was after their cattle. The poachers carried rifles, the Maasai spears and knives and throwing sticks. The poachers stayed away. So it had been and so it would be till the end of time.

Far to the north lay the city of Arusha. A relic of German and then British colonial times, its aged buildings tried desperately to cling to their facades of pink and white plaster and stucco. As the buildings disintegrated, the community grew and throve. West of Tarangire, the park, lay hundreds of miles of nothingness interrupted only by an occasional village. East was the vast emptiness of the Maasai Steppe, a vestige of the old Africa. Hundreds of miles to the south was the great joke, the new "capital" of Dodoma, reachable only by a rutted and poorly maintained gravel road.

Here between Tarangire and the Steppe there was only heat and flies and the distant milling game.

The thick vegetation encircling the water hole offered good cover for hunting lions, but no lion would approach in hopes of making a kill until the Maasai had moved off. No matter that the twelve Maasai who had gathered beneath the huge baobab were well past their prime. A Maasai, though he makes his way from child to junior warrior to senior warrior, from senior warrior to junior elder to senior elder, is a warrior always from the day he is born until he puts his walking stick aside and lies down for the Final Sleep. The lions know this. So they growl to themselves and stay away from the water hole even as the young zebra begins to drink.

The herds of game did not fear the Maasai because they knew the Maasai will eat only the flesh of cattle and occasionally of sheep or goat. Since God had given the Maasai ownership of all the cattle in the world, it was only fair that they should agree not to eat any wild animals or even to kill them, save those of course that were foolish enough to try and prey on their cattle. The wildebeest and gazelle and ostrich knew they could approach the water hole to drink in safety so long as the dozen Maasai elders sat wrapped in their blankets beneath the baobab and talked.

Of the twelve the youngest was sixty-two. No one knew the age of the eldest. They kept their walking sticks close at hand and their brightly hued cloaks close around them. None was bent or broken, for to become a senior elder among the Maasai one had to achieve physical as well as mental and emotional perfection.

All of the five clans and most of the sixteen tribes of the Maasai were represented at the gathering. Moutelli had traveled all the way from the north of Kenya to represent the Samburu, who were not considered true Maasai because they tilled the soil but whose opinion was valued in council anyway.

As befitted their station, the heads of the elders were clean shaven. Many wore bright decorative earrings in their stretched, extended earlobes. They sat in an informal circle with Moutelli of the Samburu slightly off to one side. As no true hierarchy existed among the Maasai, anyone was welcome to offer an opinion during an okiama, or council, be he Samburu, city man, passing youth, or even an ilmeet—a foreigner. The Maasai believe firmly in the equality of men. All Maasai were equal (though just a little bit better, perhaps, than everyone else).

The Samburu might have disputed that, and so would the Bantu peoples who had control of the governments. But it was not something you disputed with a Maasai to his face, not even to an elder.

It was an extraordinary okiama, a gathering of knowledge such as had not been seen in living memory. Ordinarily two elders were more than enough to settle any problem or resolve any disagreement between them. To find three arguing a problem together was exceptional. A dozen was beyond comprehension.

For each of these elders was not merely a senior among his tribe or clan, but a laibon. Where other tribes had chiefs, the Maasai had the laibon. Instead of obtaining their reputations and positions through inheritance, the Maasai laibon gained recognition from his people because of his talents at healing and adjudicating, not to mention prophecy and divination. Laibon was a title earned, not inherited.

The eleven most famous laibon of the Maasai (and one of the Samburu) had gathered at the Olijoro Wells because each had read the same discomfiting signs. They were here to talk and to do an enkitoon-giwong, a searching out of danger, an exploration of possibilities.

While there was no ranking among them and each man considered himself the equal of his brother, there was one among them all deferred to when a final decision was required. This laibon was a little more equal than the rest of them. He was not particularly tall for a Maasai, who are tall but not as tall as the Watutsi. Only a couple of inches over six feet. Certainly he was the eldest of the group, though he did not look as old as some.

Now he rose, slowly and with dignity. Though there were no cattle to be watched he still assumed the age-old position of the Maasai herder, holding on to his walking staff with one hand and balancing himself on his right foot, his left foot crossed over and behind his right calf to add stability to the stance. He was staring north past the baobabs and the acacias, past the rolling savanna toward the distant village of Loibor Serrit, where the dirt road leading to Arusha began. Then he lifted his eyes to the sky where the moon hung, sun and moon riding the air together. A propitious time for an enkitoongiwong. He began.

"Friends and brothers, we all know why we are here." A soft and paternal voice. "We know what we as laibon must do. We must cast the stones today because none of us yet knows how to deal with this thing. I also do not know."

Loqari, who among the assembled was second in age only to the speaker, brushed the flies away from his face with his zebra-tail whisk and squinted upward. He was blind in both eyes, but that did not mean he could not see.

"Can we not show the chiefs of the two great tribes the danger they face?"

"We could talk; they would not listen. They would not believe." The man standing easily on one leg continued his survey of the northern horizon. "They are not laibon; only chiefs. Talking sense to such people is impossible."

"It is only to be expected," said another of the old men. "They cannot see."

"Not so," said a fourth sadly. "They can see but do not believe what they see. They suffer but do not feel. They will learn too late and we cannot wait for them. We must act quickly."

"We twelve must decide what to do," declared the man on one leg. "We must decide because as laibon it is our duty to decide. It falls upon us to save the world."

"A burden." Avari was one of the younger elders. He scratched himself through his brilliant yellow, red, and blue blanket of office. "It means we must save the ilmeet as well. My concern is only for the cattle and the people. The ilmeet prefer to take care of themselves. That is always their inclination." There were smiles around the circle but no laughter, which would have been impolite.

The tall speaker smiled also. "Do not be so hard on the ilmeet. There are good people among them. It is not their fault they are not Maasai. We should not dismiss them all out of hand. We have determined that in order to save the cattle we must save the ilmeet as well. What we must decide here today is how." Again he regarded the heavens.

Venus was already visible on the crest of the hills. As the sun began to set additional lights began to appear in the sky. Elsewhere the non-Maasai would be hurrying to their houses to shut out the night.

But the Maasai had no fear of the night or the lions it cloaked. They stayed there beneath the ancient baobab and continued their council.

All of them watched the coming of night. A laibon needed to know how to read the stars as well as the stones. Silently, wordlessly, they began to cast, putting aside gourd calabashes full of milk and yogurt. The stones, the special stones, emerged from small wooden boxes and steer horns. By reading the patterns the stones made against the earth a laibon was able to read the future. Each did his own reading, made his own interpretation of what the stones said. Then they would council together in the manner of an okiama and make decisions.

The casting of the stones went on for hours. In the distance could be seen the cook fires of the engang, the temporary Maasai village that was serving as host to the assembled laibon. Nearby was the manyatta, or warriors' encampment. Honored by the presence of so many respected elders, the warriors of the manyatta were being extra vigilant this night. Each warrior wished to impress the elders with his alertness and courage and so hoped for something, man or lion, to try to penetrate the village perimeter while he was on guard. But there were no attacks.

Bats fluttered in and around the great tamarind trees that lined the water hole, scooping up insects. Mongooses chittered softly among themselves down in the reeds as the laibon continued to study the lie of their stones. Occasionally an elder would scoop up his handful and spit on them for luck and to increase the accuracy of the next reading. They carried no torches, but the light of the swollen moon looming over the veldt shed more than enough light for them to see by.

Impatient and hungry, the lions moaned in the distance, waiting for their chance at the water hole. It was a long, drawn-out sound, like a giant stretching in his sleep, as they talked the lion talk to their mates.

At last all save two were done casting: Umkoli and the senior speaker. The other ten waited patiently for them to finish. A last throw and it was enough. The most respected of them was aware of his responsibility and rose to speak first.

"I have cast the stones many times and studied hard the results." He pointed skyward, tracing patterns in the stars until his finger settled on the sharp-edged yellow orb that illuminated the Maasai Steppe. "This is what I see. The troubles will grow worse as the troublemakers grow bolder. In less than one month's time the moon will go out."

The laibon nodded. The old speaker was not the only one who had seen this pattern. All of them had seen it. Every Maasai knew what happened when the moon went out. It was a sure sign of death on a grand scale. They had all seen that death in the stones and there was enough of it to worry and frighten them. Not only cattle would die, but Maasai as well and the ilmeet in their millions. The cause of that death was known to them all. You did not have to be a laibon to see what was happening in the world. A child could have interpreted the signs. The ilmeet would fashion enough death for all the world, and they would not know what made them do it.

But the laibon knew who the troublemakers were. The stones told them. The stones and the stars.

"They will be coming through," said the senior speaker, and the rest of the laibon nodded agreement. The speaker knelt and drew lines in the sand as the others leaned forward to look. "Here is the place that must be sealed. It is the opening to all the other places here and in the lands of the ilmeet as well. It is the special place, the dangerous place. Awkward to get to but not impossible." He stuck two pebbles in the dirt; one to represent the place where they were now, another hundreds of miles to the south.

"That is where they will come through. It is where the Real has weakened and must be strengthened. If we can do that they will be shut in and all will be safe for another great cycle. It must be soon."

"I too saw this." Agohna spoke from the far side of the circle. "Can we start there now to do this necessary thing?"

"Yes," said another, "let us go and seal the place tonight."

The speaker looked sad as he shook his head no. "It cannot be done. They are conscious of our knowledge of them. We would be opposed. One laibon alone must go, for his presence will not draw as much attention as several. But the way is long and dangerous and even a single laibon will attract their attention wherever he goes. He must have help. Others who are not laibon, not even Maasai, must go along to screen him. They must be full of power themselves yet unaware of it. The triangle is the strongest shape. Only one of the points can be Maasai." He paused. "The other two should be ilmeet."

"How will you get the ilmeet to believe in what must be done?" wondered craggy-faced Egonin.

"You cannot hold the ilmeet responsible for their ignorance. Ordinary people are readier to believe than great chiefs, even ordinary people who hold within themselves unknown power. That power will protect and shield whoever travels with them. Their very ignorance will serve as a screen allowing him to get close to the place that must be sealed."

This was agreed upon and all considered it wise. As to which of them would chance his life to seal the place, there was no need for a vote. A consensus already existed. As the wisest and eldest among them, the speaker would go. Somehow two ilmeet of hidden power must be persuaded to accompany him even at the risk of their own lives. That part would not be easy but if anyone could accomplish such a formidable task, all knew it was the senior speaker.

"What will you do?" asked Warinn.

The speaker considered. "I will travel to the place where one of the two great chiefs of the ilmeet lives. It will be a good place to seek ilmeet alive with hidden strength. Those who do not demonstrate their own power but who sometimes feel it within themselves are drawn to such places."

"How will you find the two?" wondered Moutelli.

"They will make themselves known to me. Such people sense when they are being sought even if they claim unawareness. That will be the easy part. Convincing them to come back with me will be much harder."

"If they refuse?" said Kokoriki, the laibon with only one arm and enough skepticism for two.

"Then I must find some other way. I will begin this thing tomorrow. I have traveled in ilmeet countries and know something of their ways, though it has been a long time."

"Which chief's kraal will you go to?" asked Moutelli.

"The one that lies to the west rather than the one of the north, I think. The elders of the north make movement more difficult for outsiders. This does not trouble me, but it may trouble those who must seek me out.

"So I will go to the city of the great ilmeet chief of the west and find the two missing corners of the triangle of power. Is this not best?"

All agreed that it was. All of them would have gone, but it had already been agreed that such a concentration of laibonic power in one place would draw too much attention from the troublemakers. One laibon could deal with limited opposition far easier than a dozen with a great deal. Better to let the senior speaker journey on his own.

"Also, I will be traveling at first not toward the weak place but away from it, and when I return it will be by a circuitous route of my own devising. This will throw them off the track. They will lose my scent and perhaps be slow to acquire it upon my return."

The laibon rose then, there being nothing more to be decided. Some stood easily, others had to use their walking sticks to help them erect. A few pulled their robes tight about them. It was cool at night this time of year and good to have a warm blanket around one's shoulders. Down in the engang the women would be waiting for their men with clean places to sleep and warm words of greeting.

They shuffled away from the water hole and the old baobab, striding straight and tall between the acacia trees. There was no order of march because all were equal in each other's eyes.

The junior warrior standing guard at the entrance to the thornbush fence that surrounded the kraal tried not to stare at them as they filed past, but it was impossible not to do so. He would not have been human, much less Maasai, if he had not stolen a glance or two at this most exemplary group of wise men.

They went their separate ways, in twos and singly, toward the various houses which had been assigned to them. The senior speaker saw to the comfort of the other eleven before retiring himself. That was proper, since this was his engang and he was host.

His first wife was waiting for him inside the entrance to the house. Somewhere farther in, a cow stirred nervously. The Maasai slept with the animals who provided them with food and covering, feeling that the herd was as entitled to protection as the herder.

She removed his blanket and then watched as he slid the brown toga off his shoulders, letting it fall to the hard earthen floor. Putting his walking stick aside, he crossed his legs and sat down easily. In near darkness man and woman regarded one another.

"You're going away," she said finally. "I see the journey written in your face."

"Do not make an accusation of it," he replied. "It was inevitable that I be chosen to go. I am the best qualified."

"Where will you go?" She had been wife to the senior speaker for nearly fifty years. They could communicate much with few words.

"To the land of the great tribe of ilmeet of the west, to the kraal of their great chief. I must find two ilmeet of hidden power to help me or all is lost."

"What is going to happen?"

"When next the moon is full it will disappear." She nodded understandingly. Every Maasai knew what that portended. "The dying will be caused by the ilmeet and they will not understand why they caused it. I must try and stop this." She nodded again.

He turned and reached beneath a low cot, pulled out a battered blue suitcase. By the light of the dying cook fire he flipped the snaps and threw back the top. Within were many things he had acquired on his travels, some of which an ilmeet would have found very interesting. The first thing he removed was a small leather sack. He felt of the contents before setting it aside. He could feel his wife close behind him.

Keeko put her hand on his shoulder. The fingers were lined by age but their grip was still strong. "I would go with you. What will you eat? Who will cook and clean and wash for you? Where will you find your leeleshwa leaves to carry beneath your arm to make you sweet-smelling to the ilmeet you must talk with?"

"They do not have leeleshwa leaves in the land of the ilmeet." He looked back up and smiled at her. Not worn by age but finely polished, he thought. Her shaved skull gleamed in the firelight. She was still beautiful. "I have journeyed among the ilmeet before. They use small sticks and lotions instead of leeleshwa leaves to hide their odor. They pass these beneath their arms. I know what to do and I will be all right.

"As for food, a Maasai can travel far on little. There will always be milk to drink and the flesh of cattle to eat."

She nodded solemnly. The questions had been her way of trying to talk him out of going, though she knew her efforts were doomed from the start because of her husband's importance. He knew she knew that. By trying anyway she was demonstrating her affection.

He was examining the contents of the suitcase again. "Tomorrow we must sacrifice a bull. All the laibon will drink of its blood for strength. Do not worry for me. I will be well."

"I cannot help it, husband, for who is to say what might happen to you in the land of the ilmeet? They are strange people full of strange ways."

"I agree that sometimes they are hard to make sense of, but I will manage. Here, help me with this." She took the articles as he handed them back to her. Her nose wrinkled with displeasure as she studied them. So many pieces of clothing to be worn at the same time, restricting and closing up the body! Judging by the few ilmeet she had seen she did not know how they could stand their own selves, much less others of their kind.

But her husband was brave and wise. She had to believe him when he said he would be all right, that he would soon return to her. Nor would she cry in his presence. Let his third wife do that. As first, it was her responsibility to show more control. But she *wanted* to cry.

As a Maasai woman she could have opposed his leaving. She had that right. She would not exercise it because of the importance of this business. All she could do was be proud that it was her husband who had been chosen. Who else could they have selected? Was he not the greatest of the Maasai, the most respected of the laibon? She considered this as she sat there holding the peculiar ilmeet clothing and staring at her husband's still strong, straight back.

"I think everything is wearable, but I should try it on to make certain," he muttered. "It has been a long time. I promise it will only be for a moment."

She moved back when he was finished and tried not to laugh at him. It would not have been seemly, but she could hardly help herself. The city Africans sometimes dressed like that, but they were not Maasai. Nevertheless, she kept her laughter to herself as she assured him that the soles of his shoes were sound and that she could not find a flaw or hole in any part of the pin-striped three-piece suit, white shirt, or tie he was wearing.

4

Tupelo, Mississippi—
10 June

Feelings were not helped by the fact that the air con-ditioning in the Federal Building was broken as the men in white sheets were hustled inside for debriefing. In contrast to the drunken bluster they had displayed during the cross burning earlier that night, they were largely subdued. For one thing it was almost three in the morning. For another, the sort of Dutch courage a six-pack and the comradeship of one's fellows provide tends to dissipate rapidly when one is marched into the hospitallike environment of a large stone building whose hallways are filled with disapproving clerks and the portraits of senior statesmen.

No longer hidden by the piney woods, the men had to run a gauntlet of desks manned by unintimidated faces, had to look back into educated eyes. A few such confrontations were sufficient to convince many of them that they just might not be operating according to divine right. The most common expression they encountered was not anger or hatred but disgust mixed with boredom.

A couple of the detainees retained enough spirit to mumble curses and insults, but not too loudly, lest they be overheard. Jimmy Cousins, one of the first to be processed, wore the look of a man being led to the electric chair. His pallor was that of someone who'd just seen a ghost. In a way he had. It was the ghost of his future receding rapidly into the distance.

Cousins was nineteen and living off a football scholarship to Paar Junior College. Colleges frowned on providing scholarships to youths with prison records. The possible all-state mention, the full scholarship to Mississippi State or even Alabama, a chance at an NFL career—all of it fading away fast because he and some of the older boys had joined together in the woods to have a little harmless fun and drink a little beer. It was strange to see such a big man whine.

"I've gotta make a phone call. I'm entitled to a phone call, aren't I? You gotta let me make a phone call, please, just one."

The solemn faces that stared back at him, male and female alike, did not look very sympathetic. Cousins was starting to understand that what he was involved in was not the same thing as breaking windows or anonymously slipping hate mail in someone's mailbox. Not the same at all.

His friends hadn't warned him about this possibility. No one had mentioned it at all.

"Come on, Jimmy, straighten up." That was old man Sutherlin murmuring to him. Sutherlin was doing his best to look dignified, as would befit a leader. He had no more sympathy for the Cousins boy than the processing clerks. He had a hell of a lot more at stake here than a lousy football scholarship. Those accusatory gazes were dissolving his real future, not some teenager's imagined one, and he was struggling to compose answers to the questions he knew would be forthcoming.

Be prepared. No simple motto, that. Sutherlin had spent his whole life being prepared. But how could he prepare for a catastrophe like this? What could he say when they found the plans and explosives in his Cadillac and the machine guns in Conroy's truck? How could you plan for something that wasn't supposed to happen?

His companions watched admiringly as he strode stiff and straight down the corridor. What they didn't know was that his calm came not from some inner strength or conviction, but rather from the fact that the old man was in shock.

Then they were in a large, open room, devoid of furniture except for a couple of big desks and several of the men who had rounded them up at the burning. On one desk a large tape recorder sat running, and nearby another man quietly operated a video camcorder.

One of the men spoke to them, sounding tired. "Come on everybody, line up. We haven't got all night. The sooner we get this over with the sooner most of you will be out on bail."

Sutherlin stepped forward. "You know, suh, you're going to be sorry when the truth of this mattah comes out. You're making a big mistake heah. I know a few people down in the capital, and y'all are going to be hearing from them."

The man behind the desk that crossed the T of the single-file line glanced at his watch. "I know it's past three in the morning and I'm sorry the air conditioning is out, but we should all be grateful it's early June and not late August. It's a sorry end to a sorry evening and I don't want to have to argue with a sorry bunch like yourselves. So just do as you're told and answer the questions." A few mutters of protest came from the line of white-clad men, but there was no strength left in any of them.

Other clerks entered the room and began taking individuals out of the line, escorting them to small cubbyholes down the next hallway. They looked as hot and tired as the men they'd been assigned to question.

"Each of you will be given the chance to call home, or your lawyers, or whatever," said the man behind the big desk. "You should've been read your rights on the way in." A few sheepish nods. Jimmy Cousins actually began to cry. The big would-be linebacker looked like a six-year-old with a pituitary condition.

The chief agent made a face in his direction, glanced down at the papers that filled his desk. "At your respective individual debriefings and question sessions the specific charges against each of you will be read." As he finished saying this he looked up at Conroy and Vandorm. "The charges will vary."

Luther leaned over to whisper to his buddy. "Don't tell 'em nuthin', BJ. We're screwed as it is."

"No talking in line," said an agent standing nearby. "You'll have plenty of time to talk in a few minutes."

"Yeah, how long's this gonna take?" said one of the other men from the back of the line. "I got cows to milk in a couple of hours. If the milking ain't done it's gonna cost me and somebody's gonna pay for damages for sure."

The chief agent shook his head and muttered to the younger man standing next to him. "Can you believe this bunch?"

Luther saw someone put a hand on BJ's arm. He looked over and saw that it was the black agent BJ had confronted back in the woods.

"Well, well." The agent was smiling humorlessly. "Lookie who I get to interview. You come with me nice and quiet-like, country boy. We wouldn't want you to have an accident or anything between here and the debriefing room, would we?"

Angrily, BJ shook the hand off. "Keep your hands off me. Just show me where you want me to go."

"Oh, I'll let you know where to go, all right." The agent's artificial smile disappeared quickly. "You just give me a chance, just the slightest excuse, and I'll help you get there."

"Don't tell 'em nuthin, BJ!" Conroy and Vandorm shouted in tandem as their simpleminded friend was led off down a side corridor.

"You show 'em, BJ!" yelled another. A number of the fainthearted drew inspiration from the courage of the least man among them.

"It's all right, guys!" BJ waved back to them as he was led off between the black agent and one other. "Y'all be good and I'll see you around."

"Don't count on it, cracker." The agent's grin had returned. "You're under arrest—or have you forgotten?"

"Shoot," said BJ, loud enough for his friends to hear as they turned a corner, "you ain't got nuthin' on me and my friends. We'll be out of here by lunch."

Conroy stared as the janitor was led roughly out of sight by the two FBI men. Good man, that BJ. Stronger than most of 'em if not too bright. Should've kept his mouth shut out there in the forest. Conroy hoped the janitor would be able to hold up under the pressure they were likely to put on him. They probably couldn't break him down physically, assuming such things still went on in law enforcement, but they might be able to trick him. Yes sir, they just might trick poor slow good-natured BJ into spilling all the beans between here and Hattiesburg.

Not that it made much difference. The chapter was pretty well dead no matter what anyone said because it would take a blind man to miss the machine guns hidden in his pickup.

Who could he blame those on? He had to have someone or there'd be nothing to tell them. Suppose he said he'd bought the Uzis for a gag? Sure, that was it. He and a couple of the boys were going to go out and do some varmint shootin', easy style. Just for fun. That would do for the automatic weapons. Play it dumb. Didn't matter whether they believed the story or not. It sounded just like the sort of thing a bunch of good ol' country boys would do. A Federal judge would give it more credibility than a local one, who'd know better.

Explaining away the detailed plans for blowing up the ACLU office in Jackson was going to be a damn sight tougher. That would depend on Sutherlin and the excuses he made for the explosives in his car. Conroy worried about that. What use did a certified public accountant have for fifty pounds of dynamite?

Conroy might have saved himself the mental torment. Down the central hallway, behind the privacy of soundproof doors, the rest of his friends were already spilling their guts to their respective interrogators in hopes of getting off as lightly as possible. Jimmy Cousins in particular was willing to do anything to keep his name out of the paper, up to and including swearing in court that Sutherlin and Conroy and all the other senior chapter members were child molesters, murderers, and commie agents. As the Bureau knew, two fanatics of any political ilk constituted a potential army. Taken alone, most of them were frightened, ineffectual wrecks. Except for the true fanatics like the anarchists, who instead of being against something were against everything. That's not a condition of politics but of sanity.

It was a long way to the room which BJ was herded into, far away from any of the others and well out of earshot. The interior of the room was also different from any of the other debriefing cubicles.

Seated behind the single desk and looking exhausted was a man with curly brown hair and a tall athletic build. The physique was not fake. The agent had played professional basketball for three years before banging up a knee and joining the Bureau. Several other men stood near the far side of the office.

The agent who'd walked the prisoner in carefully shut the door behind him. The man behind the desk rose and came around to stare down at BJ. Then he reached out and shook his hand. Immediately the room was filled with shouts and laughter.

BJ Tree, whose real name was Joshua Oak, traded in the sullen glare he'd been wearing most of the night for a relaxed smile as he shook the senior agent's hand and accepted the congratulations of his colleagues. Amidst all the backslapping and guffaws he turned to the black agent who'd escorted him down the corridor.

"I hope I didn't lay it on too thick out there, Elton."

The agent's head went back as he let out a roar of his own. "Man, are you kidding? I'd have given anything for a camera when you called me 'nigger' out back there in the woods! You should've seen some of those faces. I thought their eyeballs were going to fall out and roll around on the ground and we'd have to spend another half hour picking 'em all up. Your buddy, the guy next to you, looked like he was going to shit in his pants!" He was laughing so hard he had to pause to wipe the tears from his eyes.

"All I can say is that it was a helluva day for the Bureau, Josh, when you decided to join the undercover boys instead of going to Hollywood."

More laughter all the way around. Then the senior agent returned to his seat, put his long legs up on his desk, and gestured.

"Somebody get Laurence Olivier here a chair. You ready for a drink, Josh?"

Oak accepted the proffered chair. "No hard stuff. How about a beer?"

"Can do. Red?" One of the agents nodded, vanished into a back room. "The air conditioning in this rock pile is shot but we've still got power."

"Anything cold. Beer's fine. No, cancel that. I've smelled too much beer already tonight." He twisted around in his chair. "Make it a Pepsi or an RC or something, Red."

"Got it," the agent fumbling around in the back room replied.

Drinks and ice materialized, the other men more than willing to accept the beer that Oak had turned down. They laughed and joked for another ten minutes or so, men casting aside the tension of the past months and reveling in a job well done, before the conversation turned serious.

"We found all the stuff just where you said we would." The senior agent had a tendency to conduct the conversation with his beer. "Plans, maps, munitions, the whole business. You wouldn't think a few yokels like that could plan anything so sophisticated. If you hadn't hooked on with them they might've brought it off before we'd learned anything concrete."

"I've been doing this long enough," Oak commented dourly, "to know that it's dangerous to underestimate these kinds of people no matter how simple they seem or what their background is. A dirt farmer's just as capable of assassinating a President as any professional killer. All it takes is the right, or maybe I should say wrong, combination of fanaticism, will, and luck. This bunch of bumpkins may not look like Nobel Prize material, but they're country-smart. Never sell that short."

The agent named Elton was sitting on Oak's immediate right and looking thoughtful. "You know, we found enough dynamite and blasting powder in that Cadillac to blow up half the state capital."

"One of Sutherlin's accounts is a big local construction company. He's been buying the stuff on the sly from low-level employees for months. But you guys know that already."

The senior agent nodded. "To read your reports you'd think you were getting your information off a teletype. I'm amazed at how you managed to keep us updated so regularly and so thoroughly without getting that bunch suspicious."

"Wasn't all that hard. Like I said, when you've been doing this as long as I have . . . Sutherlin and the rest don't think I'm capable of writing much more than my name."

"I've still got to hand it to you, Josh. We never could have busted this lot without your help. Oh, we could've kept them under surveillance, but there's no guarantee we could have moved on them before they'd killed some folks. As it is we can't make a whole lot stick, but you know the Bureau. Decided to move in before anybody got hurt." He considered. "Possession of automatic weapons, holding explosives for illegal purposes—and of course these wonderfully incriminating plans which everybody put their names to. Including 'BJ Tree.'" More chuckles from Oak's colleagues.

"It'll stand up in court, don't worry. Now that I've seen the principals up close, I think that a year or two in local prisons will be enough to kill any future plans of a destructive nature."

"I think so too. These boys went further than they originally intended. That's Sutherlin's doing. He dragged Vandorm and Conroy along." Oak let the ice in the glass numb his teeth. "One thing, though. I know I don't swing any weight with the prosecutors, but I've got a request anyways. You know that big kid, the one that couldn't quit whimpering? That's Jimmy Cousins. He's a local football star, comes from a broken home. His father's as worthless as anyone we hauled in tonight. Nobody knows where the mother is.

"I think he just fell in with this mob accidentally, because he was looking for a substitute family. The kid needs to belong and I don't think he should suffer because he made a stupid decision. If you can get him off quiet so he doesn't lose his scholarship, I think this'll straighten him out. He's been scared straight."

"A soft heart in your position's dangerous, Josh," said Elton.

"At least I haven't got a soft head. You know that, Laffler," Oak told the senior agent.

The tall man looked uncomfortable. "Elton?"

"If Josh thinks the boy can be made right, I think we're beholden to help him all we can."

"Huh. Josh, you know I don't have much more pull with the department than you do. It's entirely up to what Justice wants to do. But I'll give them your opinion. He didn't know about the plans for the bombing?"

Oak shook his head. "He was a fringe member of the chapter. Not inner circle. Sutherlin didn't trust that many people with the knowledge. Afraid it might reach the wrong ears."

Laffler waggled his oversized ones. "Smart. Mean and nasty. Let's see if we can't put our accountant away for a while longer than his friends."

"I think that'd be a good idea," Oak agreed. "With most of these boys it's as much a game as anything else. Party time in white sheets." Elton made a noise. "Sutherlin's different. The hate's been building up inside him for nearly forty years. He's got a vicious streak runs right through him. A real bitter pill. Don't let him out of custody."

Laffler nodded. "Don't worry. And we'll see if we can't keep the Cousins boy out of jail. Him being under age and all and not knowing about the guns and such—yeah, maybe we can do something."

That made Oak feel better than he had in several days. "Great."

"Oh, and you're going to have to go to Washington, Josh."

Oak paused with the glass of cola halfway to his lips. "Don't shit me, Frank. I'm supposed to be on vacation as of ten o'clock this morning."

Laffler looked apologetic. "Sorry. Another subcommittee wishes the benefit of your lucid explication."

"Screw that." Oak slumped back in his chair and looked disgusted. His gaze went to the ceiling. "Come on, Frank, not another subcommittee. They can read the reports. I'll do a final wrap and then I'm off to Kingston. Won't that be enough?"

"You know as well as I do that it's never enough when a few congressmen are up for re-election, Josh. You ought to know that by now. You're getting a reputation. Not only as a good agent but as good theater. The suspense, the black hood and all."

"One of these days, Frank, somebody's going to pick me out despite the disguise and the voice camouflage. That'll be the end of my undercover work."

Laffler eyes him knowingly. "Would you be all that upset with a desk job? Sitting around and pushing papers for a change until retirement time? I know training would love to have you teach a couple of classes, and students say yessir and nosir and don't shoot back."

Oak let out a grunt. "You know, that's not a half-bad idea."

"Getting tired of changing roles, Josh?" Elton grinned at him.

"I guess you could say that." He inhaled tiredly, rubbed at his eyes. "Another command performance, huh? Senate or House?"

"Senate this time. A big one, Josh, or I would've tried making excuses for you. Senator Baker's sitting in."

"Baker." The senior senator from Nebraska had presidential aspirations, everyone knew. "Good. He'll do most of the talking and I can say yup and nope a lot. He likes that." The silent star, Oak mused. The Agent With No Name. Why couldn't they just put a hood over Clint Eastwood's head for a change? He wondered if he'd be able to get his hotel deposit back. Unnecessary worry, of course. The Bureau would reimburse him.

"Why don't you do it, Frank? Or let Elton go in my place. Hell, with the hood on the committee members won't know the difference anyway."

Elton put up his hands. "Huh-uh, not me, man. I stutter if I have to speak to a crowd."

Red Coleman, who was the oldest field agent among them, came up behind Oak and put a hand on his shoulder. "You know, Josh, if you're really fed up with this undercover stuff, all you have to do is pull that hood off your head and step on the voice box and that'll be the end of it."

"Don't think I haven't thought about it, but I'm too much a

company man. Wouldn't be the right time or place anyways. Be just
my luck there'd be somebody watching C-Span on cable whose brother
or drinking buddy I caused to have put away for a while and he'd
recognize me as an old 'friend.' I'd never be able to sit securely behind
that desk Frank promised me. I haven't been what you'd call loyal
company to a lot of homicidal types these past ten years."

More laughter, and the drinking and joking resumed. Beneath the
feelings of good fellowship and camaraderie in a dangerous profession
there was admiration for the one man among them who'd performed
by far the most dangerous job of all. While they were making wisecracks
and swigging beer, Laffler and Coleman and all the others sooner or
later came to the same thought.

*Man, I wouldn't have Joshua Oak's job for all the laundered money
in the District of Columbia and points north.*

Have to get his football player off the hook somehow, Laffler
thought. That's the least the Bureau owes him. Like everyone else he
wondered how Oak got away with it, infiltrating one dangerous sect or
cult or radical organization after another, blending in with the others,
making himself inconspicuous but valuable to the fanatics he'd been
assigned to watch until the proper time came to betray them. Oak
shrugged off such questions with the thought that it was just good
acting, but most actors worked for applause. Their lives weren't in
danger every time they stepped out in front of the lights.

Ten years was a long time, a very long time, for anyone to work
undercover. Joshua Oak kept playing the odds and they got a little
longer with each successive assignment. Sooner or later someone was
bound to recognize him or find him out, and that would be the last
anyone heard of Joshua Oak.

Laffler didn't want to see that happen. The Bureau would fight
him on it—Oak was the best they had at his strange specialty. No more
than one more such potentially fatal assignment, no more than one. He
was going to insist on it the next time he spoke to his superiors.

After all, even headquarters ought to realize that a live Oak in the
classroom was more valuable than a dead Oak in the woods.

5

Seattle–Tacoma
International Airport—
17 June

The two women strode briskly through the terminal. Merry Sharrow had plenty of time to catch her plane. The fact that she was already checked in and had her seat assignment failed to slow her down. As punctual in her private life as on the job, she'd insisted on arriving at the airport two hours prior to takeoff time.

Amy had learned to live with her friend's chronological fanaticism and didn't complain. "You've got your camera?"

"Yes, and my tickets."

"What about a raincoat?"

"Are you kidding?" Merry checked her watch. She didn't want to miss her plane. This was her vacation, her choice. Her blood was rushing. She couldn't remember when last she'd been this excited. Wonderful things were going to happen to her in Washington. She could feel it. The city was beckoning to her. All very childish, really. Cities didn't beckon.

"How about Kotex?"

"Of course I've got—" Merry started to reply automatically. Then she saw the grin on her friend's face and stuck out her tongue at her.

"Tell me," Amy asked as they strode down the concourse toward Merry's gate, "why Washington, D.C.?"

"I don't know, really. It just kind of jumped into my head. Monuments and museums and maybe some excitement."

"Excitement? You?"

"I might surprise you. Heck, I might surprise myself."

"What did Donald have to say?"

"I didn't ask him. I left a message on his answering machine."

Amy gaped at her. "My, but we have taken charge all of a sudden, haven't we? What prompted this sudden outburst of independence?"

"Seemed like the time was ripe. Besides, I *need* a vacation." She stopped suddenly. People surged around her like water around a rock. "Amy, I hit a dog a couple of days ago. It really tore me up."

Immediately Amy was all sympathy. "You poor thing! Why didn't you call me? I know how you feel about animals. Where?"

"Getting off the interstate on the way home. The morning it was raining so bad. But that's not what's got me all shook, Amy. I . . . I looked at the thing out of my right eye and it looked just like a dog, a big mutt like a wolfhound or something. Then I saw it out of my left eye and it looked like something else. Not like a dog. I can't describe it."

"Out of your left eye?" Amy searched her friend's face. "Man, you do need a vacation."

"That's what I thought. Someplace far away. Washington seemed as good a choice as any, and that was the first thing that popped into my head."

"You're sure you're okay?"

Merry considered. The face and the clawed paw (hand?) were only faint images now, like those left behind on the retina when the TV is turned off. All around her busy men and women hurtled toward distant appointments. Each carried an attaché case or garment bag or both. Their eyes were vacant, their minds elsewhere, and the only time any of them looked anywhere other than straight ahead was when they glanced at their wrists to check the time. They looked like feeding flamingos, hunting minutes instead of tiny pink shrimp.

It frightened Merry, but she didn't let it show. It was as if everyone in the airport except Amy and herself was dead; unthinking, unseeing. Zombies. She shuddered.

"Chilly in here. I'd better go through security or I'll miss my plane."

"Right. I gotta go too. The old man'll be wondering if I took off with you." There was a brief, awkward pause and then they were hugging each other hard.

"Take it easy." Merry pulled back. "It's not like I'm going to Timbuktu or something."

"I know, but it still feels funny, watching you leave. I want postcards. Tons of postcards. Now go and get on that plane before I get silly."

Washington, D.C.—
19 June

" . . . and so what you are really saying, Mr. Bush, is that you believe the emphasis of law enforcement in this country insofar as these various extremist groups are concerned ought to be changed."

There was silence in the Senate chamber except for the hum of the air conditioning and the soft whirr of videocameras while the man known as Bush composed his reply. He sat behind a long, curved table facing the raised dais which protected the five members of the Senate Subcommittee on Crime and Terrorism. A hood of black cloth covered his head and shoulders. When he spoke it was into a special microphone which electronically distorted as well as amplified his voice. The result was a nicely theatrical quaver.

"Am I to understand, Senator, that you are actually asking for my opinion?"

The senior senator from Nebraska nodded. "Absolutely, Mr. Bush. If it were only facts we wanted we could just read your reports, couldn't we?"

The hooded man choked down his instinctive response and tried to view the hearings in the same light the senators did. They couldn't be expected to take him too seriously. Hearings on crime were good for media exposure but contributed little to the actual running of the country. Two of the men on the panel, Crawford of Texas and Eggleston of Michigan, were on the Armed Forces Committee that was meeting early this afternoon. They were anxious to wrap this session up.

So why was he frustrated and disappointed? It was always like this. The same questions to which he gave more or less the same answers. Radicals might differ wildly in their philosophies, but their methodologies for overthrowing the existing government by force were depressingly similar. They weren't really interested in his opinions. That was part of the show, the theater.

He rather liked the senator from Nebraska, though. Baker was an anomaly who thrived on the illusion that one man could actually make a difference in Washington. That ingenuousness was one reason the voters of America's heartland kept returning him to office. Whether he ever got anything done didn't seem to matter as much as the fact that he stood for something.

The half dozen television folks were already starting to break down their equipment. They looked bored. So did the junior reporter from the *Post.* The important questions had already been asked. Baker had requested the professional informant's opinion because the query would look good in the record.

So be it. "Well, Senator, since you've asked for my opinion, this is what I think we ought to do, based on my experiences with the shadowy side of this country over the last ten years. First off we need to legalize all victimless crimes, starting with prostitution and then marijuana use. I'm sure the American Tobacco Company will be thrilled and so will Internal Revenue. That's two *big* new sources of tax income." Crawford suddenly woke up and looked as though he wished he were elsewhere. The junior reporter from the *Post* was holding his tape recorder up high, a gleeful expression on his face. The hooded man wasn't finished.

"Next we ought to throw at least half our law enforcement resources into a war on white-collar crime. If we put away some of these bastards working for Fortune 100 companies who skim and steal millions every year, everybody in the country would benefit, not only from the reduction in crime but because all the hidden costs these crooks tack on to everything you and I buy would be eliminated. That would also make us more competitive overseas."

"Thank you, Mr. Bush—" Eggleston started to say.

"The other half of our strength needs to be focused better on organized crime. More damage is done by it in New York alone than by all the mad bombers and wacko neo-nazis in the whole country in a year."

"I see," murmured Baker, a bit dazed by the force and depth of the unexpected response. Informants, professional or otherwise, weren't supposed to go in for criminological analysis. He wondered who the man in the hood really was. "Thank you for your opinion, sir, though I confess I was not expecting a complete reassessment of the entire

United States Justice Department and its policies. Unfortunately, this subcommittee is empowered to deal only with that branch of crime which is your specialty: those terrorist and subversive organizations which pose a threat not only to our financial and moral well-being but to the very survival of our beloved American institutions as well."

The hooded man leaned back in his chair and put his hands behind his head. "Shoot, Senator, I don't think we have to worry about that too much. Everything's been pretty quiet lately. We know the location of all the nuts in the fruitcake."

"Your levity is not appreciated, sir," grumbled the impatient Crawford.

Baker hastened to move the hearing to a conclusion. "What we really want to know, Mr. Bush, is how to stamp out these radicals once and for all, so that hearings like this one will no longer be necessary and so that our thinly stretched resources can be better utilized elsewhere, just as you've suggested." Murmurs of interest came from the small but suddenly revived group of onlookers.

"Senator, I wish I had the answer to that one, but I'm afraid that the extremists are always going to be with us no matter what we do. It's one drawback to living in a free society. We can't eliminate them, so we have to do our best to keep them under control and minimize their influence. Like fleas on a hound. We've had to cope with dangerous fringe groups since before the Revolution. Every free government does. They're like weeds: you clean out one area and they pop up somewhere else.

"It's an ongoing, never-ending job. I know it's expensive and I really think we ought to put the money elsewhere. Who's more of a threat to the country? The guy who blows up a police station in Topeka or the one who doesn't pay a couple of million in taxes every year?"

Baker coughed into his closed fist. "I'd have to ask my constituents that one, Mr. Bush." Crawford leaned over and whispered to him. Baker nodded, then smiled and turned back to his own microphone. "We thank you for a job well done, Mr. Bush. You see, I *have* read the reports of your exploits. We also want to thank you for your opinions and your frank observations. Sadly, we of the Senate are compelled to deal exclusively with fiscal and historical realities and cannot allow emotion to influence our decisions." The hooded man mumbled something his mike didn't pick up, which was probably just as well.

"I must say that I personally find it refreshing to have someone appear before this subcommittee who is not afraid to speak his mind, who says what he feels and says it straight." Baker shuffled some of the paper on the table before him. "The unique and difficult services which you provide to your country are much appreciated. I am told that within a limited field your work stands out."

"I'm just an ordinary guy doing his job, Senator."

"I beg to differ with you, Mr. Bush. What may appear ordinary to one man strikes another as exceptional. I would very much enjoy talking to you face-to-face for a change. Again, sadly, that is impossible." The black hood nodded once. Baker glanced left, then right.

"Gentlemen, if there are no further questions . . . ?" Eggleston was frowning at his watch. Plenty of time until the Armed Forces Committee meeting, but he didn't want to be late for lunch. The Senate dining room offered gourmet food at rock-bottom prices and Eggleston wanted to be there before all the lobster was gone.

"Thank you again for your revealing and enlightening testimony, Mr. Bush. This subcommittee meeting is at an end." Baker stood and began chatting with Mark Delarosa, the junior senator from Oregon.

Down on the floor, two men appeared and flanked the man in the black hood. The three of them exited the meeting room together. Outside, they walked thirty feet down a narrow corridor before turning and entering a small elevator. It was just big enough for the three of them. The elevator dropped to the next-to-lowest level of the Capitol Building. As it descended, the man in the middle of the elevator removed his black hood and ran a hand through his hair.

"You did fine, Josh," said one of the agents. "I think they really appreciated your frankness even if they didn't agree with your opinions. At least you woke 'em up." He pursed his lips. "How the Bureau will react is something else again."

"Let 'em scream," muttered Oak. "I don't give a damn. Besides, I didn't say anything that could damage the program. Baker asked for my opinion and I gave it to him."

"Yeah," said the other agent, "and you know what Nettles thinks of agents giving their personal opinions in public, much less to a covey of senators." Ed Nettles was the Bureau's current Assistant Director for Field Operations. He did not consider either independence or outspokenness to be praiseworthy qualities in field personnel.

"What else could I do? I had a senator ask me straight out, while I was under oath, to give my opinion. So maybe I went beyond the bounds of his intentions. He didn't go away mad. What the hell else was I supposed to do?"

"Be oblique," said the other agent, a very pretty redhead named Corcoran. "That's what Nettles would say. Be informative and don't embroider."

Oak was folding up the hood. "I'm not real good at that. I can mask my personality and my job, but not my feelings. That kind of subterfuge I leave to the doubletalkers upstairs." He handed the hood to the redhead.

The elevator let them out in the bowels of the Capitol. This was a section of the old building that visitors never saw. It would not have struck anyone as a center of power. Exposed steam pipes and water lines ran across the ceiling like rusty snakes. The large number of fire extinguishers had been placed on the walls to deal with electrical shorts, not structural fires. The walls were solid stone.

"Something's bothering you, Joshua," Corcoran said. "Come on, tell Mama Coco all about it."

"Nothing's wrong," he muttered as they started to climb stairs.

"Happy talk? Okay." She was smirking at him.

"Won't be satisfied till you know, will you? Okay, I'll tell you what it is. I am burned-out. I've spent the last ten years being other people. My friends have been anarchists, assassins, revolutionaries, and murderers. I've played with their kids, made friends with their wives, and wormed my way into their trust just in time to betray them in the name of truth, justice, and the American way. All of which I know was necessary. It still stinks. The smell's starting to stick with me even when I'm not on assignment." He spat against a nearby wall. The Parks Department would not have been pleased.

"Not everybody I met wanted to blow up public buildings or wipe out minorities. A lot of them were just confused. There's a lot of leeway between someone who's confused and someone who's downright evil. But the grand juries don't take that into account when they hand out their indictments. The confused get dragged down with the dangerous. Once a man's private hatreds and bigotries are splashed all over the local papers for his neighbors to see it doesn't matter if the jury acquits him or not; he's ruined in that town anyway."

Corcoran's expression and the hardness in her voice mitigated her attractiveness. "You spray for roaches, you're going to kill a few beneficial bugs with them. It's tough, but that's the way it is. You know that, Joshua."

"Yeah, I know it. But I don't have to like it, and it's getting harder for me to ignore it."

"Ten years. You should see Wayland," said the other agent. Wayland was the field psychologist.

"I don't need to see Wayland. I'm not cracking up. Just getting morose in my dotage. Sometimes I wish I were a little crazy. It would make working with some of the types I've had to deal with a lot easier." They arrived in a modest, clean hallway with old framed photographs on the walls. "Maybe it's just that the longer I spend in the field, the harder it is for me to tell the real bad guys from the real good guys."

They were approaching the lower entrance to the Capitol Building. Behind them was the small private garage that was used to bring in visitors who had reasons for not wanting to be seen. Ahead lay a corridor leading to steps which would emerge at the base of the two great stone stairways that fronted the building. Beyond was the reflecting pool and the long green march of the Capitol Mall.

"If you're that fed up," Corcoran told him, "why don't you talk to Nettles about it? Everybody knows Laffler recommended you for a kick upstairs. With your record and list of commendations you could go anywhere within the Bureau you wanted to."

"Swell. Except who's the poor sucker they'd send to New York in my place? How's that for a change of pace? From Tupelo to the Big Apple."

She frowned. "New York?"

"There's a new knot of nuts up there who call themselves the Repellians."

The other agent looked mystified. "Never heard of 'em."

"Neither's anybody else. They're all from the Caribbean, some black, some white. Their philosophy's part Rastafarian, part Rousseau, and part Marcus Garvey. They think everybody ought to be able to take what they need in order to live. Too bad if it happens to belong to someone else. They have the right, see, to defend themselves against all wrong believers. I'm supposed to go up there, muss up my hair and face and sit around and smoke pot all day until it's time to rip off somebody's car when transportation's required. Besides which I'm not crazy about New York. And if I turn the assignment down, which I can do, they'll probably send some poor young inexperienced schmuck who'll get himself dumped in a Harlem alley some night for letting one lousy wrong word slip."

They were at the corridor intersection now. Garage or pedestrian exit?

"Want a lift, Joshua?" the redhead asked sympathetically. She was pretty and understanding and very married. That wouldn't have stopped many of Oak's friends, but it was enough to stop him.

"Thanks, Coco, but I think I'll walk on down to the Smithsonian and see what's new. Green is good for the soul." That was the best thing about his two years in Mississippi. The restorative of the unblemished land had been there whenever he'd needed it.

"If you're that uncomfortable with undercover you ought to get out," she added.

"You don't really understand, do you? Neither of you do. It's not that I'm fed up with undercover, or my assignments. It's not that I'm fed up with the Bureau." He pushed open the twin glass doors and started toward the broad stone steps beyond. "What I'm fed up with is myself."

6

He left the Capitol Building behind and started down Madison Drive. As he watched the clusters of gawking tourists, the city kids enjoying early summer on the lawn, the busy bureaucrats and messengers on their bicycles, he was struck yet again by the sheer beauty of the city. Once you left behind the concrete and granite walls of the Congress and other government buildings and stepped out among the sunshine and flowers and trees, you no longer felt the oppressive weight of power. Washington became just another city full of busy people, and one prettier than most.

Off in the distance the thin white spear of the Washington Monument stood out against the stark blue summer sky like a cloud that had been turned on its end and rooted in the earth. Around him people oohed and aahed at the massive piles of stone. Each structure was a monument unto itself, to whichever branch of the immense bureaucracy it happened to house. Husbands read aloud the names on the signs out front to their perfectly literate wives.

Street vendors hawked hot dogs and ice cream and Italian ices. Oak fought to lose himself in the sounds and sensations of the city, but his inner thoughts wouldn't let him be. Was he really that burned-out? Was it finally time to transfer to a desk where if he had to lie he could do it on paper instead of to another human being? How could somebody like Wayland help him? By advising him not to live a lie? Living lies was his profession. Where did that leave a man emotionally?

Corcoran had been right about the commendations. What he did, Oak did exceptionally well. A transfer anywhere within the Bureau was his for the asking. What would it be like to be himself for more than a few months at a stretch, instead of Cletus White or Andrew Booker or BJ Tree? To be able to go through a day's work without wondering in the back of your mind if you were going to wake up floating facedown in some unnamed bayou or ghetto dumpster later that night?

That had happened before. Not to him, but to others less skilled in maintaining the Lie. They had signed away their lives and usefulness in a single moment of thoughtlessness. So what kept him with undercover? Why did he continue to trust his life to the flawless maintenance of a false persona?

Responsibility. The knowledge that no matter how distasteful and unpleasant the job, he was better at it than anybody else. He'd fully intended to quit, to transfer out four or five years ago. Three years had been the maximum for anyone in his position when he'd gone into undercover. Now it was ten, because he'd done it for ten. Each additional day he stayed with undercover, he was extending the parameters of his own specialty. *I am the Lie*, he thought, *and the Lie is good.*

He felt lousy.

The Bureau needed him. His country needed him. The people needed him. But what about Joshua Oak? Was there anything left of him, or had he simply become an amalgam of all the different aliases he'd assumed during the last decade? A name on a post office box, a social security number: that much testified to the existence on earth of a man named Joshua Oak.

God, but he was tired. Maybe Corcoran was right. Maybe he ought to go straight to Nettles and say that he'd had enough, that he wanted out. Give him a nice quiet job somewhere researching kidnappings and violations of the Mann Act or something. He liked Washington. He could see himself serving out the rest of his years until retirement right here in the city. No more field work, no more getting shot at in the line of duty.

He halted, blinked. He'd long since passed his intended destination, the Smithsonian museum. Somewhere along the way he'd made a right turn, crossed Constitution Avenue, and gone straight through the Ellipse. Might as well keep going, he told himself. He crossed onto E Street and found himself walking along the back side of the White House grounds. The view here wasn't as impressive as the one from the front, with the fountain and big flagpole, but the flowers and trees were just as pretty on E Street as they were on Pennsylvania Avenue.

It was a fine day for demonstrating and a good place to do it. The serious protestors always did their demonstrating out back of the White

House, where they were more likely to catch the eye of some high government official being driven in to see the President. If you wanted to be photographed you paced around out front. If you wanted to get your message across, you hung around the back driveway.

Quite a few of the unhappy today, Oak mused. You didn't really need the signs to match up demonstrators with causes. The women in the jeans and sloppy shirts who hadn't washed their hair in a week were radical feminists. Beneath the shade of a big tree, neat and turned out as though ready for a sermon, were the anti-abortionists. Across the broad stone driveway and sharing the occasional frosty glare with their opponents were the pro-choice advocates. Yuppie fanatics versus the traditional.

There was some shoving and pushing going on among a large homogenous group that spilled out into the street. Oak identified them immediately. Beige skin, short haircuts, neatly trimmed black beards, and hints of wildness in their expressions. Pro-Khomeini Iranians, a heaping helping of Hezbollahs, asserting their right to tell their hosts where to get off. A few anti-clericals had infiltrated the carefully organized march and were doing their best to disrupt it, hence the pushing and shoving. He slowed. Pushes were starting to turn into punches as the rhetoric heated up. Both groups were utilizing to the fullest the opportunity to exercise the freedom of speech and demonstration that was denied to them in the homeland.

Oak turned his amused gaze on the other placard carriers. They had stopped marching and were staring at the riot-in-the-making. These good people were used to picketing silently, at the very most chanting in rhythm; but not too loudly or impolitely. The Iranians, never loath to allow their deepest and most primitive emotions full rein, must have looked like men from Mars to the peaceful marchers from Des Moines and Cincinnati. Anti-abortionists stood shoulder to shoulder with the Get-U.S.-Out-of-Central-Americans and the anti-vivisectionists and stared at something utterly alien to most of them: real violence, the intrusion of the outside world into their familiar venue of all-American protest.

Oak watched for their reactions with interest. After all, these were the people he'd lied for, stolen for, and risked his life for during the past ten years. Housewives, grad students with their intellectual girlfriends, professional placard wavers, all banded together unconsciously to gaze at the Farsi-spouting Middle Easterners. "How about a picnic—or maybe the beach?" he asks. "Oh no," the demure young thing replies, "let's go over to the White House and shout obscenities at the President. If you insist, we can go to Sans Souci for lunch afterward."

The middle class in microcosm, he thought. The wealthy were too busy making money to demonstrate and the poor had better things to do, like figuring out how to get enough that week to feed their kids. There they stood, the overweight and the fashionably anorexic, the blacks with their white supporters, the whites with their black supporters, claiming the right to tell Canadian seal hunters what they could and could not hunt, claiming the right to have the government pay so they could send their kids to private schools, claiming, claiming . . .

The Vietnam vets protesting against cuts in veterans' programs were the only ones present with any common sense. They pulled up their threadbare fatigues and started moving as far away as possible from the now violent mob of Iranians. Oak was nodding to himself. He didn't mind doing dirty work for those guys because they'd gone off and done some dirty work for him. The rest of them could go to hell.

No, that wasn't fair. They weren't bad people, they tried to be compassionate and understanding. They just didn't know much about the world beyond their private lives. Without the Joshua Oaks of the world to look after them they'd be defenseless. Now they stood and stared, paralyzed by the explosion of violence that had erupted before them, seemingly out of nowhere.

Something came whizzing toward his head. With instinct born of long practice, he ducked to his left. It shattered against the tall wrought-iron gate that enclosed the White House grounds. The Iranians had not been schooled in the polite formalities of dignified American protest but rather in the crucible of Third World passions where people lost brothers and wives to opposing interests instead of arguments. Their disagreement was turning ugly and threatening to suck innocent, uninvolved bystanders into the maelstrom.

Both factions had been swollen by the arrival of reinforcements who had arrived in vans and trucks with unexpected swiftness—too swiftly for their appearance not to have been prearranged. Rocks, clubs, bottles, and sticks began to take the place of flailing fists. The park across the street was raining Iranians.

Time to move. Curious to see which side would prevail, he searched for a place of relative safety against the fence. There was no reason for real panic. The Bureau, not to mention the Metropolitan Police Department, kept constant watch on such large groups of potential troublemakers. They would know in advance about any planned confrontation. Oak expected them to arrive to clean up the mess at any moment.

Unless this was escalating beyond the intentions of the organizers. That had been known to happen. The confrontation might very well have been planned as a peaceful one that had gotten out of hand despite the best intentions of the participants.

The anti-abortionists were collecting their neatly printed placards and shooing their co-opted children out of the way, casting a few venomous glances behind them. The shouting of slogans in Farsi had given way to a full-fledged Persian riot. The Vietnam vets were breaking beer out of ice chests. They seemed to be enjoying the show. But many of the remaining placard carriers were too stunned to know whether to retreat, stand still, scream for help, or leap into the fray. Their sensory systems had been overloaded.

Oak saw one middle-aged Iranian, here to visit immigrant children perhaps, fall to the ground grabbing at his face. Blood streamed from his nose and mouth.

Another rock sailed past, this one arcing far over Oak's head. It cleared the fence and landed on the perfectly manicured lawn beyond. Something to occupy the groundskeepers the next day. Additional landscaping courtesy of Teheran.

The police were late. Oak was mildly surprised at such tardiness. There was no danger of the demonstration actually spilling over onto White House grounds, of course. The Secret Service would see to that. But they wouldn't step beyond their jurisdiction to suppress trouble that posed no threat to the President or his family.

Oak felt sympathy for some of the older combatants, but not to the point of intervening. This was not his fight and the Bureau took a stern view of its agents involving themselves in outside altercations. But if the cops didn't put in an appearance pretty soon, some of the bystanders were going to get hurt. A number of them found themselves trapped between the ebb and flow of the mob and the unyielding iron fence. A couple of the women thus pinioned started to scream. Off to one side, a trio of Get-U.S.-Out-of-Central-America girls were clinging to one another for comfort. They looked scared.

Screw Nettles, Oak thought, and started toward them, shoving one Iranian out of the way. The man glanced back murderously, saw that the individual who had pushed him was not one of his brothers in Islam, and returned his attention to the holy war at hand.

Two well-dressed young men appeared on either side of the trio and started escorting them away from the fray. Oak halted, cast his eyes over the demonstrators to see if anyone else was in trouble. Most of the other placard wavers had managed to slip clear of the combat zone, but one apparently had lingered too long in the center.

She was crouched back against one of the trees that projected through the sidewalk. Clubs and axe handles were being wielded dangerously close to her with great enthusiasm. She looked lost as well as frightened. Just an unlucky pedestrian, Oak mused. Not even a demonstrator. Well, she would be all right if she had the sense to stay close to the tree.

A couple of fleeing anti-nukies rushed past her and one man bumped her right side. He stumbled, recovered his balance, and kept running. But the impact had sent her staggering away from the protective bulk of the tree and out into the mob. Her sunglasses were sent flying, to be pulverized by jostling, positioning feet.

Where the hell were the cops? Oak wondered as he forced his way through the mob. One of the rioters found the man heading toward him a worthy opponent without bothering to inquire if he was pro- or anti-Khomeini and swung a thin metal whip at him. Car antenna, Oak noted absently as he ducked the swing and brought the heel of his right hand up against the other man's nose. The demonstrator collapsed, both hands going to his face. Oak pulled the blow. He didn't want to break the man's nose, but neither was he in the mood to catch something like a car antenna across his right eye. No one else confronted him as he made his way through the loud, angry mob toward the sidewalk tree.

She was still trying to find her glasses. He reached down and gently grabbed her shoulder, pulling her erect.

"Forget it. They're gone."

"What? My . . ."

"Your glasses. Busted. Come on."

She wasn't completely paralyzed because she nodded and followed him. Despite the stunned expression she wore, she was quite attractive, Oak thought. Slim, medium build but not skinny.

"Are you a policeman?" she shouted above the babble of the mob.

"Just another spectator like yourself." They were heading back toward the fence now. Oak didn't want to be caught out in the street when the cops finally arrived and the Iranians scattered in all directions. "Which of these happy groups are you with?"

"With? I don't— Oh, you mean the other demonstrators. I'm not with any of them. I'm just a tourist. I was taking pictures around front and somebody told me I should circle the grounds because it looks different from back here. The White House, I mean."

He put a protective arm around her shoulders, pointed. "There's a guard box over there. We can't go inside but these people will stay away from it."

"Okay."

He hustled her through the mob until they were standing close to the armored guard station.

"You all right?"

She nodded once and then, as if remembering something she'd left at home, added a smile. "I'm okay, thanks." She straightened her dress and then began rummaging through her purse. While she excavated, Oak rapped hard on the bulletproof window of the station. The man inside ignored him until Oak removed his ID and pressed it up against the glass. Still the man hesitated, then finally walked over and opened the window.

"I'm breaking security talking to you. What do you want?"

"What do *I* want? Where the hell are the cops?"

"They'll be here any minute," the Secret Service man told him.

"Why so long?"

"Traffic accident at New York and Twelfth. They have to detour around."

"Figures." So much for security efficiency, he thought.

"Listen, I'm not supposed to do this, but seeing that you're with the Bureau I'll let you and your lady friend inside. Door's around back."

"She's not my lady friend. Just some tourist I pulled out of the stampede before she got trampled. My good deed for the day. No, thanks, but I don't want to compromise you. We'll be all right here. I just wanted to make sure we weren't going to be stuck here all day."

"You won't. Listen."

Oak could hear the approaching sirens clearly. In a minute the rioters would also, and then the battle which had been so enthusiastically joined would evaporate as fast as a pan of water on the steps of Persepolis. The participants would melt away in the grass of the Mall or the shadows of nearby government buildings, or retreat back into the cars and vans which had disgorged them in the first place.

"Get much of this?" Oak asked the Secret Service man conversationally.

"Naw. These guys are pretty smart. The Bahktiar supporters are here all the time, parading back and forth with their signs, but the Ayatollah ass-kissers don't show up too often. They know they're liable to be deported if they're arrested more than twice. Now me, if they'd lend me an Abrams tank for about thirty minutes I'd clean up the whole bunch of them permanently, but what the hey, I'm just a hired hand and can't set policy. You know what that's like."

"Yeah, I know what that's like." Someone was shaking his arm and he looked over into the anxious face of the woman he'd rescued.

"Look, down over there. Can't you do something? Can't somebody do something!"

Oak tried to see what the woman was pointing at. There, lying on the ground out in the open away from a tree or trash can or anything that might provide temporary protection, was an old man. He was trying to use a long walking stick to struggle back onto his feet, but every time he made the effort another of the rioters knocked him down. He didn't look like he could keep it up much longer. If he fell down and stayed down he risked taking a kick in the head or worse.

Oak tried to imagine how he'd come to be caught up in the riot. He didn't look like a demonstrator, or a tourist either for that matter. He was well dressed, though something about his attire struck the FBI man as peculiar. He might be a minor government bureaucrat, but he looked older than the mandatory retirement age and that opinion didn't jibe with the presence of the knotty walking stick. Maybe he was retired from one of the nearby bureaucracies. Oak knew people like that, unable to leave the center of power for the boredom of the provinces. They ended up hanging around the places where they'd worked, pestering former friends and slowing up the wheels of government a little more than usual.

"He'll work his way clear. They're not interested in him; only in bashing one another."

She shoved her face toward his. "How can you stand here and let him get trampled like that?"

"He isn't getting trampled."

She seemed to hesitate, fighting with herself. "Well, if nobody else is going to help him . . ."

He reached out for her, too late to prevent her from dashing back into the very crowd from which he'd just rescued her. He could see her flailing away at the two Iranians who threatened to stumble over the old man, beating them with her handbag. One of them turned and took a wild swing which barely grazed her, but it was hard enough to knock her backward. Another punch might connect and do some real damage.

"Shit," he muttered. How do you save a woman who doesn't want to be saved? He plunged back into the mob a second time.

Reaching her wasn't as difficult as he'd first thought it would be because the police were starting to pull up in their cruisers, blocking off E Street at both ends and just itching for an Iranian or two to take a swing at them.

The rioters were much too clever for that. Those who couldn't make it cleanly back to their vehicles or to the crowded Mall beyond dropped their makeshift weapons and surrendered peacefully. Most of them had been involved in similar confrontations before. They might choose to ignore most of the social customs of the country hosting them but they knew how the police operated as well as the cops themselves. They plastered big friendly smiles on their faces and surrendered without incident. Oak could see the frustration boiling in the duty cops' expressions. You couldn't clobber a demonstrator who smiled, put his hands politely atop his head, and surrendered.

The woman was still swinging her handbag as he helped her and the old man back to the guard box. The Secret Service man had shut the window and was talking on an inside phone, no doubt reporting to his superior inside the White House itself.

The demonstration was shutting down as rapidly as it had started. In five minutes there wouldn't be an Iranian in sight. Within an hour or so the more peaceful picketers would have resumed their derogatory vigils outside the President's home.

Any of them would have been outraged to wake up one morning to find picketers marching outside their own bedrooms, but who thought of the White House as somebody's home? It was a symbol, there to be picketed or toured, but not to be lived in. Oak blinked. The old man was talking to him.

"Thank you very much for your help, sir."

He appeared to be in good shape, though still shaken by the violence of the confrontation he'd found himself swept up in. Considering his probable age, Oak thought he was handling himself very well. Tough old bird. His hands weren't shaking and he'd managed to hang on to his walking stick throughout the fighting. The only thing Oak was sure of right away was that the man wasn't a paper-pusher. The muscles beneath his coat testified to that. Then Oak realized what it was that had struck him as peculiar about the old man's appearance.

It wasn't that he was so obviously a foreigner. His thick English accent and jet-black skin were proof enough of that, not to mention the stretched-out earlobes that swayed whenever his head moved. No, it was the fact that his suit, though neat and clean, was forty or fifty years out of date. So was the white shirt, which looked like a throwback to an ad from the twenties for Arrow collars. Good thing Oak had intervened, because everything about the man screamed foreign diplomat, probably from a poor country. He might just have prevented an international incident. Might be one more commendation to add to the total Corcoran had alluded to.

The man was brushing dirt from his pants. "They would not let me up," he was muttering.

Definitely British-educated, Oak decided. Too dark to come from most of the Caribbean countries. African, then. He struggled to recall his geopolitics. East African. If he was from the west side of that continent he'd have spoken with a French accent, unless he was Nigerian. Complicated place, Africa.

Not that it mattered.

"Are you okay, mister?" It was the solicitous voice of the woman Oak had been compelled to rescue twice. My day for pulling the sardines clear of the sharks, he mused sardonically. She was helping the old man wipe off his suit. "I tried to help. I'm afraid I wasn't doing a very good job of it."

"Don't get down on yourself," Oak found himself telling her. "You tried. That's more than any of these other upstanding citizens did. A riot like this can scare off soldiers. I know these types. When their blood's up they don't care who gets in their way, and they don't make accommodations for sex or age. They just start bashing away in Allah's name. As far as they were concerned both of you were just part of the scenery and if you happened to get in the way, too bad."

"Violence," the old man murmured, "so much violence in the world, and so much of it petty." For the first time Oak noted that the oldster was as tall as he was. "Where I come from you do not shame the man you disagree with by fighting with him. There are better ways to settle an argument."

"These guys aren't as interested in arguing as they are in beating righteousness into their beloved brothers."

"That is a contradiction in terms." The old man looked Oak in the eye.

Something happened. It was so quick it was undefinable, but for just an instant Oak had the feeling he was looking back into the mind and soul of an intellect as vast as it was unencumbered by the expected ethnocultural baggage. It staggered him and he blinked. Then his right eye stopped throbbing and it was all gone.

The old man looked away and now Oak wasn't sure he'd seen anything at all. Must have imagined it anyway, he knew. The specimen standing next to him was nothing more than a tall, old black man in a badly out-of-date suit.

"And you." He had a wonderful smile, Oak thought, which he was now lavishing on the blonde. "You were thoughtful enough to try to help me."

She looked embarrassed. "I just felt like I had to do something. It's not like me. Usually I don't get involved. And fighting—that just couldn't have been me out there."

"Take it from me, it was you," Oak assured her. "If that'd been a sword instead of a handbag you'd been swinging, you wouldn't have needed my help."

She really looked baffled, he thought. "It just isn't *like* me."

"Then why'd you go back in there?" Oak asked her.

She looked up sharply. "I—I don't know. I just *had* to."

"It was good of both of you to think of me," the old man told them.

Oak thought it was about time for him to resume his interrupted stroll down E Street, report in to the Bureau, go home, or turn around and head back for his original destination, the Smithsonian. Instead, he found himself looking at the woman. She'd told him she was a tourist. Was she with a group tour, was she married, or what? His social life was nothing to be envied. Finding the time to have even a transitory relationship with a member of the opposite sex was damn difficult when you spent the majority of your time not only away from home but away from yourself.

Not that there weren't plenty of opportunities to establish casual liaisons in the field, but Oak could no more lie to a woman for purposes of sexual conquest than he could to a theater manager to get in free.

So what social life he had was confined to the brief periods he was home between assignments. Like now.

Clearly this lady was a stranger to Washington, a Washington he knew intimately. He glanced down at her hand. No wedding ring—which didn't necessarily mean she was unmarried, but it was an encouraging sign. She was attractive and sensible. Though obviously frightened, she hadn't collapsed in a shrieking fit when she'd been trapped by the surging mob.

Maybe she'd like to see the non-tourist side of Washington. Maybe if she was alone she was lonely and could use some company. He certainly could. Prettier than she thought she was, he mused. Minimal makeup, and nothing to bring out the beauty of her face. He rubbed at his right eye. Plain coiffure, which was understandable in any case. She was out walking, not going to the Inaugural Ball.

Ah, why bother? He was tired and feeling down on himself and this morning's riot hadn't done anything to raise his regard for his fellow man. Better to continue his walk than chance rejection by a total stranger. And he really ought to spend some time at home. He saw the place infrequently enough as it was.

He needed time to himself, to unwind and relax. Maybe he'd run up to Baltimore for an Orioles game, or head down the coast for a few days. Just sit on the beach and have the gulls yell at him for a change, try to decide which one sounded the most like Senator Baker. They wouldn't press him for easy answers to difficult questions.

"If you'll both excuse me," he found himself telling them, "the police are on the scene and it'll be safe to continue your walks in a couple of minutes. I've got business of my own to attend to and—"

"You didn't see them, then?" The old man looked sharply at Oak, then down at the woman. "You didn't see them either?"

She looked for advice to Oak, who had none to give. "Didn't see who?"

"*Them.*" The old man was insistent. "The ones who started the fighting, the ones who incited the riot." He assumed a sly look. "Oh, they're very good at that, yes they are. It is one of their specialties, getting people to fight one another. Then they stand aside and laugh at the combatants and make obscene gestures at them. If you're in a crowd you have to be on guard against that all the time. But they moved very quickly and quietly and I didn't see them until it was too late. They're gone now, of course, so I can't point them out to you."

"That's nice," said Oak easily. "I'm glad I was able to help you. It's been fun but it's time for me to go." He took a step up E Street only to find the old man blocking his path. His voice had fallen to a conspiratorial whisper.

"They didn't fool me, though. What they really wanted to do was get inside there." He pointed at the White House. "That could have had terrible consequences."

Oak didn't want to linger any longer but he did anyway. "Someone was using the riot as a diversion so they could get into where?"

"The great chief's house. I've never seen them this bold in the daytime. But there were only two of them and they didn't have enough cover to make their approach."

"I see. You're worrying about nothing, old man. They couldn't have made it past the gate." He spoke as if explaining to a child. "You see, it's very heavily guarded, all the time. Security makes it impossible for even very clever people to get any farther than this fence without proper clearance."

"Oh, but they aren't people, don't you see?" He studied Oak's face. "No, you don't see, do you? Not completely."

Oak could have taken that two ways, chose instead to try to ignore it. "No, I guess I don't. Now if you don't mind, I have business of my own."

"I too have business. I must get inside and see the great chief." He walked up to the guard station and tapped on the glass with the end of his walking stick. "Pardon me?" The guard inside ignored him.

Oak sighed. He should turn and walk away, but what the hell. He'd already rescued the old man once. If he was a little senile, well, you couldn't just leave him standing there in the middle of the street. For the first time it occurred to Oak that the well-dressed oldster might have wandered away from a nursing home. There were several in the vicinity, and if he had enough sense to get on a bus he might've come a long way. Men in white coats might be hunting him even now. Or maybe he'd been visiting relatives and had wandered away from some granddaughter's birthday party. He walked over to him.

"I'm sorry, but you can't just walk in and say howdy to the President. That ain't the way it works."

"Are you certain?"

"I'm really sorry, but that's the way it is." He glanced at the blonde. "You tell him."

She looked blank for a moment, then smiled sorrowfully at the old man. Kind and understanding too, Oak thought. He could use a little of that right now.

"I'm afraid he's right. You can't just walk in and see the President. What did you mean when you said they were the cause of the riot, and that they weren't people?"

The old man ignored the question. "I had hoped—I have come such a long way. I had hopes that the chief of your tribe would be able to put me in touch with certain people. Special people."

He sounds crazy, Oak mused, but he doesn't look crazy and he isn't acting crazy. Tired, though. He could well believe the oldster had come a long way. Maybe down on the express from Philly.

"Say, old-timer, there's a bench over next to that tree. Why don't you have a seat and think it over." He signaled his intentions to the blonde with a nod of his head. Together they eased the old man over to the bench. It was bolted to the sidewalk to prevent its unauthorized use by frenzied demonstrators such as those the police had just caravaned away. The woman sat down next to him while Oak stood to one side feeling awkward and out of place.

"I'm sorry you can't get to see the President." She smiled at the old man and he responded with a frank stare which she handled very well, Oak thought. Lovely smile, it was.

"Perhaps it doesn't matter. Perhaps it wouldn't have done any good anyway. It would have been difficult to convince him of the seriousness of my visit. The ignorance of ilmeet officialdom is appalling at times."

"Ilmeet?" Oak murmured.

"Aliens, foreigners—anyone who is not Maasai."

"Say what?"

"It's an East African tribe, I think," the woman said unexpectedly.

"You a professor or something?" Oak's query was as much accusation as question and he was instantly sorry for the brusqueness of his tone. Take it easy, Joshua B., he growled at himself. This isn't a combat situation. "No offense. I just wondered how you knew."

"I do a lot of reading. *National Geographic, Smithsonian, Natural History.* Stuff like that."

The old man was delighted. "Yes, I am Maasai. You have been to Africa?"

"No. One day, maybe. I dream about traveling and I keep saving my money. This is about as far from my hometown as I've ever been."

Oak extended a hand. "Where's home? By the way, I'm Joshua B. Oak. Josh to most people. You?"

She took the hand politely. "Merry Sharrow, Seattle. What's the B. stand for?"

"Burton."

"Your parents must've liked his performances."

"I don't think so. It's a common name. From an old uncle or somesuch, probably."

The old man was staring at him. "Your name is Burton?"

"Just the middle one."

"A fine man, Sir Richard Burton."

"Actually, I haven't seen many of his films."

"Films? Oh, you're speaking of the actor who was named after him. I am referring to the first Sir Richard Burton, who was an explorer of my country as well as many others. A brilliant and learned gentleman

who delved into branches of knowledge shunned by his contemporaries.
He was very much misunderstood and underappreciated by his fellow
ilmeet, especially his wife, who committed one of the great crimes of
history when she burned his exhaustive personal diaries."

If this is a crazy old man, Oak thought, he's one helluva sharp
crazy old man. Still, his interest now was focused more heavily than
ever on the blonde. Contact had been established.

"You're a long way from Seattle, Mrs. Sharrow."

"Ms., but Merry will do." She smiled at him. "Like I said, the
farthest I've ever been. I was born, raised, and work up there. I'm on
vacation."

"You looked pretty lost a while ago."

"My first riot. It's been an educational morning. Thanks again."
The smile widened slightly.

Oak hesitated. BJ Tree would have known what to say. So would
any of half a dozen other aliases. But Joshua Oak did not. "I feel like
the odd man out here. Guess I'll be going. You come from Seattle and
he comes from Africa. Me, I just come from outside of town."

"Stay a moment, please," said the old man.

"I thought you were feeling okay, old-timer."

"I am much better, thanks to you both. Burton. An interesting
coincidence, young man. You are certain you were not named for the
venerable explorer?"

"Hell, I don't know. I never asked anyone. For all I know Burton
could have been the name of some bastard cousin in Boston. Speaking
of names . . . ?"

"Ah. I have been impolite. I have not even asked you the
condition of your cattle. How are they?"

One minute he sounds sane, the next screwy, Oak thought. A *rara
avis* wherever he's from.

"I don't have any cattle."

"What about you, Ms. Sharrow?"

"I've got a cat," she replied helpfully.

"No cattle. Then you are both poor, for one who lives without
cattle lives in poverty."

"I'll stick with my bank balance just the same," said Oak.

"You cannot eat what sits in a bank." The oldster waggled a finger
at him. "You cannot raise your children on it. And I am still impolite.
I am Mbatian Oldoinyo Olkeloki, which means in Maasai 'Mbatian the
Mountain Who Crosses Over.'"

"That's a beautiful name," Sharrow said. "Where do you cross over
to?"

"To Other Places. As for instance this land of yours, which looks
healthy and well but is full of many cold, dead things you cannot

understand." He looked from her back to Oak and the satisfaction was plain in his voice. "Perhaps I do not need to see the great chief. I knew that those I would need to find would make themselves known to me. The prophecy has been fulfilled. Here you are."

"Here we are?" Oak thought Merry sounded a little wary herself now.

"One named Burton and another from a far place, both come to help me in a moment of crisis. Why else would you have helped me? Who am I to either of you? There were many ilmeet who were not participating in the fighting. Why did you choose to help me?"

"You were old," Oak replied promptly, "and you were on the ground. I've been on the ground myself. I know what it's like when you're about to get stomped and it's something I wouldn't wish on any man."

"Is that the only reason? Are you quite certain within yourself?"

"Anyone with a good conscience and caring heart would've done what we did," Sharrow told him.

"Possibly, possibly, but they did not, and you two did." He looked in all directions. "They have all gone. Your presence shields me from their attentions. That is the proof of it. No, I no longer need to see your chief. I have found the people I came to find."

"Swell," said Oak brightly. "You two have a nice chat, but I really do have to get going."

"What do you do, where do you go that you are in such a hurry to leave one who would be friends with you, Joshua Oak?"

"I work for the government. I've got work to do."

"In what capacity?"

"None of your business." He'd had about enough of this. The old man's amusement value was falling fast.

Olkeloki simply looked gratified. "I thought as much." He turned to Merry Sharrow. "And you?"

"I'm a clerk. I take mail orders over the phone for Eddie Bauer Outfitters in Seattle."

"Hey," said Oak, surprised, "I bought a coat from them once."

"Really? Maybe I processed your order."

"Good coat."

"Glad you like it. We take a lot of pride in our products."

"Maybe I'll buy a vest to match someday. I hope the rest of your visit is a little more peaceful."

The old man rose with unexpected speed and grabbed Oak's arm. Josh's natural reaction was to the throw the oldster over his shoulder. He managed to restrain himself. There was no threat in the African's expression, no danger in his face.

"Please, you must—you must do one more thing for me."

"Well . . . what d'you have in mind? I mean, I really do have to be going and . . ."

"I know. I know that you are a busy man, Joshua Oak. I know that you are both busy. But what I ask of you will take but little of your time, will enlighten you, and is something you may find interesting.

"Will you listen to a story? I have come ten thousand miles to tell someone a story."

7

"It's the least we can do," Merry Sharrow finally said when it was clear Oak wasn't going to respond. Her excitement, not to mention her naivete, was refreshing in a city that ran on routine and cynicism. Still he hesitated.

"Tell you what, old-timer—Olkeloki. I'll listen to your story if you can prove to me that you're visiting here from Africa instead of General Marshall hospital across the river."

"I understand. It is natural that you should doubt me." He fumbled through one pocket, then another. It was as if he was unfamiliar with his own clothes. Eventually he produced a small leather passport holder. The gray leather was battered and worn but all in one piece. Oak wondered what kind of hide it was fashioned from as the old man passed it to him. Something much stronger than steerhide. Buffalo maybe, or elephant.

It contained a number of dusty, foreign-looking documents and a passport printed in two languages, English and Swahili. The passport picture was of the old man, but instead of his suit and tie he was wearing beads and little stamped metal arrowheads in his ears and a yellow-orange toga over his upper body. Oak gazed at the picture for a moment, then handed the documentation back to its owner. Red dust lingered on his fingers and he rubbed at it, trying to brush it off.

"The earth of Africa." Olkeloki slipped the billfold back into his coat pocket. "No matter how hard you try to leave it behind, it follows you wherever you go."

Oak nodded absently, looked thoughtful, and said abruptly, "If you needed to see the President why didn't you go through your embassy?"

"I am not a government official. Only what you would call a concerned private citizen. Such as I are not permitted access to high officials in my country. Nonetheless, I might have managed an interview or two, but it would have taken much time. We do not have much time."

Apparently the "we" kept going right by Merry Sharrow. "Please, Josh, come with us. It'll be fun. I never met an African before."

"And I have never met an ilmeet lady from Seattle, so I think we are even, Merry Sharrow. Please listen to me, Joshua Oak."

Why not? Consider it a serendipitous extension of his planned visit to the Smithsonian. An anthropological side-trip. Besides which, someone had to look after this poor innocent child of the Northwest or she was liable to do something really stupid, like give the old man money.

"You owe it to me, Joshua Oak," said Olkeloki.

"I *owe* it to you? How d'you figure that?"

"You made yourself known to me."

"I see, and if I'd let you lie there on the pavement to get your ribs kicked in and your nose busted I wouldn't owe you anything, is that it?"

"Exactly." Olkeloki looked very pleased. He hefted his walking stick, which was nearly as tall as he was. Oak gestured at it.

"You take that thing with you wherever you go?"

"It is a companion of my youth, and a useful friend. Come, I know a good place. I sought it out the day after I arrived in this city. It reminds me in its crude way of home. The food is not exceptional but the room is reassuringly high."

"You like restaurants with a view?" Sharrow asked him.

"View? No, it is not the view which is important. The higher we are the safer we are, because few of them can climb trees and fewer still can fly."

"Fewer what?" Oak cursed himself as soon as the words left his mouth.

"The gnomes, of course." Merry Sharrow had a twinkle in her eye. She looked just like Dorothy about to set off on the yellow brick road, having fallen into an adventure not included in the guidebooks. A nice, safe adventure of short duration, for she would be back safe and cool in her hotel room tonight. Amy would be proud of her.

"Gnomes," murmured Olkeloki solemnly. "Yes, that is close enough. You are very perceptive, Merry Sharrow."

"It comes from divining what people really want when they call in their orders."

Oak noted the smoothness of the old man's stride. He didn't trudge along like an old man. Probably you developed excellent leg muscles hiking through the middle of Africa.

"That walking stick of yours isn't a bad idea. Useful for making room for yourself on the subway and it might even make a mugger or two think twice."

"Mugger?" Olkeloki struggled with the term. "I am afraid I do not know all the new words. Your language is a live thing, always growing and expanding and putting out strange new shoots and buds. It is hard to stay abreast of all the new idiomatic expressions." He gestured fondly with the walking stick. "Yes, this staff has stood me in good stead for many years."

"Say that fast three times," said Merry, and she giggled quite unexpectedly. "Have you ever had to use it to ward off robbers, Mr. Olkeloki?"

"No, I have never had to use my staff to beat robbers, though I once did kill a lion with it."

Oak sputtered through his smile, choking back the derisive laughter that threatened to explode inside him. "No kidding. I don't suppose you'd care to tell us how you managed that little trick?"

"Certainly. I was quite young at the time and was caught away from my spear while guarding my father's herd. The lion saw this and thought to make off with a calf while I was unarmed. But I had this staff which had been given to me by a famous elder. When the lion charged out of the bush toward me I waited, as if for my death. Dying was not on my mind, however. It was an old male lion, but he was still very large and strong, with a black mane that was turning gray in places. As he came across the grass toward me I could see that he had my death in his eyes. It is not something you forget.

"I stood as if waiting resignedly for that death, but when he leapt at me, his claws reaching for my shoulders and his jaws for my throat, I fell to the earth and brought this staff up as hard as I could between his legs. He flew over me, hit the ground, and rolled over. As he fought to get back his breath I lunged at him and ran the staff all the way down his throat. He threw me several feet, but I landed running and went to get my spear. It was not needed, for when I returned to the place I saw that the lion was dying. Fear had given me great strength. I had pushed the staff all the way into his lungs and he had choked to death on it." Lifting the stick off the pavement, he turned it parallel to the ground and showed Oak the far end. There appeared to be several deep gouges in the upper third.

"This is ironwood. See there, the marks of the old lion's teeth."

"Let me see!" said Merry breathlessly, crowding close. An amused Oak gave her plenty of room. It was a pleasure to see such enthusiasm, such ready acceptance in another human being.

The old man led them on, turning up a side street lined with office buildings of more recent construction. They entered a bank and took one of the elevators up ten flights to the top floor. It let them out at the end of a short hall. At the other end was the entrance to a restaurant. Oak checked his watch. Three o'clock. The place would be deserted.

It was green with palm fronds and bamboos growing in pots. Fake thatch decorated the ceiling and the upholstery was full of flowers. The sign etched into one of the glass and mahogany doors identified the eatery.

THE BRASS ELEPHANT

It wasn't an establishment he frequented, but the name was familiar. Several of his colleagues had eaten here. From the little he could recall, they spoke well of the place.

The young receptionist's gaze lingered a bit longer than was polite on Olkeloki, finally said, "Can I help you?"

"A quiet table, please," said the old man. "Away from the windows and the door."

"All right. You know that we're not serving lunch anymore and dinner doesn't start until five-thirty?"

"That's fine. Something cold to drink is all we want."

"Okay. If you'll follow me, please?"

She seated them in a large, dimly lit high-backed booth surrounded by plants and carved coconut shells. Oak ordered a gin-and-tonic, Merry a pink squirrel, and Olkeloki, surprising Oak yet anew, a Midori on the rocks.

"Don't see how you can drink that stuff," he said when the glasses arrived. "Too sweet for me."

"I never heard of it," said Merry.

"It's made from honeydew melons."

"You know a lot about liquor?"

He shrugged. "A little. For instance, I'm an expert on beer. It's required in my work."

"Sounds like you have an interesting job."

"Some might think so. I used to, but it's begun to wear on me these past couple of years. Doesn't answering phones eight hours a day bug you after a while?"

"Not so far. See, I'm not what you'd call an ambitious person. I never have been. All I ever wanted was a low-key steady job, and I've found that. The pay and fringe benefits are good and the working conditions are ideal—for me, anyway. I get to talk to a lot of interesting people, even if I never get to meet them in person. I guess you'd say I have a wide circle of acquaintances but very few close friends."

"Not married yet, then?" He said it diffidently.

"No, not yet."

"Engaged?"

"Sort of." For some reason she seemed uncomfortable saying it and he decided to change the subject by turning to Olkeloki.

"I can see why you liked this place."

"Yes." The old man looked uncertain as he gazed around the cool, dark room. "Though it smells different today than it did when I was eating here yesterday. I think because there are no other people eating here now." He tilted back his head and sniffed at the air.

"Better or worse?" Oak asked him.

"Oh, much better, though the foulness lingers."

"Foulness." Oak sniffed also. "I don't smell any foulness."

"It is not your fault. You cannot help the way you smell. It is not your body odor so much as it is the nature of your clothing. It is much worse to wear so much clothing when one is indoors. Besides ilmeet, we also refer to foreigners as iloridaa enjekat. This means 'those who confine their farts.' Because of the way you dress."

Merry responded to this with a loud guffaw that sounded as much like a bray as a laugh. She quickly put one hand over her mouth and bent low over the table, looking around quickly to see if anyone else had heard. But the restaurant was deserted except for their table.

"That's quite a laugh you've got there," Oak said mildly.

"Oh, shut up."

"We believe," Olkeloki continued, "that it is better to dress one's body loosely so that the wind may carry away the unfavorable bodily odors."

"Maybe that works fine in East Africa, but try that in Vermont some January." Oak sipped at his drink. "The wind'll carry off a lot more than your odor. Is that the story you wanted to tell us?" Olkeloki smiled. "What, then? Some expensive foreign aid project gone astray? That wouldn't be news. Or maybe something you're trying to get done for your people?"

"For my people, yes," he replied excitedly. "You are more perceptive than you would like to admit, Joshua Oak."

"Let me guess. It's a dam, no, an irrigation project of some kind."

"I am on an enkitoongiwong at the behest of a special okiama of laibon." Seeing their expressions, he smiled apologetically. "I am sorry. Some words do not translate literally into your English. I am here to seek help, yes, but not just for the Maasai. For the ilmeet as well. It is my duty as a laibon."

"What kind of help?" Merry was leaning forward again.

"If something is not done to stop them, and soon, they will destroy the world as we know it. Their very nature is anarchistic. All would dissolve into chaos. Those people who did not perish in the cataclysm of their coming would live on as slaves or amusements."

"So you're going to prevent this world takeover all by yourself, with our help, of course." Oak was glad he had a full drink and a lot of patience. "Don't you think that's a pretty tall order for one laibon and a couple of regular ilmeet?"

"It is the only way." Olkeloki responded to Oak's sarcasm with the utmost seriousness. "A larger group might be no more effective and would certainly invite cooperative retaliation. I by myself attract too much attention. I must have certain selected ilmeet with me, to screen me and shield my magic from their notice as well as to complete the three points of the triangle."

"Who are 'they'?" Merry asked.

Oak threw her a look as if to say, Haven't we wasted enough of an afternoon here, and wouldn't you like to tour the Smithsonian with me, because that's where I was heading when the Iranians threw us together, and maybe none of them were named Omar Khayyam but still . . .

"The shetani." Olkeloki whispered it. "The shetani are the spirits who can cross into our world. Not often, but when they do cross over they can work a great deal of mischief and make much trouble. The ilmeet suffer from their attentions because they do not know how to make them visible. I am not sure most would believe even if they saw.

"Something bad has happened. There is a place where the wall between reality and the Out Of has weakened and . . ."

"Excuse me," said Merry, "but what's the 'Out Of'?"

"It is where everything comes from. Everything has to come out of something, and it is simplest to call it the Out Of. It is the place where nothing goes in and everything comes out. An accident of some kind. Men first came from the Out Of, the first men your Dr. Leakey studied in a place not far from where I live, a place called Olduvai Gorge. The Out Of lies a long but not unreachable distance to the south of that ancient place. Men came out of it, and many animals, and plants. Perhaps they were fleeing the shetani, very long ago. It is a thought older than legends the laibon tell to their disciples. I do not know if it is true.

"But the Out Of is real, and the shetani are real, and they will come through the weakened place in irresistible numbers unless we can seal it up again."

"Irresistible numbers?" Oak sipped at his drink. "What kind of numbers?"

"Billions, who will be but the advance scouts for the armies waiting to follow. They will overrun the earth. They will destroy mankind."

"You said spirits." Merry fingered her own glass. "Are you talking about something like ghosts, or djinn?"

"No. They are nothing like that. You have no knowledge of them, so you ilmeet can recognize them only by their actions. A few ilmeet can see them, but they are rare." Merry squirmed uncomfortably in her chair.

"Already they have begun to make serious mischief. I believe they have been trying to get the two great ilmeet tribes to fight each other for many years now. The shetani are naturally lazy. Why fight long and hard if they first can get the ilmeet to weaken each other? I know the governments of the two great tribes would not listen to laibon, so I have come here to find help of another kind." He shook his head sadly. "You ilmeet think you know everything there is to know, but much of the cosmos remains a closed book to you. Your Einstein had the key to the Out Of but went off in a different direction to work on his relativity theories. I think maybe a shetani must have toyed with his equations. That would be like them."

Oak coughed loudly, tried to smile across the table. "All very interesting, I'm sure."

"How do we stop these shetani, Mr. Olkeloki?" Merry leaned forward. "You said you need our help. I'll be glad to help if I can." Oak examined the bottom of his glass studiously.

"They must be confronted at the place where they seek to come through in the greatest numbers. That is the only way to stop them. Get to the breakthrough place and seal it permanently. This must be done immediately."

"By you?" said Oak.

"Yes, by me," replied Mbatian Olkeloki. "I am not the only one who can do this thing, but I am the most qualified."

"Where is this Out Of place?" Merry wondered. "Where are these shetani coming into our world from?"

"The weak lines meet in a place just north of the Great Ruaha River, in a game preserve that lies close by a park of the same name. This is a vast and difficult to reach region that lies hundreds of miles to the south of Maasailand."

She nodded. "That's in Tanzania, right?" and before he could reply she blinked, eyed the ceiling, and said in the same breath, "Doesn't it seem to you guys that it's gotten dark in here?"

Oak didn't follow her gaze. Maybe it was a little dimmer than when they'd come in, and maybe it wasn't. "Clouding up outside, or could be they turn down the lights between lunch and dinner to save on their electric bill. No point in highlighting fancy decor if there aren't any dining customers around to enjoy it. Tanzania's in East Africa?"

"On the Indian Ocean." Olkeloki traced outlines on the tabletop with a long brown finger. "South of Kenya, north of Mozambique, east of the rest of the world."

"Local geography's more my style. I remember that the capital of Kenya is Nairobi, but I'm afraid that's about it."

"That is more than most of your geographically ignorant people know," said Olkeloki approvingly. "South of Nairobi lies the Steppe, then the veldt and the forests. South we must go to find the place where the shetani gather."

Oak spoke gently. "Not we, I think. I said I'd listen to your story. Now that I have, it's time for me to leave." He reached toward his wallet, knowing better but unwilling to abandon the old man. "If you need taxi fare back home, wherever home is, I'll stake you up to five bucks."

"You are calling me a liar." Olkeloki's tone was even. "If this were my country I would have to kill you." He spoke without malice, as though still telling his story.

I will tell you a story, I will buy you a drink, I will kill you if you call me a liar. Poor old guy, Oak mused. "I guess I'm lucky this is Washington and not wherever you really call home."

"You are young. The young are impetuous. You wrap yourselves in self-assurance to shield your mind from what it does not recognize."

"I see; sort of like TV wrestling or Creole cooking without pepper." He looked over at Merry. "How would you like to see my city? I know this town top to foggy bottom. Might get you into one or two interesting places you won't find on your tourist map."

"That's okay. I want to thank you for helping me during that riot, but I think I'll stay and listen to Mr. Olkeloki a little more."

Oak started to push back his chair. "Thanks for the drink."

The old man put out a hand to restrain him. "Please! You were made known to me as was promised. You have the second name of a predecessor in my land."

Oak's exasperation was beginning to show despite a desire for a cordial parting. "Look, I told you, I was not named after some long-dead, obscure explorer."

"You are the right man." Olkeloki glanced at Merry. "She is the right woman. Two to shield me, two to form the remaining points of the triangle. It must be so. You have to come with me, Joshua Oak. It is your destiny. Yours, mine, hers, all are entwined."

"Sorry, but the only place I have to go is home. I've been out of town on business and I've got about a six-foot-high stack of back mail to catch up on." Gently but firmly he disengaged the old man's fingers from his arm.

"I will pay for your help," said Olkeloki unexpectedly. "Properly, with cattle."

Oak smiled in spite of himself. "That's all right. You tell Ms. Sharrow here the rest of your tale and you pay her in cattle for going halfway around the world with you. I'm afraid my neighborhood isn't zoned for cows."

"Then if I cannot persuade you with true wealth . . ." Olkeloki started to reach into his coat and Oak tensed, the muscles in his hands and arms tightening. But all the old man brought out was a small leather bag, neatly secured at the top and decorated with attractive bead work in patterns of red, yellow, and blue. Clinging to it and drifting around it like an intermittent halo was a cloud of red dust. African earth, Olkeloki had said.

"Since you will not accept cattle, perhaps I might pay you with this." So saying, he turned the bag over and loosened the drawstrings slightly. Like so many misshapen marbles, a handful of irregularly shaped pebbles spilled onto the table.

Even in the reduced light they lit up the booth. There were gemstones the size of Oak's thumbnail. Some were a unique lavender blue. Others were a deep green whose minor inclusions gave them the appearance of aerial photographs of rain forests. There was also gold in the form of nuggets larger than the gemstones, and more crystals still, some transparent, others pale yellow, still more tinted light blue.

Oak eyed the bag. Olkeloki had emptied less than half the contents onto the table. The bag might now hold a collection of lead fishing sinkers or just plain rocks, but he had a sneaking suspicion it wasn't so. He pulled his chair back up to the table. Merry Sharrow was gaping at the pile with her mouth open. The expression on her face might have been taken straight from a children's book.

"They aren't real, are they?"

Oak picked up several of the nuggets, took a long one between thumb and forefinger. It bent easily and he finally managed to snap it in half. If it was dyed lead it had been colored on the inside as well as on its exterior. Putting down the nuggets, he picked up one of the bright lavender gems.

"Sapphire?"

The old man shook his head. "It comes only from my homeland and is called Tanzanite."

Oak put it down, nudged a couple of the green crystals with a forefinger. "And these? Emerald?"

Again the shake of the head. "Tsavorite."

Oak added a half handful of the smaller, transparent gems. "Also from your country?"

"Everything I have brought with me comes from my country. Those are diamonds."

That was what he'd suspected. Oak knew a little about diamonds because a group of radicals he'd infiltrated six years back had been financed with them. He'd suspected, but hardly dared to believe. A couple of the stones would weigh in at twenty carats or more. As for the Tanzanite and Tsavorite, he suspected they wouldn't bring the same return as the diamonds, but neither were they something you'd use to decorate the bottom of an aquarium. And there was the gold, too.

"You'd pay us with this?" he asked slowly.

Olkeloki nodded once. He looked bored and impatient, as though this were a part of his tale he was anxious to be done with. When the stones had been returned to the leather sack, he looked at Merry Sharrow.

"You can have it all. I have no need of it."

Gold and jewels will allow any man to suspend his disbelief, for a little while at least. "You say these shetani, these otherworldly spirits, are slipping into our world to cause trouble and that more of them, billions of them, are just waiting for the right moment to pour in and destroy us all?" Olkeloki nodded solemnly. "Unless we can seal up some kind of passageway which is located in a remote part of Tanzania?" Again the nod. "I didn't think ghosts and poltergeists deliberately hurt people. I thought they were content to rattle a few chains and throw toast across a kitchen."

"I think you know what people can do to one another, Joshua Oak, but of the other world, of the places that cling to the dark side of reality, you know very little. You should not be ashamed of this. It is true of most all ilmeet."

Oak wanted to ask him about the first part of that statement, but Merry spoke first. "How are these shetani dangerous to us?"

"They can assume many disguises, sometimes animals, other times seemingly inanimate objects. Very rarely, they can make themselves resemble people. But they can only accomplish such transformations successfully in the absence of light. By this I do not mean simply darkness. The pen in Joshua's pocket," and Oak glanced reflexively down at the ballpoint that rode in his shirt pocket, "is black. It could be a shetani, waiting for the right moment to sign your name wrongly to an important document, or to break your fingers."

Oak removed the pen. It was a perfectly ordinary pen. He smiled at the old man.

"Or it might not be," Olkeloki went on. "The shetani are very clever, mischievous and clever. I know that both your country and that of the great tribe that opposes you are full of shetani, many more than ever before. They are the cause of much trouble between you. They tend to concentrate in certain subtribes, like the CIA and KGB."

Oak didn't know whether to laugh or frown at that one. If naught else it was a novel thought. Imagine maleficent poltergeists wandering around Langley, Virginia, and Moscow stirring up trouble, causing discontent, perhaps misfiling important papers and fiddling with secret documents. Spooking the spooks, so to speak.

"I don't know what you're trying to say, old man, and I don't understand how you came into possession of that," he gestured toward the leather sack with its precious contents, "but I'll give you this: I've met a lot of strange people in my time, and you're unique. The KGB and the CIA, huh?"

"What about the mistakes they've made over the last thirty years?" Merry was eyeing him challengingly. "Even their governments haven't been able to figure out some of the things they've gone and done."

"Any secretive organization is going to trip itself up every now and then. Take it from me. Perfectly natural. Has nothing to do with infiltrators from the spirit world. I know because—" He stopped himself sharply. Was Olkeloki grinning at him? "Now look, old man, this—"

Suddenly the elusive smile vanished, to be replaced by a complete change of expression and posture. It was as if someone had smacked the African across the face. Instead of looking relaxed and confident, he was sitting up straight and stiff. His eyes were wide and unblinking as he looked first to his left, then right.

"What is it?" Merry was looking around also.

"There are shetani here," Mbatian Olkeloki declared.

Oak scanned the empty tables, the deserted restaurant. "I don't see anything." He was trying to let the old boy down gently.

"They are here." Olkeloki took no umbrage at Oak's comment. "Do you not see how dark it has become? They bring the darkness with them, on their backs. They cannot function well without it."

"Like I said, there's no reason to keep the lights turned up when a place like this isn't serving." That was no reason to turn them off completely, though, he told himself.

"You do not see them?"

"Sorry," Oak replied, and he was.

"And you, Merry Sharrow?"

She was trying to stare past the artificial palm trees and genuine potted plants, turning her head a lot. "I'm sorry, but I don't see anything either."

Their denials did not put an end to the old man's fantasy. "That's good. It means they sense our presence but have not located us precisely yet. The eyes of the shetani serve them ill during the daytime hours."

You had to admire him, Oak mused. Nothing fazed him. There were shetani here, but if you couldn't see them it meant it was because they hadn't found us. Neat. Like the kid whose dog chased airplanes and when he was teased about this by his friends replied, "We haven't had an airplane land in our yard since we got him."

"We'd better leave," Olkeloki whispered.

"I'm with you on that one." Oak pushed back in his chair, rose, and extended a gentlemanly hand to Merry Sharrow. She ignored it and slid out on Olkeloki's side. Oak shrugged.

Then something happened which cracked his smugness as surely as lead shot breaks a duck's neck. It wasn't particularly impressive, nor was it very loud. Just something between a cough and a grunt.

It wasn't imagined. Oak owed the fact that he was still alive to his highly trained senses. He was not one of those people who hear sounds where none exist. He looked sharply to his left, saw nothing.

"Ruvu shetani," murmured Olkeloki. "We must hurry." Merry moved close to Oak, perhaps unconsciously. The old man's fingers were tight around his staff.

Easy, Josh, he told himself. Don't let a little noise get you all—there it was again! Was that a rustling there, back among the dense silk flowers and well-watered dieffenbachia?

"Must be a waitress." His voice sounded unnaturally thin to his own ears. He took a step toward the cluster of real and artificial vegetation. Really shouldn't turn the lights off completely when there's anyone at all in the restaurant, he told himself.

"Don't go over there, Josh, please." Merry looked back at Olkeloki, who was also watching the greenery. "I loved your story, I really did. But it was just a story, wasn't it? You just like to tell people stories, right?"

Olkeloki gestured with his walking stick. "To the right, I think." As he said it the rustling sound came again.

Oak was torn between the desire to remove the snub-nosed .38 he always carried with him from its shoulder holster and an equally strong desire not to make himself look like an idiot. If some busboy or waiter was moving around back there deliberately trying to frighten them, Oak was going to return the favor in kind.

The gun stayed under his arm. Waving your weapon around in a downtown restaurant was not a good way to endear yourself to your superiors. Anyway, there wasn't anything over there.

Merry sounded small and lost when she spoke into the silence. "I smell something. Over that way." She pointed.

Oak had smelled it too, but he'd been so intent on trying to see through the bushes that he hadn't mentioned it. It was a strange, unsettling, unpleasant odor, as if someone had exhumed a month-old corpse and drenched it in brandy. It was weakly nauseating, sweet one moment and putrid the next. Perfumed carrion.

Olkeloki moved up close and put a hand on Oak's shoulder. "Come. Come quickly."

"It's just a story, isn't it?" Merry kept repeating that and Olkeloki kept not answering as they turned away from the dark recesses of the restaurant. He held the staff in both hands and his eyes kept darting from right to left as he tried to see between the tables.

They were alone in the restaurant. The bamboo that grew amidst concrete and steel, the palm fans in their pots, the vines that hung from the ceiling all testified to the art of a master decorator. The tables began to thin out, recede behind them.

Oak stopped, uncertain. "Wait a minute. We came in over there. I'm sure of it. We've walked too far in any case. This isn't that big a place."

"You are right. We have come too far." Olkeloki turned on his heel and starting retracing their steps. Soon he was running, which was crazy. The restaurant wasn't that big. You could run through it in much less than a minute. Merry and Oak were running too, running hard between the bushes and plants. Because the coughing, grunting noises were all around them now, and the rustling of the bushes was becoming violent.

Something in our drinks, Oak thought wildly. He got us to look away and slipped something in our drinks. Because this running was impossible. They should have run through the whole building by now. Then he glanced down and it was like the time he'd stepped into his shower and his hot water heater had been broken and a powerful stream of pure ice water had smacked him in the middle of his back, running down his spine to chill the crevice between his buttocks. In addition to being stunned he was scared, more scared that he'd ever been except maybe for the time in Idaho when he'd been discovered by that neo-nazi group and was sure he was going to be shot.

He was frightened because he was running over grass.

8

Then the grass was gone, as fast as if someone had slipped new glasses over his eyes, and he was moving over soft, low carpet once again. Green carpet, he noted absently. He was so relieved to see tables again, neatly set with napkins and silverware, that he almost cried out. And still the expectant, nervous rustlings and gruntings came from the vegetation closing down around them.

"To the right."

"No, straight ahead," Merry argued, "keep going straight!"

"You're sure?"

"I work at night," she told him, panting hard from the endless sprint. "I've got excellent sense of direction in the dark."

"No," he said abruptly, slowing to a halt. "Not yet."

Merry stopped nearby. "Please, let's just leave."

"Huh-uh. I want to know what's going on here. Hell, I *need* to know what's going on here, Merry. I need to know if this is some kind of test the Bu—my company is putting me through, or if this old fart's got us both hypnotized, or if this is some kind of new amusement ride or what." This time he did draw the .38 from its holster, not caring what any other patrons or employees of the restaurant might think if they saw it. Let the manager call the cops if he wanted to.

More sounds and rustling from a cluster of palms and calathea, and then a glimpse of maybe-movement. Busboy? The leaves stilled as he drew near the clump and he paused. It had to be a ride of some sort, or an elaborate gag that wasn't funny anymore. Or maybe he'd just been to too many movies.

Reaching out, he swept the top layer of leaves aside.

In the darkness an enormous gray-black face leaped toward him, fiery red-orange eyes burning like coals. Jaws parted to reveal a mouth that looked big enough to swallow a Volkswagen. From the black throat came an angry growl. Oak staggered backward and gestured feebly with the pistol, too shocked by the sight to aim and fire. Then it was gone.

Something the size of a house cat skittered from behind the cluster of bushes to vanish between two tables. Merry Sharrow had inhaled sharply behind him but had been unable to scream.

The three of them retreated slowly. Oak waited several minutes before returning the pistol to its resting place beneath his left arm. He might have cursed himself for not firing, but didn't. Would a .38 be any use against a visitor from hades anyway?

"What the hell was that?" he muttered, then looked sharply at Olkeloki. "What's going on here, old man?" He was conscious of the fear in his voice and desperately embarrassed by it.

"That was your lion," Olkeloki said softly.

"I asked you what the hell's going on here! No riddles."

"Not a riddle. Your lion. Everyone has their lion. I have mine, you have yours, she has hers. Most people do not see their lion until it comes for them. The first time is usually the last."

"It wasn't any damn lion. It was just a big dark shape." Wasn't it? Or had that dirty yellowish fringe framing the horrible face been something else? A mane? He looked at Merry. "You saw it too?"

"No, but I saw the other thing." She pointed between the two tables where the cat-shadow had vanished. "It ran from behind the bushes in front of you, under there. It looked like, it looked like— I think I've seen something like it before."

Olkeloki spoke without taking his eyes off their surroundings. "Yes, you are the right ones. I was right to choose you, as you chose me."

Ignoring him, Oak stared at Merry. "What are you talking about? You can't have seen it before."

"Not 'it,' something like it. About a week ago, back home outside of Seattle. I was driving home in a bad storm and just as I was getting off the interstate I hit something. I thought it was a big dog, about collie size. I kept telling myself it was a dog. But it didn't look like a dog. It looked like the thing that ran under the tables."

All kinds of craziness were racing around inside Joshua Oak's skull, bizarre thoughts colliding with one another, bouncing off reason and crashing through logic, messing up his usual cool calculation. Get out, no matter what's going on. Get out of this restaurant, out of this building, back into the clear no-nonsense June sunshine, down on the street where people were hawking newspapers and ice cream and giant pretzels. Get away from giant lion faces and twisted parodies of humanity that go scuttling out of sight beneath dining room tables.

Another distinct growl reached them from a clump of bamboo off to their right. "We must go from this place now," said Olkeloki intensely. "There is too much darkness here. The longer we linger, the stronger they become."

Ordinarily Oak would have trusted his own senses to lead him along, but he was so dazed by what he was seeing and hearing that he allowed himself to be led. Which was just as well. Merry Sharrow hadn't been just boasting when she'd laid claim to a good sense of direction in the dark. The restaurant brightened slightly as they came within sight of the wide picture windows that overlooked the city. He was extraordinarily relieved to see that it was still there.

The cash register was locked and there was no sign of the hostess who'd seated them. The carpet behind her little podium was stained. Probably a spilled Coke, though Oak found he didn't really want to examine the stain too closely. He tried to keep his body between Merry and that section of floor so she wouldn't see the stain. The hostess might appear if they yelled for her, and then again she might not, and something else might follow the sound of their voices.

Out. He wanted outside, immediately, *now.*

There were no offices atop the building. Only the restaurant. They moved rapidly down the short hall toward the waiting elevators. As they ran Oak was sure the noises behind them were growing louder and more distinct. Besides the grunts and growls there was something else, something new. A sharp chittering sound, a drunken distorted laughter like a cloud of muffled hornets might make.

Wuzz, wuzz—run, run!

He tried to divide his attention between the lights rising toward them on the plate between the elevators and the dark, now almost black, entrance to the restaurant. A pair of steel doors separated and they rushed between them. Oak jabbed repeatedly at the "G" that would take them to street level.

He didn't allow himself to relax until the doors closed and they started to descend. Then he glanced at Olkeloki. The African was watching the lights.

"I want an explanation, old man. Any kind of explanation, but I want one. And no more of this shetani bullshit, understand?"

"He already explained it to you." Merry sounded as much angry as frightened. "You saw it. You heard."

"I don't know what I saw and heard," he muttered, upset and trying to hide it. "I saw *something,* but that doesn't mean I actually saw what I think I saw." He thought back to the strain of the subcommittee hearing, the way he'd stalked out of the Capitol Building. "I've been under a lot of stress here lately."

"So have I," she said.

A little of the tension began to leave him. "There you go. I'll bet that's it. We've both been under pressure and it's affected our perceptions. We were listening to a wild tale in an empty restaurant, all decorated to match the story, and we had some booze and imagined a few things." The revelation came to him fast and unbidden and he grasped at it the way a taxpayer would an extra deduction.

"Sure, I know what happened. Somebody spent a lot of money to make that place look like Africa, or someplace tropical, anyway. Plants, carpeting, the whole bit. My first time there, your first time there. I'll bet there's some kind of sophisticated audio system to make jungle noises, add to the atmosphere for the diners. Something like that would be a natural. I'll bet you when they're not serving lunch or dinner they're checking out the ambience, testing the electronics."

She looked unsure. "What about the lion? How do you explain the lion?"

"Big screen video, rear projection." He was feeling much better now. "That kind of stuff's easy to do." The cat-thing—maybe a big rat. Or maybe a real cat, a kitchen scavenger allowed to run around loose between serving times to keep the rats out. The grass underfoot for an instant? His own imagination, or sweat in his eyes. An easy explanation for everything.

"I've got to hand it to you, old man. You work for this place? Is your boss back there now, congratulating himself on the efficiency of his updated electronics? Or is he waiting for us below? You made me pull my gun. I think you owe us a free dinner at least." Merry was tugging at his arm. "You ought to be in Hollywood. You're wasting your talents in a place like this." The tugging grew more insistent.

"Josh." There was fear in Merry's voice.

"Now what?"

"The elevator," she said in a small voice. "The elevator."

They were still descending. The building was only ten floors high and they were still going down. The light on the control panel had fallen beyond "G" and was now locked, blinking irregularly, on "B." For basement. Blinking as they continued to descend smoothly—to where? What lay beneath the basement? Far beneath the basement, beneath ground level, beneath the unmarked sub-basement with its conduits and pipes and electric lines?

Where were they going and what would they see when they finally stopped and the doors opened?

Something landed heavily on the roof of the elevator cab. Whatever it was it was big and solid. What it definitely was not was something projected by a hidden speaker or rear-screen projection unit. Merry Sharrow moaned softly and shrank back into the corner of the elevator, which continued its steady, precipitous, impossible descent. The cab was beginning to rattle and shake, just as if they were picking up speed.

"What's going on?" she asked in a tiny voice. "What's happening to us? I don't want to be here. I want to be someplace else, please, I want to be someplace else."

Oak was watching the ceiling. He had the .38 clenched in his right fist. Something else landed on the other side of the roof. It was heavy enough to make the elevator jerk on the end of its cable. You could hear them moving around up there, whatever *they* were. He thought he could hear that chittering laughter again but he couldn't be sure because of the racket the elevator was making.

How far had they descended? A thousand feet? Two thousand? What unsuspected shaft lay beneath the city of Washington? Had something been dug here long ago and abandoned by the government or the KGB?

The cab rang like a bell as something huge and powerful smashed through the ceiling. The metal bulged inward as if it had been struck by a falling girder, and the decorative plastic grillwork shattered, littering the floor with chunks of what looked like oversized white Wheat Chex. Light from the exposed fluorescents flooded the elevator. One tube hung swaying and crackling from two wires. Merry Sharrow screamed and tried to hide her face in her hands.

Olkeloki was trying to raise his staff over his head parallel to the floor, but the cab wasn't wide enough. Another blow reverberated in their ears and a second indentation appeared in the ceiling alongside the first. The elevator rattled on its cable and the lights flickered and threatened to go out.

The second blow, or punch, or whatever, had cracked the metal roof. Oak thought he could see something vast moving in the darkness above. Holding the pistol in both hands he took careful aim and fired, three quick shots in succession. In the enclosed metal box of the elevator the sound of the .38 going off was deafening. Merry screamed again.

Something on top of the cab made a sound like a belch—or maybe it was a moan. Oak hoped it was a moan. In any event the elevator slowed to a gradual stop. The only sound was that of Merry hyperventilating in her corner.

Cautiously Oak moved until he was standing beneath the crack in the roof. His finger tense on the trigger, he tried to see outside. No sound, no movement came from above. Whatever had been up there trying to get at them, solid or ethereal, had no taste for a .38 slug. He was suddenly aware that it was downright hot in the elevator. He was sweating profusely. From the tension no doubt. They couldn't have descended *that* far, surely.

What now? Somehow he didn't think pushing the red button marked "Emergency" on the control panel would do much good. The light continued to blink steadily behind the letter "B." Being a properly conditioned creature of technological habit, he reflexively pushed the button for "G." At first nothing, and then the elevator gave a jerk like bait at the end of a fishing line and wondrously, gloriously, began to rise on its cable. The comforting whine of machinery was clearly audible through the crack in the ceiling.

Mbatian Oldoinyo Olkeloki never took his eyes from the roof as he spoke. "Do you still think, Joshua Oak, that I am the representative of some government agency or amusement park?"

"I don't know who the hell you are, or what this is all about."

Merry Sharrow had managed to get back on her feet without help. "It was real." All three of them were watching the ceiling. No one looked at his neighbor, not yet. "It was all real. I could see it and—you could smell it. I can still smell it."

Oak could too. Perfumed carrion. He forced himself to breathe slow and steady, regularizing his heartbeat, until the elevator slowed and the light on the instrument panel shifted from "B" to "G." Merry moved a little closer to him.

The doors parted.

"Christ, buddy, take it easy!"

A young man with neatly cropped hair, red-and-blue-striped tie splitting the front of a blue suit, raised both hands and stumbled backward a couple of steps. Oak blinked at him, suddenly conscious of the picture he presented: clothes reeking of sweat and fear, hair disheveled, not to mention the .38, which he hastily returned to its holster.

"Sorry," he mumbled. "Mistake."

The young man dropped his hands in stages. "Hell of a mistake."

A slightly older man came up alongside the first. "What's going on, Dave?"

Oak stumbled out into the hall. It was full of junior bureaucrats and senior paper-pushers, male and female, hurrying to and fro. The bright light made his eyes water. Merry Sharrow and Mbatian Olkeloki were right behind him as they pushed their way down the hall.

"That guy had a gun," Dave muttered as he and his friend watched the harried trio retreat. "Looked stoned, too."

His companion shrugged the confrontation off. "What do you expect in a town like this? Come on or we'll miss the meeting." Together they stepped into the elevator.

Oak lunged through the open doorway and out onto the campus
of George Washington University. The air was filled with the intermittent roar of traffic on nearby Pennsylvania Avenue. In the intense
sunlight he turned to stare back at the building they'd fled. A perfectly
ordinary office building. Restaurant decorated in a tropical motif on
top, offices below, and something impossible and unsuspected beneath.
Storage in the event of a nuclear attack? Crazy as that was, access to
anything like that would be strictly controlled. And even if you did
accidentally manage to bypass alarms and security, you'd encounter
guards. Not something much bigger than a man capable of punching a
hole in the steel roof of an elevator cab.

Merry Sharrow leaned up against him. One hand clutched at his
coat. "I—I don't feel so good."

Oak didn't feel so good himself. He grabbed her with both hands
and held her steady, looked left and right. Street vendors half a block
away. "Hang on. We'll get you a Coke or something."

"We have to talk." Olkeloki looked anxious but otherwise unaf-
fected by the nightmare in the elevator.

"Yeah, sure, you bet your ass we have to talk. But not out here
and not in any more restaurants. Someplace where I know I can chat
without putting my sanity on the line. Where are you staying?"

"I have a hotel room, but now that a few of them have found me
I fear it may be under observation."

"Observation?" He remembered what he'd seen, or thought he'd
seen, through the hole in the roof of the elevator. Shapes, outlines,
inhuman silhouettes. Ugly things. And that smell. He experienced a
sudden, desperate urge to run like mad back toward the sanity and
safety of the Bureau offices, or the Capitol Building, or the Smithsonian.
He might have, too, except there was Merry Sharrow, clinging to him.

"Let's go to my place. It's a ways out of town and I think the ride
would do us all good." He glanced along the avenue, searching for a cab.

"Your house?" Not all of Merry's reflexes were paralyzed.

Oak checked his watch, a bit surprised to see that it still ran. Less
than an hour since he'd rescued Olkeloki and Merry from the mob
outside the White House. It seemed like days.

"Are you kidding? Even if I wanted to try something, Olkeloki will
be with us. Believe me, I'm not in the mood for anything except
explanations. Hey!" He waved and whistled sharply.

The cabbie saw his arm and slid neatly over to the curb. Oak and
Merry slid in back. Olkeloki got in next to the driver and looked back
at them. "I have already explained it all once, but I will be happy to
explain again. It will be simpler this time because you have seen."

Oak gave the cabbie an address. The ride was going to be expensive but he didn't care. All of a sudden the city no longer seemed familiar and friendly.

"Seen? I haven't seen anything," he said defensively. It was not one of his usual smooth, efficient lies.

Olkeloki simply smiled back at him. "You are not blind, Joshua Burton Oak. Neither are you dumb, however much you might wish it. You are the right ilmeet man. Merry Sharrow is the right ilmeet woman. You were made known to me. You cannot stop what is going to happen."

We'll see about that, Oak thought as the cab pulled away from the curb.

9

Near Burke Lake, Virginia—19 June

It was a source of endless amusement to Oak's colleagues that someone of his temperament and profession should choose to live in a place with the unlikely name of Butts Corners. He preferred it that way. The long commute didn't bother him because he rarely had to make it, his assignments keeping him away from hearth, home, and city for long stretches at a time. When he was home he was usually off duty. From his house he could walk to Burke Park and the lake where he could sit alone among the elms and oaks and just watch the water and its inhabitants. Not for Joshua Oak the fast life of a condo on the Potomac. When he finally concluded—no, survived—an assignment, he needed to slow down, not speed up.

He paid the cabbie and led Merry and Olkeloki up the flagstone walk to the modest two-bedroom house. Trees grew thick and close around the walls, shielding it from passing eyes. A station wagon with plastic wood flanks showed its backside in the open garage. The raised door was a signal that his housekeeper, Mrs. Hernandez, had been on the job. The very ordinariness of the home was comforting.

There was nothing unusual about the house's appearance, but the special keyless entry system wasn't visible from the street. Oak was about to enter the combination releasing the twin locks when Olkeloki stepped past him.

"Wait." The old man caressed the doorknob with long, wrinkled fingers, ran them along the edges of the jamb, and finally nodded. "It is all right now."

"Glad to hear it." Oak entered the combination and the locks clicked. As he pushed open the door he wondered why he felt so nervous entering his own home. *It's all right now.* Merry was talking to Olkeloki.

"The thing I hit on the road, that I thought was a dog? That was a shetani?"

"An N'tedi, from your description. They have very bright eyes set high up on their heads, like many insects, and long tails. The right side of their mouth droops and drags upon the ground."

Oak listened as he absently shut the door behind them. The events of the morning had left him badly shaken. His neat, rational world view was full of cracks. He spent his life dealing with irrational, illogical people. There was always some way of categorizing them, classifying them. How did you classify what had happened in the elevator, or the restaurant? What was happening to him?

The first thing that struck Merry Sharrow about the interior of Oak's house was its cleanliness. She had suspected the presence of a housekeeper but even so was startled. The condition of the home bordered on the antiseptic.

Small glass sculptures here and there, neat rows of records (all alphabetized according to composer or performer, she noted), book-shelves stocked with books that had actually been read, and a kitchen as clean as the bathroom. Unintentionally she found herself comparing it to Donald's more typical bachelor pad, with its articles of clothing tossed in corners, sports equipment in the refrigerator, and general aura of comfortable chaos. Oak's house was neater than her own.

Olkeloki hardly paid his companions any attention. "I must check each room and all the furniture. Only then can we relax and talk."

"Go right ahead." Oak collapsed into a chair that looked out of place among the clean lines of the rest of the furniture. It appeared to have been made in the thirties or forties and reupholstered three or four times since. The successive upholsterers had done a bad job of matching previous fabric. The result was a kind of off-color, crazy-quilt charm.

Merry took a seat on a nearby couch. The books looked more worn than most of the furniture. She and Oak watched while Olkeloki scrutinized the den, peering beneath tables, behind the television, even removing several of the larger books to look behind them. Without a word he moved on to the next room.

"Josh, what do you make of what's happened to us?"

"What?" He'd been lost in thought, now looked sharply over at her. "What the hell am I supposed to make of it? What do you make of it?"

"I asked you first."

He sat up straight. "Okay. I can rationalize what happened in the restaurant. You heard me do it. As to the elevator," he hesitated, "I can't explain what happened in the elevator. I think the only one who can explain that is in there." He indicated the kitchen, where Olkeloki could be heard moving around among the appliances and utensils. "And I can't accept his explanation."

"You were there. You saw, you felt the same things I did."

"Oh, something happened to us in that elevator. We weren't asleep and we weren't hypnotized. I may be a skeptic, but I'm not an ostrich." He looked lost, and it shocked her. Somehow she knew Joshua Oak had never been this lost before.

"I don't know what's going on here, Merry. I'm not sure I can handle it. I've always been able to handle anything that was thrown my way, and I've been in some pretty difficult situations." He put a peculiar emphasis on "difficult." "But this—how do you handle something like this?"

"There are times when we just have to accept things, Josh. I mean, if a flying saucer were to land in your backyard tonight . . ."

He bent forward and put his head in his hands. "Please, no talk about flying saucers. Not now."

"All I'm saying is that the world is full of unexplained phenomena. Up where I come from people believe in a man-thing called Bigfoot or Sasquatch. Nobody's ever proven its existence, but that doesn't mean it doesn't exist. Maybe these shetani, maybe they're like that."

Oak found a certain amount of relief in the course of deductive logic. "Then how come if they're causing trouble, like Olkeloki claims, nobody's seeing them now?"

"Maybe you have to look at them a certain way. Maybe they flip in and out of our reality like shadows, only they're becoming stronger because of this crack or weakness in the Out Of he keeps talking about. Josh, *I* saw something. I hit it with my car and I watched it run off into the woods. I tried to tell myself it was a dog, but it wasn't a dog. Now I've seen another one like it, that little thing that ran off under the tables in the restaurant. You saw it too."

"Yeah, I saw it." It was quiet for a while. They listened to Olkeloki rummaging around in the back rooms. "Remember what the old man said, about needing our help and how we'd made ourselves known to him?"

She nodded. There was a bowl of trail mix on the coffee table and she began picking out the coconut and raisins. "He said it was prophesied."

"Right. Now, I believe in prophecy and divination even less than I believe in these shetani or whatever they are."

"How do you explain the fact that you brought us together outside the White House? Him all the way from Africa and me from Seattle?"

"I don't explain it. I can't explain it any more than I can explain any of the rest of what's happened today. But you I can understand. You've encountered one of these things previously. Maybe you're sensitized to them or something. But what about me? Why me? How do I fit into the picture?"

"He said you had the same middle name as a famous explorer of his country."

"Pure coincidence and even if it's not, so what? How does that qualify me for a role in this looney tune?"

"Josh, what do you do for a living?"

"I already told you that I can't tell you."

She was eyeing him shrewdly. "Would it be useful to someone in Olkeloki's situation?"

"No. Yes. I don't know, Merry." Useful to Olkeloki? How? He was a professional informer, able to move without detection among dangerous, unbalanced people, able to gain their trust until the time came to betray them, to render them harmless. Did that make sense? Was it enough to tie him to an old man from Africa and all that had transpired?

Merry saw the uncertainty and confusion in his face. She swallowed and forced a smile.

"You have a lovely little place here. During the riot you as much as asked me out."

So much for subtlety, he thought.

"I'm guessing you're not married," she asked him.

"No, I'm not married."

"Ever been?"

"Twice." He could see that surprised her. "What do you think about that?"

"I don't think anything about it. Neither of them worked out, huh?"

"They both tried. First Susan and then Jessica. Susan lasted two years, Jessica two and a half. No kids. I wasn't ever home long enough to make kids a viable proposition. That was part of the problem, maybe the largest part. Pretty tough to make a life with somebody when they're always getting phone calls in the middle of the night telling them they have to go away for months on end. When they call home but can't tell you where they are or what they're doing or when they might be able to come home. A lot of couples have trouble making dinner conversation. I hardly ever made dinner." The corners of his mouth turned up slightly. "Susan always thought I had a mistress."

"Did you?"

"No. Wish I had. It might have made things better. Jessica never thought that. She tried real hard, Jessy did. I loved that woman, you know? We might even have been able to work it out. Trouble was she was too much like me."

"How do you mean?"

"One day I came home and she was gone. I guess she felt it was her turn to take off for a while. Only she never came back."

"I'm sorry," Merry said quietly.

"So am I. What about you? Surely someone as pretty as you has been married at least once?"

"Simple flattery's the best kind. No, but I'm," she almost said 'engaged,' decided she wasn't in the mood to lie, "going with a special guy. Four years now."

"Four years? What the hell's wrong with him?"

"Nothing's wrong with him," she said sharply. "It's just—it's just not the right time yet, that's all."

"Four years?" Oak repeated, muting his astonishment a little. "What's he want? To make sure you don't have some gross orthodontic disease or something?"

"When two people are thinking of a commitment for life they have to be sure of themselves." Oh shit, she thought. "Hey, I didn't mean . . ."

"Skip it."

"What I'm trying to say is that sometimes intentions don't always match up with results. We'll get married one of these days, when we both agree the time's right. I'm sure."

"You're sure?"

"Sure I'm sure. I have to be sure." Something small broke inside her and the Other Words came tumbling out, the words she often thought but never said aloud. "You know what I'd like to be, besides sure? I'd like to be engaged." She held out her right hand. "One crummy little cheapo ring, that's what I'd like."

Olkeloki interrupted her before she could really get started. "This house is safe. I think we can spend the night here, but tomorrow we must go."

Oak pushed himself up from the old chair. "You're asking me to accept a fundamental change in my world view. That's a lot to ask."

"Surely after what you have seen and experienced today you believe?"

"I can't say what I believe. I'm not sure what I believe right now. I have pretty much accepted one thing, though. You're in some kind of trouble."

"If that is all you can believe for now, that will be enough. I am in trouble, yes. You are in trouble, Merry Sharrow is in trouble, the whole world is in trouble."

"I don't know about the whole world and I'm not sure about Ms. Sharrow and myself," he said impatiently. "But I can see that you need help." He didn't add that he still wasn't sure what kind of help the old man needed. "I don't like the way old folks get pushed around these days. Was always taught to respect my elders and all that stuff. Always took it seriously. So if you're in some kind of trouble and you're convinced I can help, well . . ." He extended a hand.

Olkeloki's handshake was surprisingly strong. "Thank you, Joshua Oak. It may be that with your assistance we can do this thing. And with Merry Sharrow's aid as well."

Oak glanced back at her. "You're not coming!"

"Spare me the false gallantry. What did you think I was going to do? Go back to Seattle? Besides, what's it matter to you? Remember, we just met this morning."

Teasing me, Oak thought. Somehow this old dude's talked us both into accompanying him to Africa and she's sitting there on my couch teasing me. Damn but she's pretty when she smiles like that. No, not pretty. Beautiful. Damn.

"She must come with us," Olkeloki declared. "The triangle must be complete."

"Why me? If half of what you're carrying around in that leather sack is real you could hire yourself a dozen well-armed mercenaries to follow you anywhere. I could give you phone numbers to call."

"Numbers are not important. The corners of the triangle must be filled by those who have been marked. Myself, Merry Sharrow, you."

"Bull. I haven't been marked."

Olkeloki ignored the disclaimer. "You were made known to me."

Oak sighed resignedly. "I already said I'd try to help you. Where are we headed?"

"Kenya. We cannot fly through Dar es Salaam, which would be quicker. There were shetani watching the airport when I left. They can take the form of only certain kinds of people, but they mimic policemen very well. I am sure they saw me leave. They will be waiting for me to return. We would never get out of the city alive.

"So we will fool them. We will go to Maasailand from Kenya, from the north. Once we have mixed with the northern peoples we will not be as conspicuous."

"Easy for you to say. Don't you think Merry and I will stand out a little?"

"I do not. Oh, you mean because of your skin? The shetani are color-blind. They peer much deeper into a person to identify him. If they are given the chance to see inside any of us they will see the danger to themselves and take steps to eliminate it. But I believe we can avoid them once we are on the ground. I fear the Chuni shetani while we are in flight.

"Do not despair. All is not against us. The shetani fight among themselves as much as they do with human beings. Also, they are not well organized, which is why they have never been more than a nuisance before this. But if they cross through in such numbers mere disorganization will not stop them."

"Crazy, this is crazy." Oak smiled to himself. This morning he'd been soured on life by the indifference of yet another self-serving subcommittee. Subsequently he'd lived through two waking nightmares in an ordinary downtown office building. Now he found himself in his own home, his inner sanctum, having agreed to accompany a salesclerk from Seattle and an old man in trouble halfway around the world to do battle with a bunch of ghosts. Only—ghosts didn't run beneath restaurant tables or punch holes in the tops of elevators.

"I'm going to do everything I can to help," Merry was saying, as much to herself as to Olkeloki. "Everybody's always saying that I never try anything different. Well, I've always wanted to see Africa."

"It is a truly beautiful place," Olkeloki assured her, "as long as the shetani are kept under control."

She turned to Oak, met his stare evenly. "Whatever's waiting for us over there, at least it won't be boring. Besides, I'll be back here in ten days."

"Why ten days?"

"That's when my vacation's up. If I'm not back in ten days I'll lose my job."

He looked over at Olkeloki, his tone jaunty. "How about it, old man? Can we save the world in ten days?"

"We can but try."

"Merry, you're sure you know what you're getting into here? East Africa isn't Washington. We have riots, they have wars. Restaurants here close at nine, over there people starve. I don't know for sure what kind of trouble our friend here is in but I don't think it's a joke."

"This may come as something of a shock to you, Josh, but I'm a big girl now. I've lived on my own for six years, owned my own house for the last four, and I camp out alone in the wilderness all the time."

"Wilderness, right. You get in trouble, you call a park ranger."

"Billions of people will never know enough to thank you for what you are doing, Joshua Oak," said Olkeloki. "I am grateful for your help. The presence of a Burton in Africa is always respected."

"I wish you'd quit bringing that up. For the last time, I don't know anything about the guy and I doubt either of my parents did either. I'm coming along to help you out, that's all. Let's leave it at that."

That maddening smile again. "As you wish."

Merry watched their host out of the corner of an eye. A fine man, this slightly mysterious, soft-spoken Joshua Oak. She allowed herself to believe that he was coming along as much to look after her as to aid Olkeloki. It was an entirely romantic and entirely foolish notion, but one too delicious to discard. The farthest Donald had ever gone out of his way for her was when her Jeep had broken down late one night at the Seven-Eleven outside Tacoma and he'd struggled out of bed to come and pick her up.

"So when do we leave?" Oak was asking.

"Tomorrow morning we will fly to London. There we will change planes for Nairobi. If any shetani have picked up my trail we should be able to lose them while changing planes at Heathrow."

"I'll have to get my things from my hotel room," Merry said thoughtfully. "How much should I take?"

"As little as possible. One change of clothing only and what personal items you cannot do without. We will be moving quickly and lightly."

"You can't buy hose in the middle of Africa, you know," Oak commented.

"Gee, and I had that all figured out for myself."

"I have a couple of small backpacks we can use. Be better than fooling with suitcases."

Olkeloki looked pleased now that everything had been decided. "It would be best to spend the night here. They may follow my spoor back to my hotel, but I believe we lost them at the restaurant."

"All right. Merry, you can have my bedroom. I've got a spare and I'll sleep on the hideabed." He glanced questioningly at Olkeloki.

"Do not worry about me. I will sleep on the floor and keep watch, much as I used to watch my father's cattle. That is where I have been sleeping in my hotel. Your ilmeet beds are too soft for me. When I lie down upon one my spine feels as if it is turning to butter."

"Won't be much of a party, but we'll make do. I'll send out for Chinese and maybe we can find something watchable on the tube."

While the old man was "watching," Oak mused, maybe he and Merry could get to know each other a little better. Just a nice, quiet evening at home, he and Merry staring back at Johnny or David or CNN while this tall refugee from a Bela Lugosi film kept a lookout to make sure no monsters came to devour them until the last of the popcorn had been consumed.

There was one more thing he had to do, though. He checked his watch. Just time enough for him to get through. He dialed a Washington number. The memory phone held twenty numbers, but not this one. It was too important to commit to an electronic memory which someone with the right kind of equipment could tap remotely.

While the call went through he watched Merry Sharrow as she made her way around the kitchen. He could hear the sink running. A pleasant feminine voice trilled on the other end of the line.

"Name?"

"Joshua B. Oak."

Pause. "Code?"

He rattled off a string of letters and numbers and waited while she cross-checked with the inevitable computer. Finally, "To whom did you wish to speak?"

"Assistant Director Kilbreck."

"I'm sorry. I don't know if Mr. Kilbreck is available right now. May I take a message?"

"Oh come on, Julianna," said Oak impatiently, "knock it off. Kilbreck's sitting there in his office reading a comic book or something. He's always there doing as little as possible between four and five, as sure as the sun comes up in the east and sets in the west. Put me through. It's important." To me, anyway, he added silently.

"All right, keep your shirt on. I'll try and put you through." While he was waiting on the connection, Merry Sharrow came out of the kitchen. She'd washed her face and hands and was drying herself with one of his old towels. Olkeloki was occupying himself with the several shelves of books that took up one wall of the den. Oak still couldn't figure him out.

"Oak, that you?" Kilbreck did not encourage familiarity between underlings and superiors. Still, his tone was friendly enough, if all business.

"Afternoon, sir. You busy?"

"Busy killing time, which never files any wrongful death suits. I saw the tape of your star turn before the subcommittee. You did well, though in the future it might be wise to keep a tighter rein on your personal opinions. Just because Senator Baker asked for them doesn't mean you had to be quite so voluble in your reply. But the Bureau is proud of you." Which was Kilbreck's way of saying that he was pleased.

"Thank you, sir. Then you won't mind my taking a couple of weeks off. To tell you the truth, sir, I'm flat wore out. These last couple of years down south were pretty bad. I'd just like to disappear for a while, get my mind off Bureau business completely."

"I'd say you're overdue, Joshua. As I recall you haven't taken off more than five consecutive days since you joined the Bureau."

Kilbreck's recall was legendary among his agents. Oak wouldn't have been surprised if he'd quoted the exact vacation days his informer had taken off each year in the last ten. Or he might be utilizing his desktop computer to scroll through Oak's file.

"By all means take some time off. A month if you wish. You certainly have enough time accrued and, as you know, we encourage those of our people who function in stressful capacities to relax whenever the opportunity arises."

"What about that business up in New York?"

"Nothing that can't wait, or be handled on a temporary basis by someone else. I'd rather have you fresh and eager to tackle something like that than surly and run-down. Are you going to stay around Washington or were you planning to relax further afield?"

"Actually, sir, I thought I might spend some time in Britain. I've never been there and it's about time. I've always wanted to see Stonehenge and Westminster Abbey, places like that." Educational places. He could almost see Kilbreck nodding approvingly over the phone.

"The Mrs. and I have been there several times. You'll like England. Do try to stay away from guided tours. You never meet anyone interesting that way." They both chuckled. If there was anything Joshua Oak had enjoyed a surfeit of the past ten years, it was encounters with interesting people. That was the thought Kilbreck was laughing at.

Oak was chuckling at the image of Martin Kilbreck sitting in a country pub trying to mix with the local people. Kilbreck was about as relaxed in strange company as a telephone pole. The assistant director was an odd duck. He also happened to be one of the bravest and most decorated senior agents in the Bureau's history. Oak had learned early in his career that more often than not, the truly brave man tended to look more like your neighborhood druggist than Conan the Barbarian.

"When are you taking off?"

"Tomorrow, sir."

"Isn't that kind of abrupt?"

"I don't see any point in hanging around. I've been feeling like I needed to get away for a number of months now. I just couldn't decide to where. England just kind of came up. Now that I've made up my mind to do it, I figure I'd better get on with it before I talk myself out of going."

"Makes sense. You have a good time, Joshua, a good time. Get your mind off work for a while. We'll see about an assignment when you get back."

"Check. Thanks, sir."

"No need for thanks. You've more than earned your time off, Oak, more than earned it."

Oak let out a sigh of relief as the receiver at the other end was disconnected. That hadn't gone badly at all. No difficult questions, no requests for forms filled out in triplicate. Now he could lean back and enjoy the forthcoming journey he was about to embark upon in the company of a naive total stranger from Seattle and a crazy old man from Africa.

Sure he could.

10

Near Burke Lake, Virginia—20 June

The next morning Oak had the opportunity to show that in addition to being able to handle rioting Iranians and spirits that assaulted elevators he could also cook. The three of them sat around his small breakfast table eating and looking through the glass at the lush green woods behind his house.

"You clean house, you decorate, you cook." Merry finished her toast. "You're not a typical bachelor, Joshua Oak."

"Typical bachelors haven't had to live through two failed marriages. As for the way I live, I figure if you can't organize your private life, you can't organize your work, and if I can't organize my work, I'm . . . in trouble."

So what is it you do for the government, Josh? she mused. Some super-secret spy agency no one's ever heard about? Are you the truth that's stranger than fiction? You make great coffee, and that's strange enough.

He really was an interesting man. If only he were more open. Donald was open, and on occasion he could even be romantic, but he was definitely, decidedly not mysterious. Heretofore the only mystery in Merry Sharrow's live involved the window envelopes that showed up in her mailbox marked OCCUPANT.

Olkeloki had downed a whole quart of milk from Mrs. Hernandez's stock. He refused to touch bacon or eggs, but he eagerly devoured a brace of breakfast "steaks" Oak found in the bottom of the freezer.

"Except for cattle we eat no other meat save for an occasional sheep or goat slaughtered for ceremonial purposes. We kill no other grazing animals. The wild grazers are our trust."

"But you kill lions," Merry reminded him.

"To defend ourselves and our herds. With our spears and knives. The Maasai do not carry guns. It would not be fair."

"It's certainly more sporting." Oak was shoveling in scrambled eggs and hash browns.

Olkeloki's expression narrowed. "Sporting? There is no sport in killing. That is another strange ilmeet custom. I have studied it for many years and still find no philosophical basis for such an institution. Only immature children find sport in killing."

"Whoa now, I didn't say I supported it. Fact is I'm against it. Anything you kill, you eat."

"That is human."

"What hotel are you staying at, Merry?"

"Sheraton. This side of the river, I think."

"Fine." He wiped his mouth, crumpled the napkin. "We'll finish up here and I'll shove some stuff into one of my backpacks. Then we'll shoot over and get your stuff." He turned to Olkeloki. "How about you?"

"I have one suitcase. I am somewhat attached to it."

Oak nodded. "We'll get it too and then head out to the airport. What about reservations?"

"That will not be necessary. We will buy tickets on the next appropriate plane going to London."

"It may not be that simple." Oak repressed a smile. "School's out and this is the time of year when a lot of Americans take their vacations."

"It has been my experience that they do not fly on a plane called the Concorde. It flies higher than the shetani."

"Seats on the Concorde cost 50 percent more than first class on a regular flight. How are you going to pay for that? You can't just dump gold and diamonds in front of a ticket clerk."

"I have also brought with me many traveler's checks. I am not ignorant of the ways of ilmeet commerce, Joshua Oak, and I prepared for my journey accordingly. How do you think I came from London to your city? I only wish the same machine traveled between London and Nairobi but alas, it would not be a profitable route. You ilmeet are driven by profit. We could fly one to Riyadh in Saudi Arabia, but I should prefer not to."

Oak was sympathetic. "Memories of the slave trade, huh?"

"Which did not involve the Maasai. We were not cooperative enough. No, it is simply that I would like to avoid the extra change of planes that would be necessary. And the connections are bad. I do not wish to linger in London."

"It's your money. We'll get Merry's stuff, then yours, and head on out to Dulles. How was your breakfast?"

"The milk had a strange flavor and was too cold at first. The meat was good, though not fresh."

"Maybe it was aged. Isn't meat better after it's been aged?" Merry asked.

"A common fallacy among the ilmeet."

Oak's housekeeper had made use of the station wagon. It started instantly and the needle on the fuel gauge swung right until it cleft the "F." Rush hour was fading and it didn't take long to make their way into town, stop at the two hotels, and swing back west toward the international airport. It was too early in the summer for the real heat and humidity. Spring flowers still lingered among the trees lining the roads.

Oak was startled to find that he was starting to enjoy himself. Danger of an as yet undefined kind might be stalking their footsteps, but he could live with the presence of that old companion. By God, he was on vacation! And being paid handsomely for taking one. He could thank the old man for that while trying to keep an open mind about these shetani of his.

Not only was he on vacation, but a pretty woman was riding next to him. Merry Sharrow was staring out the window, finding as much delight in the sight of a new home set back among the trees as in the White House or Library of Congress. He wondered if she would show similar enthusiasm for the delights of the boudoir.

The station wagon rolled onto the shoulder and he resolutely forced his gaze back to the road.

Traffic was light as they turned off Interstate 66 onto the section of freeway known as the Dulles Airport Access Road. The heavy station wagon might be a technological anachronism, but it provided a smooth, easy ride no compact could match. Merry continued to ooh and aah at each new scene, exuding enough energy to power the big Ford all by herself.

She really hasn't the faintest idea what she's getting into, he mused. An ordinary (well, prettier than ordinary) woman from the wilds of the Northwest on an ordinary vacation who'd fallen into something out of Frank Buck by way of James Bond. Right now she was too excited by the prospect of going off on a genuine "adventure" to consider that it might be full of real dangers. Probably all she could think about was that she was going to an exotic land to see all those funny animals you normally only encountered in zoos.

They sped past the turnoff to Wolftrap Center as he spoke to the sole occupant of the back seat.

"What do these shetani look like?" As he asked the question he remembered loading the wagon. First his backpack, then Merry's, and lastly the old man's suitcase, older and more beat-up than any piece of luggage he'd ever seen. Either Olkeloki had done a lot more traveling than he'd talked about or else that suitcase had been sitting out in the African sun for years. It reminded him of the old commercial for American Tourister luggage, the one where a gorilla spends several minutes bashing the suitcase around his cage. Ironic that Olkeloki was the only one he'd ever met who might actually have been in a position to have that happen to his luggage for real.

"No one knows for certain," the old man was saying in reply to the question. "There are hundreds, perhaps thousands of different kinds of shetani. You saw one yourself."

"All I saw was something small that went running across a restaurant floor. It might've been a house cat. Whatever was on top of our elevator could have been a man."

"What about my dog-thing?" Merry countered.

"You've already said yourself it looked as much like a person moving on all fours."

"There are shetani with more than one head," Olkeloki was saying, "and the two are not necessarily alike. There are shetani whose faces dangle from the ends of their arms in place of hands, and shetani with mouths bigger than their bodies. There are shetani as tall as giraffes, like the Likutu, or the dangerously playful like the Adinkula. Some shetani practice witchcraft. The Liyama eat only clay and water.

"The Siwawi eat fish and live in the ocean, but come out on land to suck energy out of each other's tongues, and the Chingwele eat only snakes. They have sharp blades growing from their heads and arms. There are three kinds of chameleon shetani: those who resemble ordinary reptiles, those as big as your arm, and some who grow to the size of a cow. You do not ever want to encounter one of those."

"Why not?" asked Merry.

"Do you know how a chameleon eats?" He went into graphic detail until Merry looked mildly disgusted and Oak decided to put an end to these fantasies once and for all. It was time to get serious, time to take the masks off and find out who they were really up against.

"What I don't understand," he said casually, "is that if these shetani are around us all the time, why we don't see more of them?"

"You do not know how to look for them. Also, most shetani move about only at night, when people sleep. They usually avoid people. Now that the way from the Out Of is weakening, that is beginning to change.

But once you see one clearly, you will always be able to see them. It is both a blessing and a curse, because as you become able to see them, so they will be more aware of your awareness. Sometimes it is better to dwell in ignorance. That is a luxury we can no longer afford." He looked out the right side of the car and spoke again before Oak could offer his next carefully thought-out objection.

"Never have I seen so many shetani, so bold and numerous. They must have been gathering for many years to be present in an ilmeet country in such numbers."

Oak looked sharply to his right, saw nothing unusual, and made a quick scan of the terrain ahead and off to the left. The car swerved slightly and Merry threw him a cautioning glance.

"There's nothing out there but trees and highway, old man."

"They cover themselves with darkness. That is why they cling to the forests and the night. But they are here, yes. They are all around us, clever little killers that they are. I think they are enjoying the warm sun. They must have worked long and hard to perfect such disguises."

For a second time Oak surveyed the highway, saw nothing but pavement, trees, an occasional house. Cars and trucks flashed by in the opposing lanes.

"The next time we pass one of these things, you point it out to me as we go by."

"Very well. It may be dangerous for us. As I said, the shetani usually leave people alone in broad daylight—unless they feel others are aware of their presence. Then they may react."

"I'll take that chance."

"Are you sure, Josh?"

"Look, woman," he told Merry in no-nonsense tones, "don't you understand what's happening here? This isn't a damn game. We're getting ready to jump on a plane to fly halfway around the world with an old man who may or may not be missing a few straws from his bale because something or somebody is giving him and his tribe trouble. I'm convinced something happened to us yesterday in that restaurant and elevator, but I'm still not sure what. Before I go transatlantic, I'd like to be sure."

"I do not understand all your words, Joshua Oak." Olkeloki was frowning.

"No big deal. You just show me the first shetani we pass."

"If you insist."

If Oak expected a long silence, he was disappointed. The old man looked out the window to his right and pointed. "There, three of them, hibernating as is their wont."

"What, where?" Oak hit the brakes so hard that Merry had to use both hands to keep from being thrown into the dash. Fortunately there was no one behind them or they would have been rear-ended for sure.

The station wagon skidded to a stop on the shoulder, leaving black streaks on the concrete. Oak backed up until they were parallel to the spot Olkeloki had pointed out. Beyond the drainage ditch thick with flox and ragweed lay private forest, bushes, and grass.

"Where? I don't see a damn thing. Are they back in the trees?"

"No, they are quite near." Oak snorted, started to open his door. "I wouldn't do that," the old man said hastily. "They may be sensitized to you by now."

"*What* may be sensitized to me? Look, this has gone just about far enough. I don't know what happened back at the restaurant, but I sure as hell don't see any African aberrations running around out here." Ignoring the old man's warning, he got out and walked around to the front of the car. Merry Sharrow looked on anxiously, scanning the trees. The dog-thing had disappeared into the trees, that rainy morning back home. She rolled down her window.

"Josh, maybe you ought to get back in."

The only things moving in the grass and bushes were birds and bugs. A couple of cars going toward the airport whizzed past in the fast lane. Overhead a 747 lumbered southward, probably heading for South America. When he'd first stepped out onto the pavement he'd felt nervous, then silly. Now he was getting angry.

"Why? You see anything, Merry?"

"No," she admitted.

Olkeloki slid out of the back seat and walked up to stand alongside Oak. He gestured with his walking stick, not into the woods but down into the ditch. Merry strained to see. Oak didn't have to strain. It was so sad he couldn't laugh. So the whole business yesterday had been some sort of illusion or clever cover after all.

Three large, twisted black shapes lay on the edge of the ditch. They were chunks of tire rubber, the kind of debris that's scattered along the banks of every highway and interstate in the country. Whenever a big eighteen wheeler loses a tire, the rubber shreds during disintegration, sending pieces of itself flying in all directions. Eventually the fragments are bumped or pushed to the sides of the roadways until cleanup crews can get to them.

"And I suppose those empty beer cans over there are giant insects," Oak snapped. "Maybe it's time you told us what kind of con you're really trying to pull?"

"Some of it is tire rubber." Olkeloki did not wear the look of a man who'd been found out. "Notice the color."

"Black. What should it be, pink?"

"Black is the color of the shetani, the color of night, the only color with which they can mask themselves. You have to give them credit. What a clever way to conceal themselves in the countries of the ilmeet until the time comes for them to rise up and work their chaos. This way they are able to hide in plain sight and even to move about. The shetani have been very smart."

"Sure they have." Drawing back his leg, he prepared to kick the nearest chunk of rubber into the ditch. Merry inhaled sharply.

The tire fragment sailed over the ditch and landed in the grass beyond.

Oak turned back to the car. "Did you see that, Merry? Did you see the danger we're in? See, killer African ghosts, right here on the highway." He wound up and kicked the second piece.

If he hadn't been wearing his hiking boots he probably would have lost his foot. The black strip twisted like lightning. Flat, razor-sharp teeth clamped down hard on the ankle of the boot and penetrated about a quarter of an inch. A shocked Oak stumbled backward against the hood of the station wagon, kicking reflexively, but the basketball-sized figure clung to his foot with its obscenely large mouth. It had a long body, a pencil-thin neck, long thin arms, no legs, two eyes at the end of stalks which were offset to the right side of the flattened skull, and a mouth full of four-inch-long teeth.

Unable to reach flesh and bone, the little horror released its grip on his ankle and bit down higher up. The leather there was thinner and Oak could feel the edge of the teeth. He kicked again, waving his leg around in the air. The horror hung on despite his violent contortions. A long thin tongue lined with tiny filelike teeth shot out of the top of the mouth and whipped up his pants leg. It was a good two feet long and normally lay curled up deep inside the bulbous body.

"Get it off," moaned a voice Oak barely recognized as his own, "Get it offfff!"

Olkeloki took a step to his left, raised the heavy walking stick over his head, and brought it down sharply on the shetani's back. To Oak it seemed that the staff just bounced off that incredibly tough body, but the horror's eyestalks swiveled around to glare up at the laibon. The staff descended a second time to crash against the narrow skull. The eyestalks retracted and the shetani let go.

It stood there for an instant, glaring and growling at them. Then it turned and sprinted toward the ditch, running on its two hands and occasionally balancing itself with that disgusting tongue. It leaped over a pile of broken bottles, bashed through a sack of garbage, and vanished into a drainage culvert.

A big Safeway truck went thundering past. The driver let off a blast from his air horn by way of greeting. Oak leaned against the hood of the car, listening to his heart trying to blast its way out of his chest.

Olkeloki put his hand on his shoulder and he jumped. The old man was not smiling. "Come. They know we are here. They will gather to try to stop us now."

"I don't know what to say. I—I'm sorry I—that *thing* . . ."

"Apologize later. Drive now. We do not want to be caught out in the open like this and stopped before we have begun."

"No—no." He turned and limped back toward the driver's side. There was pain above his ankle where the creature's teeth had penetrated. He could still see it clinging determinedly to his leg, the red eyes glaring soullessly up at him, could feel that grotesque tongue rasping against his skin. His sock was starting to get soggy with blood.

The station wagon left rubber behind as it squealed out into the highway. The Toyota Celica Oak hadn't seen in the rear-view screeched as its driver sent it careening wildly around the wagon. The man shook his fist and shouted unheard obscenities. Oak ignored him.

Merry was leaning over and studying his right leg. "I can see the tooth marks where it bit through the top of your boot."

He nodded absently, pushing the wagon up to seventy-five before slowing down. He didn't want to be stopped by the patrol. Not here. It took him a few minutes to find his voice.

"What the hell was it?" he asked hoarsely. "What was it, old man?"

"A Namangonye shetani, I believe. Normally they are interested only in stealing food from gardens and they leave people alone. But these are not normal times. Not with the barriers between reality and the Out Of growing so weak. Ah, there are two more of them."

Oak kept his gaze resolutely forward, but Merry looked to her right. She followed the objects with her eyes until they had receded out of sight. "They really do look like tire fragments."

"Most are nothing more than what they appear to be. It is difficult to tell. The shetani are superb mimics and can—"

"Oh shit!" Oak wrenched hard on the wheel. Merry screamed as the station wagon skidded, slid, and bumped over something. Oak glanced into the rear-view mirror. "Whole slew of 'em, lying bunched up in the middle of the road waiting for us."

"What if it was only tire rubber?" Merry said accusingly. "You could have killed us!"

"Didn't you feel it?" he replied wolfishly. "Smashed right through them. It didn't feel like running over rubber." Already the objects they'd struck had fallen out of sight behind the fast-moving car.

"But how could they know so soon?"

"They are aware of our presence now," Olkeloki explained. "They have their own means of communication, which I cannot pretend to understand, but I think that we will be safe once we are on the plane."

Merry's response was to let out another scream and try to bury herself in her seat. Something was crawling over the front grille, clawing its way over the LTD symbol on the front of the hood and making its way slowly toward them. This one had legs. It also had a gaping mouth that ran from the right side of its face all the way around and up the left jaw to end only where an ear should have been. Four spikes ran across the top of the head. They were ridged as if with fur. The eyes bulged out of the skull and a single nostril protruded from the right side of the face. Sharpened, human-sized teeth lined the vast mouth.

"Kibwenge shetani," said Olkeloki. "They are very persistent."

"Make it go away!" Merry whined.

It was right up against the glass now, staring in at them, kneeling on its thin legs and holding on to the windshield wipers. Stretching its impossible mouth incredibly wide it bit down directly in front of Merry. The teeth cracked the glass but didn't penetrate. Meanwhile Oak was trying to maintain control of the wildly weaving car while fumbling for the gun in his shoulder holster.

"Concentrate on your driving. Stay on the road or we are lost!" ordered Olkeloki in a commanding tone Oak had never heard him use before. The old man reached into his jacket and produced another small pouch. Instead of gold and gems, this sack was filled with something dry and foul-smelling.

He extracted a pinch of dried weeds and dust, leaned forward over Merry's shoulder, and slammed his dust-filled palm against the windshield just as the shetani bit down again. A rapid-fire series of coughs reached them through the glass. Both the shetani's hands and feet contracted in a useless attempt to cover that enormous mouth. With nothing left to maintain its grip, it went tumbling off the right side of the station wagon, bumped once against the underbody, and was gone. Looking into the right-side mirror, Oak could see it go bouncing and tumbling down the pavement behind them.

"Jesus," he muttered. "It must have been one of those I ran over. It must have grabbed hold of an axle or something. I was doing sixty at the time."

"Some shetani are very quick and very strong."

He glanced back at the old man. "How did you make it let go?"

Olkeloki was carefully replacing the tiny sack in a coat pocket. "I made it sneeze. The shetani do not like to sneeze. It can kill them. So it let go. It was not tire rubber we drove over, Joshua Oak. You are becoming aware of them. You are more sensitive than you think."

Oak's heart was slowing down, his respiration returning to normal. "Yeah, well, on the whole I'd rather be watching the 'Skins play the Cowboys." He could feel the warmth of his own blood inside his right sock. The wound was messy but shallow. If dogs had rabies, what did shetani carry? He decided he didn't want to know.

"And you say millions of those things are going to appear everywhere unless we can stop them?"

"Not millions," replied the old man quietly, "billions. Am I correct in assuming we will have no more of this ilmeet nonsense about what is real and what is dream, and that I may now devote my energies to the important task that lies ahead?"

"You bet your ass, old man." He looked over at Merry. "You okay?"

"Ugly. They're so *ugly*. Like parodies of people and animals all mixed up together. I'd much rather see a homey old ghost."

"There's nothing wrong with their teeth, either. Anytime I start feeling skeptical again, the pain in my leg will take care of it."

"Will you be able to walk?" Olkeloki was leaning over the front seat.

"Bleeding's pretty much stopped. I've got some stuff in my pack we can dress the wound with. From now on I'll look twice before I kick *anything*."

11

Volgodonsk, U.S.S.R.— 20 June

Petrovnich was out of breath by the time he reached the office. That in itself was of no particular significance. The engineer was badly overweight. But the expression on his face made the chief engineer sit up fast and put aside the automobile spare-parts newspaper he'd been perusing. Petrovnich was keen-eyed, nervous, and entirely too dedicated to his profession to suit the easy going Alexiyev. On the other hand, if anything went wrong you could count on Petrovnich to ferret out the trouble and fix it. This was valuable, especially when the chief inspector came out from Kiev on one of his infrequent but always disquieting surprise inspection tours.

So while Alexiyev was not personally fond of Petrovnich, he held the man's talents in high regard. Nor was his subordinate a man to waste time.

"Comrade Chief Engineer, I regret to report there is a leak."

"A leak?" This was an alien term, a foreign term, a term which had no place in his office. "In the men's washroom? That's what you mean, Petrovnich. There's another leak in the men's washroom?"

"Would that it were, Comrade Chief Engineer. The leak is on the face, dead center, about two thirds of the way down. I was walking the river road and just happened to glance in that direction. The sun was just right or I wouldn't have noticed it at all, which I suspect is why it has not been reported yet. It is definitely a leak."

"In that case," muttered Alexiyev, all thoughts of buying some parts for his laika quickly forgotten, "we'd better have a look at it, hadn't we?"

The Tsimlyansk dam across the Don was one of the largest in the Soviet Union, one of those massive utilitarian projects the Soviet government was so proud of showing off to visiting dignitaries. It was a statement of socialist dedication and a testament to modern engineering. "Here I am," the dam declared, "and like the people who raised me up, I shall not be moved." It was solid as the earth it was composed of, immense and broad, more a fold in the earth than a man-made edifice. The huge lake backed up behind it provided power for the cities of the southern Ukraine as well as water for irrigation and flood control.

Chief engineers at the Tsimlyansk station had come and gone. Alexiyev was the latest and he was no less impressed by the finality of the dam as it regulated the Don's southward flow. And yet this immovable object, this simple marvel of engineering, which had never given anyone any trouble in the decades since it had been built, had, if Petrovnich was to be believed, sprung a leak.

Chief Engineer Alexiyev hung slack in the safety harness, having been winched down from the top of the dam. The winch and the men operating it were invisible far above, the tamed river still dizzyingly distant beneath his backside. His feet kicked at the dirt wall in front of him. Petrovnich hung in a similar harness on his left, looking queasy but determined. Petrovnich didn't like heights.

Alexiyev had been staring for several minutes now. He continued to stare in disbelief as a steady stream of water gushed forth from the face of the dam exactly where the assistant chief engineer had insisted it would. Less water emerged from the unseen crack than from a garden hose on a hot summer day. That in itself posed no danger. It was the implication of what might lie behind the stream of water that was threatening.

It might be nothing more than a narrow fissure, the result of millions of tons of rock and earth settling unevenly over the years. In that case the leak should soon heal itself. The structural integrity of the thirty-million-odd cubic yards of fill might not be involved. Better not be involved. No, what mattered was not this thin spurt of cold water. What mattered was what the dam looked like on the opposite side of the leak. He would have to send down divers and he didn't want to, because requesting divers meant filling out time-consuming, complex forms as well as reporting to Kiev. It might mean a visit from the disliked chief inspector.

Not that he had any choice in the matter. There was the leak, plain as a tear on a movie star's cheek. He could not flip a coin to determine the safety of the thousands of people who lived downriver from the dam.

The divers arrived that afternoon. They went down into the cool water near the base of the dam, trailing power lines for their high-intensity underwater lights and many safety lines. They were not enthusiastic. Rumor had it that the lake was home to bottom-feeding fish big as tractors.

The divers saw none of the imagined giants but the face of the chief diver, a powerfully built sandy-haired young man named Sascha, indicated that he had seen something else. Alexiyev steeled himself for the worst.

As it turned out it wasn't quite that bad, but in some ways it was worse.

"Well?" He addressed the diver as he was doffing his tanks with the aid of an assistant. The man's face was flushed from the time spent in cold water.

"There's a hole down there all right, Chief Engineer."

Alexiyev swallowed. "How big?"

The diver held both palms out facing each other about half a meter apart. A great surge of relief flowed through the chief engineer.

"That's *all?* You're sure?"

"Yes." Sascha began unzipping his wet suit. "They were all about the same size."

Some of Alexiyev's relief was replaced by something less exhilarating. "All? There is more than one hole?"

Sascha nodded slowly. "Comrade Chief Engineer, there are dozens of them." Alexiyev suddenly felt unsteady. "Evenly spaced from each other and covering a section of the interior dam face about thirty meters wide by ten high. If I did not know better I would say the dam was infested with giant rock-eating termites. That's just what it looks like—a house that's being chewed up by termites.

"Furthermore, as near as we could tell with our lights, the holes all go straight in. They are smooth and even on sides, top and bottom. I don't see how they could have been caused by erosion. I would bet my reputation as a professional diver, Comrade Chief Engineer, that those holes have been excavated, bored, whatever you want to call it. Someone has been down there boring holes in your dam. They have been doing so in precisely the right place to cause a catastrophic structural failure." Alexiyev could see that the young man was not frightened. He was angry.

The chief engineer was thinking too hard to be angry. He was not normally a fast thinker but this afternoon his brain was functioning at near the speed of light.

"You're certain of all that you've told me, Comrade Sascha? You realize what you're saying."

"As I've said, I stake my reputation on it. My men will confirm this. You can send down other divers if you wish. I should like to go down again myself, with Gregoriov and one other, as soon as our tanks have been refilled. We want to take cameras with us this time."

"Yes, yes, of course." Alexiyev was hardly hearing what the young man was saying. He was staring out across the vast expanse of the dam, trying to reconcile its apparent solidity with what the divers had seen.

He was thinking of the hundreds of thousand of people living along the banks of the river downstream, of the farms and factories, all wiped out in minutes by a collapse of the dam. He could not conceive of anyone who might want such a thing to happen. For someone to consider doing it, he would already have had to forfeit his humanity.

"By all means go down with cameras, Comrade Sascha. Take plenty of pictures of the—holes. I'm going to need them."

"You'll have them." He turned away, hesitated long enough to look back. "One more thing, Comrade Chief Engineer. I think that since even photographs may be questioned it might be a good idea to call in some people from the army."

"Yes. They will need to be informed. Everyone will need to be informed."

San Onofre, California— 20 June

Carrington stared out at the broad gunmetal-gray sheet of water that was the Pacific Ocean. It was eighty-four outside with the hottest part of the day still to come. He forced himself to turn away from the window and the cool water. Still hours before checkout time. He took a lot of kidding from friends for the time he spent in the water so near to the plant's outfall, but he always joked back in kind.

"When my board starts glowing, maybe I'll cut down—and that'll depend on whether or not the surf's up."

Around him the great installation hummed silently at full-throated power, feeding energy into the extensive Southern California grid, keeping air conditioners running uninterruptedly in Los Angeles and San Diego. As usual, the control room was overstaffed. Why they needed so many people he didn't know. If the NRC would just let up on the industry a little they could save the taxpayers a lot of money.

But no. There had to be backups to watch the backups to watch the on-line shift. The result was that he was drawing a top salary for doing next to nothing, wasting a degree in nucleonics when he could have been doing something worthwhile with his time. His eyes drifted back to the window overlooking the empty beach below. Like sitting on his board waiting for a wave with a pipeline in it.

He waved across the room to Charlie, checked the nearest clock (the room was full of clocks). It wouldn't be long until he could check out, change into a suit, and get in an hour or two in the water before the sun went down and it was time to head home to San Clemente.

He was thinking about all that as he sat down on the edge of a colleague's desk and the earthquake struck.

It seemed to go on forever. That is a characteristic of any earth tremor that continues for longer than five seconds. This one rattled the landscape for almost a full minute. Desks were cleared by the shake, which sent pencils and pens, books, and manuals flying. Near the end of the quake the ground seemed to give one monstrous heave, as though a gargantuan hand had shoved the edge of the continent from below, raising it eight inches before allowing it to crash back against the underlying basalt.

Alarm bells were ringing all over the place, sirens were howling, and people were alternately yelling and cursing at one another. It was just like the nightmare Carrington had managed not to have in the four years he'd been assigned to San Onofre. The nightmare of the red lights.

They were blinking on now, singly and in groups, on the walls that lined the control room.

"Jesus Christ!" muttered Fossano, a huge bald butterball of a man who looked like nothing so much as a snowman desperately out of place in semitropical Southern California. He was sweating, and not from the tension of the earthquake. His eyes were scampering over one gauge after another, his hands moving like those of a concert pianist on the controls below. All he wanted out of life at that moment was for the red lights to turn green once more. He pleaded and begged as he worked, running through half the Catholic liturgy. Yellow. He would settle for yellow. Anything but red.

The son-et-lumiere display refused to cooperate, though he did manage to induce some of the red lights to wink out. But more kept flashing on, faster than he could work. He kept murmuring "Christ" over and over to himself.

Boseler, better known as The Old Man, was in the midst of it all, running back and forth from one station to another like a rat looking for an exit from its maze. He moved fast and talked quietly, displaying the control everyone else in the room wanted to demonstrate but didn't possess. He was sweating too, Carrington noted, as he dropped into his own chair. That was scary.

"Backup One through Six on-line and operating!" he yelled as he scanned his instrumentation.

"Right, let's square the circle, boys and girls." Boseler spoke as he strode back and forth between stations. He was a chain smoker who wasn't allowed to smoke on the job, so he chewed pencils. Carrington imagined The Old Man's lips must be rife with splinters by now.

From across the room Sallyanne Rogers called out in that

incongruously girlish voice which was no indication of the three advanced degrees she held.

"Unit Number Two temperature is coming down!"

"Faster. Got to do it faster." Boseler masticated his pencil and looked anxious. Rogers didn't reply, bent back to her work.

Slowly, painfully slowly, it got quieter in the control room as the clamor of bells and sirens was replaced by the chorus of professional, well-drilled voices. Boseler conducted them like a quiet demon. The snowman's fingers were slowing as the red lights reluctantly went away and bright green took their places behind the glass.

A readout screamed at Carrington. "Trouble in Unit Three."

"How bad?" Boseler demanded to know. "Never mind, I can see the numbers from here. No choice now, let's go. Emergency cooling, full shutdown. C'mon, Steve, flood that sucker!"

"Not yet, not yet!" Fossano was licking his lips as he worked switches and buttons. "We can save it."

"Carl, I haven't got *time* to—"

"I can route water from Two and One to Three by reversing pressure on all the backups. We don't have to flood the unit."

"That's one hell of a risk, Carl," said Boseler. "If it doesn't work we could lose the whole plant plus the crew in Three. You know what happens if we lose all three units?"

"Yes. You'll all reach Japan faster than me. I'm a lousy swimmer. But it ought to work. The parameters fit."

"Shit," muttered Boseler. He didn't hesitate. His job didn't go to people who hesitated. "Try it, Carl. God help us if you're wrong."

"God help all of us," Carrington heard someone mutter.

The snowman's hands were busy once more. Carrington forced himself to monitor his own instruments. There came the water from One and Two, backflushed into Three. It was already too hot by half for proper cooling, but mixed with what they were pumping like crazy into the entire system it might be enough. Had to be enough.

An awful lot of gauges went yellow and stayed there. Then they began to turn green, one by one. As still more cold water was brought into the system all the gauges began to turn, not just in One and Two but in Three as well. Meanwhile the hottest water was being expelled, much of it as steam.

They watched and agonized for another half hour before Boseler felt secure in ordering a stand-down. Somewhere beyond the plant's outfall pipes there were likely to be some very uncomfortable fish, Carrington knew. He didn't think he'd be going surfing today, or tomorrow either. He wasn't going to set foot in the water beyond the plant until the icy California current which washed the coast had had time to do its necessary scouring.

A senior technician was standing close to Fossano. Her belly was heaving and she was using his handkerchief. The snowman was the only man Carrington knew who actually carried a handkerchief to work each day. Bless you, Fossano, the younger man thought. "That was absolutely too fucking close," he mumbled.

"How close was it?" said Charlie, mimicking a well-known television announcer perfectly. Carrington smiled and Sallyanne Rogers giggled nervously.

Then Boseler was leaning over his shoulder, talking softly. "How're we doing, son?"

"We got to One and Two fast enough, sir. We were about two minutes away from full meltdown in Unit Three."

"Three-Mile Island was a damn picnic," said someone from across the room. "Be still my beating heart."

"Could've been worse. A lot worse." Standing there leaning over his console, the snowman suddenly looked neither fat nor foolish. Instead he rather resembled a savior, which was much nearer the mark, Carrington knew. Savior of what, no one in the room could say. San Onofre certainly. Maybe San Clemente, Oceanside, and Dana Point as well.

"Get on the horn, Carrington. Find out how we stand in relation to the rest of the county. There'll be damage all up and down the coast."

Now that the crisis at the plant was over, everyone was starting to wonder about their homes and families. A quake of the magnitude which had jolted the plant would be powerful enough to level schools and houses, even in tremor-conscious California. He dialed Scripps Institute at La Jolla. Assuming the telephone lines were still working, that was the nearest place likely to have a full report ready. They had their own seismographic station. So did the plant, but the quake had busted it.

His call went through smoothly, without any hiss and crackle. He asked his questions fast. He listened to the reply for a long time before hanging up.

Everyone was staring at him. "Don't keep it all to yourself, son," Boseler prompted him.

He looked up at The Old Man, then over at Rogers and Charlie and the other citizens of the control room. "That was Scripps."

"We didn't think it was Jack-in-the-Box," said Boseler curtly.

"They say—they said there wasn't any earthquake. None at all."

Fossano spoke first. "Fifty years I've lived in this state. All my life. I've been through plenty of quakes, most small, some big. That was the biggest. A seven at least."

"Maybe their seismograph's out," someone suggested.

"Yeah, but their behinds ought to be functional," snapped Rogers. "They should have felt that good down there."

"Don't fool around with those jerkoffs," said Charlie. "They're only interested in fish anyway. Call the Richter Center at Caltech."

Carrington nodded, turned dazedly back to the phone, and worked the push buttons. You could hear everyone breathing and they could hear his questions as he asked them.

"Yes, I see. You're sure? Yeah, well, it *is* pretty weird. No, everyone here felt it. Lifted the whole installation." A long pause. "Of course we'll all testify."

He hung up, turned to his friends and co-workers. "There was a quake, all right." Relieved sighs from around the room.

"Then we aren't going crazy?" Fossano was sitting down now.

"No, but the folks at Caltech are," Carrington said grimly. "They say we experienced a seven point eight tremor. The epicenter was about ten miles directly below the plant. I mean smack under us."

"Only ten miles?" Rogers frowned. "That's awfully shallow for a disturbance of that magnitude."

"That's what the people at 'Tech said." Carrington looked around. "There's no earthquake fault ten miles under San Onofre. Everybody knows that. The nearest fault of any size is thirty-five miles inland, and it's minor."

"The survey teams couldn't have missed anything that obvious." Boseler looked acutely uncomfortable. In a little while he was going to have to deal with the press. "They couldn't have."

"Caltech agrees. There's no fault under this plant. Therefore there shouldn't have been any earthquake, much less one that strong and localized. El Toro hardly felt it at all." Everyone sat silently, trying to absorb the disturbing implications of this new information. The big Marine base at El Toro was less than half an hour's drive inland. The tremor should have knocked it on its collective ear. Should have.

Hell, a 7.8 quake ought to have registered strongly as far north as San Francisco, let alone thirty miles up the road. The preconstruction geological research had been exhaustive at San Onofre. There was no earthquake fault beneath the plant.

"So what happens now?" Rogers wondered aloud.

Boseler spoke as though mentally ticking off the relevant points on mental fingers. "We experienced a quake here, we know that. Caltech confirms it. Seven point eight. Nobody but us seems to have felt it. That makes no sense. We also know there is no earthquake fault beneath us or anywhere close by."

"Which implies?" murmured Fossano.

Boseler stared at him. "That something other than mother nature is responsible for what happened here less than an hour ago. No natural phenomenon is better documented in this part of the world than the earth tremor, and what occurred here this afternoon doesn't fit any of the documentation. Caltech's already as much as said that. La Jolla's mystification only serves to confirm it."

"I know something that could cause it." Everyone turned toward Rogers. She looked as though she didn't want to say what was on her mind.

"Say it, Sallyanne," said Boseler.

"A bomb. A big-enough bomb. It wouldn't have to be ten miles down to give the impression that it was when it went off, either."

The Old Man nodded, turned back to Carrington. "Punch up a seven-sixteen number for me, will you, Steve?"

The snowman recognized the D.C. number. So did one or two others in the room. They were all lost in their own thoughts. A few yellow lights still glowed. Nothing that couldn't be dealt with by the automatics. The rest of the telltales continued to glow green—but for how long? When would another earthquake that wasn't an earthquake strike? And what might it be like the next time? An eight? If that happened, a magnificent if underutilized section of California coast might be rendered permanently uninhabitable.

Washington would want to know two things foremost. How, first of all. Second and more important—who?

12

Heathrow International Airport, England—21 June

The closest thing Merry Sharrow had ever seen to the organized hysteria that filled the International Terminal at Heathrow Airport was the minor riot which had taken place following a closely contested championship football game her senior year in high school. No world traveler himself, Josh looked equally frazzled. That made her feel a little better. Only Olkeloki appeared relaxed amidst the multiethnic rush of people bound hither and yon. He knew exactly where he was going. She and Oak tagged along behind, lugging their backpacks through the crowd. Merry bounced off Savile Row suits and chadors, positive that if she lost sight of the old man she would be swept away by the babbling tide of humanity, to be washed up later that evening in some backwater eddy next to the gift shop or the Thirty-One Flavors ice cream stand.

Four women of unknown age slipped past her like the oil of their homeland, their eyes alive and searching while the rest of their bodies were concealed beneath thick black veils. A gaggle of Japanese businessmen waddled by, so many chattering geese dressed in interchangeable three-piece suits. They formed an island unto themselves, a small piece of stable Nippon holding firm against the surge of undisciplined humanity. Of course, compared to the evening rush hour in Tokyo or Kyoto or Yokohama, the anarchy that was the airport would seem no worse than normal.

The backpack wasn't getting any lighter and she was glad Olkeloki had insisted they bring as little as possible in the way of baggage. Incongruous enough that she found herself on her way to East Africa with a fifth of what she'd taken from Seattle to Washington, D.C. Most of her clothing lay in Oak's bedroom dresser awaiting her return. Olkeloki told her she would need little. Tanzania in winter was not unlike D.C. in summer.

Like the signposts indicating the conclusion of a marathon, the numbers of the various check-in gates loomed overhead. Since they were carrying tickets, reservations, and all their luggage, they had actually managed to avoid the worst of the crowds on the ground floor. They could proceed straight to the waiting lounge. Then she could rest.

"It is just as well that you are tired," Olkeloki told her. "You will both sleep on the plane. It is a long flight from here to Nairobi. A shame no Concorde plies this route. We must travel instead by fat plane."

"That's jumbo jet," Oak corrected him.

"Is it? I do not travel often enough to keep up with all the colloquialisms. They are both a joy and a curse to English." He led them down a glass and steel maze toward the promised land, Gate 42, where they would finally be able to rest.

Olkeloki looked thoughtful as he strode along clutching his battered old suitcase in one hand and the omnipresent walking stick in the other. "The last time I flew out of Nairobi the planes had propellers. Jets are infinitely better. We will make the journey nonstop, whereas the last time I went from London to Rome, Rome to Cairo, Cairo to Khartoum, and thence to Nairobi."

"No wonder you really know your way around here," said Merry. "What were you doing in England?"

The old man smiled at her. "Going to school. I am a graduate of Oxford University. As a leader of my people, I feel it incumbent upon myself to update and modernize my education from time to time, so I try to get back to the old school as often as possible."

That explained a great deal, Oak mused. Olkeloki's poise in strange surroundings, his excellent command of the language, and his ability to adapt to customs radically different from his own. Cattle herder and witch doctor he might be, but he was an *educated* cattle herder and witch doctor. Oxford, no less.

"When did you do your undergraduate work there?"

"Let me think a moment. It was some time ago. I finished in thirty-eight, I believe. Why do you wish to know?"

"Just curious," Oak replied, "and I also need for you to keep talking."

"Certainly. About what?"

"Anything. So we don't alarm the man who's following us."

Merry Sharrow reacted admirably, keeping her voice even and not turning sharply to look behind them. "Shetani?"

"How should I know?"

"It would be most unusual," said Olkeloki casually, likewise resisting the urge to let his gaze wander over the crowd that filled the concourse behind them. "It is difficult for them to mimic human beings."

"You're sure we're being followed?" Merry asked him.

"Pretty much so. I keep seeing the same figure too many times. When we stop, he stops. When we go, he follows. That's about as conclusive as you can get. How subtle are these shetani of yours?"

"Where shetani are concerned," said Olkeloki gravely, "all that is certain is that nothing is certain."

"That's reassuring. I could've sworn someone was watching us when we passed that first gift shop, and again when we went through security. You two stay here. I'm going back for a doughnut or something. Here, hang on to this." He handed his backpack to Merry. "Just keep talking like everything's normal."

He turned and made his way back against the tide of expectant passengers. Their conversation was inconsequential and he was able to ignore it without much trouble. Most of them were tourists going to Africa for the first time. They babbled endlessly about the great adventure which lay ahead of them and who had the better hotel. The children wanted to know when they were going to see the animals, the women argued about whether they would be able to handle the heat and the food, and the men were already beginning to regret the expense.

Oak's eyes flicked over each of them like a customs' inspector on the hunt for illegal ivory. A good inspector could pick out a smuggler with a single glance. Would he be able to spot a disguised shetani as easily? Or was he getting jumpy, starting to imagine things? A crowded terminal struck him as an unlikely place in which to encounter the shy, malevolent spirits. Certainly Olkeloki thought so. But the old man didn't know everything there was to know about their adversaries, and Oak knew from experience what it was like to be under surveillance. *Someone* was watching them. Hadn't Olkeloki claimed Oak was sensitive to their presence?

Horsepucky. Oak was sensitive to everyone's presence. That was what had kept him alive the past ten years. As for being jumpy, there'd been three times when he'd jumped without provocation during the preceding decade. Twice he'd come off looking like a prize fool. The third time he would have come off looking dead. Wiser to play the fool every now and again.

He walked quickly past the gift shop without feeling alien eyes on the back of his neck, stopped at the tiny snack bar beyond, and ordered coffee and a plain doughnut. While chewing he checked his watch. It was a dual time zone job, full of cheap chips and useful functions, so he hadn't had to change the time when they'd left Dulles. Their 747 would start boarding in less than half an hour. He didn't have much time to check out his feelings.

He was a little uneasy about leaving Merry to the care of Mbatian Olkeloki. The old man seemed harmless enough, but harmlessness was one thing and trustworthiness another. In spite of what had happened on the highway between his house and the airport he still wasn't quite ready to swallow the old man's nightmare whole. His right leg throbbed where something that had been a piece of truck rubber one second and a piece of a bad dream the next had tried to amputate his foot. There *had* to be another explanation for what they'd seen and experienced this morning, but he was damned if he could think of it. Just because he couldn't think of it, however, didn't mean it didn't exist.

He froze, reflexively sipped at his coffee to maintain the appearance of normalcy. There were two of them, he was sure of it, and they were both very good at not wanting to be seen. Oak, whose perceptions had been honed by a decade of dealing with dangerous radicals and extremists, saw them nonetheless.

Just a glimpse of two tall shapes, then the crowd swallowed them up. Leaving his coffee behind but for unknown reasons hanging on to the rest of the doughnut, Oak went after them in time to see one disappearing into the men's room off on the left. That made him hesitate. There was no familiar, comforting bulge beneath his left arm. FBI or not, the local authorities would have taken a dim view of any attempt to bring a handgun into England, much less onto an international flight. His unease was balanced by a burning desire to know what was shadowing their progress. He couldn't imagine how spirits or anything else could have tracked them across the Atlantic. Olkeloki claimed some shetani were capable of flight, but flight at Mach 2? Oak doubted it. The most likely explanation was that he was imagining things and that they weren't being followed at all, but he was a firm believer in the instincts which had kept him alive while working for the Bureau and he had no intention of abandoning them now.

Another glance at his watch indicated he had barely enough time to take a leak. If he hung around here any longer the plane would leave without him. That decided him. He pushed his way into the restroom.

It wasn't crowded. His gaze went immediately to an Englishman who was washing his hands. He held them beneath a dryer, then turned and left. Oak was alone in the men's room.

Cautiously he paced the line of urinals, bending low to check the empty stalls opposite. There was another row of each on the other side and as soon as he finished with the first aisle he walked around to inspect the second. He kept his back to the urinals and bent over no farther than was necessary to see under the swinging doors.

The exit door rattled as someone went through in a hurry. Whoever it was must have been standing on one of the toilets on the first aisle. Oldest trick in the book. Cursing silently, he whirled and raced back the way he'd come. As he drew even with the first aisle, his eyes intent on the doorway, something like a lead pipe caught him behind his haircut. Afterward he couldn't tell for sure if he'd been hit from the front or from behind, much less what with, but he knew he hadn't run into the wall. There was a brief, watery glimpse of a tall figure, though whether man or spirit he couldn't tell.

He didn't black out completely. The light from the naked overhead fluorescents was painful. Somewhere close by, a little boy was saying clearly, "Daddy, why is that man lying on the floor?" Then another figure leaning over him, sounding concerned.

"Say, friend, are you all right?" Heavy accent, Oak thought. The man sounded Italian.

Water on his face had him sitting up fast and blinking. By now several men had gathered around him in addition to the father with his kid. None of them were cops, for which Oak was grateful. He wondered what might have happened if Daddy hadn't arrived to take a piss when he had.

More than anything else he was furious with himself. It would never have happened back home. He'd let down his guard and received a cheap lesson in return.

"I'm okay. I slipped and hit my head, that's all." Willing hands helped him to his feet. "I'll be all right now." He managed a smile as he staggered to the door and out into the bustling concourse beyond.

Outside he paused long enough to check directions and the back of his skull. There was nothing spiritual about what had clobbered him. He had a feeling it had been a man. A shetani would have taken out his throat instead of going for the head. What a pretty mental image *that* made; him lying spread-eagled on the dirty tile with his jugular vein severed and blood spurting all over the place. The little boy screaming instead of questioning.

A glance at his watch cleared his mind fast. It felt like he'd lain on the bathroom floor only for a minute or two, but it had been a lot longer than that. If he didn't move his ass fast he'd miss the plane. Suddenly he found he wanted very much to be on that flight, not only to look after Merry Sharrow and to help Olkeloki, but because when the old man gave the shetani the evil eye or whatever it was he planned to do, Josh wanted to be there when he did it.

And if men were somehow behind all that had happened in the past couple of days, he was looking forward to meeting them again, too.

He relaxed once he joined an anxious Merry and Olkeloki on the plane. "Somebody clobbered me when I wasn't looking, in the men's room."

"Did you get a look at them?" Merry asked. "Are you okay?"

"No I didn't get a look at them and yes I'm okay."

"I don't understand how anyone could follow us all the way from Washington."

"Neither do I. It makes absolutely no sense, which means it fits right in with everything else that's happened."

"The ways of the shetani are not the ways of men."

"You don't say?" Oak said. "Now that's profound." His hand went to the lump forming on the back of his head. "Whatever hit me was a lot solider than any spirit."

They were interrupted by standard interminable preflight safety instructions in the form of a film displayed on the movie screen. It provided a respite for him to gather his thoughts. The flight should be a comfortable one, he mused. The first class compartment in the nose of the big plane was barely half full. He never got to fly first class. The Bureau was reluctant to lavish such extravagances on mere field agents and it would have been out of keeping with his various undercover personae. Only once had they sprung for the fare. That was the time up in Idaho when he'd been severely wounded. Before long they would start serving dinner. He was looking forward to the obligatory hot fudge sundae.

Men or shetani, spirits or skeletons, at least nothing would be able to bother them for the next ten hours or so, he thought as he scrunched back into the leather padding.

"You're sure you're all right?"

He smiled up at Merry. "I've been hit before. I'd rate this one about five on a scale of one to ten." He closed his eyes.

She continued to stare at him. I'll bet you have, Joshua Oak. Will you ever relax enough to tell me just what it is that you do for our mutual Uncle? If nothing else he was the most remarkably self-possessed man she'd ever encountered. Monsters had chased them out of Washington, D.C., someone or something had tried to fracture his skull! just prior to takeoff, and here he was already half sound asleep, resting like a little boy. Olkeloki was staring out the window. The old man never seemed to get tired.

Good for him. The transatlantic leg of their journey had worn her down more than she'd thought it would and the mob at Heathrow had finished the job. Dinner wouldn't be served for several hours yet. Ignoring the familiar FAA regulations she let her seat recline. By the time the jumbo jet had banked sharply to the right to swing out over the Channel she was sleeping as soundly as the man next to her.

Mbatian Oldoinyo Olkeloki spared his ilmeet companions a glance and smiled. It was good that they rested now. In the days ahead there would be fewer opportunities to do so. As for himself, he longed to join them in sleep but could not. He had to keep looking out the window, had to keep alert.

He had no intention, having come so far and already accomplished so much, of letting anything sneak up on them from behind.

13
Over Sudan—22 June

Africa.

Merry Sharrow stood next to the empty seat and stared out the window. The sun was just appearing over the Indian Ocean and the rest of the first class passengers were still asleep. The cabin crew wouldn't turn the lights on until it was time for them to serve breakfast. But Merry had been awake for an hour. She'd spent most of it moving from window to window to get different views of the ground six miles below. After all, it wasn't the same as flying over Boise and Des Moines. Details were impossible to make out, but she'd been struck immediately by the absence of lights on the ground.

A rearward glance revealed Mbatian Olkeloki lying back with his sleeper seat fully extended. He was wearing the same benign, contented smile he'd adopted soon after they'd entered French airspace many hours ago, just as he was wearing the same earphones. He must have gone through every selection in the plane's music library at least three times already, she mused, and still he continued to listen.

Oak lay straight beneath his light airline blanket, sound asleep. She didn't understand how he could rest so soundly. Africa was as new to him as it was to her. She thought about waking him, decided that the morning light would do it soon enough.

In fact, the light would wake everyone, and they would all need to make use of the same facility. Before the bathrooms filled up she ought to wash her face and hands.

Her backpack lay in one of the big overhead bins. Flipping open the cover, she fumbled through the unfamiliar sack until she found the compact handbag she'd insisted on bringing along, reclosed the compartment. One of the flight attendants, looking sleepy, stepped out of the aisle to let her pass.

All four of the first class bathrooms were empty. Merry entered the first and locked the door behind her, began searching the handbag for her hairbrush. As her fingers closed on the plastic something grabbed her hard from behind and yanked her inward. A hand went around her mouth, others around her waist and arms as she tumbled backward. The fingers over her lips belonged to a black skeleton.

She should have struck the wall behind the john but she didn't. When she saw why, her eyes widened even further. The bathroom should have been no more than a couple of feet wide and equally deep. Instead, she found herself in a room at least ten feet long and six across. The little flush john clung to the back wall, impossibly far away. For the bathroom to be as big as it looked it would have had to extend five feet beyond the exterior of the 747.

With her right hand she scratched frantically at a ten-foot-long vanity. A mirror of equal length ran above it and she was able to see the image of her captors. The reflections were not as alien as the impossibly large bathroom because she'd seen something like them before.

They looked like the dog-thing she'd hit on the way home that rainy morning east of Seattle.

No two were exactly alike. All had the same long, thin limbs, but many had true feet instead of a second pair of hands. In the dim light from the single attenuated fluorescent bulb above the mirror she saw that they wore neither clothing nor adornments of any kind.

The heads of the females looked almost normal except for the jaws, which extended outward like those of an ape. These vast mouths were lined with small, sharply filed teeth. The male skulls were long and narrow like those of the Easter Island statues, only rounded instead of sharply angled at the sides and top. They grinned at her through slightly smaller protruding jaws. Neither sex had any ears and only the males had visible nostrils. At least a dozen of them had crowded into the bloated bathroom. As she stared, another pair of long arms emerged from the inside of the lavatory bowl. With a grunt, the thirteenth shetani emerged from the stainless steel depths.

They were as big as she was, though with their thin bodies and impossibly skeletal limbs the most massive of them couldn't have weighed more than a hundred pounds. They were trying to pin her arms behind her. Wrenching loose her left arm, she swung at the grinning shetani trying to crawl on top of her. Her fist smashed into the gaping mouth and sent it tumbling backward.

The racket they were making was deafening and she wondered why no one had come to investigate. Bulbous eyes goggled wildly at her as they tried to drag her down to the floor, chittering and grunting. The face of one of the females kept bumping up against Merry's cheek. The taut skin was as cold as ice. Glaring at her, the shetani reached down and dug long fingers into Merry's right breast. Gasping in pain, Merry jabbed backward with her elbow. The pressure was released as the hideous little creature was sent sprawling.

They weren't very strong, but there were so *many* of them! Then the hand that had been clamped over her mouth slid off and she screamed as loud as she could. The shetani giggled madly and made obscene gestures in front of her face. She screamed again, loud enough to wake sleeping passengers all the way back in economy, but no one came to investigate. Whatever had exploded the space inside the bathroom also muffled any sound from within.

Two of the males were working on her legs now, trying to drag them apart as a third worked on the belt of her jeans. All three of them had gigantic erections.

This can't be happening, she wailed silently. But there was nothing dreamlike about the pressure on her arms and legs, nothing imaginary about the horrible chuckling noises that filled her ears. They had her belt unbuckled now. Long spiderlike fingers were dragging the Levi's down her thighs and groping for her panties.

A soft snap came from the vicinity of the sliding door latch and a querulous face peered inside as the door opened. "Hey, what's going on in here?"

It was the flight attendant Merry had passed in the aisle. If there was any doubt remaining in her mind that what was happening to her was real, it was erased by the expression that came over the other woman's face. All the horror of her situation was reflected in the flight attendant's eyes.

Several of the shetani trying to pin Merry to the floor let go of her and jumped the intruder. Hands went over her mouth in time to shut off her incipient shriek while others quickly pulled the door shut behind her. One of the shetani had a chameleon riding on its shoulder. The lizard was as black as its master, except for the independently mobile red eyes. Its long tongue snapped out and struck the flight attendant in the face, plucking out her left eye as neatly as if it had gone after a beetle. It swallowed the prize with obvious enjoyment.

The attendant went crazy, sending shetani flying in all directions as the pain assailed her. More spidery fingers let go of Merry as their

owners switched their attention to the bigger woman. As they did so
Merry thrust her right arm forward and sent one shetani flying over
the vanity with enough force to shatter the safety glass mirror. A kick
of her leg dislodged another.

Now she was on her feet with two of the distorted harridans
clinging to her shoulders as she staggered toward the door. One of them
put an arm around her neck and started to choke her even as it swung
around to get between her and the exit. Stiffening her fingers the way
she'd been taught to do in self-defense class, Merry didn't hesitate as
she drove them forward into that grinning face. Both protruding eyes
popped and sent black jelly splashing over bony cheeks. It had no effect
on the shetani, which continued to pull and push at her.

Another jab loosened its grip and sent it falling to one side. With
both hands Merry reached around, grabbed her remaining assailant, and
ripped it off her shoulder. She threw it into the vanity sink. Its skull
split when it struck the spigot. Dripping black blood and brains, it
struggled to roll back onto its feet.

She was free with the door at her back. The rest of the shetani
were concentrating on the flight attendant, shredding her clothing while
the trio that had been preparing to assault Merry fought for position
between the younger woman's legs. Merry flailed weakly at the doorknob.

Please God, don't let it stick, let it open!

The last sight she had of the flight attendant showed the shetani
dragging her, headdown, into the lavatory at the far end of the
impossibly long bathroom.

Then she was out in the aisle between the galley elevator and the
bathroom. The door was wrenched out of her hands and slammed tight.
She stood there alone in the quiet aisle, swallowing and trying to get her
wind back. The little light above the doorknob was on, illuminating a
single word.

OCCUPIED

A couple of sleepy, just-awakened passengers glanced in her direction as she stumbled down the aisle, pulling up her jeans. She practically
fell in Oak's lap as she clutched at his shoulders.

"Josh, Joshua! For God's sake, wake up!"

"Hmph, what?"

No time, she thought desperately, and maybe the wrong man. She
abandoned him and yanked the earphones from Olkeloki's head. She
wouldn't have to wait for the old man to wake up.

His eyes snapped open immediately, alert and startled. "Woman,
what are you—?"

She was already pulling at his arm. "Mbatian, you've got to come with me, you've got to! We have to help her!"

Maybe it was the timbre of her voice, still touched with terror, or maybe something he saw in her face. In any event the old man was on his feet and following her back up the aisle as she fastened her belt.

"Shetani," she mumbled, half crying.

He put a comforting hand on her shoulder. "I know. I can smell them now."

They stopped outside the bathroom. The OCCUPIED light still glowed steadily. No sound came from within. Olkeloki twisted the doorknob. It rotated, but with the interior latch secured the door wouldn't open.

"Stand over there, please." She moved aside and watched as he clamped down hard on the knob with both hands. As he twisted, the veins in his arms stood out and his face went taut with the effort. She heard a muffled *ping* as something snapped inside the door. The old man slumped slightly, took a deep breath, and pushed.

Merry retreated as the door swung inward, but nothing sprang out to attack her or the old man. Olkeloki looked inside for a long moment. Then he closed the door quietly and let the broken latch catch. The OCCUPIED light winked back on. It was lying.

She stared expectantly at him as he escorted her firmly back to her seat and made her sit down. "What did you see? You saw that it's much too big in there, didn't you? Much too big for any airplane. They—they were waiting for me. They came out of the toilet and they grabbed and at first I couldn't scream, and then I *could* scream."

"But no one heard you."

"No, until Andrea—that was the name on her tag—checked on me. They grabbed her too, but she fought them, and then a chameleon took out her eye and she went crazy and they all had to go for her. That's how I was able to get free and get away." She started to rise. "But Andrea, the flight attendant, she's still in there and they've got her and they're going to . . . to . . ."

Olkeloki gently pushed her back into her seat. "The woman you speak of is not inside. Nor are the shetani. All have gone. All."

Merry's fingers were working, twisting. "They were pulling at my jeans. They were going to rape me. And they were grinning and laughing and it was horrible, horrible and—"

"Describe them to me." Olkeloki was purposely brusque with her. Anything to stop her burgeoning hysteria.

She had no trouble describing them. The hard thing would be to forget what they'd looked like.

"Ukunduka," he told her when she'd finished. "Very dangerous shetani. I do not know how they got on the plane, but it is clear that

we are not as safe as I thought. You must stay in your seat until we
have disembarked, Merry Sharrow."

"Don't worry. But what about the flight attendant, what about
her?"

Olkeloki's expression was grim. "The Ukunduka feed only through
sexual intercourse."

"Feed? You mean—No, don't tell me, I don't want to know what
you mean." If he explained it to her she might apply the explanation
to her last sight of the doomed cabin attendant, and she was going to
carry nightmares enough off this flight as it was. There was no need to
embellish them.

"Are you feeling all right, miss?" Merry jumped. Another flight
attendant was standing in the aisle alongside her seat, a concerned
expression on her face.

"She just had a bad dream," Olkeloki said smoothly.

"Oh." Clearly the woman hadn't expected the tall Maasai to
answer for Merry. "I'm sorry to hear that." Her professional smile
returned. "We'll be serving a full English breakfast shortly and then
we'll be landing in Nairobi. I hope you're feeling better by then."

Merry's reflexes must have taken over because she managed to nod.
She noted that her hands were shaking. Interesting phenomenon, she
told herself. The flight attendant took Olkeloki off to one side.

"That must have been some dream."

"She'll be all right. I'll look after her."

"Very well," the flight attendant said reluctantly. Of course, the
passenger's business was her own. She shrugged mentally and continued
down the aisle. There were other passengers to rouse.

Merry was trying hard to get her trembling under control. "I never
did get to go to the bathroom." Olkeloki found a blanket, tucked it up
under her arms. The tremors weakened. "I don't think I could go now."

"You must not give them another opportunity. Stay in your seat
until we land. I will warn Joshua Oak that he must do the same. The
Ukunduka make no distinctions between sexes."

He wouldn't have to tell her again, she thought. She wondered if
she'd ever be able to go the bathroom on a plane again. If necessary
she'd stay in her seat until her bladder ruptured.

Hungry as she was, she ignored breakfast. When the cabin lights
came back on she moved over to sit in the unoccupied seat next to Oak.
He listened quietly to her story, then glanced at Olkeloki for confirmation. The old man nodded somberly.

"You're sure you saw something in there?" he finally asked her.

"Josh! How can you say that?" She barely managed to keep her
voice down. "With everything that's happened to us the last couple of
days you still need more proof? Go ahead then; get up and go use that
bathroom!"

"I'm tempted to, except that I'm sure you saw something in there. Maybe shetani and maybe something else, but whatever it was left its mark on you. You're white as a sheet. So if Olkeloki says not to take a piss until we're on the ground, I'm not going to argue with him. I'm stubborn, but I'm not a fool. He's been right too many times or I wouldn't be here now." He broke off as the cabin attendant set eggs, sausage, and muffins in front of him.

"Of course you know it's impossible to fit a bathroom of the dimensions you describe on any plane."

"I know," she admitted, pulling the blanket up high around her neck. "It's also impossible for something alive to come up through a toilet bowl with a throat maybe four inches in diameter. At least, those were things I used to know. Now I know different. Remember one of the flight attendants? Taller than me, blonde, kind of pretty? Name of Andrea? Why don't you ask her what *she* saw? If you can find her."

Oak hesitated. "You said the shetani pulled her down the john with them."

"That's right, know-it-all. So unless she grabbed herself a parachute and decided to quit work early she should still be on the plane, shouldn't she? But she isn't. Why don't you look for her, Josh? I pray to God that I'm all mixed up inside and that you find her. Olkeloki doesn't think you will. He doesn't think anyone will, ever again, because those Ukunduka—"

"Spare me anything Olkeloki told you. It doesn't sound pretty."

"It wasn't pretty," she whimpered. "It almost happened to me. If she hadn't come to check on me . . ." Merry let the thought trail away.

"You want to go home? I'm sure there are several planes leaving Nairobi today. From everything Olkeloki's said it's a busy airport. We could get you on the next flight out."

"I'm not going home."

"No? Not even after what happened to you in there?" He nodded in the direction of the bathrooms.

"*Because* of what happened to me in there. Those—those filthy things tried to assault me."

"I see. Back in Washington they tried to kill you, but attempted rape only makes you more determined."

"You're damn right. First they just frightened me. Now I'm mad. I think you'll find I can be pretty damn relentless when I've got my dander up, Josh."

"If you say so. I never saw anyone with their dander up before." He leaned back as if trying to peer behind her. "Where exactly is your dander?"

"You're trying to be funny, aren't you?"

"Sorry," he said seriously. "Just trying to put some color back in your face. You're really going through with this, aren't you?"

"Yes, and you're going to say that you believe me. Go on, use that bathroom. Olkeloki says the Ukunduka will screw anything that moves. Go on, tough guy."

"The OCCUPIED light is on."

"So what? Haven't you noticed it's been on ever since I went in there?"

"The length of time it takes for someone to move their bowels is not an indication supernatural forces are at work. There has to be somebody in there."

"Oh, there's somebody in there, all right. Lots of somebodies. Go check 'em out, Joshua Oak."

"I've already told you why I'm not going to do that."

She pounced triumphantly. "Then you *do* believe me."

"All right. All right, damn it, I believe you." He eyed the door warily. "Why not, after what happened to us on the way to Dulles? From now on I take anything you say as the literal truth." He grinned at her. She grinned back. Something connected and both of them looked away nervously. Oak turned his attention back to his rapidly cooling breakfast while occasionally glancing toward the now threatening bathroom door. It stayed shut and the OCCUPIED light on. Merry found a magazine and tried to lose herself in its chromatic inanities.

Time to speak of other things, the Walrus had said. Oak wished the Walrus were in the row opposite. Maybe he'd help make some sense out of the last forty-eight hours. Soon they would be landing in a city considerably farther east than Baltimore, which was the farthest in that direction he'd ever traveled previously. Then they'd be relying for their safety and guidance on an old and maybe not too sane gentleman of uncertain intentions, who'd managed to involve himself with something dangerous and incomprehensible.

"If they took the flight attendant," he said suddenly, "why hasn't the rest of the crew reacted?"

"Long-flying jumbo jets like this one have a cabin staff of fifteen to twenty people, sometimes more." She smiled apologetically. "We're always finding out about stuff like that where I work. They even have their own curtained-off sleeping compartments. Probably her friends think she's napping somewhere, or maybe getting it on with one of her co-workers, or a passenger. Or they might think she's up with the pilots, or down in the lower galley. There's an elevator to a lower compartment on these planes. And I've heard that the flight attendants in coach don't mix with those in business and first class. They wouldn't miss her for a while yet."

While he mulled over this disquieting explanation the OCCUPIED light on bathroom number one continued to glow. It was still glowing when the big jet touched down at Jomo Kenyatta International Airport.

The light followed him as he and Merry and Olkeloki gathered their hand luggage and disembarked. They gave the bathroom a wide berth. Merry didn't even look in its direction.

Soon after the last passenger had departed for the terminal, the cleaning crew swarmed aboard. The heavyset woman assigned to the forward johns started in Number Four. She didn't get around to One until the first group of passengers had long since cleared customs. In that group were Oak, Sharrow, and Olkeloki, along with a couple of younger travelers, none of whom had to wait for additional baggage to be unloaded from the 747-B's cargo bay because they'd brought only hand luggage with them. They were in a shuttle bus heading for downtown by the time the cleaning woman reached first-class bathroom Number One.

She barely glanced at the glowing OCCUPIED sign. It wouldn't be the first time one of the white man's clever pieces of electronics was out of order. Sure enough, the doorknob turned easily when she tried it. Almost too easily.

She had five children by her first husband and two by her second and so one would not have thought the sight of blood would have shocked her. She fell back against the bulkhead opposite and stood there with the back of her right hand over her mouth, hyperventilating.

"Now what's wrong, mama?" asked the tired crew supervisor. He'd attended college in Nairobi and he resented the fact that he had to prove himself in such a lowly position with the airline before they would let him train to be a mechanic. He glanced inside the bathroom. Instantly his stomach turned over. He barely managed to stumble the couple of feet to the open galley sink before his insides tried to spray themselves all over the interior of the aircraft.

His violent reaction provided the catalyst the cleaning woman needed. She started screaming and didn't stop, not even when the rest of the crew had gathered around her. She had to be led off the plane. By now the cabin attendants counted one of their members as missing, which was quite impossible. People didn't disappear from a 747 in flight.

Someone had the presence of mind to call the police.

By the time they arrived nearly every passenger had cleared customs. The more than three hundred people who'd been on the London–Nairobi flight had scattered to the four winds of East Africa. It would have been difficult to hold them in any case because there was no evidence. Only the cabin attendants' insistence that one of their number was missing. The captain and co-pilot backed up the flight crew.

But there was no body, the chief of airport security pointed out, and even if you could somehow silently murder and cut up a woman into pieces tiny enough to flush down an airplane toilet the bones would surely jam it up. And as anyone could see, he demonstrated readily, the john flushed perfectly. Perhaps the lady in question, for reasons of her own, had chosen to change from her flight uniform into civvies without notifying any of her colleagues and had slipped off the plane with the first passengers? Perhaps the remains they had found were those of some animal, ritualistically slaughtered by a wealthy passenger with ties to one of the many primitive cults that were still popular in this part of the world?

But how had this been accomplished in total silence? And it would have had to have been a fairly large animal, for there was a great deal of blood. Blood on the floor and blood on the walls and what about those bloody very human handprints on the broken mirror? Had the chief of airport security thought to look closely he might also have seen bloody handprints not only on the toilet seat but on the bright metal of the bowl itself. They were positioned almost as if someone had been grabbing at the rim of the seat from below. His demonstration flushed them away.

No body, no bone, just blood everywhere. It was only much later when the forensic team arrived from the city that the fragments of fingernail and strands of hair were found, along with a few threads of blue cloth. They gave the head of Nairobi's forensic medicine department nightmares for weeks because they were eventually identified as belonging to the vanished flight attendant. And yet there was no body, not anywhere on the plane or on the ground or even in pieces in the aircraft's septic system.

The head of forensics was a modern African, well educated and dedicated to his profession, but try as he might he could not reconcile the grisly scene in the bathroom with what was never found.

14

Nairobi, Kenya—22 June

Oak didn't know what to expect in the way of pre-arranged accommodations, so he was only mildly surprised when Olkeloki led them through the doorway of the Nairobi Inter-Continental. The lobby might as easily have been in a fine hotel in Dallas or New York. The only immediately obvious difference was that the faces behind the desk were as black as those of the bellmen who tried to carry their backpacks. Clearly the lobby and nearby coffee shop were popular places for well-off locals to meet and socialize.

The rooms were equally comfortable and modern, though the television was limited to one local station which was only on the air from five to ten in the evening, and that largely in black and white, plus an in-house movie channel. In spite of Oak's urging that they get out and see some of the city, after endless hours on two intercontinental flights all Merry wanted to do was soak in a hot tub until her skin began to wrinkle. For his part Olkeloki was busy trying to find a driver to take them to the border town of Namanga. There, he informed them, they would have to abandon their vehicle, walk across the border with their baggage, and hire a Tanzanian matatu or taxi on the other side. Kenyan vehicles were not allowed to travel in Tanzania and vice versa. Olkeloki found this rule idiotic, but then he was not a politician. He was only a simple laibon.

Oak was damned if he was going to spend the whole day in a hotel room. He'd spent more than enough of his life in hotel rooms already.

The bell captain provided him with a small map of downtown Nairobi and sent him on his way. Give Joshua Oak a map and he could find his way through hades.

Out the banquet entrance, down to the first cross street, then left to the broad, divided avenue known as Jomo Kenyatta Boulevard. Off on the far right was the towering international conference center of the same name which had been designed to look like a traditional African hut. Crowds of anxious Africans, Indians, and the occasional tourist milled around him. Hordes of shoeshine boys tried to sell him a shine for his walking boots, low-investment capitalists on the move.

The traffic jam he stepped around was international in scope, consisting of an eclectic mix of Volvos, British, Japanese, and American cars. He was a bit surprised to see the latter, which consisted largely of four-wheel drive American Motors products. Poking its flat top above the newer, shinier vehicles like a country cousin come to town was the ubiquitous Land Rover.

The shops he passed were well stocked and only a minority of them catered to the tourist trade. Curious, he entered one electronics store and was amazed at the range of products displayed, including the latest flat-screen TVs and videorecorders. In the back of the store was a booth where locals could rent videocassettes. Half the titles were in Tamil or Hindi, a reflection of the large Indian population which Kenya had had the sense not to kick out of the country after gaining its independence from Britain. As he watched, a tall African in a neatly pressed business suit was renting out *The Best Little Whorehouse in Texas*.

The Soviets haven't got a chance here, he told himself as he exited the store and headed down the avenue in the general direction of the central market.

As he entered an area of small shops, street hawkers tried to sell him crudely carved wooden giraffes or elephants, bracelets of twisted copper wire, and small, obviously fake, Maasai knives. At least there were no ashtrays that said "Welcome to Kenya," no matching salt and pepper shakers similarly decorated, no rubber Mau Mau spears—though he suspected if he searched long enough he could find them too.

He spent most of the day rummaging through the central market and the surrounding shops, particularly regretting the solid malachite box he left gleaming on its display table. Maybe when they'd finished helping Olkeloki they could come back to Nairobi and make like tourists.

Back at the hotel, he was working his key in the room lock when the door next to his opened. Merry was wearing a short-sleeved cotton shirt and matching pants, having stuffed the heavier Levi's into her backpack. She all but glowed from her long stay in the tub. Oak stared for a long moment, then self-consciously looked away.

"Olkeloki's not in his room," she told him.

"He told me he had to arrange transportation for us to the border tomorrow, to this Nimga place."

"Namanga," she corrected him. "So that's why he didn't answer his phone. I was beginning to worry."

Oak couldn't keep from smiling.

"I didn't stuff myself on the plane the way you did," she said. "I could use a good breakfast, if they're still serving it downstairs."

"And I could use lunch. Wonder if you can get an ostrich egg omelette?"

"I understand the local coffee is wonderful. I'll settle for starting with that."

The security guard on their floor nodded politely as they entered the elevator. Downstairs Merry was immediately drawn to one of the many hotel gift shops.

"Let's go in, Josh."

"We're here to save the world, remember? Not to buy trinkets."

"I just want to look."

Like most of the shopkeepers within the hotel complex, the owner was Indian. He didn't bow and scrape, but he smiled a lot and made an attempt to sell Merry one of everything in the store, assuming she would be the easier touch of the pair. In that he was dead wrong, just as he was unaware that he was talking to another salesperson.

While he was unsuccessfully haranguing Merry, Oak passed over the malachite and lapis trinkets in favor of examining the less flippant items for sale. There were masks from West Africa and buffalo hide shields, intricately carved wooden animals, including a six-foot-tall reticulated giraffe, and several striking carved African heads of highly polished ebony. One head even looked familiar and it took Oak a moment to think of who it resembled.

Then it struck him that the ebony carving was a fine rendition of a much younger Mbatian Olkeloki. In fact, all of the heads were Maasai.

The luckless shopkeeper abandoned Merry in favor of new quarry. "All Maasai."

"Why is that?"

The shopkeeper shrugged and smiled. "They are the ones the woodcarvers prefer to carve." He chose a spear from a barrel in the opposite corner, showed it to Oak. The center section was fashioned of wood. From its base protruded a two-foot-long metal spire, while the blade which crowned the top was more than a meter in length and made of solid steel.

"Separates into three pieces." The shopkeeper proceeded to demonstrate. "Traditional Maasai, very clever."

"Old?" asked Oak casually. He was surprised by the honest reply.

"No sir, contemporary."

"For the tourist trade?"

"Oh no, sir, not at all. This is a Maasai lion spear. That is why it has the long blade, so it will penetrate all the way to a lion's heart. A Maasai moran, or warrior, killed a German tourist with one of these just last year. The tourist wanted to take his picture. The moran warned him not to. Last picture he ever took. All moran still carry these."

"For what?" He thought back to what Olkeloki had told him about the current East African government policies regarding lion-spearing. "I happen to know the Maasai no longer are allowed to kill lions just to prove their manhood."

"That is true enough, sir, but they still carry them. It is a sign of adulthood among the warriors. It is also very functional, just in case a lion should charge from the bush. The government cannot prevent a man from defending himself." He handed it to Oak. "See the weight of it, sir? A functional device, not merely something to place on one's living room wall."

"Josh." The voice came from the landing above. It was half whisper, half moan. Craning his neck, he saw Merry standing atop the stairs leading up to the miniature mezzanine. She was staring at something. She looked as though she'd just seen a ghost. As it developed, he was not far off the mark.

"Merry?" The proprietor followed him up the stairs, looking concerned.

"Is your wife all right?"

"She's not my wife," Oak said absently. "Merry, what's the matter?"

"Look." She pointed.

Lining the back wall was a crowded collection of ebony and blackwood statues. Few were more than a foot tall, though one towered more than a meter above the floor. All depicted grotesque, distorted figures that were loathsome mutations of animals and people. Oak recognized the outlines immediately.

"That one there." Merry kept pointing. "That one's just like the one that I hit on my way home from work that morning." Oak started toward it and she tried to hold him back. "Don't."

He smiled as he pulled away from her. She didn't relax even after he picked up the carving. "See? Just wood." He examined with interest the disgusting parody of a dog-man, turning the carving over in his hands.

"Shetani." The shopkeeper looked more confused than worried now. "Beautiful work, the best. I have locally made cheap imitations downstairs. These are all from the south coast and the Tanzanian interior. True Makonde."

"Makonde." Oak put the carving down. "These aren't done by the Maasai, then?"

"No, no." The Indian appeared surprised. "The Makonde are a small tribe that lives mostly in Tanzania, though a few have migrated to Kenya. They are noted for their woodcarving and they are the only ones who can do true shetani. They do little else."

"Does the word mean anything?"

"In the Makonde language shetani means 'spirit' or more often, 'devil-spirit.'" He grinned. "Silly primitivism, but the art is striking, is it not?"

"Very striking," said Oak dryly. "You okay, Merry?"

She nodded. "I just wish you wouldn't handle it, that's all. Just looking at it makes my stomach turn over."

Oak continued to study the carving. "How far back do these shetani stories go?"

"There are records in which such spirits are described by a Greek traveler to this part of the world in 450 B.C. He must have been well and truly taken in by the coast Makonde because he makes reference to the shetani as real creatures. Herodotus, I believe, was his name. The Makonde say there are hundreds, perhaps thousands of distinctly different kinds of shetani. They come in all sizes and shapes. Some are benevolent, most are not." Again the half-apologetic smile. "Native superstition. Animism is still more popular than Islam or Christianity in many parts of Africa."

"I see." Oak fingered a tall elephant carving. "So the Makonde just continue making use of these spirits to satisfy the art market?"

"Oh no, they truly believe in them. Stories of actual sightings of shetani are handed down from father to son, generation to generation. To see who is the biggest and best fakir, I imagine. People laugh at their stories, which makes them sullen. The other tribes call them the Maweea, which means The Angry Ones."

"Do the Maasai laugh at them too?"

"I do not know, sir. I am not Maasai. That is a strange thing to wonder. Angry or not, they are wonderful woodcarvers and their shetani work resembles nothing else anywhere in Africa. Their visualizations are closer to the later works of Picasso and the twentieth-century abstractionists than to the work of their neighbors."

"Do you know a place called Ruaha?" Merry suddenly asked him.

He frowned. "No. Why?"

"I was told it's a big park in Tanzania."

The shopkeeper shook his head. "In Tanzania I know Ngorngoro and Kilimanjaro parks, and Lake Manyara and the Serengeti, but this Ruaha I have never heard of. It must be very obscure and isolated."

"Would any Makonde live near there?"

"If it is in the southern part of the country, perhaps. You are going to Tanzania then?" She nodded and he responded with a disapproving frown. "You should stay in Kenya if you want to see East Africa. Things are bad in Tanzania, very bad. Not as bad as in Uganda, but very difficult for foreigners traveling alone.

"On the surface all appears calm, but underneath . . ." He shot both hands into the air, palms together, and then opened them like a flower over his head. "Any month now, any week, maybe even any day—boom! The Tanzanian governmental infrastructure is like a house of sticks. It will collapse at a touch. Who knows what will happen to those poor people then? They deserve better but they are too poor even to make a revolution.

"That is why you should buy a fine Makonde carving now, because soon the carvers may not be able to work. They will be conscripted into the army or some terrorist band and the art world will lose a fascinating legacy. Not to mention a profitable one. I still have a good selection left. Which can I sell you?"

"None today, I'm afraid."

The shopkeeper sighed. "I understand. Many tourists are excited when they first see them, but then they think of keeping them all the time in their homes and their first enthusiasm fades. There is something about them that makes many people uncomfortable."

"You say some of the shetani are benevolent?"

"A very few, according to the stories the carvers tell my buyers. Most you would not care to meet even in bright daylight. Legends." Another shrug. "See how the eyes tend to follow you around the room, even though they are only smooth black orbs and have no pupils? This too makes people uneasy. I do not understand it myself. I live with them every day and they do not trouble me. In them I see only the skill of the carver. To me they are more clownish than terrifying. You are sure you do not wish to take one with you? You are more interested in them than most of my customers."

"Maybe when we come back from our travels in Tanzania," Oak half lied.

"Ah, you are going on safari. That explains it. There is no need to drag a big woodcarving around with you. I will be here to serve you when you have had enough of looking at animals and poverty. But I wish you were not going across the border."

"We have a good guide," Merry told him.

"Then it may be all right."

"Thank you for letting us look around."

He winked at her. "Pretty lady is welcome anytime, if only just to talk. We can pack and ship anywhere in the world for you."

As Merry and Oak headed up the concourse toward the restaurant, the shopkeeper stood in the doorway of his establishment and watched them go. They did not look well-off, but that was probably deceptive. All Americans traveled with thick rolls of traveler's checks or, even better, credit cards. Hopefully they would return.

Up on the little mezzanine, unseen by the owner or his recent visitors, something moved back by the wall that was lined with twisted, distorted ebony figures. It had a circular mouth like that of a lamprey. Two elongated ears drooped to the floor. It was about the size of a poodle and had only two arms.

Balancing itself on powerful fingers, it danced over to the top of the stairs and glared down, clinging to the edge of the first stair with its strong digits. Its mouth was pulsing in and out like a carp's. A tongue as long as the drooping ears dangled from one corner of its mouth, idly caressing the linoleum. Each time that oval mouth puckered it made a soft sucking noise.

As Merry and Oak disappeared around the front desk, the proprietor turned back into his shop. The shetani saw him coming, pivoted, and hopped back to the place it had vacated on the shelf of carvings. It looked just like its wooden cousins, but this time it chose not to mimic their frozen poses. Instead, it shimmied up a curtain until it was against the ceiling. Reaching out over the floor it latched on to an open air conditioning duct. Letting go of the curtain, it swung easily across the open space until it was gripping the edge of the opening with both hands. It vanished within.

A high wall separated the hotel pool from the street beyond. The indoor-outdoor cafe overlooking the turquoise blue rectangle was crowded with tourists eager to consume a final meal of familiar food before disembarking for such exotic destinations as Amboseli or Tsavo. They were joined by a sprinkling of Nairobians, mostly businessmen socializing during their lunch hour or elegantly dressed wives out for a day's shopping. Skin color aside, it was easy to tell locals from tourists: the locals were far more formally dressed.

Oak studied the menu with some trepidation. In his various guises he'd eaten food both bizarre and simple, but it had all been of the domestic variety. He relaxed as he read further. The hotel's international clientele required it to offer such staples as club sandwiches and bacon and eggs in addition to such surprises as gazelle stew.

Their food arrived in tandem with steaming cups of Kenyan coffee that was every bit as good as Merry had claimed. They were sitting and making small talk when he unexpectedly burst out laughing. A local couple seated nearby eyed the ill-mannered muzungu disapprovingly and it was all Oak could do to stifle his laughter. Merry just smiled that uncertain smile people put on when they're not in on the joke and waited for him to explain himself.

"What's so funny, Josh?"

He finally got himself under control. Tears were running down his cheeks and he dabbed at them with his linen napkin. He couldn't remember the last time he'd laughed so hard and spontaneously. His profession was not conducive to regular outbursts of hilarity.

"Are you kidding me? I mean, look around you." Merry glanced right, then left, finally back at Oak. "Look what we're doing, where we're sitting. As soon as I extricated you from that riot back in Washington it occurred to me what a really attractive woman you were. That combined with your demonstrated naivete appealed to me, so I thought I'd ask you out on a—hell, I can't call it a date. That's high school stuff."

"An assignation?" She was trying to share his high spirits.

"Whatever. I was going to take you out to get something to eat. And it just hit me. Here we are together, sharing a meal, only I had to travel ten thousand miles or so to make it work out." He coughed, wiped at his eyes again.

"You know something, Josh? This is the first time I've seen an honest smile on your face since we met. I don't know if the reticence you've displayed is personal or professional, but I'm glad something's finally put a dent in it. I kept hoping it wasn't an ingrained part of your personality."

"Come on, now, Merry. I distinctly recall smiling once or twice before this."

"I know," she agreed somberly, "but those weren't real smiles. They were surface smiles. They didn't come from within Joshua Oak. They were like casual handshakes. It's hard for you to smile and mean it, isn't it, Josh?"

Such perception made him uncomfortable and he looked down at his plate. "I haven't had a lot of happy times the past few years, Merry."

"I'm sorry. I know you must be involved in something dangerous and sensitive or you would've told me about it by now. Josh, are you a spy?"

A different kind of smile now. "No, Merry, I'm not a spy." Not the kind you're thinking of, anyhow. "Do I look that much like James Bond?"

"Not only don't you look like James Bond, you don't look much like Sean Connery or Roger Moore either. You don't even look like George Lazenby."

"I thought everyone had forgotten that film." Oak didn't try to hide his surprise. "You like the Bond films. A lot of women don't."

"A lot of women lead busy, interesting lives. Me, I sit behind a telephone all night selling equipment to people who are preparing to travel to interesting places that in all likelihood I'll never get to myself."

He gestured toward the high-rise office buildings of downtown Nairobi, visible over the wall that surrounded the swimming pool. "What do you call this?"

"Unplanned. The point is I like any escapist film that's well made. The Bond pictures, anything by Lucas or Spielberg or Zemeckis, even the halfway good Disney films. Living vicariously is better than not living at all. I'd give anything for a little excitement in my life. That's why I was so ready, willing, and eager to take off with Olkeloki. He wanted me to come here with him, to *Africa*. I didn't much care what he was coming here for, only that he was coming *here*." She paused, watching him. "You're laughing again. At me?"

"No, not at you, Merry. What's funny is that my life's been the exact antithesis of yours. I've been trying for the last three years to find some of what you've been trying to get away from. I'm no James Bond, not even a George Smiley, but I've seen a little of the stealth business and it's nothing like the way it's portrayed in the movies. Most of it is dull, boring, and only dangerous when you're convinced everything is running smoothly. It isn't much fun being unable to relax for fear of having your throat cut in an idle moment. That's not exciting; it's scary as hell. Up until a couple of years ago I had to take blood pressure medicine every week."

"What changed? Obviously you didn't quit your job."

"No. I just resigned myself to the dangers. I reached the conclusion that if I was going to end up dead it was going to be by someone else's hands and not my own."

"That's heavy."

"Not as heavy as jumping on a plane to Africa with a half-crazy old man and a saleslady from Seattle. I mean," he went on, leaning forward and lowering his voice, "I have this feeling that any minute now a voice is going to say 'thank you for visiting the outer limits: we now return control of your television set to you' and I'll wake up back in Butts Corners with a beer in my hand listening to some local yokel shill used cars for the late-night movie."

"I don't have that feeling at all. I know the difference between fantasy and reality, Josh. My movies are fantasy. This is real."

"Is it? I wish I was as certain as you. But I'm not going home until this cockeyed caravan produces some answers. I just wish I had a better grip on the questions. I'm afraid I may have left part of my sanity in an elevator back in D.C. and the rest of it out on a public highway."

"What about saving the world, like Olkeloki says?"

"Sanity first. Any extra added benefits acquired in the process gratefully appreciated."

"Do you know what I think, Josh?"

"No, but I have this inescapable feeling you're going to tell me."

"I think you're scared."

"Haw! Now there's a revelation. Of course I'm scared. I'm scared out of my senses, Merry. I'm scared from my receding hairline to these old hiking boots that bring back old scares of their own. Are you going to tell me you're not? After what happened back on the plane?"

"I was scared before that," she confessed, "but I'm used to being scared. You work for some secret government agency. You're not supposed to be frightened."

"I'm not frightened of anything I understand. I don't understand these shetani. I'm not sure Olkeloki does either. What do you mean you're used to being scared?"

She looked toward the pool. "Everything scares me. Always has, ever since I was a little girl. I'm scared of making any long-term commitments, which is why I don't press my boyfriend to make one, and then I'm scared that he won't *ever* make one. I'm scared of quitting my safe, stable, secure, dull, boring job for one that might pay more and be more stimulating as well." Her eyes met his again and in her expression he saw the little-girl fear Merry Sharrow had never been able to outgrow.

"Josh, I'm even scared of the daytime; the crowds, the hustle, the real world. That's why I chose a night job. There's less to be afraid of. It gives me a way to hide."

It was a propitious time for the waiter to arrive with their food, giving each of them time to digest what the other had said. Oak's eggs were slightly overcooked but he didn't say anything. The bacon looked wonderful.

"Aren't we a fine pair to be running off to the ends of the earth together," he finally murmured.

"Mbatian seems to think we're just right."

"'Mbatian Oldoinyo Olkeloki,'" Oak snorted derisively as he began cutting the bacon. He picked up a slice of toast and gestured with it as he spoke, like an Italian traffic cop directing Fiats with his baton. "I believe in these shetani a lot more than I believe in him. They've shown me what they're capable of. He hasn't shown us a damn thing except that he's aware of them and that they seem to follow him around. All he's done so far is run. He ran from here to Washington, ran around the city, and now he's run back here with the two of us in tow. And he's the one who's supposed to stop these nightmares or whatever they are from infecting our world or whatever the hell it was he said they were going to try to do."

"He found us, didn't he?"

"Some accomplishment. I don't have any special talents. I'm no secret sorcerer and neither are you. Any two people gullible enough to follow him back here might have done just as well. For all we know, maybe he needs two people back in Maasailand for some sort of special ceremony. Virgins to sacrifice."

She actually blushed. The last time Oak had seen a woman blush it had been in a magazine photo and the pink hue had been airbrushed on.

"In that case," she shot back, eyes down, "I don't think either of us qualifies."

The explosion caught him with the toast halfway to his mouth. He dropped it as he ducked under the table, bumping it and spilling the coffee. His eyes went toward the source of the sound, professionally alert, his whole body tense and every muscle taut. Merry simply stared toward the wall ringing the pool, as did the rest of the tourists.

As soon as it was apparent there was not going to be a follow-up to the initial explosion, Oak had time to note that many of the African patrons had also made a dive for cover in their fancy suits and dresses. They were retaking their seats as cautiously as he was. Slowly the sounds of conversation and people eating, of waiters and busboys going to and fro, of silverware clattering on plates and street noises beyond the wall, resumed.

"Car backfire," Oak said, swallowing. He beckoned a waiter over. "What was that all about?"

The man looked apologetic. "There was a coup attempt here a few years ago, sir. More of a military mutiny, actually. It was put down, but everyone remembers. They are a little nervous."

"I understand." The waiter left to attend to his customers. But Merry didn't pick up her fork. She just stared at the man across from her.

"You ducked also, Josh. You weren't here years ago. You've been shot at before. I knew you had to be involved in something dangerous, and you said you weren't a spy, but you've been shot at."

He looked sheepish, said nothing.

"I never saw anybody react like that. Does it happen every time you hear an unexpected loud noise?"

"Just about."

"It doesn't bother you? I'd be terribly embarrassed."

"I'd rather be embarrassed once in a while than dead once. It wouldn't matter if it did bother me, Merry. Once acquired, a reaction like that's hard to shed."

"What other reactions does your job require of you?"

He told as much as he could. Once he got started he found himself telling her a great deal more than he intended. Not because she was an especially good listener, though she was (and why not—listening was part of her job) or because he thought he was obligated to tell her, but because there was a lot more bottled up inside Joshua Oak than he believed possible and it was an immense relief to finally be able to let a little of it out.

After they finished eating they went back to her room and talked until dark. Not about his job. About his life. And about hers.

15

Nairobi, Kenya—23 June

They didn't see or hear from Olkeloki all that night, nor did he answer his room phone the following morning. Oak began to wonder if maybe he'd been right all along and they were involved in some kind of elaborate scam, the extent of which had yet to be determined. If the old man had deserted them, they'd be stuck for the three-way hotel bill. Merry was equally convinced that he was just having some trouble finding a good driver and had gone out early to look for one. But his continued absence made for an uneasy breakfast.

Oak paused with the coffee cup halfway to his lips. While not dying out completely, the babble of the breakfast crowd was definitely reduced. Everyone was staring—at him. So was Merry. Looking closer, he saw that she wasn't looking at him but past him. So he turned to try to locate the object of all the attention.

He didn't have to look far. Someone had come up so quietly behind him that he hadn't been aware of the man's approach. Oak always sensed when another person invaded his personal "space," but this time his senses failed him.

The tall, regal figure was shrouded in a heavy red and yellow blanket which fell to just below the knees. Beneath the blanket he wore a loose toga or caftan of royal blue, secured at the shoulder. Hanging from a leather belt decorated with bright beadwork was an intricately carved ebony stick, about eighteen inches in length. The calabash fashioned from a thick gourd that hung from a leather shoulder strap held liquid that sloshed softly as its owner shifted his feet from his right foot to his left. Simple leather sandals protected his feet. A beaded circlet hung from each elongated earlobe while thin metal arrowheads dangled from the base of each loop. Similar beadwork decorated the calabash with lines of blue, red, and white.

The only part of the elegant ensemble Oak recognized was the solid, hand-smoothed walking stick.

"You were not in your rooms, so I came here." Mbatian Olkeloki surveyed the table. "You have eaten enough. A long ride on a stomach too full can be uncomfortable. We should go now. I have a driver waiting."

"Where are your—?" Merry began, but the old man anticipated her query.

"My ilmeet clothes? In my suitcase, which is in the back of the matatu I have hired. So are your backpacks."

Oak's brows drew together. "How did you get into our rooms? We haven't been down here that long."

White teeth flashed. "Does it matter? You will find nothing missing. We should make use of the daylight. In this part of the world it is not wise to travel at night."

"I don't mind traveling at night," Merry told him. "I do it all the time."

"This is not Seattle. I have settled with the hotel. I will pay for your breakfast. Are you ready?"

"Well, I—Sure, why the hell not?" Oak replied, exchanging a glance with Merry.

"Then come." Olkeloki spun on his heel and flowed out of the dining area, trailed by the amused stares of the sophisticated Nairobians and the delighted ones of the tourists.

Oak and Merry had to move fast to keep up with the old man, whose change of attire seemed to have rejuvenated him. The face was the same, but his bearing and attitude had undergone a subtle alteration. From the neck down his movements were those of a thirty-year-old. The swirl of blanket and toga hovered about him like a red and blue cloud as he paused at the cashier's station, then led them toward the front doorway.

The doorman did not move to help. Olkeloki ignored the younger man and opened the door himself. He did not hold it for Merry.

Their driver was a short, thick-set Bantu clad in jeans, T-shirt, and a sharp-looking forties-style hat that he wore cocked down over his forehead at a rakish angle. He was leaning against his vehicle and reading the morning paper. He dumped the paper inside and straightened as his passengers approached.

"Could we take a minute to look in the trunk?" Oak asked when he finally managed to catch up with the old man.

"Why waste time? If I had wanted to steal your pitiful few belongings, Joshua Oak, why would I return? Nor do I have anything to gain by leaving them behind in your hotel rooms."

"No, of course you don't." *Idiot*, he shouted at himself. *The man may be half crazy but he's not a thief. Settle down!* He followed Merry into the back of the matatu.

The taxi was a survivor from the early sixties, an Australian Ford that had been sandblasted to a pale gray except for the places where rocks and rust had punched holes in the chassis. The rear right taillight had recently lost an argument with a large projectile of unknown pedigree. The driver slid behind the cloth-wrapped wheel, jammed a key into the ignition, and, to the surprise of both American passengers, started the machine instantly. They were rapidly learning that in Africa looks meant little, at least where machinery was concerned. Function did not necessarily follow form.

By the standards of the African bush the interior of the matatu was clean, which was to say that the layer of ochre dust which coated floor, windows, and seats was relatively fresh. The driver pulled away from the front of the hotel in much the same way a space shuttle clears its launching pad. Similarly, as soon as they pulled out onto the highway the acceleration became tolerable and the number of G's the matatu's passengers were expected to endure declined. Oak wished he could say the same for his lingering apprehensions.

The freeway direction signs suspended over the roadways were identical to those found back home and he wondered if American engineers had worked on the road. The driver did not know. The names on the signs, however, were anything but familiar. Thika, Naivasha, Machakos. Similarly, while Nairobi had the comfortable feel of a large, modern city, the country they drove through as soon as they left the city's outskirts behind did not.

Their driver was friendly and cheerful, especially when they got far enough out of the city for him to boost the aged matatu's speed up to a chassis-shaking rate. The same thoughts must have occurred to Merry because she leaned forward for a look at the speedometer.

"Are we really going a hundred and forty kilometers an hour?"

"Oh no, missy." The driver turned around to grin at her while displaying utter lack of interest in the narrow two-lane highway they were rocketing down. "You think from the speedometer?"

Merry nodded, watching as the needle fluttered about the far end of the dial.

"No need to worry about speedometer. It's broken." Keeping one casual hand on the wheel and his foot flat on the accelerator he turned to Olkeloki and reached past him with his right hand. "Your pardon, laibon." The deference in his voice was in sharp contrast to the way

Olkeloki had been treated back at the hotel, yet the driver was obviously non-Maasai. Perhaps that was why the old man had hired him.

He twisted a dial and the radio slid neatly out of the dash, revealing a hidden compartment from which he extracted a pint bottle of clear liquid. Having been in similar situations back home, Oak knew instantly it wasn't water. Vodka most likely, or perhaps gin. He was wrong on both counts. The bottle had a fascinating zebra-striped label.

"Kenya Cane," said the driver after taking a sip directly from the bottle and noticing Oak's curious stare in the rear-view mirror. "We are not like the rest of Africa, not here. People in Kenya know how to make good things. The market for sugar is bad. The market for liquor is always good. Myself, I think the sugar growers make this for themselves to drink because the sugar market is so bad." He giggled at his own joke.

He wasn't completely irresponsible, Oak reflected. Any man who could steer a refugee from rent-a-wreck down a country highway while simultaneously quaffing sugar spirits and discoursing on the state of domestic economics had to have his wits about him. At the same time it was obvious he'd never attended a formal driving school. His approach was straightforward, though. Press the accelerator all the way to the floor and try to keep the car pointed in the direction you want to go, and don't confuse the issue by trying to make use of such unnecessary Western appurtenances as brakes or turn signals.

Fortunately, they had the road almost to themselves after the first hour.

"Where are all the people?" Merry asked. She might equally have asked where was all the country.

The land around Nairobi had been green and fertile. Now they were careening over a vast, dry plain bordered by brown hills. Isolated acacia trees waved thorny branches at them as they roared southward. They looked like oversized, out-of-place houseplants.

"These are the Athi Plains." The driver sniffed. "From here to the border is not good land, but I am not a farmer or herder so I do not care. Soon we go through Isinya. It is nothing, a cesspool. But Kajiado has a cafe and I may stop there to get petrol. From there it is maybe another hour to Namanga and the border. Maybe less. The laibon says you are in a hurry. Not to worry. Manu and his bibio will get you there." He rapped the dash with an affectionate palm. Not too hard, either, Oak noted.

"Ah, look there." He pointed to his left.

At that moment it all came home to Merry Sharrow. Until the driver gestured a faint air of unreality had clung to her since they'd left Washington. The sight of the two adult giraffes loping along the side of the highway wiped out the last lingering wisps of disbelief. Instinctively, she looked for walls and bars. But there were none here, just as there was no national park or game preserve. Only the speeding matatu, the acacias, the empty brown plains, and the two ambling giraffes like signposts from a vanished age.

"In Swahili are called twiga," the driver informed them. Merry clapped her hands together like a little girl, turning to watch as the giraffes fell behind.

"That's perfect."

"I will tell you one better. Leopard is chui, pronounced in English chewy." Even Oak had to smile at that.

Olkeloki did not turn around, stared resolutely straight ahead. "Language is a frayed thread between peoples, but a fascinating one."

Oak wondered what held his attention so unswervingly. Looking at him sitting there in the front seat across from their thoroughly urbanized driver, cloaked in his bright blue toga and red blanket, his walking stick resting on his right shoulder, it was difficult to believe he was the same man Oak had rescued from a riot behind the White House. The same man who had spoken calmly to them of impossible creatures and an unimaginable threat from beyond while planning to convince them to accompany him back to Africa on the fastest form of transportation yet devised by humanity. Now he looked like an illustration from an anthropology text, a cardboard cutout from an African studies program at Georgetown University suddenly come to life.

But he was real enough, was Mbatian Oldoinyo Olkeloki. Whatever he was. As real as this rattletrap taxi cannonballing through the dry plains of East Africa. As real as the pair of giraffes that had watched them speed past with nary a glance up from their daily business of denuding acacias.

"Look out, *look out!*" Merry lunged over the front seat and grabbed the wheel.

For five seconds all was chaos inside the cab. Oak barely had time to shout a startled curse, Olkeloki stiffened perceptibly, and the driver screeched something in frantic Swahili as he tried to regain control of his vehicle. Moving at a speed somewhere between eighty miles an hour and that of light, the aged taxi leaned hard on nonexistent shocks. Tires screamed and rubber evaporated as it swerved into the fortunately empty opposite lane. They squealed a second time as the driver fought wildly with the wheel for control. They crossed back into the southbound lane, slid into the sandy shoulder and threw up a dusty roostertail an unlimited hydroplane would've been proud of, and finally straightened out back on the pavement. How the driver missed the acacia tree growing just to the right side of the road Oak could never quite figure out, but he was more than willing to accept the reprieve without an explanation.

Somehow the rusty body held together along with all four of the nearly bald tires. It was a miracle they didn't roll. The old Ford was no Land Rover and Oak didn't doubt for a second that if they had rolled, all four of them would have been crushed to death inside. Suddenly wide awake and stone cold sober, the driver clung to the wheel like a limpet, alternating his gaze between the road ahead and the mad ilmeet in the back seat.

Merry was on her knees, staring out the back window. Oak bit back his instinctive response and waited. Eventually she turned and resumed her seat, blinked as if suddenly aware that she'd done something out of the ordinary.

"I—I'm sorry. There was some truck tire rubber in the road and I thought I saw one piece move. A big piece. There's no wind outside." Their driver heard this and leaned forward until his chin was practically touching the wheel.

Oak put a hand on her shoulder. "Are you sure you saw it move?"

She didn't meet his gaze. "I thought I did."

He eyed her a moment longer before glancing up at Olkeloki. "What do you think?"

"I do not know, Joshua Oak. I am so happy to be back in my own land that I have not been paying as much attention as perhaps I should to our immediate surroundings. As such it may be that she has saved us all."

"By almost killing us," Oak mumbled.

"Look, I said I was sorry," said Merry belligerently, "but damnit, Josh, I swear I saw the thing *move.* I must have."

"It's okay. Where these shetani are involved I'd rather react first and argue about it later."

"Shetani?" The driver looked up at him.

"Nothing." Oak offered him a placid smile. "Just an old story. The mama was daydreaming, that's all."

"Crazy muzungu," he growled softly.

For the remainder of the drive he didn't speak, just clung to the wheel and stared straight ahead. The only casualty of Merry's action was the easy camaraderie which had previously prevailed inside the matatu.

Oak wasn't sure what had happened. He hadn't seen anything move, but then he'd been looking out a side window and not straight ahead. More troubling was the fact that Olkeloki hadn't seen anything either. Up until now he'd only had the old man's sanity to worry about. From now on it seemed he was going to have to keep a close watch on Merry Sharrow as well. Not that he thought she was unhinged. Just maybe a little—emotional.

We're all crazy here except me and thee, he thought silently, and I'm not so sure about thee.

16

Gstaad, Switzerland— 23 June

Alexis Bostoff was the fastest-rising star in the Soviet firmament. A full member of the Politburo at the unheard-of age of thirty-four, he held the important post of assistant minister of armaments. Because of his military training and connections he understood not only the needs of the vast Soviet military complex but its operational stratagems as well. In this respect he was unique.

He was also brilliant, articulate, and handsome enough to have had a career as a movie star in the Russian cinema. It was premature to speak of him as a successor to the still young Dorovskoy, but already the whispering had begun. Here was a young man who someday might be able to charm the West into a reasonable disarmament without concurrent weakening of the motherland, a man who could keep both the party and the generals happy. He was totally dedicated to his work. Most important, he got along well with Dorovskoy himself. The Premier valued the young assistant minister's advice. Everyone was amazed that Bostoff had not succumbed to the disease which had aborted so many similar promising careers: that of premature ambition.

This was his first visit to the West and he'd immediately set about charming both his Swiss hosts and the media. The sight of a Russian armaments minister tearing down the ski slopes with the slickest of the Beautiful People was a novelty the press was quick to seize upon. It was nothing remarkable to Bostoff, who'd grown up in the northern Urals. He'd had to learn how to ski at an early age in order to get to school in the depths of the raw Russian winter. He'd continued skiing on into maturity for both exercise and recreation. Perhaps incidentally, it made him stand out in a cluster of typically overweight officials.

Earlier that week in Bern he'd shown himself to be as comfortable at a press conference as he was on the slopes. When one of the reporters had inquired if he had any personal problems that were giving him trouble he'd replied that some people suffered from a persecution complex, others from an inferiority complex, but that he was burdened by a military-industrial complex. From that point on the attitude of the media had changed from hostile to sympathetic. No one had even asked him about Afghanistan.

The conference itself had gone better than anyone in the Soviet delegation had hoped, due in no small part to his own aggressive analysis of the world economic order. He was feeling very pleased with himself as he schussed down the medium-degree-of-difficulty slope toward the town below. He was also enjoying a rare morning of solitude, since none of the KGB men assigned to watch him knew how to ski. They could only grumble and watch him depart unescorted from the top of the lift. Others waited below, he knew, surveying his progress from time to time with high-power binoculars. But out on the slope, he was free.

All vacations eventually came to an end, even working ones. Soon he would be back at his desk in Moscow. There was so much to do. True disarmament could only proceed from a position of strength and equality. The problem was to explain to the West why it had to modify its definition of equality. It wasn't going to be easy, but if anyone could do this, Bostoff knew he would be the one. He was convinced he could make progress toward a real peace between the superpowers. He had the energy and enthusiasm of youth on his side, thoughts of a different approach to disarmament, and enough power to fend off the extremists within the Kremlin. It was a breakthrough that had to be made and he might as well be the one to make it.

He bent his left knee and slid smoothly across the next slope. As he did so he was startled to see a large black rock sticking out of the otherwise perfectly groomed run. It shouldn't have been there. The Swiss maintained their ski slopes as methodically and obsessively as they did their streets. Such an obstacle would not be permitted on the bend of a curve. It would be removed immediately by heavy equipment or blasting.

It looked like a big chunk of basalt. Bostoff had to make a decision instantly. The drop-off to the right was steep and while he was a decent skier, he was no Jean-Claude Killy. Similarly, there was not enough space or time to allow him to stop.

But there was just enough room between the rock and the up-slope for him to squeeze through. He planted his right pole hard in the powder and angled upward instead of down. It would be all right; he would shoot neatly through the gap. And when he reached the bottom he would have a word or two for the resort's operators.

He was skimming by when something like a length of black hose whipped out of the rock. The hose ended in five long, looping fingers. They crunched across his right knee with terrific force, simultaneously shattering the patella and his balance. He careened wildly forward, the pain shooting up his leg as he wondered what had hit him. He knew something was broken just as he knew that the ever-alert security men below would reach him in minutes. Major resorts like Gstaad kept medical teams on twenty-four-hour standby. There was no reason to panic.

That relaxed confidence stayed with him right up until the instant when he lost his balance and fell forward. His forehead struck something solid and unyielding that lay just beneath the masking layer of white powder.

The first reaction of the Swiss medical team upon reaching the motionless body of the Russian minister was disbelief. The entire right side of the skull had been caved in as if by a blunt object. But there was nothing there, nothing beneath him except four feet of snow and nothing nearby to show how he had broken his kneecap. Everyone was puzzled as to why he'd fallen in the first place. The run he'd been coming off of was smooth and simple. Even a novice should have been able to handle it easily.

Speculation ran rampant through the minds of the KGB men. There were no natural obstacles visible which might have contributed to the fatal fall, nor were there any signs of foul play. Therefore whatever had induced the accident had somehow been taken away before the medical team arrived.

They couldn't prove a thing, but they could imagine a great deal.

Namanga, on the Kenya-Tanzania Border— 23 June

The dusty little town with its single street and collection of ramshackle structures was an accident of history. There was no reason for its existence until the split-up of British East Africa. Now it was the only formal border crossing for many miles in either direction.

None of the permanent structures made of wood, stucco, or concrete blocks rose higher than a single story. This included the government building at the north end of the street. Beyond the solider edifices, like the lace trim on a lady's fan, was an undisciplined sprawl of sheds and huts fashioned from discarded poles, scrap lumber, and sheets of corrugated steel. Framing this urban orphan of independence was a pale-blue sky utterly devoid of clouds, brown hills marching southward, and the occasional feather-duster silhouette of an acacia.

None of Nairobi's sophistication here. Hordes of traders and nomads, travelers and squatters raised a cloud in front of the shops that lined the central street. Others with nothing to do and nowhere to go sat on wooden steps and porches and stared at the minutes of their lives ticking past. They came to Namanga because it was a destination, and any destination was a better place to be than the dry, empty plains. The town was poor, but it was not boring.

It was also a jumping-off place for Amboseli, one of Kenya's smaller but better-known game parks. As they parked next to the government office Oak watched a police officer in neat tan and khaki uniform wave a Volkswagen bus crammed with overdressed tourists eastward.

Their own driver was obviously delighted to be rid of them. He seemed genuinely surprised when Olkeloki favored him with a generous tip, however, and now that he had discharged his obligation a little of his original good humor returned.

"Good luck to you all. Ji hadari, be careful."

"We'll be fine." Even as she said it Merry wondered if she believed it herself.

While Olkeloki waited outside, she and Oak entered the government building and were directed to an office where a man in a dark suit sat behind a desk and stamped papers.

Amazing, Oak mused, how interchangeable bureaucrats were. He'd seen this man's twin countless times in Washington. Change the suit to a uniform and he'd have been right at home in the Pentagon. This is the species that *really* rules the world. *Bureaucratis paperpushii internationalis.*

Off in one corner two men in Arabic dress and narrow, pointed beards were arguing with a police officer. One wore a Muslim cap of embroidered white cotton that kept slipping off his head as he spoke. The officer leaned against the wall and listened patiently, arms folded and eyes half closed. As best Oak could make out the men were trying to come into Kenya from Tanzania with visas that were something less than in order.

The official inspecting their own passports noticed Oak's stare. "You see, sir, most of our traffic here is one way. There is nothing to buy in Tanzania, so whenever the people there can accumulate any hard currency or Kenyan shillings, they try to cross the border so they can shop here in Namanga. First they have to bribe their own officials to let them out, then they have to bribe them so they can get back in." He tactfully left off discussing what bribes if any might have to be paid at the Kenyan end of such shopping excursions, and handed back their passports.

"Thank you for visiting Kenya."

"We hope to be back in a few days," Merry explained.

"You have extended visas. We will be pleased to welcome you back when you have concluded your safari in Tanzania." Suddenly he glanced sharply up at her companion and Oak was immediately reminded of some of his colleagues in the Bureau. The man's main job might be the checking and stamping of passports, but he clearly did a little police work on the side.

"You are going just for safari, aren't you?"

Among the various guises Oak had perfected over the years to hide his real feelings and intentions was a vacant smile of surpassing blandness. "We're just tourists. We like traveling by ourselves. I think you can see and learn a lot more when you're not traveling with a group."

The official wasn't finished. "But you are not married."

"Do couples have to be married to travel in Tanzania?"

"No, but I advise you to stay as far away from the provincial authorities as possible. They do not usually harass well-organized groups of tourists traveling with professional guides, but one or two foreigners such as yourselves traveling by themselves are likely to provoke their interest. They are very suspicious over there. The Tanzanians think all foreigners are South African spies."

"Is there anything to spy on?"

The man grinned up at him. "Of course not. And should the South Africans want to spy on Tanzania, it follows that they would choose people who would be inconspicuous and would blend in among the locals, like a white man and woman with American accents. But that is what Tanzania is like today."

The sarcasm made Oak homesick for the corridors of Washington. He slipped his passport back into his backpack. At the same time a family of Indians stepped forward and the father dumped a dozen passports on the official's empty desk. He sighed and opened the one atop the pile.

Back outside they were momentarily dismayed not to find Olkeloki waiting for them. Merry finally spotted him standing across the street, poised on one leg and balancing himself with his staff. His ancient suitcase looked very out of place. He waved and gestured for them to join him. Oak shouldered his backpack.

As they crossed the street Merry was conscious of many eyes following their progress. They were the only white people in the town and it was a strange feeling to be the minority for a change. Probably the tourists who paused here on the way to Amboseli from Nairobi didn't bother to get off their air-conditioned buses. Certainly they didn't walk down the middle of the main street carrying their own luggage.

"Don't you have to get your passport checked too?" she asked Olkeloki.

He smiled at some private joke. "Not in Maasailand, Merry Sharrow."

"This is still Kenya." She pointed down the street. "Over there is Tanzania. Everyone in the office was having a passport checked."

"It is time to go. You will see." He picked up his suitcase and started down the street. Shopkeepers ceased their haggling to observe the unique passage of two muzungu trailing a laibon with a suitcase.

From time to time they would pass Maasai herders who had come into town to trade. There was unmistakable reverence in their voices when they spoke to Olkeloki. Seeking his blessings, perhaps, Oak thought. His opinion of the old man rose another notch. The Bantu did not speak to him, but they gave him a clear path. This unspoken deference extended to a cluster of half-naked children. They interrupted their soccer game to watch solemnly as the laibon strode past.

The street here was devoid of vehicular traffic. All cars and matatus were stopped at the barricade back by the government building. Nothing on wheels was allowed within a hundred yards of the border.

They were approaching a tall chain-link fence. It was initially impressive, until you noticed that it only extended for about fifty feet in either direction. Oak almost laughed aloud. Anyone could drive right around the barrier at either end. For that matter smugglers probably struck out across country and avoided the town altogether. But this was the formal border crossing, so it had to look formal. The fence was window-dressing, not a barrier.

Then they were walking in Tanzania instead of Kenya. Same dirt, same sun, but everything else was different. There were no crowds and no shops, just a couple of fading structures off to the left. The government building dated from colonial times. Next to it was a makeshift garage with a couple of pumps out front. A number of trucks and smaller vehicles stood parked wherever their owners had left them. No one was doing any trading because, as the Kenyan official had said, the people of Tanzania had nothing to sell to Kenya. What trade there was, as in illegal ivory, for example, would not pass through government hands.

Olkeloki directed them to the government building. Instead of the neatly uniformed Kenyan who'd escorted them to his passport office, a single tired-looking overweight cop in pants and short-sleeved shirt boredly gestured them inside.

The building consisted of one large room with a few desks and filing cabinets. A fan turned lazily overhead, making life difficult for the flies. The single official was short-tempered and busy. Busy? Busy with what? Oak thought as they stood quietly and waited. He kept them waiting for an hour before he deigned to motion them forward. There followed another thirty minutes of inane questions until Merry began to fidget and Oak had to fight down the urge to toss the man out the nearest window.

Looking out the window as the man questioned Merry, Oak could see Olkeloki standing in full view of the cop on the porch. Surely he'd seen them cross the border. But he made no move to accost the old man or shoot questions at him.

A glance in the direction of the fence showed a line of men crossing back into Tanzania. They did not even glance toward the government building. They were clad in togas of light red or yellow and wore no blankets. Instead of staffs they carried long spears tipped with blades of varying length. Oak did a double take: it looked like they were wearing designer hose.

A closer look revealed that the differing designs composed of stripes and chevrons, dots and circles, were painted on. Their hair had been braided tighter than the tightest corn-rows with some cordlike material and the result dyed brightly with ochre. Like the leg paintings, each man's hairdo was different in design. Some wore long, straight braids while others preferred a pleated mat ending in a single short pigtail. They padded along silently in single file. A few carried calabashes similar to Olkeloki's, though not as fancily decorated.

As they passed the old man, each of the marchers executed some sort of salute.

Eventually the insufferable, insulting customs official consented to stamp their passports and they were allowed to depart. As soon as they rejoined Olkeloki Oak asked him about the line of marchers.

"Ilmoran. Junior and senior warriors."

"I notice they didn't check in with our slug of a customs man either."

"The Maasai have no need of passports in Maasailand. The governments of Kenya and Tanzania know this."

"And they let it go?"

"It is safer that way. Insistence upon unreasonable regulations would anger the Maasai. Neither government wants to anger the Maasai."

"They all saluted you or something."

"Yes." Olkeloki started toward the garage. "It is well that they did. It does not do for a moran to show disrespect before a laibon. They are good boys, most of them. A little high-spirited, but that is the nature of ilmoran."

"You must have been a moran yourself when you were younger," said Merry.

"Yes. It is a wonderful time, full of energy and excitement. We can rest a little easier now. We are in Maasailand and there will always be ilmoran around to call upon if we should need help. When there are warriors about, the lions leave."

"What about the shetani?"

He looked thoughtful. "That is something we may have a chance to find out, Merry Sharrow. Ah, here we will find transportation." He gestured toward the vehicles parked nearby.

The drivers were sitting in the shade of their machines, chatting or playing cards, but when the two muzungu appeared talk and play was instantly forgotten. Perhaps the travelers would be able to pay in dollars or sterling.

Oak studied the assortment of wired-together hulks and brakeless wonders with a jaundiced eye. "This lot makes the car we came down from Nairobi in look like a Rolls."

"Singularly unimpressive," Olkeloki agreed. "Nevertheless, we must hire one or walk."

"How far is it to where we're going?" Merry asked.

"Perhaps ninety kilometers. Sixty miles. But the way will not be as smooth as was our journey from Nairobi." They were walking around an old, abandoned bus pursued by pleading drivers when a miracle appeared. The miracle took the shape of a nearly new Subaru station wagon. It was white without any decoration or customizing whatsoever but it stood out like a winged chariot among its chunky, older relatives. Not only a real car, but four-wheel drive as well.

"Purchased for an outrageous price from some foreign-aid worker leaving Tanzania," Olkeloki explained. As they drew near, the mini-wagon disgorged what seemed to be half the population of Calcutta: mother, father, grandmother, mother-in-law, and an endless stream of bright-eyed children. Each of them down to the littlest infant clutched an empty shopping bag.

"Going over the border," Olkeloki said unnecessarily. "A major expedition. Perhaps all the way to Nairobi."

The driver was sitting behind the wheel with his door open counting his money as they approached. Olkeloki didn't appear to mind that Oak took the lead.

"We need transportation."

Obviously well-to-do, the driver looked up at him from beneath his cap. He wore faded blue jeans with only one visible hole above the left knee and a Mickey Mouse T-shirt. Mickey's two-button shorts had faded from red to pale pink as a result of endless washings.

"Certainly, bwana. Where you want to go?"

Now Olkeloki spoke up. "West."

The driver eyed him up and down, very modern and unimpressed by this paragon of traditional African power. Then he casually turned his attention back to the foreigner.

"I will take you east as far as Kitumbeine. The road to there is okay, but beyond is very bad. Washed out in places. Why you want to go west? If you want to go to Ngorngoro I will take you, but is best to go south to Arusha and then follow the main road to the parks. You want to go Serengeti? I take you Serengeti."

"No," said Olkeloki firmly. "My kraal should be near Engaruka now. That is where we must go."

Again the sideways appraisal before the driver smiled up at Oak. "I will take you and mama anywhere you want to go, but not him."

"Sorry. The old man goes with us or we don't go. He's our guide."

"Then let him guide you. I don't take him in my car." He pulled his legs in and started to close the door.

Olkeloki stepped past Oak, spoke softly. "Your vehicle is easy to describe. I know your license number and vehicle identification from the plate fastened to the upper dash." He gestured slightly with the walking stick. "I have friends in Dodoma."

"What is that to me?" said the driver, but he hesitated with the door closed only partway.

"How did you get a fine automobile like this?"

"I bought it" was the proud reply. "With my own money and money contributed by my family."

"Yes, but who did you buy it from, and how?" Olkeloki looked back at Oak and Merry. "You see, there is no way an ordinary African can purchase such a vehicle in Tanzania and it is illegal for departing foreign workers to sell their cars to local people."

"I bought it in Nairobi." The driver was chewing his lower lip and looking defensive.

"Do you take me for a fool? You and your whole family could not afford the duty you would have to pay to bring this back into the country. You have a black market license. The car has papers because they were transferred from the muzungu who sold you the car, and you paid off your local police. That is tolerable in small towns, but not in the capital. There are people there who will go out of their way to take this away from you."

The driver looked resigned. "All right then. But the old man sits in the back. I don't want his flies up here with me." Clearly he was hoping that Merry would slide in front next to him. Oak quickly disabused him of that notion by taking the other front seat while Merry and Olkeloki put their luggage in the back end. A few words of Swahili between Olkeloki and the sullen owner settled the price. The Subaru pulled out of the garage area with the other drivers looking on enviously.

They had encountered little traffic on the road from Nairobi to Namanga. Now they saw none. Like the highway on the Kenya side, the road they were bouncing southward on was also paved, but there the similarities ended. The Tanzanian road was showing the effects of inattention and disrepair. It didn't slow them down. Their driver seemed to know the exact location of every crack and pothole in the pavement. He drove as though he was anxious to be rid of them.

Several miles south of the border he pulled over on the shoulder and stopped. "I want one hundred U.S. dollars to take you to Kitumbeine or you can get out and walk."

"We settled on a price." Olkeloki was clearly restraining himself. They'd never seen the old man mad. Oak wasn't sure he wanted to. "And you said you would take us to Engaruka. That is too far to walk from Kitumbeine."

"Strange things have been happening around Engaruka. I do not see for myself, but I hear. One hundred U.S. dollars to Kitumbeine."

"You drive this new car with all its innovations and you are still superstitious?" Olkeloki taunted him.

The driver pushed his cap back on his forehead as he turned to face Oak. "Where did you find this slippery-tongued laibon and what are you doing with him? What do you do in an empty place like Engaruka?"

"He's our guide. He's showing us around."

"Huh." The driver glanced in his rear-view mirror. "He's no tourist guide. You want to go to Engaruka, you have to pay fair. Maybe I wreck my car. Not much road between Kitumbeine and Engaruka."

Olkeloki had a small leather pouch attached to his belt. Now he unfastened the bone button that secured the flap and withdrew a wad of green paper. The driver's eyes got very wide as the old man counted out ten American fifty-dollar bills.

"I do not have time to argue with a thief. Take us to Engaruka."

"N'dio, laibon! Immediately! But if anything happens to my car it will cost you more."

"If you get us to Engaruka with a minimum of delay I will give you two more American fifties. If you try to cheat us I will give you the sharp end of my knife."

The driver did not look afraid. "Don't try to frighten me, old man. I will get you there without threats. I am not one of these simple country folk."

Oak thought the man's response smacked of false bravado, but then what did he know of local customs? Speaking of local customs . . .

"You said strange things have been happening around where we're going. What do you mean by 'strange things'?"

"Like I say," the man told him as he pulled back out onto the highway, "I don't see for myself, I only hear. Many storms. It is the dry season and the rest of the country is dry, but in the mountains above Engaruka it is said that it rains and thunders all the time. Others say they hear voices up in the sky and that the voices are not those of human beings. I believe none of this, of course. I am not backward."

"Right. That's why you didn't want to take us there."

"A wise man avoids the panic of others whether there is reason for it or not. An elephant can step on you accidentally as easily as on purpose. The result is the same. And then there are all the moran. It is better to avoid so many. When they gather in large numbers they look to pick fights. Ilmoran are crazy."

Olkeloki leaned forward intently. "What about the ilmoran?"

"From all over, from all of the sixteen tribes of the Maasai as far

north as the land of the Samburu. Why they are gathering in some
nowheres bush town I do not know. Some say it has to do with a special
celebration. The government leaves them alone because they are afraid
to make trouble." He laughed. "The government is too frightened to
ask. I do not believe it is a celebration. There are better places to have
celebrations. Even the Maasai know this.

"But they are going there for something. I myself have seen
hundreds of ilmoran heading that way. They have been coming for
many days now and they say that Engaruka is surrounded by manyattas." Again he glanced slyly into the rear-view. "It is said that they
have been summoned to Engaruka by a council of elders."

Olkeloki's face had become an impenetrable mask, impossible to
read.

They stopped in a place called Logindo for the driver to refuel and
took turns using the restroom, making certain two of them stayed with
the car at all times. Then they retraced their route for a few kilometers
before turning off westward toward distant mountains. Oak felt a little
more sympathetic toward their driver. The "road" was little more than
a jeep track, though he seemed to know exactly where they were going.
He spoke little and drove hard, which was fine with his passengers.

They were delayed only once, by a flat tire. "See? Acacia," said
the driver as he extracted a three-inch-long thorn from the right front
steel-belted radial. While Oak looked on interestedly he proceeded to
replace the tube in the tubeless tire. With no service stations handy
and no automobile club to call upon it made more sense to carry a
supply of spare tubes, replace a punctured one with a fresh one, pump
it up, and drive along on the punctured tire instead of wasting time
trying to patch it. The tube was much simpler and cheaper to fix than
the tire itself.

They drove on as afternoon began to give way to evening.

17

Engaruka—Evening of the 23rd

It was still light when they finally pulled into the village. If they had driven on through and blinked twice in passing they would have missed it. The houses were actually built of mud and sticks. One a little larger than the rest had a tin roof. The general store boasted a porch of milled lumber. As Oak emerged from the car he had a glimpse through one of the glassless windows. There was no need to worry about thieves sneaking in because there was nothing to steal. The shelves were empty.

As if by magic a dozen naked children materialized alongside the car, dividing their attention equally between it and its passengers. The village was situated in a slight depression and there was a single communal well located at the lowest point. A young woman or old girl was filling a battered wooden bucket and trying to watch them at the same time.

The character of the land had changed. There were more trees and not all of them were acacias. Just ahead a few palms hinted at the location of open water, probably a seep from some subterranean river.

Olkeloki handed the driver his final payment. He pocketed the money carefully, then headed back to his vehicle. He hesitated before climbing in and looked back at Oak and Merry.

"Come with me. I will take you into Arusha. No charge. I have to go there anyway. It is my home. You don't want to stay out here in this place. This is not for tourists. If you go with him," he indicated the silent figure of Olkeloki standing quietly nearby, "maybe nobody ever see you again."

"We'll take our chances," Oak told him.

"He's our friend," Merry added.

"Your friend? No friend brings people to this place." He snorted derisively, then climbed into the Subaru. The dust it raised hung in the air long after the car itself had vanished from sight.

Oak hefted his pack. "Well, what now?" A few adults had gathered to gawk at the visitors. Children continued to erupt from the earth like maturing cicadas.

"We walk." The old man gestured westward with his staff. "That way. Not far."

"It better not be." Merry was squinting into the sky. "It's starting to get dark."

"Don't worry," Oak told her sardonically, "we can't go too far. We're not carrying any water with us."

"There is water where we are going. Water, and food, and good company." Again the laibon gestured to his left. "My kraal and my people are waiting for us over there."

Oak had prepared himself mentally for an arduous hike, but they'd gone less than two miles when they reached the crest of the third hill and Olkeloki looked proudly out onto the sloping plain beyond. For her part, Merry had expected a single dusty Maasai encampment with thornbushes ringing mud and dung huts.

Spread out before them in the warm glow of the fading equatorial sun was a small, temporary city.

"So many," she murmured, adjusting a pack strap.

Olkeloki was clearly pleased. "Ilmoran, of all the sixteen tribes of the Maasai."

Dozens of manyattas, or warriors' encampments, had been erected on both sides of the small stream that meandered across the plain parallel to the hill on which they were standing. Each was home to between fifteen and thirty fighters. Oak tried to count them, settled for a rough estimate of more than a thousand.

Children from the nearby kraal appeared to greet the three travelers as they neared the passage which had been cleared through the thornbush wall. They were taller and brighter of eye than the children of the "modern" village. They were also not the least bit shy, pulling at Oak's pants legs and giggling delightedly at the sight of Merry's blonde tresses. Oak noticed none of them danced around or pulled at the attire of the old man. They glanced at him while maintaining a respectful distance.

"There will be an olkiama tonight, a council of elders. I must find out what has happened in my absence." Abruptly, four junior warriors materialized from a patch of tall grass like brown ghosts and fell in around the travelers, two in front and two behind. They carried spears and throwing clubs and tried with little success not to stare at Merry.

"What's that they plait their hair with?" she asked Olkeloki.

"Sisal. It used to be a major Tanzanian export, until the government nationalized the plantations. They are beginning to return them to private ownership now, much chastised, I believe. The Maasai have always used it." He spoke briefly to the pair of warriors in front. They responded with nods and words and loped off ahead of the rest.

"They go to announce our coming so that we may be made comfortable on arrival and be given food to eat and milk to drink."

"If it won't insult anybody," Oak told him, "I'd just as soon stick with water. I'm not a big milk drinker." Especially if it smells anything like the stuff you've been carrying around for days in that gourd, he thought. Olkeloki sipped regularly at the contents of his calabash, which actually looked and smelled more like thin yogurt than milk.

"I am cognizant of ilmeet requirements," said Olkeloki understandingly. "We will slaughter a sheep or goat. I will do my best to see that your needs are met and that you are made to feel at home."

"How long before we push on to this Ruaha place?" They were close to the kraal now and the thick, pungent aroma of people and animals was everywhere.

"As soon as I determine what is going on here. Warriors do not gather in such numbers unless they are needed." That sounded ominous, Merry thought. "It may be that we cannot proceed farther for now."

"You mean, they aren't here for some sort of annual ritual or celebration?" Oak asked him.

Olkeloki shook his head. "Warriors gravitate to danger. I think that whatever is going to happen will happen soon. Certainly the place is significant." With his staff he pointed beyond the encampments.

Dominating the western horizon was a singular mountain. It was not as high as Kilimanjaro, which lay many miles to the east, nor distinctively craggy like the crest of the Sierras or Alps. Like Fujiyama it formed a perfect cone, but instead of the Japanese mountain's cloak of pine trees and snow, it was deeply eroded by monsoon rains and boasted growths no higher than thornbushes. It was an old mountain that had somehow held its shape despite century after century of tropical downpours and scouring wind. High grass grew up its flanks, which rose smooth and unbroken from the plain below. No other peaks crowded it for space. It sat alone like an old man in the desert, and its skin was just as wrinkled.

While the sharp light of sunset turned the surrounding plains gold and brown, the mountain assumed an unexpected purple cast that made

Oak's skin crawl. Its crown was veiled in rapidly thickening dark clouds.

"Ol Doinyo Lengai." The note of reverence in Olkeloki's voice was unmistakable. "The Mountain of God. It is sacred to everyone in this part of the world, not just the Maasai. A place of power."

"Good power, or bad?" Merry asked.

"That depends whether Engai Narok, the good black god, or Engai Na-nyokie, the evil red one, is dominating the mountain. I think that tonight we will find out. See!"

Lightning split the gathering thunderhead boiling above the now hidden peak. The thunder reached them a moment later.

"They fight for control; Engai Narok with lightning and Engai Na-nyokie with the thunder."

"It's just an ordinary thunderstorm," Oak pointed out politely.

The old man looked back at him. "I hope that you are right, friend Joshua. We will find out during the olkiama. I have a feeling we have returned just in time."

The interior of the engang, or kraal, was every bit as primitive as Oak anticipated. Yet the closer he looked the more he felt that here were a primitive, seminomadic people who had managed to preserve their traditions while coming to terms with the twentieth century. They displayed assurance and confidence in everything they did, along with an assortment of Rolex and Seiko watches and a silvery Hitachi boom-box that squatted in a corner outside a hut muttering music and Swahili.

Further confirmation came from an unexpected source. Olkeloki had disappeared into a large hut, leaving Oak and Merry to wander around outside. They were confronted by a tall, spear-carrying warrior who said to Oak, in perfect English, "I know that you are those who arrived from America with the old laibon. Please, can't you tell me how the Celtics did this year?"

"The Celtics?" Oak gaped at the young man. With his saffron toga, spear, painted legs, and ochred hair he looked like a citizen of the seventeenth century. But he spoke as an inhabitant of the twentieth.

"My name is Asembili. I have been home for only half a year. Prior to that I was attending Harvard Boys Academy in Boston. Next year I hope to be sent to Harvard itself, or Princeton if I must."

"Harvard or Princeton?" Merry looked him up and down. "But then how can you . . . ?"

". . . walk around dressed like this? I am Maasai. This is how Maasai warriors dress." Oak thought of Olkeloki and his ancient but well-fitting three-piece suit. "Every few years a tribe or clan will choose one of its brightest boys and pay his way to England or America so he can go to school there. This is done so that he can return to help the Maasai deal with the modern governments of Kenya and Tanzania. In that way we 'itinerant nomads,' as the government people call us, are not cheated." His pleasant smile faded and he pointed with the tip of his lethal-looking spear toward the cloud-shrouded mountain.

"You have come to help the illaibon?"

"I don't know—no, I guess that's what we're here for." Oak watched the lightning dancing around the cone of the old volcano. "Olkeloki seems to think it's important for a couple of foreigners to accompany him south."

Asembili looked solemn. "We are to go up the mountain tonight. To fight."

"Fight what?" Merry wondered.

"Whatever fights back."

"That sounds pretty nebulous," said Oak.

"The ilmoran do what the elders advise. Are you a warrior?"

"I've done my share of fighting." He saw Merry staring at him.

"Will you come with us? I will let you fight next to me."

"No thanks. If you end up fighting who I'm afraid you're going to be fighting, I'd just be in the way. Besides, I had to leave my own weapons at home. You must know what airport security's like these days."

"Sometimes the most honest weapon is one that has no trigger." Asembili pulled a two-foot-long ebony stick from his belt. It was similar to Olkeloki's. Oak thought it was some kind of insignia of office, like a baton. As the young moran demonstrated, it was rather more than that.

Grasping the upper six inches, he separated the carved handle from its ebony scabbard. Attached to the handle was an eighteen-inch-long triangular blade.

"Fight with Asembili's knife. My clan will be proud." Ignoring Oak's protest, he handed him the weapon. Then he spoke frankly to Merry. "A little old, but still worth many cattle."

"Hey, now you listen here . . ."

Laughing, he skipped out of her reach. "In America I could not say that. Perhaps I will see you on the mountain." He turned and ran easily toward the entrance.

"Nervy bunch," she muttered. "I'm old enough to be his sister. I can see he didn't pick up any Boston manners."

"This isn't Boston. You ought to be flattered."

"I like a little subtlety. These people aren't subtle. It's not just the men, either. Haven't you noticed how many of the young girls have been giving you the eye?"

"Whaaat?"

She shook her head. "Some men are so naive. Where've you been for the last hour? Half the women in this place have done everything but proposition you by telegram. I suppose that's 'Maasai' too."

"I'm not sure where I've been for the past couple of days, much less the last hour. You're putting me on."

"Sure I am." She nodded past him. "See those two over there? In the bangles and beads?"

"Where?" Oak turned, saw two girls who looked to be in their late teens walking toward a hut. The instant his eyes met theirs, both of them cocked their heads sideways and smiled explosively back at him. The first one bent and disappeared inside the structure. The second ran her long tongue slowly over her upper lip before following her friend.

"Whew." Oak turned back to Merry. "That's been going on ever since we got here?"

"I'd better keep a close watch on you. If I let you get off by yourself you might never be seen again."

"I guess the Maasai are just a little, uh, promiscuous."

"Why Josh, I do believe that you're blushing, though it's getting so dark it's hard to tell for sure." Torches mounted atop poles were being fired up by an older man carrying a butane cigarette lighter.

With nothing to do but wait for Olkeloki, they wandered outside the thornbush wall. Hundreds of lights from ilmoran torches speckled the plain and the lower slope of Ol Doinyo Lengai. Lightning continued to illuminate the clouds and thunder rolled in waves down the mountainside.

"I still can't believe the local government wouldn't be interested in an armed gathering of this size, even if the ilmoran are armed with nothing more than spears and clubs."

"Remember what that driver told us," Merry reminded him. "Not only are local officials leery of offending the Maasai, communications aren't too swift around here. By the time the word was passed up to anyone in a position to do anything about it, the ilmoran would probably be gone. So why make waves?"

"You're right. Let's go back inside."

"Worried about lions?" she teased.

"Not with all these warriors around. I don't buy all those stories about lions avoiding ilmoran, but if I were a big cat I wouldn't come anywhere near an encampment of this size."

Sheep and goats were being slaughtered, the dressed meat ending up on sticks slipped over open fires. While they watched, a cow was brought forward but not slain. Instead, a warrior used a sharp stick to jab a hole in the jugular vein while another caught the steady stream of blood in an empty calabash. A third moran held the animal's head up. It did not appear to be in pain.

When enough blood had been collected, the wound was sealed with a mixture of water, leaves, and dung. Then another calabash was brought forward and they watched while the fresh blood was mixed with milk. The warrior who had collected the blood offered Oak a drink. He declined.

They were assured that the cow would heal with no ill effects. No Maasai would risk the life of one of his cattle simply to obtain a little blood.

Oak halted outside the hut which had swallowed Olkeloki. "Ever have the feeling you were being watched? And I don't mean by young men or women."

She eyed him questioningly. "You feel it too. Shetani?"

His expression twisted. "Can't tell. Just—something, out there, watching." He spun around sharply. Nothing but flickering torches, women going about their evening work, and ilmoran moving to and fro. Yet there was something out there watching him. He could feel its eyes on his back. He knew when he was being stalked. He'd felt it twice before, once in Alabama and again in Idaho. It was an unpleasant sensation.

Then Olkeloki was standing next to them, looking sepulchral in the dim light. The shadows exaggerated the gauntness of his face and filled in the hollows around his eyes. This was a different man from the one who had smiled and joked with them on the flight from D.C. He'd seen something inside the hut which had scared him. Olkeloki wore the look of a troubled spectre.

"It is time," he told them quietly. "Come." His eyes met Merry's and some of the sprightly old gentleman they knew returned. "You will come also, Merry Sharrow. I argued for it. It is not traditional for a woman to march with elders and ilmoran, but I reminded them that this is the twentieth century."

"Where are we going?"

"Up! Up with the ilmoran." He swept his staff toward Ol Doinyo Lengai, which thundered in response.

They followed him out of the kraal at the head of a procession of elders. There were more than twenty of the laibon, each man distinguished by a blanket different in color and pattern from his brothers. They chatted among themselves as they walked, sometimes agreeing, often arguing, never silent for long.

Off on the moon-swept plain that fell away to their left, lines of torches were beginning to form as the ilmoran commenced their advance on the mountain. Like the elders, the warriors moved in single file. Gradually the lines coalesced until it looked as if a solid line of fire were crawling up the mountain. In the still of the African night you could hear men talking to one another, but no shouted orders or barked commands. He remarked to Olkeloki on this apparent lack of a unified command.

"The Maasai have leaders but no kings, senior warriors but no generals. We have a hierarchy of wisdom without a parliament or congress."

"Aren't you in charge?" Merry asked him.

"My advice is sought, but I do not give orders. I am only one of the spiritual and temporal leaders of the Maasai." He gestured at the line of old men trudging along behind them. Oak thought he could see right through the tallest of them. A moment later he saw that it was only an illusion caused by torchlight. The man smiled at him as though he knew something Oak didn't know. It made Oak uncomfortable and he turned away from the marchers.

Except for the soft, distant chants of the ilmoran as they climbed and the chatter of the elders, the night was dead quiet. Even the cicadas were silent, their miniature air-raid sirens turned off. Somewhere a single bird chirped, sounding lonely and out of place.

"Events are progressing even faster than I feared," Olkeloki told them without taking his eyes off the thunderstorm that was raging around the crown of the mountain.

"The shetani," whispered Merry, and he nodded.

"The elders know. They say that because this is a place of power, the first thrust will come here, where the mountain weakens the walls of reality. We must try to stop them. If we can, they will hesitate. Here we must buy time until we can seal the main lesion in Ruaha."

This is wild, Oak thought as his fingers tightened around the long knife the young warrior had given him. "What will they be like? The thing that climbed onto our windshield back in Washington?"

"That—and other things. There are many different kinds of shetani, remember. You wanted revenge for what happened to us in the elevator, Joshua Oak. Tonight you will have all the opportunity you could wish for to gain it."

"Fine, but I wish I had my gun with me." Olkeloki did not reply.

They halted at the end of a steep drop-off. From this modest promontory they had a clear view of the mountain and the plains off to the left and below. Shouts of defiance rang against the rocks as the ilmoran yelled encouragement to one another. Ahead of them the gradually increasing slope of the mountain was still deserted; mongoose and fox, hyrax and hyena having long since been driven to their burrows by the tramp of so many feet. Thunder rolled over the Maasai.

"Engai Na-nyokie," declared Olkeloki. "A night of evil. We must be ready for anything. We have to prepare. Excuse me." He left Oak and Merry and made his way back to the line of waiting elders.

"I have to prepare too," said Merry. She turned and headed for a high clump of boulders nearby, searching for a comfortable bush.

Too nervous to stand alone, Oak followed Olkeloki, waited patiently while the old man conversed with his colleagues.

"You once told us that guns aren't much good against these shetani."

Olkeloki looked back at him. "Bravery and determination can often succeed when guns and bombs fail, Joshua Oak. A little magic can also make a difference. Watch, and learn."

Oak wanted to ask more, but the old man turned away from him. Feeling useless as well as foolish, he watched as the line of laibon stepped to the very edge of the promontory and raised their walking sticks, holding them out toward the mountain. They began chanting softly in unison. Oak looked on interestedly, wishing he could make sense of what they were singing. Then he happened to glance back toward the mountain. His breath caught in his throat.

The torches of the ilmoran continued to advance up the mountainside, but now their glow was eclipsed by the pale blue fluorescence that shone from the edges of a thousand spear blades. Each slice of steel had been kissed by something like Saint Elmo's fire. Nor was the blue glow steady and unvarying. Instead, each spear pulsed, the intensity of the light varying according to the volume of its owner's voice.

The thousand warriors began to chant, their heads bobbing forward and back as they climbed. Gradually their grunts and the light of their spears were synchronized. They began to move faster. Oak remembered to breathe.

A muffled noise reached him over the near-hypnotic singsong of the laibon. Shetani—or something less ethereal? Olkeloki lowered his staff and moved close.

"What troubles you, Joshua Oak?"

"Thought I heard something. Getting jumpy, I guess."

"Now is the time of jumpiness." Together they gazed out over the sea of torches and glowing spears.

"Merry sure is taking her time."

"It is the nature of women to take time for their insides. Why do you think they live longer than men?"

Instead of offering an answer, he asked the question he'd been unable to ask until now.

"I know I've been something less than a true believer through all this, old man. This looks like something major coming up. Who's going to win?"

Olkeloki shrugged. "The Maasai do not worry about the outcome of a fight. As the ilmoran say, the war will be won by our side, or theirs. It is the fighting they are concerned with."

"Fatalism."

"Determination."

Both men were silent for a long moment, listening to the rhythmic chant of the thousand. Then Oak looked back toward the boulders, frowning. "I don't want to miss anything, but I'd better go see what's keeping her."

"The impatience of the ilmeet. You will embarrass her."

"To hell with embarrassing her. Maybe a snake bit her, or something."

There was amusement in the old man's voice. "If that were so then I think she would be here describing it to us now, no matter how deadly the snake. Go look if you must. I must help my brothers." He raised his own staff and moved to rejoin the line of laibon.

Oak pushed his way through the brush around the rocks. He didn't call out. If Olkeloki was right and Merry was simply taking her own sweet time with her business he wanted to find out without making himself look like an idiot. And if she was in some kind of trouble, cornered or paralyzed with fear by the sight of some poisonous reptile or pack of wild dogs or something, he wanted to approach without startling it lest it react by attacking.

With the ease of long practice he made his way silently through the rocks and small trees until he saw movement ahead. He slowed still further, moving forward until he could see her standing with her back to a low granite arch. She was in trouble, all right, but the threat came not from any native of the African veldt. It was a lot more dangerous than that.

The abomination had a head twice the length of its body. That head was mostly mouth and teeth save for a pair of bulbous eyes which dangled loosely from the tips of long stalks. One short ear clung like a leech to the left side of the skull while the other listening organ flopped about with every move the creature made. Dark drool dripped from the lower jaw as it reached with long, thin arms toward the cowering Merry.

Oak looked at his tiny spear, then bent and picked up the biggest rock he could find and heaved it with all his strength. In school they usually put him on the line in football, but he still had a pretty strong arm. The stone struck the monstrosity in the back of its skull and bounced off. It whirled and he found himself staring into eyes that were not the product of any normal evolution. They did not shock him, did not paralyze him, because he'd seen them before.

He'd seen them through the hole in the roof of an elevator in an office building in Washington, D.C.

It turned, arms dragging momentarily on the ground, and reached out to draw him into that unholy chasm of a mouth. He readied the

knife, wondering where to strike first, when another spear flew out of the
trees nearby, a thin shaft of fluorescent blue against the night. It struck
the Likutu shetani square in the center of its narrow, bony chest. The
shetani uttered a sound halfway between a laugh and a gurgle. A second
spear followed close behind the first, then a third, and a fourth. Black
goo began dribbling from the shetani's lips and it swayed like a tree in a
gale.

A running silhouette appeared atop the rocks behind Merry. It
leaped onto the monster's back and Oak saw moonlight flash off a
two-foot-long knife as it stabbed again and again at the muscular neck.
Other ilmoran began to emerge from the bushes to hack at the tottering
Likutu. It reached for one of its tormentors and the Maasai warrior
nimbly dodged the groping claws. Then the shetani stumbled and fell.
The ilmoran swarmed over it like army ants butchering a caterpillar.
As bits and pieces of the creature were sliced from the body they
exploded, evaporating like black soda bubbles in the warm night air.

Merry ran to join Oak and he grabbed her shoulders with both
hands.

"You okay?" An unearthly stench rose from behind them.

She nodded. "It just jumped out at me. I couldn't even scream.
It—it was going to kill me, Josh."

"Maybe it just wanted to say hello, shetani-like."

She took a deep breath. "I think that's the same thing." She looked
past him. "We'd better get back to Olkeloki and the others." He
nodded. They turned and left the ilmoran to their butchery.

On a rocky outcropping that overlooked the holy mountain the
assembled laibon worked at their magic. A warm breeze blew off the
flanks of Ol Doinyo Lengai, blowing the blankets the old men wore back
against their bodies. Some of them thrust their walking sticks defiantly at
the mountain. Others spat into their calabashes and shook the contents
at the distant slopes. Olkeloki stood on the highest point of ground,
slightly apart from the others. As Oak and Merry emerged from the
bushes it struck him that all this chanting and gesticulating was merely a
prelude to something of much greater import. He halted, sensing instinctively that now was not the time to bother the old man. Merry leaned
against him for support, still weak from her confrontation with the
Likutu.

Olkeloki turned toward his brothers and raised his staff over his
head as he shouted a command. It was repeated by the other laibon.
Calabashes were set aside. Each man raised his own walking stick above
his head, clutching it firmly in both hands and holding it parallel to the
earth. Twenty staffs formed a line above twenty rock-steady old figures.

"What's happening?" Merry rubbed at her left eye.

Oak squinted into the wind that blew down off the mountain, trying to penetrate the darkness. "Can't tell for sure, but *something's* happening. You can feel it."

Three times they uttered a single ululation: three times the words were repeated by the massed warriors on the mountainside. Then the roiling clouds that hid the crest of the sacred mountain split asunder and hell came running down the slope on inhuman feet.

Jumping and rolling, loping and crawling, moving on four arms or four legs or two limbs alone, the horde of shetani poured down on the assembled ilmoran like a mutated zoo. Some of them were thin, gangly giants like the Likutu. Scrabbling around the long legs of the Likutu were stunted monstrosities without arms or legs, all jaws and teeth and long, muscular ears. Oak and Merry could hear them chittering and giggling as they pushed themselves downhill with the bulbous lobes of their hearing organs.

There was something that ran along on yard-high legs attached to an eight-inch body. Swaying atop this minuscule torso was a huge, narrow skull that ended in a flattened, bony blade. It smiled horribly as it ran. Alongside it loped a couple of very human figures that had no faces at all. In place of a head was something like a serrated tuning fork. There were goliaths with skulls in the shape of narrow arrowheads. Tiny round mouths sucked air beneath a single eye.

There were shetani with hollow cheekbones, not hollow from lack of food but truly hollow: you could see clear through the skull behind the arching bridge of the nose. One shetani galloped along on eight-foot legs that were no thicker around than a man's thumb. Two huge ears stood straight up on either side of the head while bright orange eyes glared out from beneath thick ridges of bone. The nose was a long strip down the front of the face. Beneath it a pair of jaws faced each other, flexing horizontal fangs.

Another's teeth protruded upward from its lower lip, while the face of its companion seemed to be falling off in dribs and drabs as it ran, melting into the earth. A few of the shetani carried spears and clubs, but most came racing wildly downhill unarmed.

A thunderous war cry shook the ground as the ilmoran lowered their spears and advanced to meet the alien army. Now the shetani in front could see that the volcanic slope they were tumbling down was already occupied. A few slowed and were nearly run over by those following behind. There were signs of confusion in the shetani ranks.

Some changed the direction of their descent as they tried to find a way around the advancing warriors, but the ilmoran had spread out to form a line across the whole lower slope of the mountain. Nor were there any gaps for the shetani to slip through. The ilmoran marched upward shoulder to shoulder.

"Look!" Merry grabbed excitedly at Oak's arm. "They're confused. They expected to come through untouched, unopposed. They don't know how to react."

A few of the shetani started to retreat back up the mountainside, but the momentum of the majority was such that they had no choice but to fling themselves on the line of warriors.

The Maasai plowed into them, stabbing and slashing with their spears, some of which mounted blades a yard long. Such blades were designed to penetrate all the way to a lion's heart. Pulsing with the pale light which was a visible manifestation of the laibon's magic, the warriors dispatched one invader after another. Sizzling and crackling, the cut and pierced abominations exploded into nothingness with each successful spear thrust. The night air began to turn putrid with the stench of evaporating shetani.

Then something happened which proved that the shetani were not blind, mindless entities. A group detached themselves from the main battle, circled around the right end of the line of ilmoran, and began to climb the hill atop which the laibon stood chanting. They had located the source of the warriors' magic and intended to put an end to it. As soon as their intent became clear to the senior warriors who were directing the fight, a platoon of ilmoran was dispatched to intercept the climbing shetani.

Nor did the advance go unnoticed among the laibon themselves. A few put down their staffs and made ready to defend themselves. Someone shoved a glowing spear into Oak's startled hands. The wood and metal lance was cold to the touch.

"Can you use that thing?" Merry asked him. The noise around them now, the chanting of the laibon, the war cries of the ilmoran, the hellish babble of the shetani, was almost deafening and she had to shout to make herself understood.

"I don't know," he yelled back at her, "but I'm sure going to try." A .38 would have felt better in his hands but he was glad of any kind of weapon.

Several of the shetani broke through and reached the line of elders. Belying their age, a trio of the oldsters began swinging their staffs enthusiastically. Each had been a warrior in his youth and eagerly demonstrated that old skills are not necessarily forgotten skills. The shetani inflicted a few bites and bruises, but no serious injuries.

One charged straight at Oak. It stood some four feet high. Long blades of bone protruded from each elbow and it used these as weapons, swinging them at the human and aiming for his legs, grinning and laughing as it fought. With the long spear Oak was able to fend it off easily.

Then something landed on his back. Merry cursed and searched frantically for something to use as a weapon. The shetani ranged in hue from dark brown to jet black and it was difficult to see them at night. As Oak went down under the weight he twisted around and found himself inches away from a face of pure petrified ugliness. It grinned at him as it raised its right arm, which was lined with a razor-sharp sliver of bone, and brought it down straight toward his face.

Abruptly the shetani's head was separated from its neck. Gushing black liquid, the body collapsed. As Oak slid out from under it the flesh began to effervesce and vanish.

Standing over his prone form was a figure that appeared to have been carved from solid obsidian, a figure that rose higher and higher into the night sky, until its braided headpiece seemed to brush the moon. It neither smiled nor frowned. Oak rolled over, blinking at the pain that was shooting through his shoulders where the shetani had latched on with clawed feet. As soon as he had satisfied himself that the ilmeet was all right, the moran whirled and rushed back to rejoin the main battle. Oak guessed that his savior had stood just a shade under seven feet tall. The spear he carried was almost as big as its owner.

Someone else was standing next to him then, holding a long blade. "Josh, I found your knife." He smiled at her.

"Looks like you were getting ready to use it."

She studied him closely. "That awful thing was trying to split your head wide open. I—I couldn't find anything to hit it with."

"The Maasai cavalry beat you to it. Don't worry. Some folks never have a bloody nose, some never catch cold. Me, I've got a thick head."

Another figure joined them. This one was familiar and no less concerned than Merry. "How are you, friend Oak?"

He smiled reassuringly at Olkeloki. "I've felt better. How goes the war?"

"The shetani are not good fighters. They have little stomach for an open battle. Some have no stomach at all. They prefer to overwhelm one or two people at a time, and to attack from hiding or to make trouble and cause people to kill one another. The waiting ilmoran took them by surprise. Now the surprise is wearing off." He looked solemn. "The laibon have discussed the matter. The ilmoran can beat the shetani, but many will die. So the old men have decided to do something else." He put a helpful arm around Oak's shoulders. "We must leave now."

"Leave? But the fight's not over." He hefted his spear. "Somebody saved my neck. I'm not running away while I can still help."

"I am sure you are a strong fighter, Joshua Oak." Olkeloki favored him with a smile that might have been complimentary or might have been patronizing. "But the time for fighting draws to an end. The laibon have decided how best to end this. We would have done it first, but such things take time and a great deal of preparation."

Oak's ready response was overwhelmed by a new kind of thunder, the likes of which he'd never heard before. Merry Sharrow, however, recognized it instantly.

"Mount St. Helens," she shouted above the intensifying din. "I was home asleep when it blew up. It threw me out of bed. Seattle isn't that far from the site and—"

Before she could finish, the sky and storm clouds above the Mountain of God lit up with multiple bursts of red lightning. A wave of hot air swept down the mountain's flank to stagger the onlookers. Merry clung to Oak to keep from being knocked down while Olkeloki leaned hard on his walking stick.

Explosions of lesser intensity continued to sound from deep inside the mountain. Peering through the hot wind, they watched as the shetani began to retreat, scrambling and clawing their way back toward the clouds. At the same time the ilmoran turned and began to retrace their steps down the mountainside. Not a victory, then, Oak thought. Stalemate.

Something was burning the back of his right hand and he shook it off. Pumice and ash were starting to rain down as Olkeloki led them back beneath the shelter of the trees.

"We must get back to the kraal," he told them. "I do not think this stage of the eruption will last long, but we should seek shelter."

"How would you know?" Oak grabbed at the old man's blanket. "This isn't an old volcano. Even a non-expert like myself can see that."

Olkeloki nodded. "Ol Doinyo last erupted in nineteen sixty-seven."

"Okay." Oak let go of the blanket. "Just don't try telling me that a bunch of old men had anything to do with it blowing its top tonight. You just timed everything well, that's all."

"I would not try to tell you anything, Joshua Oak." Was the old man smiling at him or not? "What matters is that we have turned back the shetani. They will consider carefully before they try to come through again in such numbers. They will wait until the opening from the Out Of is widened and made permanent. Then they will use it to come through in places where people will not know how to stop them. Unless we can seal the weakness first."

"Ouch!" Merry slapped at her arm where a hot ash had landed. "What you're saying is that they can use the actual split in the Out Of to come through elsewhere, like here?"

"Yes. Or in downtown Manhattan, or Piccadilly Circus in London."

As they crouched beneath the trees Oak tried to envision the nightmare that would result from a sudden outbreak of shetani in a densely populated urban area. Frightening enough to confront an army of such horrors here on an open plain. Imagine thousands of them suddenly materializing on the Mall in Washington or in New York's Central Park. He could just see the municipal and Federal governments trying to decide how to deal with an invasion by supernatural forces. Meanwhile the ravening shetani would take a city apart.

Washington seemed impossibly far away as he retreated from the erupting Mountain of God in the company of hundreds of silent Maasai warriors. Modern weapons might take care of the shetani; if not the guns and bombs Olkeloki spoke contemptuously of, then lasers and flamethrowers. Even so, thousands of people would perish and civilizations would quake. And hadn't the old man spoken of billions pouring through from the Out Of? Since everything came from the Out Of, it stood to reason it had to be a much bigger place than the real world. Under the shetani assault civilization might give way to something straight out of Dante's Inferno.

He thought of all the shetani who'd already slipped across, who had been coming through for years, infiltrating the real world in a steady stream, disguising themselves as chunks of shredded tire rubber, lining the highways and byways of the developed countries. Now they were getting ready to move, to make a final assault on an unsuspecting mankind. No way could a bureaucracy cope with that. And when the last remnants of an enslaved humanity had been exterminated, the shetani would turn on one another, murdering and slaughtering, until the earth had been transformed into a lifeless globe.

Of course, he reminded himself, none of that appalling scenario need come true. All they had to do to prevent the world from being turned into a charnel house was to reach the source of the main breakthrough without attracting the shetani's attention and seal it off forever.

"This way," shouted Olkeloki, pointing to his left. "If all has gone as planned we will not have to run all the way to Ruaha."

They followed the laibon into the bushes and practically ran into a brand-new Land Rover. A single very young moran stood in front of the vehicle. He raised his spear until he recognized the laibon, then grinned and put the weapon up. Old warrior and young embraced.

"Muani," Olkeloki told them, making introductions. The teenager nodded, lighting up the night with his smile. Ash continued to rain down around them. "One of my grandsons. When we arrived at the manyatta I was concerned at our lack of transportation. Muani has been to school. Someday I think he will make a very fine mechanic." He spoke to the youth in Maasai and the young moran beamed with pride.

"You can drive such a vehicle, Joshua Oak? I would do so myself but my eyes are not what they used to be."

"You bet I can," Oak told him.

The three of them piled into the big four-wheel drive. A five-pound lump of hot lava smashed into a thornbush nearby, setting it afire. Ol Doinyo Lengai continued to fulminate and roar behind them.

The engine turned over instantly. He flicked on the lights and powerful halogen beams sliced through the darkness. Another lava bomb landed on the roof, sounding larger than it was. His spirits rose when he saw that the gas tank was nearly full.

"Which way?" Even inside the Rover the thunder of the fractious mountain made it hard to make oneself understood.

Olkeloki murmured a few last words to the young warrior. The two embraced again and the youth dashed off into the brush to rejoin his fellow ilmoran. Then the laibon climbed into the seat next to Oak. For a long moment he sat there, staring out of the windshield as though aligning some built-in compass, then pointed.

"That way. I must confer with the other elders. Then we must go south, to Lake Manyara. There is another there I should speak with. From there we go to Dodoma and thence to Iringa, which lies but a few hours from Ruaha itself."

Oak put the Rover in gear, began picking his way down the slope. "Where'd your grandson rent a car like this, anyway?"

"Rent?" Olkeloki looked amused. "This is a CCM Land Rover. Do you not recall our matatu driver telling you on the way to the border that only the local political party has ample transportation? But since this is a socialist country where everything belongs to the people, Muani knows that the Land Rovers of the CCM belong to him as well. It will not do a few politicians any harm to walk for a while because we have temporarily borrowed their transportation."

Oak grinned. "Wouldn't hurt if he'd borrowed it from Washington, either."

Merry let out a yelp as a huge figure suddenly materialized alongside the Rover. It was no shetani, Oak saw immediately. Olkeloki rolled his window down and spoke to the new arrival while Oak kept them moving away from the mountain at a stately five miles an hour.

"Relax, Merry," he called back to her. "I know this guy. He's the one who saved my life back there on the hill."

Olkeloki glanced sharply at Oak. "That decides it, then. He is marked."

A few more terse, shouted words passed between the warrior and the old man. Without breaking stride the giant disassembled his huge spear. Then he jumped into the Land Rover as Olkeloki held the door open for him. Merry made room as he crawled in back. He had to bend forward so his head could clear the roof.

"This is Kakombe. He is an Alaunoni, or leader, among the senior warriors."

Oak shifted gears, enjoying the feel of the Land Rover. It looked brand-new. Leave it to an impecunious government to supply its field operatives with the best (and most expensive) equipment available.

"Pleasure's all mine. I didn't get a chance to thank you back there. You took off before I could find my tongue again."

"Shetani would have ripped it out," he replied in lightly accented English. He grinned at Merry. "Hello. Sorry it's a little cramped back here. I don't mind if you don't."

"Do I have a choice?" She smiled back at him. "I'm Merry Sharrow, that's Joshua Oak."

He nodded understandingly. "Yes, the two il—two Americans who returned with the laibon to help us against the shetani."

"We're helping our own people, too. They're in as much danger as you are. Probably more so."

Kakombe looked solemn, then spoke softly to Olkeloki. The old man translated.

"He says that he's pleased to meet both of you. That you fought bravely, Joshua Oak, if not as well as a Maasai, and that he respects both of you for coming all this way to do battle against such great evil."

Oak glanced into the back. "Why didn't he say that himself? He speaks excellent English."

"Kakombe is an Alaunoni. As such he is expected to be perfect in all things. He will speak English when he feels confident with the words, but he is too proud to make a mistake. This comes from when he was a child and had a speech defect. The other children used to make fun of him."

Merry studied the powerful bulk scrunched up on the other half of the seat. "I bet they only did it once. We're glad to have you with us, Kakombe."

"Be careful of what you say and how you say it, Merry Sharrow," Olkeloki said.

She sounded suddenly concerned. "Did I say something wrong?"

"No, but you must also be careful not to say things too right." The old man spoke firmly to the giant and Kakombe responded irritably.

"Remember," Olkeloki explained, "that Kakombe is an Alaunoni. When a woman smiles favorably on him and speaks words of praise, it would be natural for him to think she might have more than casual conversation on her mind. Kakombe knows your language but not your ways, and you are not yet familiar enough with his."

"Oh. I didn't mean to give him the wrong impression. How do I correct myself?"

"Stop smiling at him like that, for one thing."

"It's the only way I know how to smile."

"Um." Olkeloki assumed the look of a confused parent.

"Are you telling us that after fighting for his life against a few thousand nightmares the hulk here can still have sex on his mind?" Oak inquired.

"Josh!" Merry's jaw dropped.

"Grow up, Merry. Some guys are turned on by fighting. Plenty of women, too."

She looked as though she wanted to say something but couldn't find the right words.

"It is the business of a senior warrior," Olkeloki intoned, "to think only of three things: fighting, cattle, and women."

Oak nodded understandingly. "I've got friends back in the Bureau who'd go along with two out of three." He squinted into the night. "Hey, isn't that the road?"

"Yes." Olkeloki did not squint. "Turn to the right here. Soon we will be back at the kraal. There we will find food and rest waiting for us. In the morning we will rise early and start south."

Oak looked thoughtful. "Who do you have to see at this Manyara place?"

"Lake Manyara. There is one there who has lived long and knows much. His perception differs from ours and he is more sensitive to the places between the real world and the other. Between the worlds lies a hollow space, like the cavity between the two panes of an insulated window. I cannot see into it, but the Patriarch can."

"Sounds like an interesting person," Merry opined.

"Most interesting. I have talked many times with him and have always emerged from such conversations wiser than when they began. No one knows how old the Patriarch is, but as you will see, his age is written in his skin and his teeth."

"Lost them all, has he?" Merry sounded sympathetic. "My maternal grandfather went through that."

"No, he still has his teeth. The sign of age is not that they are gone, but that they are crossed. Now let me rest. This has been a strenuous evening and I am tired." Merry sensed he would answer no more questions that night.

18

Lake Manyara—24 June

The vast sheet of open water shimmered in the morning sun, a quicksilver valley between two escarpments. As they drew near, Oak and Merry were able to gauge its true extent. And according to Olkeloki, Manyara was one of the Rift Valley's *smaller* lakes.

During the morning they'd stopped twice, once for a cold drink and again to top off the Land Rover's water bags. Both times they overheard tourists discussing the previous night's brief but violent eruption of Ol Doinyo Lengai.

Ever attuned to irony, Oak conjured up an image of the busloads of tourists standing on the laibon hill snapping away with their little automatic cameras as ilmoran did battle with shetani and complaining about the poor lighting. Many would be incapable of seeing a battle for survival as anything more than another attraction staged for their benefit. That's all Africa was to most Americans and Europeans: a gigantic exotic tourist attraction, Disneyland with real animals instead of audio-animatronics. No doubt such people found the little towns Oak and his companions had driven through all morning "quaint." Back home they would be called slums. Location was everything.

As the single-lane road crawled down the escarpment they entered a real forest, the first they'd encountered since leaving Virginia. Birds sang from secret places in the canopy. The forest clung to the well-watered slope of the escarpment. Beyond lay open plains and the lake. Wildebeest and hartebeest roamed the shoreline in uncountable number, the herds spotted here and there with clumps of zebra and gazelle. Looking like water-worn brown boulders, hippos lined the far shore of the main stream that fed the lake. Their stentorian oinks reverberated across the banks, a lexicon of unsullied grouchiness.

After his surprisingly sound night's sleep on the floor of a laibon's hut, Oak was full of confidence and high spirits. The shetani had been thrown back into whatever black pit they'd emerged from and he, Merry, Olkeloki, and Kakombe were on their way south to fix things so such an intrusion could never happen again.

Merry wiped sweat from her forehead and cheeks. "It's hotter here."

"It will be hotter still in the south," Olkeloki warned her. "And it is not hot enough to use the air conditioning. We must conserve petrol."

She studied the crank set in the center of the roof. "Why don't we open the top, then?"

"That would not be a good idea here."

"Why not?"

"Yeah, why not?" Oak added. "I could use a little fresh air myself. These windows don't let much of a breeze in."

"Because the forest of Manyara," the old man explained as they bounced down the narrow dirt track, "is the only place in Africa where lions are known to live in trees. If one were to roll lazily off a branch beneath which we happened to be passing, it would become too crowded in here and the lion, being the guest, would immediately set about rearranging the seating to suit his own preferences."

That was the last time either Merry or Oak suggested opening the roof. Oak, who had been driving with his left elbow stuck out the window, discreetly tucked it against his side.

"How much farther?"

"There is a small stream, Maji Moto. Hot water in Swahili. The Patriarch can often be found camped near there. If he is not there we will have to search him out."

"I'm not too keen on hiking through the jungle," Merry told him.

"You can stay with the car, Merry Sharrow. The Patriarch will not have wandered far. He is old and does not travel as he did in his youth. And," he could not keep himself from adding, "this is woodland forest, not jungle."

"What's he like?"

"You will see. I personally find his company charming."

Yeah, but you talk to ghosts and spirits, too, she told herself. Olkeloki didn't understand. Maybe Oak could handle the heat—summer in the eastern U.S. was no picnic. But she was from the Northwest, for crying out loud! It was like an oven in the crowded Land Rover despite the fact that all the side windows were open.

Go ahead and complain, she admonished herself. Catch the looks
on their faces: Shouldn't have dragged a woman along. She could
imagine Kakombe's response. Well, she'd melt into her walking shoes
before she'd ask for the air conditioning. If the big man could handle
riding for hours practically bent over double, she could damn well sweat
a little. She could stand to lose a few pounds anyway.

Between the trees and the lake they caught glimpses of vast herds
of tanklike Cape buffalo. Beyond, the water was stained pink in places
by immense flocks of flamingos. Olkeloki finally decreed a halt where a
small rivulet cut across the track in front of them. It was singularly
unimpressive and stank of sulfur and brine.

"We can rest and eat. If the Patriarch does not join us soon we
will go and look for him."

While Maji Moto was a lukewarm disappointment, the glade in
which they parked the Land Rover offered shady compensation. High
green grass grew in the open space beneath the trees. Nearby a herd of
impala grazed contentedly, seemingly indifferent to the newcomers but
in reality very much aware of the humans' presence. From time to time
the male would lift his pale head to search with limpid brown eyes for
signs of bachelors intent on making off with one or more of his harem.

Having met too many copperheads and cottonmouths in the Deep
South, Oak was concerned about encountering snakes in the high grass.
Olkeloki assured him that the best way not to find one was to look for
one. The old man and Kakombe shared milk and yogurt while Merry
and Oak stuck to the dried meat and fruit that had been packed for
them by the women of the kraal.

Beneath that wavy green sky it was easy to forget why they'd come
to this part of the world. Time itself seemed to have stopped for a siesta.
Tall trees masked the sun. Except for the chirp of birds and the
occasional shrill cry of a ground hornbill it was as quiet as good old
Burke Lake on a weekday morning. Had the impala been deer, Oak
could have imagined he was back home.

He'd wandered a short distance away from the others, inspecting
the trees and trying to edge a little closer to the herd, when he thought
he detected a rustling in the grass. If it was a snake it was too big to
be one of the local venomous ones. Cautiously he leaned forward for a
better look.

His legs went out from under him. Something damp and sticky
slapped over his mouth as he tried to cry out. He hit the ground hard
and found himself being pulled into the bushes. As he rolled over,
waving his arms wildly, he saw his companions standing oblivious back
by the Land Rover. No one had seen him go down. Kakombe stood on
one leg sipping milk. Olkeloki was sitting in the grass contemplating
something unseen while Merry was leaning against the car chewing on

a strip of goat meat. They were figures on a tiny screen that was getting smaller and smaller as he was dragged backward through the high grass.

In another couple of minutes he would vanish into the bushes. Frantically he tore at the moist tentaclelike limb which was wrapped around his head. If it had covered his nose as well as his mouth he wouldn't be struggling now.

Sudden sight of what had him almost paralyzed his efforts. The first shetani he saw was a short, dark homunculus with long teeth hanging from the four sides of its mouth. A long nose protruded from just above that collection of deadly cutlery, dividing bright, bulging eyes that were watching him expectantly.

It was riding a black chameleon the size of a shetland pony. The chameleon's eyes were independently motile pools of fire.

There were at least three of the paired nightmares. It was the tongue of the first shetani that was wrapped around his head and mouth. Two more had their tongues fastened securely around his legs. At that moment he knew that if they succeeded in dragging him back into the undergrowth, the only part of him his friends would ever find would be his skeleton.

He dug his nails and teeth into the black, fleshy organ over his mouth and pulled on it with all his strength. It had no effect whatsoever on the squat reptilian shape that was pulling him steadily closer to oblivion. The chameleons worked silently and inexorably, but he could hear the humanoid shetani on their backs beginning to laugh. The short hair on the back of his neck rose. It was a sound he'd heard before. In a restaurant in Washington.

New sounds then, muffled and unexpected, a rumbling moan followed by a breathy *chuf*. All three shetani turned atop their mounts. Their devilish laughter died along with their predatory smiles. The long damp tongues released Oak's head and legs as the chameleons whirled to vanish into the bushes. As he lay on his belly panting hard he could hear them crashing through the underbrush.

He rolled onto his left side preparatory to standing and something like a gray telephone pole smashed into the ground inches from his right hand, flattening branches and grass and insects. Half a foot to the right and it would have pulverized Oak's fingers as well. The earth shook with the impact. The pole supported a shadow the size of a railroad boxcar. As the shadow moved past him another leg appeared. At the same time his nostrils were overwhelmed by a pungent but not unpleasant odor.

Turning to his left, he saw another immense shape looming over him. Merry's cry reached him from a distance. It was followed by a loud salutation from Olkeloki.

The shadow-shapes halted. Slowly Oak got to his feet and walked backward to rejoin the others.

"Josh!" Merry exclaimed when she got a look at his face.

"Shetani," he told her, wiping unnatural saliva from his forehead and hair. "Riding chameleon shetani. They almost got me."

"They favor the dark places," Olkeloki reminded him. "The Patriarch and his friends arrived just in time."

"Patriarch? Where?"

"I guess he means them, Josh." Merry indicated the glade and the line of elephants that stood staring back at them, trunks weaving, ears flapping rapidly as they strove to cool down enormous bodies.

"You can relax, Joshua Oak. The shetani run from the elephant, as does everything else in Africa. Now I must have my talk with the Patriarch." He strode past a still-dazed Oak, walking confidently toward the waiting herd of behemoths. There were at least thirty of them, though you had to look hard to pick them all out. They blended into the trees with the ease of much smaller animals.

"Saved by elephants. I thought that only happened in old Tarzan movies."

"I think it was an accident," Merry told him. "They were coming to meet with Olkeloki and they just happened to show up in time."

Oak remembered the massive foot that had come down inches from his fingers, whispered softly, "I'm not so sure, Merry. I'm not so sure."

Neither of them knew anything about elephants, but one didn't have to have a degree in vertebrate zoology to know that the mountain which emerged from the forest to confront the waiting Olkeloki was not merely old but ancient. The old male's skin was twisted and wrinkled into huge folds that covered most of his back and legs. It was as if an even bigger body had shrunk over the decades, leaving the skin with less mass to cover. Sad wisdom gazed out from beneath convoluted, overhanging brows and what hair was visible was white as the salts which stained the banks of Maji Moto.

"Remember what Olkeloki said about the Patriarch's teeth," Merry said with unconscious reverence.

Crossed. He said the Patriarch's teeth were crossed, Oak remembered. As indeed they were, the two immense tusks all but scraping the earth where they intersected in gently sweeping curves. In the incredible length of that ivory was a bold declaration of the elephant's age. The Patriarch carried them with dignity. How old was he? Oak wondered. How long did elephants live? The impression of age was overpowering.

"He even walks like an old man," Merry whispered.

True enough. Though supported by four massive legs, he searched out each step carefully. As they stared the Patriarch raised his head slightly, just enough to lift those huge tusks off the ground. He looked like a bulldozer with its blade dropped, Oak thought. The trunk rose slightly further and the tip caressed Olkeloki's waiting hand. Then the two old ones turned and strolled off into the forest together.

Oak became aware he'd been holding his breath. Now he exhaled and sucked in fresh air. So the old man was talking to an elephant. He'd seen too many impossible things the last few days not to believe the evidence of his eyes. What was a little harder to accept was the equally obvious fact that the elephant was answering him. Olkeloki spoke in soft Maasai and the Patriarch replied with sounds like an old boiler.

How old? A hundred years? Two? How long had this Ur-elephant wandered the forests and plains of East Africa? Did he remember relatives cloaked in hair who'd had high humps on their shoulders?

"They're talking, aren't they?" said Merry.

Oak managed a weak shrug. "Sure. Isn't that what the old man said they were going to do?"

"You know, it's funny. You watch them in zoos and circuses and you get this feeling that they could talk anytime they wanted to, but that they don't think humans have much to say."

"Maybe they're right. Or maybe Olkeloki has more to say than the rest of us."

"They talk in the manner of the old ones." Kakombe's tone was full of respect. From his great height he looked curiously down at Merry. "You are not afraid?"

"Not now. Once you've had a bunch of shetani try to rape you, nothing much else frightens you."

He glanced at Oak. "This happened and she survived?"

Oak was aware Merry was looking at him too. "I think so, yes."

Kakombe looked back to Merry. "Unusual woman." Then he turned his attention back to the herd.

Oak watched for another couple of minutes, then hunted through the supplies stored in the back end of the Land Rover until he found a clean towel. There was chameleon slime on the back of his neck, in his ears, and all over his pants and shoes. Bad enough to have to deal with murderous spirits, they had to be slimy spirits as well. Merry helped him dry off.

"Elephants would make good hunters, but they do not hunt," said Kakombe conversationally. "I did not hear them coming. They can move as quietly as any lion, for all their size. There are some laibon who say that when they wish to move quietly their feet do not touch the earth." He held thumb and forefinger almost together. "They walk this far above the ground so that they will not be heard."

Oak said nothing. Back in Washington he would have treated such an assertion with the contempt it deserved. Here in Africa anything seemed possible. How could you tell if Kakombe was telling the truth or a story? Oak had no intention of trying to peer beneath the toes of an elephant to find out.

An hour passed before Olkeloki rejoined them. As he strode back toward the Land Rover the herd turned, the other elephants forming a protective cordon around the Patriarch like so many destroyers escorting an aircraft carrier. As Oak watched they shuffled back into the woods, their extraordinary grace apparent even from behind. They became gray ghosts, then gray shadows, until eventually they again became one with the green.

Oak could hardly believe it was his voice, the even, pragmatic voice of Joshua Burton Oak, that asked the question.

"What did he say?"

Olkeloki looked troubled. "The Lords of the Veldt are disturbed. They are not immediately threatened by the shetani but they worry over the trouble the shetani may cause among men. Shetani they do not fear, but the poisons and weapons of man they fear very much. They worry that the shetani may cause men to loose such poisons upon the whole world." He straightened.

"We cannot go south from here. The shetani will be waiting for us. So claims the Patriarch. Therefore we must go around."

"Won't that cost us a lot of time?" asked Merry worriedly.

"Perhaps not much. The way is longer but the road better. We have to return to the main highway, then go east through Arusha and Moshi before we can again head safely south. We will parallel the ocean all the way to Chalinze, where we should be able to refuel. Then we will turn west toward Iringa and Ruaha. The shetani will not expect us to come from that direction. If they are watching us now it will look like we are giving up and going back to Nairobi. If they continue to follow our scent it will be more difficult for them to do so in the forests along the coast, and in this good vehicle on the better sections of road we can outrun them." He looked thoughtful. "This may be for the best. There is someone in that part of the country I should see." He smiled at Oak. "A man, this time."

"Sounds like a good plan. Tell me one thing, though." Oak nodded toward the forest. "How old is that elephant, anyway?"

"No one knows the age of the Patriarch. He himself does not know. Elephants measure time differently from humans. Once he told me he vaguely remembers a time when men walked with their backs bent and their knuckles scraping the earth, when they were eaters of insects and gatherers of fruit instead of herders of cattle like the Maasai. You ask me how old the Patriarch is. How old is Africa?"

"You'd think an elephant as old as that one would have been photographed a hundred times by now," Merry commented.

"The Patriarch values his privacy. If he does not want to be seen he stands a certain way until the tourists and cameras have left. Elephants can do that. They can stand so still they disappear."

19

Moscow, U.S.S.R.—24 June

First there was the inexplicable train derailment out-side Chelyabinsk. Forty-three killed, several hundred injured, many excuses, no explanations. If the engine crew knew anything they took their knowledge with them to the grave. The station chief insisted the cause was outside his jurisdiction. Nonetheless, acting rather hurriedly, regional officials had him shot.

No such fate awaited the technicians at the Novosibirsk Nuclear Power Plant, either because the local dispensers of Soviet justice were more circumspect in their use of power or because the people under suspicion were too valuable to be cavalierly disposed of.

In spite of all the safeguards and precautions, in spite of the experience of the monitoring team, meltdown took place. The suburban areas in the immediate vicinity of the plant were hastily evacuated. The loss of the station to the regional power grid was felt immediately, and officials predicted periodic brownouts for months to come. Industry would suffer along with the citizenry. The first heavily shielded experts to take a look at the station reported that the pile could not be approached in safety for twenty to thirty years. A piece of Russia had been rendered unapproachable.

It was only due to great good fortune that no one had been trapped in the reactor housing at the time of the accident. Most assumed that the unknown cause of the catastrophe lay buried somewhere beneath tons of highly radioactive rubble, but a few had other ideas. It could not happen the way it had, they insisted vehemently. There were too many backup systems, too many safeguards to permit so complex an installation to fail so completely without some kind of intervention. The plant had operated safely and efficiently for two decades. If anything, its accident record was superior to that of similar installations.

No, they insisted, the failure had nothing to do with the design, manufacture, or operation of the plant itself. It had to have been caused.

The meltdown was insignificant compared to what nearly happened ten time zones away outside the city of Aldan, near the Aldanskoye Nagorye plateau. Only the last-minute actions of a brave and exceptionally quick-thinking captain of the Rocket Forces prevented the theoretically impossible accidental firing of the big pretargeted SS-18 missile. So near a thing was it that it was not reported immediately. Not from a desire to keep the incident quiet, which could not have been managed in any case, but because everyone at the base who learned about it was too emotionally drained to do anything but try to regain their lost composure. As it was, the base commander was rushed to the city hospital with what proved to be a fatal heart attack.

But the missile was not launched.

There were plenty of other annoyances and catastrophes, though none so potentially cataclysmic as the one that occurred at Aldan. The crash of a small military plane near Omsk, the destruction of the big television tower at Pskov, the inexplicable explosion and fire which gutted the facilities of the largest vodka distillery in the world (which would not have overly troubled the government except that most of the vodka produced at the plant was destined for export), and on and on, a seemingly endless and mystifying litany of catastrophes major and minor.

On one thing the statisticians and experts agreed: at the very least, half of these disasters had to have been caused by outside sources. They could not be attributed to accident or neglect. All that was missing in each case was a motive. Some could be invented, but why would anyone want to sabotage a liquor distillery or make a giant barbecue of half a year's warehoused beef supply?

There was no pattern to the destruction, no rhyme or reason. Just devastation on a broad and increasingly frequent scale. But enough strategically important facilities were targeted to make some people begin to wonder if perhaps the blowing up of meat warehouses and tourist facilities and beach cabanas was merely a cover designed to inflate the overall statistics of destruction and divert attention from some sinister and as yet unperceived plan.

To these doomsayers and jingoists rational people pointed out that the United States and for that matter Western Europe and Japan as well were suffering from similar unexplained disasters. Take for example the utter impossibility of two jumbo jets, one carrying two hundred and fifty-three people, including a U.S. senator, the other three hundred and four, colliding in midair only fifty miles north of the Minneapolis–St. Paul air control center in perfectly clear weather. Such an aerial accident defied common sense, but it had happened nonetheless. Several similar fatal "accidents" had roused a normally lethargic U.S. Congress to fury. Explanations were demanded, and when none were forthcoming, right-wing radicals and fundamentalists were quick to offer their own reasons for what had happened.

That was the Americans' problem, Dorovskoy reflected as he considered the stack of reports on his desk. It had continued to grow throughout the morning and it was threatening to ruin much more than his day.

As he was trying to decide what to do next one of his secretaries, an earnest young man named Nicholas, came stumbling in without so much as buzzing for admittance. As a breach of protocol the intrusion was unprecedented. If Karnovsky found out about it he was going to be furious. But Dorovskoy was not as concerned with the formalities as his predecessors and in any case he was too tired and worried to waste time and energy giving the anxious young man a dressing-down.

"What is it, Nicholas? Please, not another train derailment. Already this morning we have had three, two on the same line."

"Sir, we . . ." The youth was having trouble finding the right words, but his face was as easy to read as that of a Kabuki puppet. He was in torment. Unable to speak, he approached the Premier's desk and dumped a printout on the report pile. To Dorovskoy's surprise the young man's eyes were wet with tears. What catastrophe could provoke such a reaction from so solid and stable a youthful assistant? He picked up the printout and began to read.

As Dorovskoy's eyes traveled rapidly down the page his hands began to tremble. Not with fear or sorrow but with anger. When he'd finished, it was all he could do to keep from shouting aloud.

"How dare they!" He repeated it over and over. "How *dare* they." Anything but this, he thought. The Politburo could handle anything but this.

"They don't know who's responsible yet, sir," said Nicholas. "But they'll find out. The city chief of police and every agent he has been able to conscript are going over the ground and the evidence a centimeter at a time. The culprits cannot escape. The only trouble stems from the investigators being hampered by their own anger."

"I sympathize." Dorovskoy was fighting to keep himself under control. "How dare they," he muttered again, as though by repeating the phrase he might somehow be able to exorcise the unthinkable blasphemy. He went to read the report again and in so doing discovered he'd crumpled it in both hands. The words seared themselves into his brain.

Of all the memorials to the folly and sacrifice of war which existed in the Union of Soviet Socialist Republics, none was more revered or solemnly impressive than the Piskaryouskoye Cemetery outside Leningrad. Four million people were buried there, most of them civilians who had starved during the Nazis' long siege of the city. One could walk along the silent rows of grass-covered mounds and read the simple signs set in the ground at each end.

HERE LIE BURIED TEN THOUSAND

On and on, sign after sign, row after row, mound upon mound containing the bones of the heroic who had perished together and now lay entombed side by side, their extinction a never-to-be-forgotten monument to the city which they had loved and the triumph over the fascists.

And now someone, or rather many someones, Dorovskoy corrected himself, for desecration on such a scale could not have been carried out by a single individual, had entered the cemetery during the night and opened grave after grave. They had removed the bones of the valiant, the men, women, and children who had starved to death rather than surrender to the invaders, and used them to spell out obscenities on the sacred ground. It smacked of the Nazis' use of treated human skin to make lamp shades. No words existed in the Premier's extensive vocabulary to express the outrage and shock he felt. It would be the same with any Russian, be he warmonger or peacenik.

No evidence had been found, nothing but a lot of strange animal footprints no doubt employed by the desecrators to conceal their own movements. It had been simple for them to move about. There was no need to mount a round-the-clock guard over Piskaryouskoye for the simple reason that no Soviet citizen would dare to disturb so much as a single wildflower or blade of grass within.

No *Soviet* citizen.

Then who was responsible? Leningrad was by far the most accessible Russian city to the West. If you could avoid the border guards you could hike to the city from Finland. But who would do such a terrible thing, and with what end in mind? It made no sense. Therefore, Dorovskoy decided, whoever had perpetrated the blasphemy was not sane. Their insanity was defined by their actions. You could not reason or negotiate with such people.

Whispers and murmurs he had initially dismissed now drifted back to him, the opinions of his more radical advisors. Brilliant young

Bostoff's still unexplained death in Switzerland. The undermining of Tsimlyansk dam. The inexplicable and just-aborted launch of the ICBM at Aldan. Coincidence? Or part of some carefully disguised pattern of sabotage and disruption designed to fatally weaken the country? Dorovskoy was an expert at identifying patterns.

True, if the Americans were responsible, as some of his radicals insisted, they were taking unprecedented steps to disguise their activities. It was not like them to kill their own people and destroy their own infrastructure to divert suspicion from themselves. Insane. The word was inescapable. Dorovskoy had met with President Weaver and his top advisors twice in the past three years and considered all of them to be reasonable men.

But what of the hidden American government, the international bankers and militarists? Of what madness might they be capable in their relentless quest to secure domination over the world? Would they attack even their own citizens? Such a thing was common enough in ancient times, but relatively unknown to recent history. But there was precedent, especially when the power brokers thought they could get away with it.

He had to make decisions. The people expected it; the Politburo would demand it. If he continued to vacillate in the face of continued disaster he would be replaced, quickly and efficiently.

"Sir?" He looked up into the anxious face of the secretary. "Are you all right, sir?"

"Yes. I am all right, young man. I am certain the police in Leningrad are doing the best they can. Meanwhile I would like for you to contact the Ministry of Defense and inform them that I will be arriving in a quarter of an hour. There are decisions to be made, difficult decisions. I will expect Field Marshal Kusnetzov, Admiral Bezinski, and Air Marshal Dzhirgatal to be present when I arrive, in addition to representatives of the Ministries of Armaments and of Heavy Industry."

"Yes sir, I will take care of it." The secretary turned to go, hesitated uncertainly. "Excuse me, Comrade Premier, but there is only going to be talk, isn't there? I have a wife and we just had our first child."

Dorovskoy liked the young man for his straightforwardness. "You may convey my messages in confidence, Nicholas." He managed a smile despite the pain which still enveloped his heart. "This is only a time for talk."

The secretary looked immensely relieved. "Thank you, Comrade Premier." He hurried from the office.

A time for talk. Dorovskoy sat at his desk thinking hard. Talk today, yes, but what of tomorrow? Another Piskaryouskoye incident and it would be impossible for him or anyone else to keep the lid on the pot. If it boiled over, everyone would get scalded. There came a time when people grew too angry to listen.

But he had to have irrefutable proof before he could issue any irrecallable directives. Even the extremists had to grant him that. Direct complicity if not responsibility had to be established. You could not threaten war over suppositions. That was sensible. That was logical.

Sitting alone in his Kremlin office Arkady Dorovskoy, Premier of all the Soviet Socialist Republics, had the uncomfortable feeling that despite his best efforts events were speeding forward out of his control and beyond the reach of logic and reason.

20

Arusha, Tanzania—24 June

As they made their way slowly through the center of the city, Oak worried that a curious cop might recognize the Land Rover as belonging to the local political party. Unlikely, he tried to tell himself. This wasn't rural Mississippi or Idaho. He mentioned his concern to Olkeloki, who was quick to reassure him.

"It would not matter if someone did recognize this vehicle, Joshua Oak. Tanzania is so poor it cannot afford patrol cars for its police. A few have bicycles. As the same is true for most criminals, it does not matter. The policeman on foot catches the thief on foot."

Despite this Oak was relieved when they left the city behind. In the shadow of Mount Meru, Kilimanjaro's less publicized but no less beautiful sister mountain, they filled the Land Rover's tanks to over-flowing. According to Olkeloki they were unlikely to find petrol for sale anywhere along the highway between Moshi and Chalinze. They drew plenty of stares, but then Kakombe would have drawn stares anywhere. Oak was glad. It shifted some of the attention off himself and Merry.

"From here it is almost two hundred miles to Korogwe, then a little less to Chalinze," Olkeloki informed them.

"Relax," Oak told him. "After the last couple of rides I'm looking forward to doing my own driving."

Once they left Moshi and turned south through the vast sisal plantations, there was no traffic to speak of. Once the plantations had been left behind there was no traffic at all. Oak opened up the Land

Rover as much as he dared, swinging smoothly around potholes big
enough to swallow a full-grown hippo.

To their left the towering green-clad Pare Mountains poked holes
in the sky while off on the right the endless brown plains known
collectively as the Maasai Steppe stretched unbroken toward far Tabora.
Wrecked and rusted-out buses lined both sides of the highway like the
skeletons of dead dinosaurs.

"In the last twenty years the lack of spare parts has become
endemic," said Olkeloki. "These old hulks lie here because the government cannot afford to have them towed away. The locals scavenge what
they can and the remainder sits out in the open, prey to insects and
rain."

"Don't they even try to fix them?" Merry asked.

"Why should they, when it is so much simpler to ask Sweden or
Hungary to give them fifty new ones and there are not enough
mechanics to fix the broken ones in any case?"

Having been raised in a family noted for its thrift, Merry found
the whole concept appalling. "Doesn't seem like a very practical way to
run a country."

"Maasai ways are better," Kakombe added with a grunt.

"Not always, Alaunoni, not always." Olkeloki was eyeing the
mountains with unusual intensity as he spoke. "Part of the problem is
that Tanzania no longer qualifies as a third-world country. Fourth or
fifth world would be more accurate. Its infrastructure is collapsing around
us. This road is an excellent example." He indicated the moonscaped
monstrosity that stretched out before them.

"This was once a smooth, modern highway. Now the government
says it has no money for repairs. This is true. It also does not have the
necessary equipment or skills. The best the government will do is send
out a truckload of gravel every now and then. It does not require much
skill to shovel gravel into a hole. Then it rains and washes away what
gravel hasn't been stolen by the local people for use in their own yards."

"You don't have to tell me about washed-out roads," Merry said.

Kakombe peered at her from around his scrunched-up knees. "It
rains often where you live, mama?"

"I'm not a 'mama.'"

The giant received this news with interest. "I did not mean to
offend. That is a common reference for any mature woman in this part
of the world."

"I'd rather you called me Merry."

"Well then—Merry, does it rain a lot where you live?"

"All the time. Much more so than here. And it's colder, much
colder."

"We have to pray for rain. If it doesn't come, it means a hard
year. Cattle die and children cry."

"The government doesn't help you when times are difficult?"

"We do not accept government aid," Kakombe told her haughtily. "Those who do become dependent on it. Why work when you know the government is there to feed you with foreign grain? Then a day comes when there is no grain and people starve, having forgotten how to take care of themselves. Such aid is like a drug. Once you are . . ." he hesitated, hunting for a word, "addicted, there is no cure. The Maasai would rather starve as free men than grovel for food like slaves."

"Except that the Maasai rarely starve," Olkeloki put in. "So long as there is rain, we have plenty. The secret to the success of the Maasai is cattle. Cattle provide milk, blood, meat, and leather. Cattle are better than tilling the land. The earth is fickle with its bounty. Cattle are our constant."

Kakombe leaned toward Oak. "How many cattle do you own, friend Joshua?"

"None, I'm afraid. My work requires me to travel and be away from home a lot. It would be hard for me to keep cattle." He forbore from trying to explain the concept of zoning to the senior warrior, who took his cattle home with him wherever he went.

"It is not seemly to work for hire. Can you not set yourself up independently?"

"Not in my line of business." Trying to change the subject, he noticed that Olkeloki was continuing to stare out the window. "Looking for something, old man?"

"Not something. Someone. It is important to see if he smiles favorably on us as we pass. Such omens are important."

Oak frowned. "If who smiles on us?"

"The old mzee." He gestured off to his left. "Over there."

Oak scanned the side of the road, the brush beyond. Nothing.

"You must look higher." Oak had the feeling Olkeloki was teasing him. "Much higher."

"Oh!" Merry's jaw dropped. Oak saw it at the same time.

"That's a natural rock formation. You pull this gag on everyone who comes by here with you, right?"

Olkeloki was not smiling. "It is not a gag, Joshua Oak." He indicated the face that glared down at them from the sheer cliff above the highway.

"That is the greatest laibon of the Maasai. When Oti was two thousand years old he took all of his clothes and worldly possessions and burned them. Then he prayed to Engai Narok, the good black god. For all the services he had rendered to the people of Africa and for being a gentle and wise soul, Engai Narok rewarded Oti with immortality by making him a mountain."

"Right, sure." Oak turned his gaze resolutely back to the road lest the Land Rover vanish into a pothole. Just because these shetani things had turned out to be real didn't mean he had to buy every wild story the old man chose to invent. Merry, on the other hand, kept her face tight to the window. As they roared down the highway, and as the hundred-meter-high face in the mountain receded behind them, she was certain its expression changed from a glower to a faint smile.

Sheer cliffs and dusty plains fell behind as the highway turned south into dense miombo forest. They were less than eighty miles from the coast. The increasing humidity was a reflection of the ocean's proximity. Broken pavement began to give way to long stretches of gravel mixed with dirt.

"We must not become bogged down here," Olkeloki warned them.

An hour later it began to rain. Not hard, but steady and unvarying as though an unseen tap had been opened. Oak grimaced as they plunged through a deep crater. You couldn't judge the depth of a pothole when it was filled with water. He found himself driving on the shoulder. Big trucks had cut the heart out of the main part of the road. Where it wasn't covered with water the highway looked like it had suffered a heavy bombardment.

The constant jouncing threatened to shake the skin off his bones. It was much harder on Merry, but she gritted her teeth and didn't complain. The Land Rover he wasn't worried about. It was built for this kind of terrain. Human beings weren't.

Sweat streamed down his neck. His clothes were soaked. "How much more of this?" They had left the village of Korogwe far behind. Surely Chalinze wasn't much farther.

"Perhaps a hundred miles," the old man told him.

Oak groaned. He was exhausted from trying to guess which water-filled potholes were shallow and fordable and which went halfway through the continental plate.

"If it keeps raining like this we're going to need a boat."

"We have no boat and we must not stop. This will get worse before it gets better, Joshua Oak. Sometimes this road stops even vehicles with four-wheel drive. Big trucks disappear in these woods. Not beer trucks—beer trucks never get lost. But eighteen-wheelers, as you call them, and whole busloads of people. They try to drive this road in the rain and they vanish and are never seen again.

"People say that bandits kill the passengers and drivers and then take the vehicles off to hidden garages in the forest so they can dismantle them and sell the parts, but we wise ones know better. They sink down into the mud or—"

"Or?" asked Merry anxiously.

"Or the shetani get them. Remember, they love dark places. What is darker in the daytime than a rainy forest?"

"Then what the hell are we doing here?" Oak sputtered. He

swerved to miss a big hole and almost sent them crashing off into the brush.

"We are here because we cannot waste time. We must reach Chalinze tonight. If we are caught out here in the darkness it will be dangerous."

"I'm going as fast as I can, damnit! It'll be a helluva lot more dangerous if I hit one of these potholes wrong and we bust an axle." He wiped sweat from his face. His eyes stung. "I'm no professional driver."

"But you said—" Kakombe began.

"I said that I liked to drive, but on roads, not through swamps! Just because I like it doesn't mean I'm good at it."

"If you are tired, then I will drive." Kakombe started to unfold himself.

"No, no, it is all right, Alaunoni," said Olkeloki quickly. "If necessary I will drive. I have more experience with automobiles than you."

Merry had been listening; now she broke in. "Hey, like I told you, it rains all the time where I come from. I have my own four-wheel drive and I know how—Wait a minute. I know what's going on here. None of you have asked me to drive because I'm a woman. That's it, isn't it?" She put both hands on the back of Oak's seat and pulled herself forward. "For Christ's sake, Josh, is that why you've been driving yourself into the ground? Because you didn't want to ask me for help?" He didn't reply, licked sweat from his lips.

She flopped back in her seat and folded her arms angrily. "That's just terrific. Here I've come halfway around the world, fighting off spirits all the way, so I can drive through a storm with three male chauvinist pigs."

Kakombe frowned and looked at Olkeloki. "What does she mean?"

"She means this!" Oak brought the Land Rover to a sliding halt on the side of the road. The highway stretched on ahead like a pale-gray tunnel through the trees. He turned to look in back. "Merry, I've been straight with you through this whole fantastic business. One of the main reasons I'm here is because I was worried about you getting in over your head from the start. I always thought that was called chivalry, not chauvinism."

"You came because you thought you were going to get rich!" she snapped.

"Well, yeah, that too. I said it was only one of the reasons. But it was an honest one."

"Great! Then why don't you let me drive?"

He hesitated only briefly. "Because I thought I could play superman and impress the hell out of everybody by making the drive all by myself.

But I didn't count on the highway turning into a tributary of the Congo. Get the hell up here." He shoved open his door and stepped tiredly out into the rain.

Merry glanced first at Kakombe, then Olkeloki. Both Africans stared expectantly back at her, waiting to see what she would do. What she did was crawl forward between the split front seats and assume Oak's place behind the wheel. At the same time he hauled himself into the back seat and settled down opposite Kakombe. He was sure the water was beginning to soften his bones.

"She's all yours, Merry. Take us away."

"I intend to. You get some rest, Josh." She glanced at Olkeloki. "I assume I don't have to worry about taking a wrong turn anytime soon?"

"Not for the next hundred miles," the laibon told her.

"Swell." She slammed the car into gear and splashed the nearby trees with mud as she sent them careening back out onto the highway.

As soon as she got the hang of aiming the big, boxy vehicle she peered into the rear-view. "How about it, Josh? I haven't killed us yet. What do you have to say now?"

He looked at the mirror. "This male chauvinist has to say that you've got the most beautiful eyes he's ever seen."

"You're avoiding the issue."

"You bet I am." He turned onto his side. "Wake me up when we get to Chalinze or when the rain stops, whichever comes first." By turning he missed the look she gave him via the mirror. That was a shame, because it would have made him feel very good indeed.

By late afternoon the gentle shower had turned into a tropical downpour, slowing their progress further. Each pool of standing water was an obstacle that had to be avoided. Once, Merry had to bash a path through the woods to circle around a small lake.

The thunder awakened Oak, but didn't upset him. It was a wonder he'd been able to sleep at all, between the sound of the rain and the bouncing of the Land Rover. Merry's eyes flashed at him in the rear-view.

"You're awake."

He checked his watch, then straightened. "Two hours. We're not there yet?" The Land Rover whammed into the ground, threatening to send his stomach up into his throat.

"Are you kidding? Look what's doing outside."

Oak could hardly see out the window. "You've been driving all this time?"

"Kakombe offered but I thought I'd stick with it until you woke up."

"I could have driven," the giant grumbled.

"You are better at driving cattle." Olkeloki wagged a finger at the senior warrior. "If you would one day become an elder or laibon, you must first learn to recognize your limitations."

Kakombe acknowledged the lecture with a grunt. "I could have driven."

"Want me to take over?" Oak was rapidly being bounced awake.

"It's okay. Olkeloki says we're less than thirty miles from Chalinze. I can handle it that much longer."

"Okay, but if you start feeling tired let me know. I had a good nap."

"Take another if you feel like it. I'll—Oh *shit!*" She wrenched the wheel hard over and the Rover slipped through the muck as Oak and the others grabbed at the nearest support.

Not only the pavement but also the underlying gravel ahead had been washed away by rushing water. In its place was a muddy bog ten feet across which they slid into despite Merry's best efforts to avoid it. As the Land Rover began to settle she worked the gear shift back and forth. The engine roared dutifully, but the Rover was not an aquatic vehicle. Water and mud rose to within an inch of the floorboard before the tires touched bottom.

Six lousy feet away from the front bumper the road rose out of the bog like a rainbow from a cloud. There was even some real blacktop just ahead. Merry kept at it for another couple of minutes, but the wheels just spun in place, throwing up geysers of mud behind them. She slumped back in the driver's seat and rubbed at her eyes.

"That's it, I give up. You want to give it a try, Josh?"

"What's to try?" He put a sympathetic hand on her shoulder. "Nothing I can do that you haven't tried."

Her tone was bitter, full of self-directed anger. "I should have seen it. I should've gone around it."

"How?" He nodded forward. "There's a damn river running across the road here. We'll have to pull it out."

She smiled regretfully back at him. "Sorry. At least we're already in four-wheel drive. You won't have to go skindiving to unlock the hubs."

Olkeloki was trying to see through the storm. "We must leave this place before nightfall. We cannot stay here. This is a bad place to be stuck."

"Tell me about it," sighed Oak. He looked over at Kakombe. The senior warrior looked strong enough to lift the Land Rover all by himself—if they could find some solid ground. "Come on, big fella. Let's unlock the winch and find ourselves a tree. The winch is that thing mounted—"

"I know what a winch is, ilmeet," Kakombe interrupted him curtly.

Oak nodded once, then leaned between the front seats until he located the right switch on the dash. "We'll give you a holler when she's all hooked up."

"Right. I'll keep the engine running. Don't want it to die here." Or anything else either, she thought worriedly as she scanned the trees.

It was like stepping into a steady, tepid shower, Oak reflected as he exited the Land Rover and promptly sank up to his waist in thin mud. He envied Kakombe. The muck barely rose over his knees.

Together they slogged forward until the ground began to rise beneath them. The road ahead was in better condition than anything they'd driven over for the last three hundred miles. All they had to do was prise the Land Rover from the bog and they'd be in Chalinze in forty minutes, if the pavement held up and the rain didn't get any worse.

How could it get any worse? he asked himself. You could hardly make out the forest for the rain.

He found a suitable tree firmly rooted alongside the road. There was more than enough cable on the winch drum to reach.

"I will get it," said Kakombe. Oak didn't argue with the giant. The mud was much less of an obstacle to him. As he watched the senior warrior wade back toward the Rover it occurred to Oak that this was the first time he'd seen Kakombe without his spear. His massive torso looked like a tree floating through the water.

Merry released the cable catch from inside. Kakombe nodded to her, wrapped the end of the cable twice around his midsection, and slogged back to rejoin Oak. Together they wrapped the excess cable several times around the trunk of the tree before slipping the big curved steel hook through one loop. Oak walked back to the edge of the bog and waved both arms over his head.

He couldn't see Merry through the rain-slicked windshield, but the Rover's engine revved and it gave a perceptible lurch forward. It advanced about a yard before the wheels resumed their tractionless dance. Steam rose from the straining winch.

"Must be slicker than greased owl shit under those tires," Oak muttered. Droplets of water flew from the taut cable, but the winch couldn't pull the heavy vehicle out of the muck by itself. What they really needed was something solid under the wheels, but any rocks they could slip beneath would likely just be ground deeper into the mud.

"Come on," Oak said. Kakombe followed him back into the bog.

Feeling as though he'd never be dry again, Oak fumbled through one of the two steel boxes bolted to the roof of the Rover. He found the emergency cable he was looking for in the second one, splashed back down into the water with the heavy nylon coils draped around his shoulders. While Kakombe watched, he secured it to the right corner of the front bumper.

"If we can get the car turned at an angle," he shouted as he spat out water and mud, "maybe Merry can break it out of the trenches the tires have dug!"

Kakombe nodded, took the front position. Together the two men heaved on the nylon. Pulled by the two men, the winch, and all four tires, the Land Rover began to turn. Sweat mixed with rainwater on Oak's face. It was in his eyes, in his nose, and any minute now, he thought a little hysterically, a tidal wave was going to drown his brain.

A faint voice reached him. Looking back over his shoulder he saw that Olkeloki was leaning out the open window of the Rover. That's stupid, Oak thought. He's going to get the cab soaked. The old man was gesturing wildly toward the forest with his staff while Merry raced the engine.

Oak turned and tried to see what the laibon was pointing at. Nothing but rain, rain, and jungle. Not a shetani in sight.

Then Kakombe was pointing too, and the movement Olkeloki was trying to draw their attention to could no longer be ignored.

Part of the forest was alive and slithering toward them.

At first it looked like the branches of the trees were falling off and making for the bog, wiggling and squirming with some horrible, artificial life. Then Oak saw that it was an army of four-foot-long worms, each as green as an Irishman's bouquet on St. Paddy's day, a bright, reflective pale green that was somehow not reassuring. Not when it was coming toward you with sinuous deliberation.

Of course, they weren't giant worms, any more than they were animated branches.

Oak yelled at Kakombe as he pulled with all his strength on the nylon line. "Those snakes—are they poisonous?"

The giant hesitated long enough to study the oncoming legless horde. "No, but they can still bite. All snakes bite. We do not want to share this water with them."

We sure as hell don't, Oak murmured to himself. He was no squamataphobe, but neither did he count snakes as among his favorite inhabitants of the earth. The last thing he wanted was a couple dozen exotic varieties curling around his legs. There were hundreds of them squirming and slithering through the undergrowth and they were all heading for the bog. A glance to his left revealed that the other side of the forest was equally alive with rustling bushes and leaves. But why had they appeared here so suddenly and in such numbers?

As he leaned into the rope he tried to remember some of what Olkeloki had told them about the shetani. There was one variety, the Mbilika, that fed exclusively on snakes. Maybe these bright green beauties were being driven toward the bog by something farther back in the trees, by horrors as yet unseen. Apparently the shetani were not ignorant of simple tactics. The snakes would attack and confuse the prey, and when the inhabitants of the Land Rover had been suitably worn out and weakened . . .

"Come on, pull, damn you!"

Kakombe whirled to glare back at him. "Pull yourself, ilmeet." Then he saw that Oak was grinning at him and, after an instant's hesitation, the giant was grinning too.

A new sound, a delightful, mellifluous, altogether exquisite sound: an aria of rubber on gravel as the Land Rover's tires found solid purchase under the mud. As the two men scrambled clear, Merry drove the Rover halfway out of the water, swung the wheel back to the left, and in seconds had it idling high if not dry on the cracked pavement above the bog. Olkeloki was leaning out his window and motioning anxiously.

"Quickly, quickly!"

Oak unfastened the emergency line and heaved it onto the roof of the car while Kakombe unhooked the tow cable from the tree. There was something on Oak's boot. Looking down, he saw tiny dark eyes staring back up at him out of a triangular green head. The snake was trying to bite through the leather. He stomped it with the heel of his other shoe and it let go, sliding back into the mud.

He turned to face the car—and froze. A second streamlined skull was staring directly into his face. The snake must have gone up his back. Now it was resting on his shoulder, pausing while it decided which portion of his face to sink its teeth into.

The head vanished and snake blood struck him in the eye. It was warmer than the sweat and rainwater. A glance showed Kakombe beckoning to him as he retreated toward the Land Rover. In the giant's right hand was one of those oversized Maasai knives. The rain was already rinsing the blood from the blade.

Shaking as much from exhaustion as from the near encounter, he stumbled up the slight slope and fell into the back seat alongside the equally fatigued senior warrior. Up front, the winch was reeling in the rest of the steel cable like a fat man sucking spaghetti.

"Drive, Merry Sharrow, drive!" he heard Olkeloki say.

"As soon as the cable's all in or we're liable to foul an axle—there!" The Land Rover lurched forward—and started to slide backward on the slick blacktop. Oak twisted around and stared out the back window. The surface of the bog was alive with thrashing, twisting serpents slithering over one another by the hundreds and biting at rocks, broken branches, one another, anything within reach of their teeth.

The transmission growled as the tires bit in. The Rover held its ground, shuddering, and then began moving forward: an inch, a foot, a decisive yard. Faint crunching noises came from beneath the floorboards as they rolled over several dozen legless bodies. The Rover's speedometer needle rose slowly and like a bad dream the bog began to recede behind them.

No one relaxed until they neared the outskirts of Chalinze. Here a small piece of the primeval had been pushed aside and cleared for human settlement. The sun was down and the rain made it impossible to see more than a few feet in front of the car. But Olkeloki seemed to know where they were and where he was going. Merry was more than content just to follow his directions.

The old man pointed to his left. "Over there, there is a place I know. A good garage. We will sleep there tonight. It will be cleaner than the local rest house."

The owner of the garage was a Sikh named Jana Singh. He greeted Olkeloki effusively, leading Oak to suspect that the garage owner and Maasai gold were old friends. He led them to a back room of the garage which turned out to be a vision lifted straight from paradise: dry cots laden with clean linen and real pillows. Half an hour later Singh's wife and two elder daughters appeared carrying bread and a curry that smelled like ambrosia. He was not in the least dissuaded by the fact that the principal ingredient of the curry was goat meat. As for Merry, she finished two bowls and asked for a third.

"We're both going to end up with the trots." She giggled. Her face was streaked with mud and grime. "You know what? I don't care. This garage has a real bathroom, with a real john. I'm going to sit on it for a while just to enjoy the feel of it."

Merry's fears were reasonable but premature. The curry, spices and all, warmed their bellies and stayed down, even refusing to be drawn into a fight with the saltine crackers and Rumanian pâté they'd had for lunch.

Suddenly Oak was more tired than he'd ever been in his life. Olkeloki and Kakombe refused the cots, opting to sleep on straw mats on the floor. As they were preparing to extinguish the lights, the garage owner came to bid them good night. He smiled sympathetically at them through his neat beard.

"My old friend Mbatian says that tomorrow you go to Morogoro."

"That's right," Merry told him.

"You are tourists?" The way he asked the question indicated that he wouldn't believe their reply, but he accepted Merry's nod of affirmation politely and did not press for details.

She lay on her back on the cot and stared at the ceiling. The steady rain on the corrugated metal roof sounded like Japanese drums. "This is a long way from Seattle," she whispered.

"What?" Oak mumbled sleepily. "You still awake?"

"I'm listening to the rain, Josh. Isn't it beautiful?"

He made an impolite noise.

"You were very brave out there today."

Oak thought her disembodied voice was lovely in the darkness. He also wished she would shut up.

"I never could have gone out there with all those snakes."

"Neither would I. Kakombe and I were already up to our asses in mud when they started pouring out of the woods around us. It was either stay out there and get the car moving or spend the night in that bog. It had nothing to do with being brave. Bravery and self-preservation aren't the same thing. Better to get bit a couple of times than stay stuck there."

"Oh no." In the darkness of the garage she sounded surprised. "One bite would have killed you, Josh."

His stomach muscles began to knot and he felt a coldness on the insides of his thighs. "Say what? Kakombe told me they weren't poisonous."

"I don't know what Kakombe told you, but I read through two guidebooks on East Africa on the plane down from London. Those snakes were mambas. You can't mistake them for anything else. Green mambas. If any one of them had bitten you, you would've been dead inside thirty minutes without an injection of the proper antivenin. If three or four had bitten you nothing on this earth could've saved your life. No, you were very brave, Josh. Good night."

"Good night, Merry." He heard her roll over on the cot.

Instead of closing his eyes he turned to his left and stared across the floor to where Olkeloki and Kakombe were already sound asleep. Had the senior warrior been ignorant of the true nature of all those snakes? Hardly likely. This was his country. It seemed more than unlikely that an experienced herder would mistake hundreds of green mambas for harmless forest snakes. The lie had been deliberate.

Why? To keep Oak from panicking and running for the cover of the mired Land Rover? Would he have panicked? That was something neither of them would ever know. Better to be insulted and alive than an unoffended corpse. Tricky son of a bitch.

Under different circumstances Oak might have shaken the other man awake and demanded an apology. He did not. Because Kakombe had stayed out there in the mud and dragged on the cable despite the fact that he wore only sandals and a thin toga instead of thick boots and tough Levi's.

He closed his eyes, listening to the rain on the roof. Sleep would come fast and easy. Off in the distance he thought he heard something rise above the rumble of the storm, above the occasional burst of contented thunder. It sounded vaguely like a growl.

We all have our lions, Olkeloki had told them more than once.

Hell with that. After swimming with a few hundred venomous snakes, any lions they met would be a picnic.

21

Ubenazomozi, Tanzania— 25 June

"Turn off here."

Oak glanced at the old man, who was staring out the front window. "What, here? There's no road."

"Just beyond the big tamarind tree."

Oak eased forward along the side of the main road. Yes, there, a barely visible gap between the huge tamarind and another tree. They would have missed it last night in the rain, and without Olkeloki to indicate the way they would have shot past despite the morning's bright sunshine. Even so, the "road" was little wider than a game track.

"You think we can get through here?" Branches were snapping against the sides of the Land Rover.

"If not we will have to walk."

"Walk where?" asked Merry from the back seat.

"To Nafasi's house."

"Another friend like Jana?"

"No. Nafasi is," the old man seemed to hesitate for a moment, "he is like a laibon, except that the Makonde do not have laibon in the same sense as the Maasai. The Makonde do not have much of anything except one particular skill."

She recalled the conversation with the owner of the craft shop in their Nairobi hotel. "Woodcarving."

Olkeloki nodded. Oak dodged around one small tree and ran over another. "Yes. That, and the fact that they know the shetani better than anyone else in Africa."

Vegetation pressed uncomfortably close around the car. It was like driving down a green tunnel. Oak had to do some tricky maneuvering. He was expecting to find some kind of bush village at the end of the track.

There was no village. The Land Rover emerged into a clearing only slightly more devoid of trees than the surrounding forest. Chickens pecked and scratched in search of centipedes and other morsels. A milk goat grazed quietly nearby, hardly bothering to look up as the heavy vehicle ground to a halt.

In contrast to the bare yard, the house was substantial. It had concrete block walls, glass in the windows, and a tile roof. Steps led up to a raised covered porch. Four healthy-looking children materialized to stare silently at the visitors out of deep, dark eyes. They were either well trained or else used to company.

There were no dogs, of course. As Oak and Merry had already learned, Africans hated dogs. A stray was likely to end up in the family cookpot.

The fine house bespoke wealth on the local scale, but the true indication of the owner's success sat under a connected carport where not one but two late-model Honda dirt bikes stood parked. One was equipped with automatic transmission and a radio-cassette player.

They piled out of the Rover and stood next to Olkeloki. "What now?" Merry asked him.

"We wait. It is best not to disturb Nafasi when he is working. He will greet us when he is ready."

"Is he a woodcarver?"

"Yes, a woodcarver. A special woodcarver. One might go so far as to say a unique woodcarver. The carvers of the Makonde put their heart and soul into their work. Nafasi adds something more."

So the four of them stood there waiting while the children stared down at them and the chickens pecked around their feet in search of any bugs they might have stirred up. The goat allowed himself a single desultory *baaah*.

It was still early enough to be cool, though it was a humid and sticky coolness. Oak found himself glancing nervously at the dense woods, though there was no reason for anyone else to be uneasy when Olkeloki was relaxed. Still, he felt exposed out there in the open.

Eventually a slightly built ancient came out of the house. He ignored the rest of them while he squinted at Olkeloki. Then a wonderfully youthful smile split his face above a curly white beard. He picked his way down the steps and the two old men embraced. Olkeloki dwarfed the woodcarver.

"Habari," Nafasi said.

"Habari aku." Olkeloki spoke to him in Swahili for a bit. Then he gestured for them to follow him inside.

The house was quite large. There were no interior doors. An old woman looked out at them from the kitchen. Nafasi led them through a sparsely furnished den or living room into a big converted porch which served as the workroom. Two younger men, one burly, the other tall and slim, looked up from their work. Nafasi introduced them in Swahili.

"These are his sons," Olkeloki explained. "The little ones out front are his grandchildren. He welcomes us to his house."

Nafasi shook each of their hands in turn, beaming last at Merry. "Si kitu. Nafurahi sana kukuona. Mama wazuri."

"He says you are welcome and that he's pleased to make the acquaintance of such a fine-looking woman."

Merry grinned down at the elfin woodcarver. "Is that why he left his wife in the kitchen?" Olkeloki translated this and Nafasi laughed delightedly.

Oak was examining the extensive workroom. Recently felled trees stripped of branches stood propped against one wall. Other chunks of half-finished sculpture stood on rough wooden tables. In a back corner on a solid ebony table stood a selection of finished, highly polished pieces, awaiting inspection by potential buyers. Oak recognized one as the creature he'd seen skittering across the floor of a certain Washington restaurant, oh, a century or so ago.

Shetani. Rendered with supreme accuracy, though not life-size. As Nafasi later explained it was usually impossible to render a carved shetani exactly as it was in life because the ebony and blackwood trees rarely grew to more than a foot in diameter. The majority of the sculptures, many of which involved several connected figures, averaged five or six inches across and one to two feet in height.

The exception was a single piece that dominated everything in the room. It stood off on a pedestal of its own, three feet high and almost a foot in diameter. Once it had formed the base of an ebony tree, for unlike the other carvings, which were perfectly vertical, this one branched off at the top into a huge black root. The root had assumed the likeness of a monstrous, toothy face with jaws that would put a crocodile to shame. Doglike ears dangled from a skull which looked too narrow to support such jaws while bulbous eyes bulged from either side of the head. The jaws were four times the size of the head, which in turn was twice the size of the hunchbacked body. Carved fire and smoke rose from the two nostrils at the end of the upper jaw while a third nostril gaped empty and open between them.

Oak found that no matter where he went in the room, those bulging orbs seemed to move to follow his progress. If this behemoth among shetani sculpture was in proportion to the rest of the carvings, how large would the shetani itself be?

One of Nafasi's sons noticed the direction of Oak's stare and said in quite good English, "Spirits of the Earth. Father did that one all by himself. He wouldn't let anyone else touch it. He worked on it off and on for several years and finished it only this past month."

"It's beautiful. Grotesque, like a Giger painting, but beautiful. And I wouldn't have it in my house."

"It does not matter. Father won't sell it. As you can see, all the other carvings are straight. It is very rare anyone finds a large ebony root like this attached to the heartwood. Father says it's full of power. He keeps it to protect the house."

"Interesting. What do you say?"

The younger man smiled softly. "I say that I am still learning about such things." He nodded to where Olkeloki and Nafasi were engaged in animated conversation.

"We tell the foreigners who come to buy carvings that these are the spirits of the ocean or the forest, the animals or the sky. But you have seen them, as have some of us, as they truly are."

"That's right," said Merry. "Not only have we seen them, we've fought with them."

"So the laibon says. Word has come down to us of the battle that took place on the slopes of Ol Doinyo Lengai. The Maasai are a great people."

"So are the Makonde, judging by the quality of what's in this room."

He shrugged. "The Maasai fight, we carve. No one carves the shetani properly but the Makonde. My name is Paul, by the way. My brother is Samuel. We are Christian, though father is not."

"Are most of the Makonde Christian?" Merry asked him.

Paul shook his head. "This is a difficult country to be a Christian in. Many are Muslim or animist."

"You're converted, yet you carve these things," Oak said.

"We carve what we know to be real." His expression turned wistful. "Someday I would like to take our carvings to America. The laibon says that we would do well there, but father will not go. He says only muzungu like yourselves can take the carvings out of Africa. We are too close to the shetani and he says they would stop us."

"Maybe things will change when Olkeloki finishes his work," Merry suggested.

Paul grew serious. "They *must* change! If the laibon does not succeed there will be no more sculptures, no more carving. The shetani do not like to be revealed."

"It is time to leave." Olkeloki beckoned and everyone followed Nafasi to the back of the workroom.

Merry drew in a breath as the old carver dragged a dropcloth from a hidden mass. It was an enormous and very old wooden chest fashioned of ebony slats too tough for termites or wood ants to penetrate. Every inch had been carved into intricate patterns and whorls. Ivory and brass inlay gleamed through the dust. A fat iron padlock of ancient design secured the lid.

"Zanzibar chest," said Kakombe. "The design is very old but it shines like new."

It did more than shine like new, Oak reflected. A glow seemed to emanate from the black wood, as though a faint electric charge were running through it. Though he did not recognize it, it was the aura of history.

Nafasi bid them all stand back. Then he produced a key the size of a railroad spike and inserted it into the padlock. A musical note sounded as he turned key in lock and the air in the room seemed to darken. Merry unconsciously moved a little closer to Oak.

The old woodcarver raised the lid. A tiny shower of particles erupted from within; splinters, or tiny things with legs and arms. A glow came from inside the chest and threw the carver's features into sharp relief. Bending over the pulsing chest there in the darkened room he looked more than ever like one of his own ebony carvings.

Oak stepped forward before anyone could stop him and peered into the chest. His eyes bulged.

The chest had no bottom. He was looking through the rectangular window of a spacecraft into the emptiness of the abyss itself. Stars and nebulae glowed beyond. A thin gust of vacuum struck him with a chill so deep it froze the saliva in his mouth. He could feel himself falling, falling, not down but out, could feel the surge of weightlessness as he started to tumble into the open chest.

Hands grabbed him by the arms and pulled him back. The coldness receded. There was ice in his throat and around his lips. He blinked at Samuel.

"Father keeps everything in that chest. *Everything*. It is dangerous for someone who is not used to handling everything to look upon it."

Everything? Oak wondered, dazed. He looked back toward the open chest. But the chest had no bottom. It was full of vacuum. Vacuum, and a universe.

Fog and swirling particles obscured the chanting woodcarver. Oak was afraid what he'd seen inside might come out to swallow them up, but it stayed within. Something else did emerge from the chest, however.

Nafasi straightened, holding an armful of carvings. These he laid on one of the worktables while Paul secured the chest. Oak noted that the younger man kept his head averted and did not look into the chest.

Light returned to fill the workroom. The particles that had enveloped the old carver in a dark cloak fell to the floor. Oak scuffed at them with a shoe. Ebony sawdust.

Samuel handed his father a towel and the old carver proceeded to wipe sweat from his face and upper body. Then he spread out the objects he had taken from the chest. Four wooden knives lay side-by-side with a trio of long-bladed blackwood spears. The knives were shorter and thicker than those carried by the Maasai. The wood gleamed with a sheen richer than that adorning any of the other carvings in the room. It was not the product of polish as much as it was an inner glow that emanated from the wood itself. Oak reached down to pick one up.

Nafasi put out a hand to block Oak's. The carver seemed to have aged several years in the space of a few minutes. He shook his head warningly.

"Ji hadari!"

"He is telling you to be careful," Olkeloki explained. "Pick them up by the handle only."

The master carver hefted one of the wooden spears and caressed it lovingly. Then he pointed to a bench top fashioned of two-by-fours that lay propped on its end against the far wall. Drawing back his arm, he threw the spear with surprising but not exceptional force. Oak half expected the shaft to splinter against the bench top or at most stick a couple of inches into the softer wood.

The blade went clean through one of the two-by-fours and continued on to bury half its length in the wall beyond. Satisfied, Nafasi recovered the weapon and offered it to Oak—handle first.

An awed Oak held it up to the light, but squint as he might he couldn't see where the blade ended and the air began. A faint rippling clung to the edge of the blade, like the heat distortion one sees above a highway on a particularly hot day. Very slowly, very carefully, he touched the sharp edge with the middle finger of his left hand, then brought it away. He'd felt no pain on contact, but when he looked down at his finger a thin red line was visible. It was like a paper cut, only there was no pain. A clean, almost magical cut. He might as easily have placed the skin in the path of a surgical laser.

"How the hell," he whispered in disbelief, "can he put that kind of an edge on a piece of wood?"

Olkeloki cleared his throat. "Nafasi says now you will be careful not to pick up by the blade."

"Tell him I'll treat it like the detonator on a bomb."

Nafasi listened to the translation, looked satisfied. Then he passed out the rest of the weapons; knife and spear to each man, knife alone to Merry. As he did so he passed his hands over each blade and murmured softly. Paul brought wooden sheaths of thin ebony to slip over each weapon. As he watched him work Oak was reminded of a falconer slipping hoods over his favorite birds. Or an Indian snake charmer hooding his cobra.

"These can't just be ordinary wood," Merry murmured.

"They are wood, but they are anything but ordinary. There are no other such weapons anywhere in the world. They are blackwood plus history, blackwood plus a little of every weapon that has ever been. There are the spears of the great Zulu impis in each edge, the power of Tamerlane's hordes, the thrust of Caesar's legions. On the very edge of each swim things that cannot be seen except in circles of great magnets that race the components of existence around racetracks on which the beginning and end of the universe is the bet. They contain weapons that have not been and weapons that will never be. They are blackwood plus all that plus Nafasi. Into them he has put his heart and soul and much more. They will cut well. I think they will even cut a shetani."

"Weapons of worth," Kakombe added.

Before they departed, Nafasi went to each of them in turn and clasped their hands.

"He is entrusting you with his skill and says he hopes you will use what has been given to you well. He would come with us, but he is a builder, not a fighter."

"Tell him thank you, and that we'll try to put his spearpoints where they'll do the most good," Oak replied.

The expression on the old carver's face showed that he was content.

Nafasi and his sons stood on the porch of the house and watched as the two Maasai and the two ilmeet departed. Chickens and children swirled around them. Oak glanced in the rear-view mirror and for an instant thought he saw instead of the tin-roofed simple structure a formidable redoubt of dressed granite and steel, but when he looked back over his shoulder there was only the one-story building surrounded by trees and brush. No moat, no gleaming towers, no exotic guns poking their snouts through slits in the walls.

Sunlight in the mirror, he told himself, and concentrated on the narrow road ahead.

They had turned west on the main road when Oak thought to look sharply at the old man riding next to him. "Those weapons were waiting for us."

"Nafasi has kept them for many years. You saw yourself, Joshua

Oak, the age of the chest in which they were stored. Do you think such things can be fashioned in a day or two, a week, a month? Too much is invested in each blade. They are not like the toy spears one sees in the tourist shops which everyone makes to sell to the visiting ilmeet."

Oak refused to be put off. "He knew we were coming, damnit. How did he know we were coming?"

Olkeloki devoted his attention to the road ahead. "Pay attention to your driving, Joshua Oak. The way will become uncertain."

Merry was turning her sheathed blade over and over in her hands. "What am I supposed to do with this? I've sold plenty of knives: hunting knives, fishermen's knives, Swiss army knives, but I've never used one on anything bigger than a trout."

"If a shetani springs at you waving its long arms and dripping black spit from its teeth you will know what to do with the knife, Merry. No one will have to instruct you." Kakombe had laid his own set of weapons on the floor beneath his feet.

"I don't feel comfortable with it. Maybe you ought to take it, Kakombe."

"I already have a knife. And a spear."

"We all do," said Oak. "The old boy gave it to you, Merry. Hang on to it. If nothing else it'll make a great conversation piece when you get home. That sucker'd do a roast turkey in three minutes."

"Okay, I'll keep it, if you'll stop talking about real food. I've about had it with milk and dried jerky and goat curry."

"When the task is done we will make a great feast." Kakombe's eyes shone. "We will slaughter many cattle. It will be a celebration to sing of."

"I hope we'll have reason to celebrate." Oak indicated the towering green-clad mountains that now dominated the southern horizon. "We go up through those?" he asked doubtfully.

"The Ulugurus," said Olkeloki. "No, the road continues west. We will not begin to climb for many hours yet."

"I wish you hadn't mentioned that damn roast turkey," Merry grumbled.

McFARLAND, Kansas (AP)—A Union Pacific train carrying binary nerve gas derailed east of this small farming community today, scattering potentially lethal cannisters of gas for hundreds of feet on either side of the tracks. Army representatives succeeded in separating the components before high winds could combine gas from broken cannisters and sweep it eastward. Major Nathaniel Davis was quoted as saying, "If the decontamination team had been ten minutes late getting there, we could've lost half the population of Topeka."

ELECTRIC CITY, Washington (UPI)—As spiderweb-sized cracks in the face of giant Grand Coulee Dam were being repaired today, a major hydroelectric turbine tore itself apart, requiring a full shutdown of the facility that resulted in loss of power to six Northwestern states. "It was just as if somebody had tossed a girder into the blades," one of the plant's technicians was reported as saying. No such object has been found, but the possibility of sabotage by some unknown subversive group is not being ruled out, says Washington's Governor Shackleford.

MERRITT, West Virginia (CNN)—The fire which has been burning in abandoned coal seams beneath this small West Virginia mining town for the past fifty years suddenly erupted in violence as it moved into a narrow and previously unsuspected vein of anthracite lying just beneath the surface. More than one hundred people, including women and children, are known dead and hundreds more are reported injured. The town of Merritt itself is reported to be totally engulfed in flame. Long-time residents of the area are still wondering how such a rich coal vein so close to the surface could have been missed by coal prospectors for so long.

LONG BEACH, California (UPI)—A Liberian-registered oil tanker inexplicably ran aground this morning in Long Beach Harbor and broke apart. The resultant explosion was heard as far north as Santa Barbara and south to the San Onofre Nuclear Power Plant, where engineers are having troubles of their own due to a recent shutdown of the plant for a complete safety inspection. Fortunately nothing but the dock the tanker ran into and a couple of nearby warehouses were consumed, but if the blaze from the burning tanker had been allowed to spread to a nearby tank farm owned by Standard Oil, officials say the entire harbor area could have been devastated. More than half the tanks were full of highly volatile aviation fuel, Standard Oil representatives reported.

WASHINGTON, D.C. (CNN)—Informed sources in the capital say that extreme conservative senators and representatives are demanding the President go public with a theory being propounded by certain members of the intelligence community here that the recent spate of seemingly random and natural disasters is actually part of an elaborate plan to weaken the country preparatory to military movements overseas by an as yet unidentified aggressor nation. While the majority of Congress continues to regard such a theory skeptically, the continuation of such disasters can only strengthen the hand of the extremists, sources report. The President was recently seen meeting with Michael Suffern, head of the CIA.

WOLBACH, Nebraska (AP)—Three grain elevators exploded here today, killing . . .

SHORT, Utah (UPI)—The flooding of a molybdenum mine here today killed . . .

CHARLESTON, South Carolina (UPI)—Two tractor-trailer rigs collided head-on outside this city this evening. The driver of the southbound truck, which was loaded with toxic chemicals, was killed instantly, along with . . .

22

East of Morogoro, Tanzania—25 June

"Tell me something," Merry asked Olkeloki as the Land Rover hummed down the main highway, "once we've gone into this Out Of and done whatever's necessary to keep the shetani from coming through into our world, how do we get back?"

"It will not be easy," the old man told her. "But then, none of this since the beginning has been easy."

"What happens if we can't get back the same way? We find another weak place somewhere?"

"There is no other weak place. We must seal this one and return the same way. Otherwise we will be trapped in the Out Of."

"And this has never been tried before, right?" Oak didn't try to hide his concern.

"As a matter of fact, Joshua Oak, it is known that two men have traveled into the Out Of and returned. One was the great laibon whose face you saw in the mountain. The other—the other was my father."

"What happened to him?" Merry asked gently.

"I was too young to understand. It was explained to me when I was older that he returned to a spot different from where he had left. Sadly, that happened to be in the middle of Lake Victoria, which as you may know is the size of a small ocean. My father, the laibon Taikoisia, was a very great laibon indeed. Unfortunately he was also a very poor swimmer. Somehow he managed to reach the eastern shore near the village of Bukima, but it was clear to those who found him

that he would not long survive. He gasped out what little he could to
the villagers, and they in turn told my people the story. Then they left
him alone on the shore to meet his lion. This was a very long time ago."

"Too bad," Oak murmured. "Maybe if they could have got him to
a doctor . . ."

"No, my friend. As I said, this happened a long time ago. It would
not have mattered. His heart and body both were worn out from his
journey."

Not for the first time Oak wondered just how old Olkeloki was.
He was about to ask when something loud and bright shot across the
highway at treetop level to explode somewhere back in the woods. He
fought to regain control of the wheel, cursing wildly.

"What the hell was that?" He finally brought the car to a stop in
the drainage ditch that paralleled the road.

Kakombe grabbed his spear from the floorboard. "Shetani!"

"I think not." Like the rest of them, Olkeloki was staring intently
through the windshield trying to see into the forest. "Surely they are
not yet strong enough to move about so boldly in broad daylight. If
they are, it means that we are already too late."

However, it was not shetani that had confronted them, but rather
spirits of a radically different and more contemporary kind.

The terrified man who came up to the car drew back when he saw
the odd collection of muzungu and Maasai inside. A second explosion
that ripped into the earth a quarter mile up the road overcame his fear.
Gesturing for them to join him, he promptly slid beneath the motionless
Land Rover. Olkeloki and the others contented themselves with climbing out and huddling on the shady side of the vehicle.

Oak bent over to peer beneath the car. "Do you speak English? If
you do, can you tell us what's going on?" A third explosion made him
wince, but only momentarily. It was at least a mile away.

The man turned his head to look at Oak. "Where do you come
from that you don't know?"

"North," Olkeloki informed the man. "What is happening here?"

"It's the government. The military, actually. Each time this year
they test their secret project. Everyone knows about it. Today is the
day they test their new weapons. Instead of buying them from others
they are trying to build them themselves."

"Build what?" Merry asked. A roar came from the vicinity of the
city up the road and something screamed by overhead, trailing a white
contrail. The streamlined shape hung in the air for a moment before
veering sharply off to its left. A distant *crump* as the object impacted
the ground echoed back to them.

"It should end soon," said the farmer.

"Rockets." Oak rose, scanned the sky. "Surface-to-surface missiles."

"Missiles, yes, that's what it is." The farmer started to crawl out from beneath the Rover. "Every year at this time they try to make them work. But our military people are not very good, because everything they shoot off lands everywhere except where it is supposed to." He glanced at the sky, then accepted a helping hand from Kakombe. "I think they are finished for this year."

Oak leaned back against the car, the tension oozing out of him. "And we thought they were shetani. Shit."

The farmer eyed them askance. "Shetani? That is a Makonde word. For spirit-things. There are no such things as shetani. That is just a name they give to the ugly carvings they make. Certainly you muzungu don't believe in them?"

"Certainly not," said Oak. "I was just kidding. Only a total fool would believe in something as absurd as spirits." He looked at Merry. "Isn't that right?"

"Oh, absolutely. You'd have to be a complete moron." Then she began to laugh. Oak laughed back at her, while Olkeloki was unable to restrain a dignified chuckle. Even the relentlessly serious Kakombe smiled.

The farmer stared at them, wondering if perhaps it might have been more sensible to take his chances with the wayward rockets. "What are you all laughing at?"

This somber query caused Oak to slide down the side of the car. Tears were coursing down his cheeks. Merry was leaning against the hood and struggling to keep her balance.

"Crazy muzungu I understand," muttered the farmer, "but Maasai don't laugh. It is not funny." There was anger in the man's voice, which only made Oak laugh all the harder. "My neighbor Liliwa lost ten chickens and a cow last year when one of the missiles landed near his house!"

Merry promptly lost control of her legs and had to sit down next to the hysterical Oak. Kakombe turned away. They could see his massive shoulders heaving up and down as he tried desperately to smother the laughter welling up inside him.

When they finally managed to get themselves under control again, they offered the disgruntled farmer a ride into town. Since the most recent attempt of the Tanzanian armed forces to independently enter the twentieth century had apparently fizzled out, the man reluctantly accepted. As they drew close to Morogoro they saw soldiers boredly taking down roadblocks and would-be ballistics experts fanning out across cornfields in search of their errant children.

From what they could see as they drove through town the city had been spared. A few distant plumes of smoke stained the perfectly blue sky like brown watercolor. Merchants were removing heavy planks from windows and doorways. Already the streets were full of people hurriedly going nowhere. As Merry had noted elsewhere, that look of empty urgency was characteristic of urban Tanzania.

The city itself was a dour collection of old stucco colonial buildings and a few feeble attempts at modernization. A sign in front of a chaotic construction site announced the ongoing construction of a six-story modern hotel. As with similar Communist-directed projects, those parts of the building that had been finished were already starting to fall down.

They drove slowly past the central market. The open-air square, which should have been a hive of local activity, was empty except for a few old men and women selling what modest produce they'd managed to sequester from sight of acquisitive government inspectors. Merry identified bunches of stunted bananas, a few pineapples, some unimpressive fish. The only vendor doing real business stood behind a stall selling used clothing, mostly battered and faded blue jeans and T-shirts he'd acquired God knew where. She saw one sweatshirt emblazoned with the legend "New York University." It was full of holes. She wondered what the dealer was asking for it.

More people, people everywhere now, clad in shorts and sandals and old shirts. Then out the western side of town and past the university, with its distant white buildings and single sleepy gate guard. Bicycles instead of cars.

"Wish I had a camera," Merry mused aloud as they drove past.

"You would not want to take picture here," the farmer told her. "Government facility, very dangerous."

Merry didn't believe him. "What—a school?"

"Last year," the farmer explained solemnly, "a visiting muzungu was arrested for taking pictures on university grounds. Police hold him for ten days. There is a big tamarind tree in front of the administration building. That's what the muzungu was taking picture of. But the police don't believe him. They absolutely cannot believe anyone would want picture of a tree." He sniffed derisively. "School is rotten anyway. Farming is better."

"Your children will never get ahead thinking that way." Merry, Oak had noted already, had many virtues, but diplomacy was not one of them.

"They would not get ahead by going there," the farmer shot back. "I tell you what kind of school that place is. Six months ago the government decides to make special grants. Morogoro University gets one hundred thousand shillings to spend any way it wants to. So the teachers, they argue and fight for weeks how to spend the money. You want to know what they finally decide to spend it on?"

"Books?" Merry guessed.

"Beer. One hundred thousand shillings worth of beer."

"That's terrible."

"You think that is terrible? They drank all of it in three days. That I can teach my children myself. No, I will stick to my farm. I have corn and some papayas and I raise pigs for the non-Muslims to eat. Perhaps one day things will be better."

By the time their guest asked to be dropped off, he had become a friend. It was all they could do to beg off spending the night with the farmer and his family.

"We're on an important errand and we can't spare the time," Oak told him as he leaned out the driver's window. "Maybe we'll catch you on the way back."

"An errand." The farmer nodded knowingly. "I guessed as much. I knew you could not be just tourists. Not traveling with Maasai." He shook his head in wonder at the sight. "Two muzungu, a laibon, and an Alaunoni traveling together. I will not ask you the nature of your errand because I am not sure I want to know, but I will wish you good luck."

They shook hands all around and Merry overwhelmed the man by making him a gift of one of the disposable razors from her stock. He was still waving when Oak glanced in the rear-view mirror a couple of minutes later.

"There stands the heart and future of this country, if his government will recognize him. Typical third-world country. They all want to build steel mills and new capitals and giant dams. Meanwhile the small farmers and businessmen go broke and are forgotten. Nothing personal, old man."

"I am not offended," Olkeloki replied. "None of it matters to the Maasai. We have grass and cattle. We do not need steel mills, dams, or farmers and businessmen. We never have and we never will."

"You're going to have to change," Merry told him. "Maybe not right away, but sooner or later the twentieth century is going to overwhelm Maasailand too. You can't ignore it and you can't just keep sending only your brightest kids to school."

"We will try to adapt and also to retain our traditions. That is all we can do."

Oak didn't really want to ask the inevitable next question but found he was unable to keep from doing so. "What happens if the governments of Kenya and Tanzania decide to break up the open grasslands and make workers and civil servants and farmers out of the Maasai?"

"We will resist. If necessary, we will become workers and civil servants. But we will always stay Maasai, and we will never become farmers. To cut open the earth would be like cutting open our own bodies. If the old traditions are lost, we will make new traditions. The Maasai will never become a footnote in ethnographic histories.

"I know this must come to pass someday, and the sadness it will bring will lie heavy on many hearts. But not mine. I will be gone. I will not live long enough to see the open plains and wandering game vanish. That will be a problem for new laibon and younger ilmoran to cope with."

"How?" wondered an angry Kakombe. "How can a man be a warrior and fight for his way of life if they take away his spear and his land?"

Olkeloki had no simple answer for the senior warrior. It was quiet in the car for a long time.

"Well," Merry finally said into the silence, "there's always football."

"An all-Maasai football team. Now that's something I'd pay to see," chuckled Oak, feeling a little better.

"An interesting idea, my friends." The concept appeared to please the old man. "New traditions. He speaks of American football, Kakombe, and not the kind the village children play. Much hitting is involved, besides running and kicking. Throwing as well."

"Spears?" asked the senior warrior hopefully. "War clubs?"

"I fear not. An oblong ball is employed instead."

"Can we carry our knives when we play this game?"

"No," Oak told him, "but don't worry. If you can recruit a few more players like yourself you won't need 'em."

They had to drive through Mikumi National Park. Oak was worried about having to answer the questions of local authorities, but not for long. There were no local authorities. Only a pair of game wardens who didn't even bother to look up from their station as the Land Rover trundled past. Nor were there any gates; only signs. Gates would be useless, Olkeloki explained sensibly, because the elephants would either push them down or eat them.

For that matter they saw no tourists so far from Kenya. Only a few local Indians sipping tea inside an open-walled park boma. Outside the city, traffic vanished. They passed only an occasional truck as they began to climb through the river gorge that split the Rubeho Mountains.

"The Ruaha," Olkeloki informed them, indicating the river running far below the winding road. "It flows east from the Kipengere Range, past the place we must find, until it joins with the Rufiji. Together they enter the ocean near the isle of Mafia."

Eventually the road leveled out and ran straight across a high plateau. Villagers sat by the sides of the road selling bushel baskets full of the ripest tomatoes Merry had ever seen. Then on to Iringa, the first town they'd seen since leaving Arusha which boasted buildings that didn't appear on the verge of collapsing.

They filled the Rover's tanks and jerry cans at a small garage. Idle men drifted over to stare frankly at Oak and Kakombe. They avoided Kakombe's shadow and failed miserably to avoid looking at Merry Sharrow. There was no hostility in those stares; only a vast and unsatisfied curiosity.

Sitting against the wall of the garage, five men were trying to patch a tire. They were taking their time and making a major project of it.

"It will take them two, perhaps three hours," said Olkeloki. "Why hurry? They could do it faster, but then they would have nothing to do with themselves. So they linger over it. They have no work. They have no cattle. Their government gives them nothing to do. A terrible waste."

Outside Iringa they left the highway for a dirt track angling north. They passed through one small town, a second, and then there was nothing: no buildings, no people, no animals, for endless miles. Only thorntree and acacia forest and red dust. Finally Oak had to turn on the Rover's air conditioning. Olkeloki thought this a terrible waste of petrol but said nothing.

In this difficult and empty land they finally encountered Africa's toughest denizen. Not crocodile or rhino, neither elephant nor Cape buffalo, this scourge of the veldt and savanna was perhaps half an inch long, clad in steel-gray armor, and well-nigh invulnerable.

One of them found Merry and nearly sent her through the roof. Kakombe finally crushed it with the butt end of his knife.

"Tsetse fly." Olkeloki didn't have to inspect the remains to identify the attacker. "These do not carry the sleeping sickness which affects humans, but they are deadly to cattle. That is why there are no Maasai here. See." He ran a finger along the inside of the window. Tiny bulletlike shapes were bouncing off the glass. "They will attack anything that moves in search of blood. They think the car is alive. But if you stand still they will usually leave you alone."

It was like driving through a hail of BBs. Eventually the flies gave up and flew off in search of prey with thinner hide. As Merry had discovered, however, once inside a vehicle they had a disconcerting habit of hiding until the passengers relaxed. Then they would come straight at exposed flesh like darts fired from a tiny gun. Nor did they waste time the way horseflies did by searching around for the best place to bite. First contact was always made with the lancetlike proboscis. About all that could be said in their favor was that the pain faded rapidly and left no swelling behind.

Killing one was another matter. Their bodies had the consistency

and resiliency of tire rubber. A flyswatter was useless against them. So
was anything smaller than a Webster's dictionary or hammer. The best
method of extermination consisted of trapping one against the glass and
pressing a shoe heel, tire iron, or other unyielding object against them.
The result was a messy window but peace of mind.

Several times in the gathering twilight the road ahead seemed to
disappear into the trees, but Olkeloki always chose the right path. As
the sun was starting to set, the forest abruptly gave way to a steep slope
at the bottom of which flowed a lugubrious stream. Here the Great
Ruaha River was no more than a hundred yards across. There was no
sign of a bridge.

There were, however, a couple of curious game wardens living in
round steel huts that were metallic duplicates of traditional African
bomas. One had them sign their names in a register while eyeing them
suspiciously. He accepted Oak's story that Olkeloki was their guide and
Kakombe his son with great reluctance. Why get into a fight with two
muzungu over purpose of visit, however? So they didn't look like typical
tourists—neither did they look like poachers.

Payment of a small fee brought a barge ferry from the other side
of the river. Two men sat on one side and pulled it across by means of
a thick steel cable and pulley system. Oak carefully drove the Land
Rover onto the ferry, which was barely long enough to hold it, and
then watched while the two men started pulling them back the way
they'd come.

Eyes blinked at them from the surface of the river. After a casual
inspection, the crocodiles sank out of sight in search of the huge tiger
fish that occasionally broke the surface and sent droplets flying over
the ferry. An impatient Kakombe sat down behind the two ferrymen
and wrapped huge hands around the cable. Their progress across the
river was noticeably faster as soon as the senior warrior lent his bulk
to the effort.

Once safely on the north shore, Oak took a moment to admire
the sunset, a sky of pink and cerulean blue silhouetted by low mountains. Then he spoke to Olkeloki.

"Which way now?"

"Upriver. I think you will be surprised, Joshua Oak. And pleased."

Ruaha River Camp was an oasis in the middle of East Africa. The
entire complex had been built from scratch using local materials by a
determined English family named Wolf. A few other vehicles were
parked around the camp, which they soon learned belonged to members
of various foreign aid projects. They drove hundreds of miles to the
camp from their project sites because it was the only place in that part
of Africa where one could enjoy a decent meal out.

Individual huts, or bomas, built of native river rock clung to the flank of a massive granite outcropping that overlooked the river, looking like so many fat birdsnests in a baobab tree. Merry expressed the belief that she'd never seen a more beautiful place in her life. The cataracts that roared below the camp generated a cool breeze which not only made the temperature more bearable but kept most of the tsetse flies away. Elephant and giraffe could be seen grazing in the shallow water upriver where the water flowed less rapidly around grassy islets.

Screened-in rooms had beds with foam mattresses and linen, chairs, and kerosene lamps. The calm before the storm, Oak reflected.

Olkeloki confirmed his suspicions. "We are very near to the Out Of, Joshua Oak. No tourist would find it, just as few have found this park. Tomorrow we will attempt to seal the weak place where the fabric of reality is tearing. Tonight—tonight we will eat well. The people who run this camp know how to cook for muzungu and Africans alike, though where they obtain some of their food in this country is as much a mystery as the nature of the shetani. Sometimes I think they must find it in the Out Of."

They were sitting in the open-air restaurant atop the smooth rock, enjoying the view upstream. "I thought all the hotels in this country were nationalized."

"Not this camp. It is too small and too isolated to bother with."

"Then there aren't any government people here at all?"

"No." Olkeloki looked at him sideways. "A strange thing to ask."

Oak shrugged. "Just curious."

"You know what I think, Joshua Oak? I think life has soured a part of you. I think you are uncomfortable with it at times and do not see all the beauty that surrounds you. A part of you sleeps. Perhaps someday it will awaken."

"Look, old man, don't try to tell me how I feel about life. Stick to your evil spirits and your world-saving and leave me alone, okay?"

"Ah, here is Merry. Kakombe will be along shortly, I should think."

While they ate an astonishingly tasty supper they watched bright turquoise agama lizards scurry across the rock walls in search of bugs drawn to the lights. After days of nothing but roast pork interrupted only by the occasional serving of roast goat they were served something that tasted remarkably like beef. It was so tender and flavorful Oak forbore from asking what kind of animal it had come off. There was also fresh fruit and, wonder of wonders, ice cream. In the middle of Africa.

Feeling very full and contented (fatted calves, Oak thought darkly) they hiked to the crest of the granite outcropping. A small bar with tables and chairs had been set into the rock. From below rose the liquid rumble of the Nyamakumu rapids. Somewhere an elephant trumpeted to its mate. Silent staff brought coffee and drinks.

"This is wonderful." Merry sipped at a cup of heavily sugared local coffee. There was no cream. Small furry shapes skittered furtively over the rocks. "There's something over there."

"Hyrax," Olkeloki informed them. "Very tasty, though I think they look too much like rodents to suit muzungu palates."

One came cautiously into the light. It looked at them out of dark, challenging eyes. Oak thought of an overweight, tailless squirrel. Then it whirled and darted back into a crevice, tiny claws scratching against bare stone.

He leaned back in his chair, listening to the river. The magic of the place was insidious. The breeze from the rapids kept the mosquitoes away at night just as it warded off the tsetse flies during the day. A warm lethargy spread through his whole system.

The spell was shattered by a query in thickly accented English.

23

"**A**nd where are you from, pretty lady?"

Oak recognized the speaker and his three companions from supper. Italian engineers assigned to an irrigation project near a town called Mbeya. They'd chatted with them only briefly before eating. He decided immediately that he liked them better before they'd visited the bar. Not that you could blame them for overindulging. They were far from home, living among people they weren't fond of, and their work was continually frustrated by the Tanzanian government's habit of taking two steps backward for every one forward.

They'd attempted to drown their frustration in a small ocean of beer. The one who'd spoken leaned, or rather swayed, close to Merry and put a proprietary hand on her shoulder. She shrugged lightly. He didn't remove his fingers and Oak straightened imperceptibly in his chair, acutely conscious of the fact that what passed for local authority lay more than a hundred miles to the south.

"We're visiting. Tourists," she told him.

"Tourists?" The burly engineer seemed to find this uproariously funny. "No tourists come here, this place. You get to go home. We all got to stay. Work here, when you can't get anything done in this stinking country." Behind the bar, the bartender's expression tightened, but he made no move to intervene. One of the engineer's companions noticed, however.

"You, what you looking at, eh?"

"Nothing, bwana." The man kept his voice carefully neutral, but Oak could see the disgust in his face as he turned back to his slim stock of bottles. The first engineer was far too drunk to notice subtleties of expression. The hand on Merry's shoulder began to rotate slowly.

"We don't see many white women here. The black whores are nice, but you get tired of anything after a while." He whispered something in Italian to his companions and the four men enjoyed a private guffaw.

Oak smiled up at him. It was a smile he'd had occasion to make use of in other places. Except for possible additional difficulties that might be caused by language, he knew how to handle the present situation. There was just no backup to call upon. He was on his own.

"Why don't you fellows relax and let's all have a beer together. I'm told the local stuff's not half bad."

"Half bad?" The man who spoke looked like an athlete. He was a tall, rugged redhead in his forties and he clutched a bottle of the brew under discussion in his right hand. "No, it's not half bad. It's worse than that. It tastes like elephant piss. But it's all we have." He chugalugged the rest of the bottle's contents before hurling the empty over the stone wall. Oak heard it shatter far below. One of the man's friends gave him a friendly shove. Laughing, they opened two more beers.

"If it's that bad," Oak said quietly, "maybe you shouldn't drink any more of it."

Instant silence and sudden glares. The effect was the same as if he'd shot off a gun.

"Sure, we've had enough." The first speaker wiped foam from his lips. "We've had enough of this country, enough of these lazy, stupid people, and maybe I think enough of noisy Americans too." Grabbing his bottle by the neck, he smashed the body against the rock wall, kept a tight grip on the jagged handle that remained.

"Josh." Merry tried to rise but the athlete put both hands on her shoulders and shoved her back down in the chair.

"You stay, pretty lady. Ludovico know when to stop. He an engineer. I know when to stop too." He leaned over and jammed his mouth against hers, forcing her head and body back until her chair was balanced on the rear pair of legs. She kicked futilely at the air.

Meanwhile Oak found himself backed against the wall, a steep fall-off behind him and two of the Italians advancing from the front. The third was circling around to the right to block the stairway.

The chair Oak picked up was heavy, simply made, of local wood. If it made contact with a man's skull it was the bone that would shatter. A glance to his left showed that the barman had already beat a fast retreat. To save himself, or to get help? With his attention divided among three grinning adversaries, Oak couldn't afford time to speculate.

A shadow appeared behind the engineer who was assaulting Merry. It lifted the man off the ground as if he were a child. A moment later Kakombe gently set the unconscious man down and then moved silently forward to put an arm around the neck of the big engineer clutching the broken bottle. His other hand went around the man's right wrist and squeezed. The jagged bottleneck fell to the floor to shatter harmlessly against the stone.

By now the other workers had turned to warily study the newcomer. Kakombe waited until the engineer stopped kicking before lowering him to the ground. Then he turned to the remaining pair. Both men drew knives; short, heavy-bladed weapons. Chair raised in front of him, Oak advanced on the nearest. Now it was the turn of the two Italians to commence a slow retreat.

"You killed him," one of them muttered angrily. He held the knife loosely, as if he was thinking of throwing it. Oak took a second step toward him and he slashed with the blade. It glanced harmlessly off one leg of the chair.

"He only sleeps," said Kakombe. "It is better to sleep than fight over such things. I have had too much honey beer myself, sometimes."

The other engineer raised his knife and Oak could see him taking aim at the giant. He'd have to make a rush with the chair and hope the two didn't know how to fight together. If Kakombe could get his hands on the other one . . .

"That's enough!"

Eyes flicked toward the top of the stairs. The barman was standing there holding a kerosene lantern. Next to him stood Axel Wolf, holding the biggest rifle Oak had ever seen. His gaze shifted rapidly between the two armed Italians.

"This is a Chesterton Express, gentlemen. It will drop a bull elephant at two hundred yards. I hope I will not be compelled to demonstrate what it can do to a human being."

The engineers exchanged a look. Slowly, knives slid back into leather sheaths. Wolf nodded.

"Better. Now pick up your friends and get out. You're not welcome here anymore. Be good chaps and maybe I won't find it necessary to speak to your project supervisor about this the next time I'm in Mbeya, right?"

Glowering, the two men shouldered their companions and started down the stairs. One of them considered spitting at Kakombe, thought better of it, and contented himself with mumbling unintelligible obscenities.

Everyone in the bar waited quietly until the sound of a four-wheel drive starting up and leaving the parking area was heard. Only then did Wolf set the big gun aside. He spoke in Swahili to his waiting men, who took the weapon and vanished down the steps.

"My askaris will make sure our drunken friends don't sneak back to cause trouble later on. I don't think that's likely. As much beer as they drank they'll be lucky if they can still find their pants in an hour. I only hope they're sober enough to make it back across the river. If not, the crocs'll get 'em. I wouldn't like that. Bad publicity, y'know. You folks all right?"

Merry was fixing her hair. "Been a long time since I saw a bar fight. Most bars are closed when I'm off work." She rubbed at her mouth. "I'm okay. Kakombe?"

"Cowards. Muzungu are nothing without their guns. Some muzungu," he added hastily, smiling at Oak.

"My apologies. Next drinks are on the house." Wolf pulled up a chair. He was the same age as Oak, but the lines in his face hinted at a hard life. Most of his hair had turned gray prematurely. "Some people handle MMBA better than others. Not easy livin' out here among strange folks without, if you'll excuse me, madame, womenfolk of your own persuasion. Some people go a little crazy and have to be slapped down. Some go a lot crazy and have to be sent back home in white overcoats." He nodded toward the river.

"Most likely that lot'll wake up in the morning with bad headaches, bad memories, and stomachs they'd as soon pass on to somebody else. When they sober up they'll probably be more embarrassed than anything else. The foreign workers here are a mixed bag. The Scandinavians are the best, the Bulgarians the worst, and the Chinese are inscrutable. The Italians and Brazilians fall somewhere in the middle."

"Thanks for the help," Oak told him, "though I think Kakombe and I could've handled things ourselves."

"I don't doubt that, old chap, but I don't allow bloodletting in my place. Not that the government gives a damn if a bunch of drunken muzungus want to spill each other's guts, but they won't stand for anything that slows up one of their pet development projects. Putting a visiting engineer in the hospital's the local equivalent of blowing up a tractor. The tractor would get the better burial. Beer?"

"I think I'll stick to double cola, or whatever that local soft drink's called."

"Right." Wolf rose, smiled at Merry. "Apologies again. Check your sodas for bugs. We do our best here but I can't inspect every case personally. This isn't Hyde Park, you know. G'night."

Merry sipped at her glass, made a face, and pushed it aside. "Warm. Thanks, Josh." She looked up and to her left. "Thank you too, Kakombe."

He shrugged and settled his massive frame into the chair next to her. Watching her face closely, he picked up her glass. "I will finish this. My throat is dry and I am used to warm beer."

She smiled at him. "Help yourself."

Satisfied that all was well for at least the *next* half hour, Oak turned and gazed out over the dark river, thinking back to what Wolf had told them. "MMBA." They'd heard the term used in Nairobi. It stood for "miles and miles of bloody Africa." Not so much a derogatory description as one of resignation. If he didn't know better, he could imagine the forest below was the piney woods of Georgia or the hardwood forest fringing his beloved Burke Lake back home in Virginia.

The sounds rising from below suggested otherwise. Exotic hoots and chirps, shrill whines and mechanical buzzings identified the surroundings as anything but familiar. Suddenly he peered harder into the dim light. A large shape was squatting on a curve of rock not far below. Wolf had warned them on arrival that it was rare but not unheard of for leopards to wander into camp. At the time Oak thought it was a ploy to ensure that guests did not make unnecessary use of the limited outdoor plumbing facilities. Now he wasn't so sure.

Then he relaxed. Shifting its position slightly, the shape identified itself as human. He thought he recognized the outline.

"Mbatian Olkeloki?"

A head turned and moonlight flashed from upturned eyes. "What is it, friend Joshua?"

"How long have you been sitting there, old man?"

"A long time. I like the coolness of the smooth stone against my backside and the slant of this slope suits my spine. The hyrax come to nibble at my toes. They look at me questioningly, but I have neither food nor answers to give them."

Oak jerked his head toward the distant glow from the bar. "Didn't you hear what was going on up there?"

"You were there. Merry Sharrow was there. Kakombe was nearby. There was little need for me to intervene. I did not doubt the three of you could deal with four drunken ilmeet. If you had not been able to then I would have known I made a mistake in choosing you. Besides, I am an old man. My time for fighting is past. Knowledge and wisdom can prevail against spirits and shetani, but they are of little use against drunks." He turned away, staring out across the hissing rapids and blackened forest, then tilting back his head to regard the stars. Oak wondered what he saw there.

"The time of crisis draws near, Joshua Oak." Sitting quietly with his arms locked around his folded knees, he looked like one of Nafasi's blackwood sculptures. He didn't object when Oak, a much younger man from another time and culture, sat down next to him.

For a time they sat without speaking, sharing the silence and something else—an all-pervasive certainty. Though neither man knew it, the feeling was similar to what Oppenheimer and Szilard and the others at Trinity Site had felt that certain evening in 1945 as the world had been about to be dragged kicking and screaming into a new and not always reassuring era.

"Mbatian? What's on the other side? Besides the shetani, of course."

In the shadows the old man turned to look at him. His eyes reflected the starlight. Somehow they seemed bigger than in the daytime.

"Everything. That's what the Out Of is all about, my young friend. Whatever is not here is there. Everything that is real becomes real only when it enters our world from there, and everything that is not real but only imagined stays on the other side. Considering the nature of much of what is not real, it's better that way. The real world is confusing enough. Every now and then a small unreal something slips through a temporary weakness or gap in the fabric of the real and floats around our world. Then people see ghosts and goblins, have dreams and hallucinations.

"So it is not only the shetani we have to fear. There is much more in the Out Of to avoid. The longer we stay there, the more likely such things are to find us. Specific unrealities are drawn to specific people. I would not be likely to encounter your nightmare, for example. It would gravitate to you."

"Nightmare?"

"Yours and mine, Kakombe's and Merry Sharrow's; they're all over there, drifting aimlessly, waiting for a weak place to let them across to trouble our sleep. When we cross into the Out Of it will be much easier for them to find us. Then we may have something besides the shetani to cope with. You have shown me that you can deal with the shetani and with drunken ilmeet, Joshua Oak. Are you prepared to confront your own nightmares?"

Oak peered into the darkness. Small furred shapes were huddling around the base of a tree that grew from a crack in the rocks. He could sense them listening and watching. What might a hyrax encounter in the Out Of? Perhaps its missing tail?

"I don't know," he said finally. "Can any man answer that honestly? All I can say is that I've been dealing with nightmares of a sort my whole life. One of them did this to me." He touched his right eye and Olkeloki looked sympathetic. "My own fault. I got lazy. The nightmare who did this to me was smiling when he did it. Never trust a smiling nightmare. That much I know." Very carefully he removed the glass eyeball and held it in his open palm, knowing the darkness would render the empty socket relatively invisible.

"I noticed it right away," the old man told him.

Oak was surprised. "Did you? Interesting. Most people can't tell the difference unless the light's just right and they get right up close.

My family always got a kick out of telling people that the same company that made ET's eyes made one for me." He removed a small bottle of special fluid from a pocket and lightly cleaned the glass before replacing it in his face. The orbital muscles clamped down reflexively, holding it in place. "I used to do the cleaning and moistening in public, until I saw the effect it had on people. Since then I take care of it in private."

"How did this happen?"

Oak didn't mind telling the old man the story. He'd long since outgrown the associated trauma. "It was in a place called Boise. Not as bad as some cities I've worked in. Not where you'd expect something like this to happen. I was one of several people arresting an old man. He was angry because of what I'd done to him and his friends. He wasn't a very nice old man and his friends were no cupcakes either. My friends and I thought we had everything under control; routine, you know? We'd searched him and his friends for weapons and we were taking them into the local police station when he pulled a handful of keys from his pants and swung on me. In addition to being a lot meaner, he was a lot faster than I thought. My friends and I had kind of relaxed."

He tapped the glass eyeball with a fingernail. "Hit me right here with a key. If it had been a screwdriver or knife or something a little longer I wouldn't be here telling you about it now." He blinked, displaying his control over the restraining muscles.

"Sometimes I wake up in the middle of the night in a hot sweat—I never can understand people when they talk about a cold sweat—and I can see that key coming straight at me and I know I can't stop it. It's just a brass-colored blur. Then I feel the pain again and I have to touch myself to make sure I'm not bleeding. They say I bled a lot. So you see, old man, I'm used to dealing with nightmares."

"I suspected as much. Remember, Joshua Oak, you were made known to me."

There on the smooth rock beneath the calm mantle of the African night, Oak's last remaining shreds of skepticism and disbelief left him. "All right, I'm about ready to concede that there are forces at work here that I don't understand, that maybe nobody understands. I can see how somebody with my background and experience could be a lot of help to you in this." He gestured uphill.

"What I can't figure is how Merry fits in. She's a telephone salesclerk. Okay, so she works at night and as a result she isn't afraid of the dark. Maybe she can handle her nightmares too. But she doesn't have any kind of martial arts or military training. She's not used to fighting. If she were a lady cop or something, then I'd understand, it would make some sense. Go on, explain to me what she's doing here, why you picked her."

"Some things I may not tell you yet, friend Joshua. All I can say

is that she was made known to me, just as you were. When we enter
the Out Of you must be on my right hand just as she will be on my
left. She is as much a key to the outcome as you or I."

"If you say so, but I still don't understand."

"Who understands the Out Of? I can only tell you that this is the
way things must be. There is much darkness and little light in the Out
Of. It is not a place that cries out for illumination. As you say, Merry
Sharrow has no fear of the dark. That may be reason enough for her
to accompany us. Or possibly she is here to make sure that you are
here."

"Hey, now wait a minute. I came with you of my own free will.
Sure, Merry's insistence on following you had something to do with my
decision, but I still—" He broke off when he sensed that the old man
was laughing at him. Was his face burning? He was glad of the dark.

"Tomorrow we will find out why any of us are here, my young
friend, when it comes time to enter the Out Of."

Oak accepted the change of subject. "You say we're going to have
to seal this break that's opening between the real world and the Out
Of. How do we do that? With dynamite? Or with some kind of spell
or something?"

"Something like that." Oak wished the old man sounded a little
more confident. "Since the Out Of is a place of darkness, we must seal
it in with light."

"A few pounds of dynamite would make plenty of light."

The old man sounded disappointed. "All you ilmeet think alike.
Always thinking in terms of explosive devices. Your physics have no
soul. I will provide the light. That is my job. You and Kakombe and
Merry Sharrow must give me the time to do what I must do. That is
your job. To keep me alive long enough to finish the work." He
indicated the night sky. "That may take some doing. The portents are
not good."

For a moment Oak didn't grasp the old man's meaning. Then he
frowned at the half moon. A small piece of it was missing.

"I'll be damned. An eclipse."

"Yes. A sign of forthcoming death among the Maasai. By the
readings I have been doing at least two will die as we try to enter the
Out Of, and many more if we fail. Too many more to contemplate. But
then, this you know already."

Oak's gaze fell to the smooth, shadowed stone beneath his feet.
He swallowed. "Which two?"

"The reading did not say." He shrugged, though not to make light
of the matter. "I may have been wrong in interpreting the signs. On a
night when the moon is going out, even death may not act reasonably.
Remember, it was only a reading, and readings are nothing more than
hunches. They are not predictions engraved in stone."

Oak considered this for a while before asking quietly, "What about the other? What happens if we're successful? Are you sure this light you're going to produce will let us back across?"

"It should."

"And if it doesn't, or if something screws up at the last minute?"

"Then we will be imprisoned forever in the world of the Out Of along with the trapped shetani and our own worst nightmares. I think we would go mad very quickly. But do not worry about that. I am sure it is possible to kill oneself as quickly in the Out Of as in the real world."

Oak scuffed the smooth stone with the heel of his boot. "You're a real comfort, Mbatian Olkeloki." The old man rose and Oak eyed him curiously. "Going up for a drink?"

"No. To sleep, my young friend, but first I must make a telephone call. It is good that they have a phone here."

"Last minute call to your wife?"

"No. To settle my conscience and also, perhaps, to prick some others."

24

Moscow, U.S.S.R.—26 June

The Premier was more than usually solemn this morning, the minister reflected. In fact, Dorovskoy was downright grim. Certainly he had reason to be. He was the man who had to make the hard decisions. The questions he was putting to the men assembled around the great oval table were as precise and sharp as a surgeon's scalpel. Replies were of comparable brevity. Eventually the questions came round to the minister of transportation.

"Seroff, you're certain the Dnieper bridge was destroyed by sabotage? It could not possibly have been caused by anything else?"

"In conjunction with army specialists my department has researched the incident thoroughly, Comrade Premier. Although no physical evidence has been turned up at the site thus far, the lack of any other reasonable explanation compels us to believe in the sabotage theory."

Dorovskoy's expression did not change, but inside he was seething with frustration. The destruction of the Volga bridge at Volzhskiy was one more in an accelerating sequence of dramatic "accidents" that were driving him, his ministers, indeed the entire country to the edge of paranoia. It was as though whoever was responsible (and who could deny that some force was responsible?) was gaining strength and confidence with each successive incident, secure in the knowledge that without conclusive identification they could continue operating with impunity. The fabric of Soviet life was being pulled to pieces around him.

Dorovskoy could not allow it to continue unpunished. More than his own future was at stake.

"This cannot go on, gentlemen. Most of you know me fairly well. It was with your support that I became Premier and it is with your support that I continue to govern. All my life I have shied away from giving ultimatums. I didn't like them when my father gave them to me, I didn't like those I received in school, and I especially resented them in the army. But sometimes when everything else has been tried they are all that is left. My father would find it amusing that I now must issue my first.

"I desperately wish there was another way, but I have no choice. Those whom the Agency for State Security deems responsible for the catastrophes of the past days continue to disavow any knowledge of the causes. Concrete evidence is lacking, but in the absence of any other reasonable explanation the circumstantial evidence appears overwhelming. It is agreed, then?"

It was unanimous. Every minister gave his assent, albeit some reluctantly. Even those who disagreed with the decision realized the Premier had exhausted his options. The unanimity of opinion brought forth no smiles. This was anything but a pleasant occasion.

Even those who were confirmed atheists prayed the Americans would be reasonable.

Washington, D.C.—26 June

None of the usual small talk or joking banter filled the hall outside the cabinet room as the members of the National Security Council filed out and headed for their waiting limousines. President Weaver bid each of them a private goodbye. They all knew what they had to do and not a man among them was looking forward to it. He checked his watch. In half an hour he would have to go through essentially the same sequence of events with the cabinet. After that the media would have to be told. The press conference had been called for 11:55, in order to catch as many people at lunch as possible, when they were more likely to be sitting in front of a TV set.

He spent the next thirty minutes talking to his wife. She tried to think of a reason for cancelling the announcement but she'd spent too many years in politics, had become too logical and methodical to dissuade him. It was hard for her to be objective in any case. A brother-in-law had been a supervisor at the Baton Rouge refinery which had been blown up. But it helped Weaver to talk with her.

It helped as much as all the useless messages and demands and near-accusations they'd sent via satellite. As words had failed to stem the tide of inexplicable tragedies, now something else would have to be tried. Weaver dreaded the upcoming press conference. He wasn't worried about lack of popular support for the decision. Polls revealed that public opinion had been roused to fever pitch by the extremists. He was worried about the absence of strong opposition, both among

234

the general population and in Congress. It shouldn't have been a surprise, really. An angry American public could take only so much without striking back, even if they weren't completely sure they were striking back at the right enemy.

Worst of all, the Soviets seemed to feel exactly the same.

Cabinet meeting in five minutes. He kissed his wife, harder than he had in some time, and sat down at the head of the table to wait for the department heads to file in. A couple of them, Harkins and Thierry, also served on the NSC. They would be filling in their curious colleagues out in the hall. That would make it a little easier, but only a little.

The bright red telephone under the desk rang. He frowned, let it ring a second time before picking up the receiver.

The two men had talked directly before, Dorovskoy being the first Soviet Premier in history to have a working command of the English language and Weaver reciprocating with a smattering of Russian. Nevertheless, simultaneous translation was still vital to proper understanding. Especially this morning.

What happened was so extraordinary and puzzling and caused so much discussion on both sides of the planet that it refocused not only everyone's attention but their curiosity and anger as well. Perhaps it was nothing more than one of those inexplicable and fortuitous coincidences on which so much of history turns. In any case, what happened was this:

Dorovskoy insisted he had not called Weaver. The President of the United States was equally insistent that he had not rung up the Premier of the Union of Soviet Socialist Republics. There had been no click in Washington and no click in Moscow. Both men had picked up their handsets at precisely the same instant the call had gone through, which was not quite but almost theoretically impossible, given the amount of preparation that always went into making the necessary connections.

The extraordinary coincidence was immediately remarked upon. It was decided that a third party *had* to be involved. This determined, individuals on both sides suggested that perhaps the same still unknown third party might be responsible for the long series of equally inexplicable events on both continents. Threats about to be made were retracted. Cooler heads were allowed to make their suggestions without fear of being stigmatized as cowards and appeaseniks. Neither side trusted the other enough to relax, but talk of ultimatums and absolutes was put off while this new possibility was to be looked into. The mysterious coincidental telephone call notwithstanding, neither side was willing to permit itself more than a modicum of optimism. Everyone backed off just the same.

What harm in talking for a few more days?

Ruaha, Tanzania—26 June

While the representatives of the two world powers talked and the rest of the world trembled, a battered Land Rover containing four tired but determined people was bouncing along a dirt track paralleling the Mdonya Sand River in south central Tanzania. Not even Mbatian Oldoinyo Olkeloki knew how much time they had left. All he could tell them was that they had no time to spare and that there would be no second chance.

Olkeloki had come for them before five, when it was still dark out. Bleary-eyed but tense with excitement, Oak had thrown some water on his face, dressed, and warmed up the Land Rover while they waited for Merry. There were no jokes about the habitual tardiness of women. Not on this morning.

Now the sun was rising over the rolling hills through which the sand river sliced. Soon it would begin to warm up and the tsetse flies would leave the shelter of their bushes in search of blood. No one at the camp questioned their early departure. Morning and evening were the best time for viewing game.

Except that we're going to see something a lot more dangerous than a lion or leopard, Oak thought.

Since leaving camp behind they hadn't seen another human being. For all the marks humanity had left on this stretch of Africa they might as well have been driving over the sands of Mars. Unvarying guide and companion, the river was as pure an expanse of yellow-white sand as his favorite Carolina beach. Under Olkeloki's direction they kept it on their right as they followed it northwestward.

Water ran not far beneath the sandy surface, the old man explained. Occasionally they would drive past shallow holes dug by elephants. When the pachyderms had drunk their fill, other animals would emerge from the woods to make use of the temporary well.

"*Ow*, damnit!" A quick search located the culprit and Merry smashed him against the door on her side. Windows were rolled up and Oak turned on the air conditioning. Olkeloki offered his personal theory that the tsetse flies were actually the offspring of certain shetani. This accounted not only for their unnatural toughness but also for their persistence and malign disposition.

They were heading toward a long, low escarpment of dark stone that resembled a gray whale resting on the earth. Another twenty miles revealed the source of the Mdonya: a gorge cut by flood waters through the basalt cliffs.

"We go up there," Olkeloki informed them. "Up above, the waters of the Mdonya rise to the surface and form the Matopotopo swamp. It is not large when compared to the basin of the Amazon or your own Mississippi delta, but it is wild and remote enough to preclude visits. Up there, in the shadow of a mountain called Kibiriti, we should find the place we seek."

Eyeing the damp, vegetation-covered slope, Oak was afraid they were going to have to walk, but there was enough dry ground for the Rover to negotiate and the river fell gradually to the plains below. Once they gained the crest of the escarpment, he was able to relax a little.

About time we got a break, he mused.

Olkeloki, too, seemed pleased. "We will be able to drive through. That will be much better than walking."

Oak looked over at him. "What, into the Out Of? In this thing?"

"I do not see why not. The shetani live here. Why should this machine not live there?" He was tapping on the dash with his long fingers. They reminded Merry of the fingers of a pianist. What silent melody was he playing, in which she and Joshua Oak were merely notes thrown in for spice?

"Besides, the English company which makes this vehicle insists it will go anywhere."

"If it doesn't, we'd have a hell of a time collecting on the warranty."

"Fear not, Joshua Oak. Magic will not stop us. Shetani will not stop us. Not now, not here, not this close. If the gap in reality is wide enough for so many shetani to pass through, it will surely be large enough to admit one Land Rover." He said nothing about the possibility of two of them dying, Oak noted.

Several miles ahead the river vanished into the outskirts of the swamp. Oak worked the Rover around isolated baobabs and boulders, keeping the broad expanse of sand on his right.

"Laibon," wondered Kakombe, "if we are so near, why do the shetani not attack?"

"Perhaps they are afraid of us, or perhaps their attention is concentrated elsewhere. We have moved fast and in unexpected ways. They may not realize we are so close. We should not be here, in this place, at this time. No human being should. The shetani are clever and dangerous, but they are not organized. They are too wild to track well."

"How are we doing on time?" Merry asked him.

The old man looked out the window at the last stars. "I cannot tell for certain, Merry Sharrow. I have said often that we had little time left. Now we have less than little time. Certainly we must be done and away by nightfall."

The character of the terrain changed as they neared the swamp. Baobabs gave way to dense forest. Complaining noises came from the vicinity of the Rover's transmission, but they had no time to make a mechanical check. It didn't matter anyway. They would go on until the car quit. Then they would have to walk.

A mile east of the first open water the woods grew too dense even for Oak to navigate. Olkeloki gestured anxiously to his right.

"Turn off here."

"What, into the river?"

"We must continue to go westward. We walk only if we have no other choice." The sun was high in the sky now, bright and reassuring.

Oak cast a dubious eye on the sand river. "You're the boss, but there's no telling how soft it is under that sand."

Down a steep bank they plunged. Oak turned upriver, the rear tires throwing up yellow fountains behind them. They got another hundred yards before forward momentum ceased.

No one spoke as they piled out of the car. Turacos shouted at them from the trees. Squawking raucously, a trio of ground hornbills glided past overhead, their enormous bills making them appear too top-heavy for flight. Still higher soared a Balateur eagle, hunting for reptiles and rodents with telescopic eyes. A single tsetse fly buzzed Merry, who stood still until it gave up and flew off in search of something moving.

Just your average June morning in East Africa, Oak mused, with the fate of the world resting not-so-lightly on your shoulders. He knelt near the rear left wheel. It was completely buried in warm, fine sand.

"What about the winch?" Kakombe was peering over his shoulder. Oak looked toward the riverbank.

"I don't think the cable's long enough, not even if we add that emergency rope to it. Stuff growing on the bank would pull right out and the big trees are too far away."

"Then we will have to try and pull it out, like we did near Chalinze."

"I don't think even you can do that, Kakombe." Merry was on hands and knees digging at the sand. "It's right up against the floorboards. We're in too deep." She sat back on her legs and shaded her eyes to look up at Olkeloki. "How far?"

The old man scanned the empty riverbed. "We are very near. I sense it. I would rather drive, but if we must walk, we should get started."

Packs and spears were removed from the back of the Rover. They'd hardly had time to shoulder their loads when Oak turned sharply to face back the way they'd come.

"What is it, Josh?" Merry moved up close to him and joined him in staring downriver. "Shetani?"

"No, though you'd think this close to the break we'd have seen some by now."

"They come through at night," Olkeloki told him. "They are not yet confident enough to move about in the daytime in large numbers. For a little while longer yet they are restricted to moving in the dark places."

"Another vehicle," said Kakombe abruptly.

"I'll be damned." Oak could see it now, bouncing toward them. "What's it doing up here?"

It was a Suzuki four-wheel drive, much smaller than the massive Land Rover. Weighing a thousand pounds or so less, it scooted along like a water bug atop the sand without sinking in. As they watched, it rolled to a halt, sat there in the middle of the river.

"Hey!" Merry waved at it. "Can you give us a hand?"

The driver appeared to be debating whether to turn around and go back the way he'd come or to continue his path upriver. Oak whispered to Olkeloki.

"What do you think?"

"Unusual to see tourists in this place, but not impossible. We are still within the park boundaries, though most ilmeet are afraid to stray off the indicated tracks."

The Suzuki's engine revved and it started toward them again.

"They see us," Merry said. Which also meant that those inside the four-wheel knew they'd been seen, Oak mused, but since he had no conclusions to jump to, there was no point in worrying about them. Yet.

The Suzuki coasted to a halt a few yards away. Two men emerged. The driver knelt to examine the imprisoned Rover. "Stuck good. If you'll all get back inside we'll try to pull you out." His tone was cool, carefully neutral, Oak thought, the English lightly accented. "You need to keep a lookout for the gray-colored sand. That's where the soft spots are."

"We'll keep that in mind." He nodded toward the front of the Suzuki. "Want some help with the winch?"

"We'll handle it." The man managed a thin smile. "Just get back in."

"We must hurry." Olkeloki looked nervous. Oak had seen him worried before, but never nervous. And if Mbatian Olkeloki had reason to be nervous, everyone else in the immediate vicinity ought to be trembling in their boots. "It is dangerous to stay long in one place so near the Out Of. We must move quickly."

The driver stood and frowned. "What's he talking about?"

Oak tried to make light of the laibon's comments. "Who knows? I mean, how can anyone figure what they're talking about? We just happened along these two walking through the park and agreed to give them a lift."

"Uh-huh, sure." The man was frowning as he started back to his vehicle.

He stopped cold. His assistant, a tall Bantu dressed in shorts and a cut-off T-shirt, was frantically trying to intercept Merry as she approached the Suzuki.

"What a cute little four-wheel drive," she was saying. "Back home we don't have any—" She stopped in mid-sentence, staring into the car.

Several things happened very fast. The Bantu pulled a rifle from inside the vehicle and pointed it at Merry. The driver broke into a trot, reached inside, and brought out an automatic weapon which he turned to point at Oak.

"You shouldn't have done that, miss. Didn't you hear about what happened to the cat?"

"Cat?" She was staring open-mouthed at the gun. "What cat?"

"The one curiosity killed." The man looked very unhappy.

"What's wrong?" Oak was trying to see past the man. "What's with the guns?"

Kakombe was nodding to himself. "I know this kind of ilmeet. He is no tourist, this one. He is like the hyena that sneaks into the village to steal the cream from the top of the milk bucket and then pisses into what he leaves behind."

"Cheeky one, your tall friend," said the driver. He stepped aside and gestured tiredly at his vehicle. "Might as well have a look yourself. It doesn't matter now."

Oak took a couple of cautious steps forward until he could see inside the Suzuki. The back end was filled with animal skins. He recognized zebra and wildebeest, but what caught his attention immediately were those of several big cats. Leopard and cheetah. From what little he knew about regulations concerning the killing of endangered species, there were enough pelts in the back of the Suzuki to put the man and his assistant behind bars for the rest of their natural lives.

And Merry, curious, cheerful Merry, had to go and see them.

"Poachers," muttered Olkeloki. "Lice on the skin of Africa."

"Cheeky and colorful." The hunter gestured with his gun. Oak nodded at it.

"Kalishnikov. Very sporting."

"I'm not in the sporting game, friend. Move over there. You too, miss."

A disbelieving Merry stumbled back through the sand to stand next to Oak. "You—you're not going to shoot us?"

The man muttered something in Swahili to his assistant, who came around from the far side of the Suzuki with his own weapon raised.

"I'm afraid I'm going to have to, miss. I can't very well let the lot of you finish up your sightseeing and then drive back to inform the local game warden that I've been working his territory, now can I?"

"We won't tell anyone, honestly. Besides, we're not sightseeing. We're here on important business."

The poacher affected an ingenuous expression. "Business? Two whites and two Maasai have business out here?" He looked around at the empty sand river and the brushland beyond. "Now what kind of business could you have out here, miss?"

Quite indifferent to the fact that he was about to be shot, Olkeloki was staring up at the sky. "This foolishness must end. The sun continues to move."

"You have to let us go," Merry told the poacher, "because if you don't, billions of things called shetani are going to break through into this world from a place called the Out Of and everybody's going to die horribly."

The poacher looked at her askance for a minute, then chuckled. "That's very good, very good indeed, miss. Maybe you're all escapees from an institution somewheres, but it doesn't matter. In my business, you see, you can't take chances and you can't do things by halves. I am truly sorry, but witnesses to my business are the one thing I can't afford."

Oak knelt, picked up a handful of sand, and let it run through his fingers, savoring its warmth and consistency. So life was a joke after all, with irony the punch line. The poachers could have cared less what they were doing there in the obscure sand river. It didn't matter. All that mattered was that they had seen the forbidden pelts in the back of the car. Enough to murder four people over. They had come all the way from the U.S., had helped to defeat an advance army of shetani on the slopes of a sacred mountain, had made their way past snakes and crazy Italians and everything else to get to this point right on the edge of the Out Of, only to have it all end because of some opera buffa encounter with a paranoid poacher who happened to be in the wrong place at the wrong time. Or were they the ones in the wrong place at the wrong time? Not even Olkeloki knew that.

The ground shifted slightly underfoot. The poacher frowned and glanced back toward his companion. As he did so, Oak flung his handful of sand. It caught the man right in the eyes. Oak was on top of him in an instant and they rolled over and over in the sand while the poacher's assistant tried to get a clean line on Oak so he could shoot him without shredding his boss. Quite aware of this, Oak tried to keep the man he'd tackled between himself and the other. If he could just get a hand on the hunter's gun . . .

The earth erupted and he felt himself falling toward the sky.

He knew he wasn't dead yet because he could hear Merry screaming and Kakombe bellowing in Maasai. Then he was lying on his back looking up, paralyzed by the sight before him.

Two immense black pillars were rising out of the ground on either side of the poacher's assistant. Deep ridges scarred the inside of the pillars. The man had been knocked off his feet and now struggled erect as his boss tried to get control of his weapon. The pillars slammed together with an explosive *crunch*. A thin scream came from between, followed by a spurt of blood.

Oak wiped sand from his own eyes. The ridges he'd seen lining the insides of the pillars were teeth, the pillars themselves enormous massive jaws rising from the sand. They swallowed convulsively, shaking the ground again, and continued to emerge from beneath the sand river.

An eye the size of a number six washtub popped out of the sand less than a yard from Oak's kicking legs. Olkeloki was dragging Merry clear while Kakombe fought to keep his feet. The poacher was staggering backward and trying to circle around the behemoth which was rising from the depths between him and his vehicle.

Most of it was out of the sand now. The body was as big as an elephant, the jaws those of a whale. From deep within its chest came a booming noise like the breathing of an idle steam engine.

The poacher unleashed his Kalishnikov on it. Shells struck the dark rubbery flesh without visible effect. It was impossible for that comparatively small body to support those gargantuan crocodilian jaws, but somehow the monstrosity managed the necessary leverage in defiance of common sense and gravity, swinging them easily from side to side like the tip of a three-story-high construction crane.

"Quickly!" Olkeloki made a run for the Suzuki while the colossus stalked the hysterical poacher. The man was running away now, firing wildly back over his shoulder and babbling incoherently. Long fingers trailed in the sand as the shetani hunched rather than walked forward.

Then it reached out with twenty-foot-long arms and let out a sound that made Merry's skin quiver. She knew she'd stained her pants but that didn't matter. Nothing mattered now except getting away, away from that horrible giant that had emerged from the earth beneath their feet. Smoke and fire spewed from nostrils at the tip of those immense jaws. At that moment she recognized the otherworldly mutant for what it was. Because they'd seen it before.

"Spirit of the Earth!" Olkeloki was already tossing gear and weapons into the back of the Suzuki, taking advantage of the shetani's preoccupation with the unlucky poacher. "Hurry, my friends, hurry!"

By now the poacher had been reduced to a gibbering madman as he raced for the forested riverbank.

"It came for us." Olkeloki yanked the front seat forward so Merry and Kakombe could pile in the back. The disgusted senior warrior immediately began throwing the still odoriferous pelts out the side window. "It came for us and found others with weapons to occupy it, but it will not remain so occupied forever."

Oak had piled into the driver's seat and was studying the dash with an intensity he hadn't known he possessed. There were fewer gauges and dials than in the Land Rover, but only one or two whose function wasn't obvious. He turned the key and threw the shift forward.

The Suzuki started to kick up sand. For an awful moment he thought the addition of their extra weight would cause it to dig in and stick as tightly as the heavier Rover, but as Kakombe continued to toss out pelts the tires started to bite. The little vehicle slid sideways. Oak wrestled the wheel and managed to straighten them out.

"Which way?" he yelled at Olkeloki.

"Straight ahead, Joshua Oak!" The old man was leaning out the window on his side and looking behind them. "Straight ahead and turn for nothing this side of hell! We are very close."

Merry was leaning over the shift console and straining to see ahead. "There's nothing there. I mean, nothing out of the ordinary." The sand river stretched unbroken before them.

Far behind them now, the poacher ducked and rolled as cavernous jaws slammed shut over his head, missing him by inches. Unable to scramble up the steep riverbank, he ran back out into the middle of the river, chasing after the retreating Suzuki.

"Wait, please, oh God, wait!" When his words had no effect he let loose with the Kalishnikov.

He managed to get off a couple of bursts before gigantic jaws swooped down to snip him neatly in half at the waist. The Spirit of the Earth gulped flesh and bone with a single birdlike swallow as the bottom half of the man's body remained upright for another moment, squirting blood in all directions. It took a few seconds for the circulatory pressure to give out. Then hips and legs keeled over into the sand.

Emitting another blast of flame and smoke, the abomination lifted its immense skull and struck out in pursuit of the fleeing four-wheel drive with thirty-foot-long strides.

"Faster, Josh," Merry pleaded, looking back through the rear window, "for God's sake, faster!"

"I'm doing the best I can!" In the slick sand the Suzuki slued two feet sideways for every foot it advanced. "You want me to roll us?"

The gargoylish shetani was making up the distance between them rapidly. Too rapidly. As it leaned toward them noisome flame gushed from its running nostrils. Merry shrieked as the fire licked at the back of the car and ducked toward the floorboard while Kakombe uttered a quiet prayer.

The fiery exhalation slammed into the back of the Suzuki like napalm. Oak felt the heat of it sear the hair on the back of his neck as the blast blew in the flimsy rear window. Glass exploded around him. Instinctively he shut his eyes.

So this is how the world ends, he thought. Not in ice but in fire, demonic at that. They were to be incinerated on the verge of crossing over. He could feel the flame licking at his skin, teasing his cheeks, incredibly hot and intensely red-orange.

Only—the fire was cool instead of hot, and the flames had wings. He opened his eyes all the way. The terrible heat which had touched him and had threatened to fry them instantly had vanished.

The flames had become a blizzard of brightly colored butterflies.

They had entered the Out Of.

25

In the Out Of—Elsewhen

Daylight was a feeble imitation of what it had been, weak and dim. The sky looked and smelled of decay and the air was sour with freshly renewed fetidness. Outside the slowing Suzuki a rotten breeze blew through cancer-laden trees. A shrunken, diseased sun hung uncertainly overhead. While its position corresponded to that of the sol they had left behind, the light it cast was uneven and sickly.

There was no sign of the pursuing Spirit of the Earth.

They drove on through the faint purple twilight. Although only a single sun was visible in the sky, many of the twisted, gnarled growths that clung to the riverbank cast multiple shadows on the sand below. Some of the shadows hinted at unpleasant shapes moving invisibly among the disintegrating wood.

Here and there young plants thrust hopeful stalks skyward, only to be sickened and bent as they matured by unseen poisons in the air and earth. There were no clouds, but Merry thought she could see thin, slightly phosphorescent green outlines flickering overhead. Some kind of unnatural auroral glow come too near the ground. The dead cold of space pressed close here.

The floor was littered with dead butterflies. Their brightly hued wings turned to gray ash as they perished from contact with the same atmosphere that had transformed them from flame into living things.

"Get out of the river," Olkeloki finally said into the silence. "The

Spirits of the Earth are many. What went looking for us in the real world may come hunting for us here."

Oak glanced into the rear-view as he swung toward the left bank. Still no sign of the monster which had nearly incinerated them. Only the purple twilight and a faint reddish glow clinging to the sand like animated fungi.

They found a place where the loose soil of the riverbank had recently crumbled. Even the exposed rock looked ill. It took two tries, but Oak got the Suzuki out of the river and brought it to a halt atop the bank. They were surrounded by forest once more, but it was not the familiar miombo woodland they'd grown accustomed to seeing.

The forest was composed of all those trees and bushes and flowers that had failed the test of evolution before they'd been able to sow a single seed. Here grew unhealthy species that had existed only as a broken strand of DNA floating in the protoplasm of a cancerous gene. Some showed leprous, warty trunks. On others the thin bark had sloughed away to reveal what looked like bloody skin underneath. Mold and fungi grew everywhere, feeding on other plants and the roots of dying trees. Oak was reluctant to turn off the engine out of a sudden stomach-churning fear that once off, the car would never start up again. Olkeloki hastened to reassure him.

"It is only a machine, not unlike you and me. So long as our hearts function, so will this vehicle." He winced in sudden pain.

"Hey, you okay?"

The old man nodded slowly. "That was a strain."

"What was a strain? I didn't see you do anything."

"It was done and over with quickly, as it had to be. One instant the way into the Out Of is malleable as gold; the next it becomes as unyielding as steel." He smiled weakly. "Be of good cheer, Joshua Oak. Now all will be made well again. We have succeeded. I will begin the preparations to seal the breach before it weakens further." Despite the feeble light and the cooler temperature Oak could see that the old man was sweating profusely. "A difficult passage swiftly accomplished. It is one thing to pass into the Out Of, quite another to do so in the company of three friends."

He had Kakombe hand him his calabash and a small leather sack from their stock of supplies, then opened the door on his side and stepped out. Merry held her breath, but nothing shot from the forest to blast the old man from the face of the earth.

"Wait in the car if you wish, but preparation will take a little time."

Keeping a wary eye on their surroundings, they joined him outside. Oak discovered he could look straight at the feeble sun. That didn't mean it couldn't damage his remaining eye, so he turned away from it.

Besides, the dim perfect circle looked too much like the dark muzzle of the Kalishnikov which had nearly ended his life.

It wasn't the first time he and death had brushed close by each other. There was the time in Idaho when the key had exploded in his eye, one rainy evening in the swamps of Louisiana, once in the Chicago ghetto. Each time he'd seen death looking at him, and each time it had waved and passed him by. Just as it had only waved from behind the Kalishnikov.

How long before casual acquaintance passed into permanent embrace? Peering into the depths of the diseased forest, he half expected to see his old friend moving back among the shadows. There were no sidewalks full of people here, no streams of life to separate them. This was the Out Of, and he knew it for a certainty that if he encountered the dark shade here it would not wave but would come smiling grimly to grasp him firmly by the hand.

"Here." Kakombe handed him his Makonde knife and spear. Oak slipped the leather thong that ran through the knife's handle over his belt. It bounced against his right leg but was not uncomfortable. A faint coolness seemed to radiate from the highly polished black wood.

Kakombe assumed a one-legged herder's pose, using his own spear for balance. Oak kept shifting his own weapon uncomfortably from hand to hand. No matter how he held it, it still felt like a garden rake. No doubt it was a unique weapon, able to kill even shetani, but he still wished for the solid butt of a .38 in his palm.

"I've got to make a pit stop," Merry announced.

"Go behind the car. I won't watch and neither will Kakombe."

"Not on your life. Olkeloki's over there muttering to himself and drawing pictures in the dirt."

"Well, if he's drawing in the dirt then he won't pay any attention to you either," he said irritably.

"I've always been convinced that men and women have entirely different notions as to what constitutes privacy. Maybe it comes from using different sides of the brain." She pointed to a large pale-gray bush. Limp blue flowers trailed from drooping branches to lie flat upon the ground, as though the entire growth was suffering from heat prostration. "I'm going behind there. Nobody look."

At what, Oak thought as she walked away. His first wife had been like that. It wasn't enough that you didn't look into the bathroom when it was in use. You weren't supposed to look toward the bathroom, either. He glanced skyward. The sun had moved slightly westward but also a little north. Maybe it just wandered haphazardly across the sky here and never set. The twilight was bad enough.

Then he noticed the small bulges which had begun to cut into both sides of the sun. Two moons, or a single moon moving in opposite directions until it met itself coming? What would happen if the first was the case and the two collided in front of the sun? Fireworks? Disconcerting to contemplate.

He left Kakombe standing storklike and walked around the Suzuki. Olkeloki had cleared a small area of weeds and large rocks. The laibon now squatted in the center of the circle, inscribing symbols and words in the dirt with the butt end of one of Nafasi's spears. He barely glanced up at Oak.

"The seal must be made secure on the first try, Joshua Oak."

"How can you seal up something we didn't even see?"

"You did not see it. That does not mean it wasn't seen. Do you still pine for your dynamite?"

"Wish I had a few sticks. The air here stinks. Makes my skin crawl."

"In the Out Of everything crawls, even electrons. Cells crawl, nuclei crawl. Everything here is sick, or it would not be here. It would be in our world. Here even the strong force is weak, and particles have bad flavor and weak color."

"I can't figure you, old man. Haven't been able to since the day we met. Just when I've got you pegged as pure witch doctor you up and slap me with talk like that."

The laibon smiled as he continued working with the dirt. Now he was setting carefully selected pebbles from his leather sack in small hollows he'd scooped from the soil. When all the hollows had been filled, he began covering them up.

"Today's science is yesterday's magic, friend Oak. Today's magic is tomorrow's science. All disciplines are tangent and the differences between them often nothing more substantial than semantics. Scientists or laibon who dismiss conclusions out of hand because they do not countenance the methodology utilized to reach them forfeit their title. Energy arises out of learning, not contempt."

"Is that what you're trying to produce here? Some kind of energy?"

Olkeloki laughed softly. "Your cultural background will not let you get away from the concept of explosion as savior. Ah well. What I am trying to produce is something that has not been produced before. Different laws to achieve a similar end."

"Magic?"

"Magic, science—it is results we seek, not definitions."

Magic. Surprising how natural and unthreatening it sounded. All you had to do was say it. Like "love." Now, why should that analogy occur to him?

Olkeloki kept working his way around the little clearing, never rising from his squatting position. He must have muscles of iron in those lean thighs, Oak thought admiringly. Consider what the old man had accomplished already: not only had he made it into the Out Of, he'd cajoled three others into coming along with him. This in spite of his advanced age.

"I asked you how old you are. You never have told me."

"I look younger than I really am, Joshua Oak." He spoke without lifting his gaze from his work. "How old do you think I am?"

"I never was real good at guessing ages. Seventy-five? Eighty?"

Olkeloki chuckled to himself as he drew three lines between several buried pebbles. "I am seven hundred and seventy-six years old, my friend. As I have already told you, my father was a great laibon. My mother was a therasi, a water spirit. I was born in the year 1210 on an island in Lake Victoria during a raging storm. My father was a poor swimmer, but a great lover."

Oak just stared at him for a moment. Then the corners of his mouth lifted slightly. "I thought you went to school in England. Oxford, wasn't it?"

"That's right." Briefly the old man's expression turned wistful. "How well I remember the lectures and exciting debates, with myself the only 'Moor' in the student body. I particularly recall the days when Roger Bacon came to lecture to us, often reading from his *Opus majus* or *Opus tertium*. He was a great one for prophesying, Roger was, and I tried to teach him a little of the Maasai way of looking into the future. He was good with the stars and the rocks, but he hated milk. He did rather well at predicting: aircraft and telescopes, steam engines." Olkeloki shook his head sadly. "No one believed him, of course. I tried to tell him to quit the Franciscans, but he preferred to stay and argue. He was a great arguer, but stubborn."

"Okay, so don't tell me how old you are. But if I happen to guess it right, will you let me know?"

The laibon's smile returned. "Yes, Joshua Oak, if you guess it I will tell you."

Oak was about to guess eighty-three when something heavy slammed into his back, nearly knocking him off his feet.

"I didn't see it," a voice rasped as he turned.

"Christ." Oak had to catch Kakombe to keep the senior warrior from falling. Despite Oak's support the giant dropped to one knee. Blood was dripping from his fringe of ochre braids. A glance was enough to locate the bruise on the back of his head.

"I did not see it," he mumbled again.

Oak looked past him, past the car. "Where's Merry?"

Olkeloki left off his preparations and rose to stare in the same direction. "I fear they've taken her."

Oak found he could hardly mouth the word. In this place it sounded doubly obscene. "Shetani?"

"Not necessarily. Many nightmares besides shetani inhabit the Out Of."

"She tried to scream, to tell me." Kakombe swallowed, rose shakily to his great height. "I heard a muffled noise from behind the bush she had chosen. I went to look and something struck me from behind. I did not hear it coming. I am shamed."

"Probably jumped you from a tree." Olkeloki lectured the warrior sternly in Maasai before switching back to English for Oak's benefit. "Didn't you think of that when you went to check on her?"

"I could not look everywhere at once. I have only two eyes." His tone was surly, but he was angry at himself, not the old man.

Oak turned to stare into the forest, into the fetid recesses and lavender shadows. So Merry was gone. What did he really know about her, anyway? Oh, they'd shared some hard times together these past few days, but he'd shared difficult times with several female agents. In that respect the experience of the last week wasn't unprecedented. The important thing, the only thing that really mattered now, was to make sure Olkeloki was allowed to complete his work. Merry Sharrow had been a reasonably rational gal. She'd concur with that opinion.

Anyway, it didn't matter. Finding her in those nightmare woods would be impossible. Anyone foolish enough to plunge blindly in there would never come out again. Gallantry was one thing, stupidity another.

"I'm going after her," he heard himself saying. At least, it sounded like his voice. "I have to try."

For a moment Olkeloki was silent. Then he nodded briskly. "Yes, of course you must look for her."

"Kakombe, you stay here with the laibon."

"The laibon can look after himself," Kakombe replied sharply. "She was my responsibility. I was looking after her and I did not look good enough. I am coming too."

"Hey, man, I said stay here. I mean it."

Kakombe stared down at him. "If the two of us fight now, ilmeet, only the shetani will benefit. Also, I do not want to have to hurt you."

Oak backed off a couple of steps, crouched slightly. "I've brought down bigger trees than you, Kakombe. Don't make me prove it."

"Both of you go." Olkekoki sounded disgusted and Oak suddenly found himself feeling foolish instead of macho. "Draw the shetani to you, as you will, and I will be safe enough here. You must try to find Merry Sharrow and bring her back. She must be here when the time comes. She is part of this." He glanced at Kakombe.

"Do not disdain the ilmeet. He is deceptive and cunning." His gaze shifted back to Oak. "You will need Kakombe to track. From what I know of your country that is a skill most ilmeet are not adept at."

Steppe Maasai and metropolitan man glared at each other. Then Oak made a face and gestured with his spear toward the forest. "We're wasting time arguing."

"That is something about which I will not argue." Kakombe retrieved his weapons and together they headed into the woods.

Perhaps the senior warrior was the better tracker, but Oak was no stranger to the forest himself. In any case one didn't have to be an expert to follow the trail of Merry's abductors. Branches littered the ground and the grass and fungi had been beaten down. There were numerous tracks. None of them were faintly human.

"A child could follow this." There was contempt in Kakombe's voice.

"Olkeloki never said the shetani were subtle. No reason for them to be, here. This is their place."

"*If* shetani have taken her. Come."

Oak had always taken care to stay in shape, but Kakombe set a relentless pace and the smaller man had to exert all his energy to keep up. Suddenly he pulled up short and slapped at the back of his neck. Kakombe turned impatiently.

"Tsetse flies here too? I am not surprised."

Oak stood there and inspected the hand he'd slapped with. There was no blood or crushed chitonous carcass. He was breathing hard and his heart pounded against his ribs.

"Didn't feel like a tsetse. You're going to have to slow down, tall brother, or—ouch, damnit!" This time he slapped at his cheek. Kakombe grinned at him, but only for an instant. Then he was smacking his own shoulders.

Oak's hand came away damp, but not with insect blood. His head tilted back and something hot and sharp struck him on the nose.

Boiling rain.

They sought shelter beneath the expansive leaves of something that looked like a seborriac pandanus. The steaming drops sizzled where they struck the earth, yet none of the diseased vegetation appeared adversely affected. Some plants stretched out blasted flowers to suck the hot precipitation.

"God, what an awful place."

"No need to blame God," said Kakombe. "He will not get you out of this. I may."

"If you can fight as well as you can boast we might have a real chance. I've spent my life in tighter spots than you've ever dreamed of. So don't get tougher-than-thou with me, understand? Where I come from the prey carries guns and shoots back."

"That is not the same as killing a lion with a spear."

Apples and oranges, lions and radicals—you couldn't compare the two and Oak saw no point in continuing the conversation. They waited in silence beneath the sheltering leaves for the blazing storm to move on. Steam rose in clouds from the forest floor.

"I must ask you a favor before we go farther," Kakombe said quietly.

Oak shrugged. "Ask away."

"When this is done with, when the laibon has worked his magic and we are safely back in the real world, will you sleep with my first wife?"

Oak blinked, looked around sharply. "Say what?"

"It is because of your hair, you see. Maasai women have short hair and shave their heads, but someday I would very much like to have a girl child with long hair. If you will sleep with my first wife and let us keep the child I will pay you in cattle. Or if you must be paid improperly, in gold. The laibon is not the only one who knows where to find gold in Maasailand. My first wife, Eseyo, is comely and very enthusiastic. You would like her.

"I know from my time in your country that such unions are frowned upon by American wives, so I would make sure to obtain permission from Merry."

"Merry and I aren't married."

Olkeloki eyed him in surprise. "You're not? She is not your asanja?"

"Nope. We're just friends. We're only here together because the old man latched on to both of us at the same time."

Kakombe let out a Maasai whoop of exclamation, a cross between a whistle and a yelp, and unfolded himself from beneath the leaves. The rain had nearly ceased.

"Wonderful news! I do not need you to sleep with Eseyo. Merry and I can have a child of our own."

"Hey, whoa, hold on a second!" Oak scrambled to his feet. "Just because she and I aren't married doesn't mean you can sleep with her."

Kakombe looked back down at him. "Have you slept with her?"

"No, but I—"

"Is she betrothed to you?"

"Not exactly, but we—"

"Then do not tell me what I can and cannot do." He started forward.

Oak hurried to block his path. "Now wait just a damn minute. Stay away from Merry. She's been through a lot lately and she doesn't need any more complications in her life."

"We will let her decide if my proposal is a complication." The warrior took a step forward and again Oak confronted him.

"I'm warning you. Lay off her."

"If you are interested in bedding her, or wedding her, you may make her the same proposition. We will let her choose. If you are not that interested you should shut up. Get out of my way, ilmeet."

"You don't understand. Where we come from we don't—you can't just walk up to a woman and . . ."

"Are you interested in her or not?"

Oak considered the question, enveloped in the stink of rotting vegetation and otherworldly purple twilight. Hadn't he come along on this crazy odyssey as much to look after innocent, naive Merry Sharrow from Seattle as for the gold and jewels? Hadn't he wanted to take her out from the time he'd first set eyes on her back in Washington? They'd been through a lot together and that was no lie, was it? Didn't that count for something? He'd been dodging his feelings about Merry Sharrow ever since they'd left Heathrow. Now this African herdsman with the Boston education was forcing him to confront them. Hell of a note.

So—how *did* he really feel about Merry? Was his interest in her honest and heartfelt or just macho-proprietary? Did he want her or did he just want to deny her to Kakombe? And was the Maasai voicing intentions he, Oak, hadn't had the guts to put into words?

Ten years of phone calls in the middle of the night. Ten years of hiding out and pretending to be people he wasn't, all in the line of duty. Was it possible to fall in love with a woman *before* you went to bed with her? Could he have fallen in love with silly-strong Merry Sharrow when he wasn't looking? Damn Kakombe, anyhow! Damn him for his forthrightness and his uncomplicated attitudes, and damn him for forcing an examination of emotions easier left glazed over.

Okay, so he'd face himself for a change. He'd tell Merry as soon as the moment presented itself. He hadn't waited too long. He ought to thank Kakombe for forcing it out of him.

"You bet your ass I'm interested in her," he said finally. "And as soon as I get the chance, I'm going to ask her to marry me."

"Excellent. And I will ask her the same, and we can let her choose between us."

Oak started to laugh, held back. It wasn't Kakombe's fault. He just didn't understand. Merry wouldn't have anything to do with him. Oh sure, they were friends and all that. You didn't bounce around in the rear seat of a four-wheel drive for days without making friends with your neighbor. But the herdsman-warrior was a member of a primitive, tradition-ridden African tribe. Maybe he knew English, and maybe he'd had a taste of formal Western education, but he was utterly unsophisticated in other matters. He didn't have a thing to offer Merry Sharrow, who'd lived a sheltered middle-class life in Seattle, Washington. Just because he was nearly seven feet tall and muscular and pretty good-looking and articulate and brave and considerate and thoughtful and exotic and . . .

All of a sudden Oak didn't have to work to hold back the laughter.

Evidently Kakombe had been watching him carefully. "Strange. First you are angry, then confused, then amused. Now you look uncertain again. University or no, I will never understand the ilmeet."

That made Oak smile again. He started to chuckle, then to laugh quietly.

"Amused again. What do you find so funny in this unwholesome place?"

"Me. You. Us. Both of us dancing for days around the fact that one member of our party is an attractive lady."

"I thought Merry was your woman. Otherwise I would not so have danced."

"Elephant crap. I don't buy that. You didn't know how to handle it and neither did I. It's damn ironic. In this place we both ought to be scared shitless. Instead we're standing here arguing over a woman."

"There is no special time or place for arguing over a woman, Joshua Oak. Any time or place will do. You learn that as a junior warrior." He kicked at the dirt, gazed off into the woods. "I have been tracking too fast for you. It was intentional. In trying to make you smaller, I was trying to make myself the bigger man. That is the wrong way for an Alaunoni to act. You take the lead, friend Oak, and I will follow. If you make a wrong turn I will still be able to correct our path from behind. In this way you can set your own pace and will not get too tired."

"Who says I was getting tired?" Oak turned angrily and pointed off between two trees. "That way, damnit."

Kakombe approved. "You have done some tracking yourself. I never met an ilmeet who knew how to track." They started down the path Oak had chosen. "What animals have you tracked, my friend?"

"Only the two-legged kind."

Kakombe considered this, then nodded solemnly.

The forest grew thicker around them, slowing their progress. Unnatural sounds filtered through the trees, cries of birds that weren't birds and small broken things that hugged the earth in fear. Tiny eyes glared at them from between leaves and branches. They glowed red-orange and occasionally a faint bilious green.

Once they stumbled into a school of silver-sided fish swimming through the damp air. All of them showed the imprint of an unknown aquatic disease. They raced away to the south, flying beneath the trunks of tortured trees. As they passed beneath an overhanging branch they were attacked by half a dozen sparrow-sized birds. The birds sang as they struck; harsh, rasping notes. Their oversized eyes bulged out of their sockets. Except for their unevenly feathered wings their small bodies were naked and pink, and they sliced at fish-flesh with minuscule needlelike teeth.

The aimless sun did not set, but it did plunge lower on the horizon. In the gathering darkness a swarm of tiny white-glowing shapes feasted on the corpse of a three-legged quagga. The quagga's stripes were as uneven and broken as its body, a mutated version of its recently extinct self. Oak and Kakombe detoured around the bloated corpse, whose smell rose even above the perpetually rank atmosphere. As they circled, all the glowing grub-things paused in their feeding. They rose on their hind legs and began to sway back and forth in unison, their tiny black jaws leaving phosphorescent trails in the air. A faint breathy whistling rose from their collective throats. Oak felt the gorge rise hot and sour in his throat, and was glad when they'd left the concourse of maggots behind.

What happened then should not have shocked or surprised him, but it did. Olkeloki had tried to warn him that they might encounter other things in the Out Of besides shetani and dancing maggots and flesh-eating sparrows. Blasphemous horrors that might manifest themselves at any time, without warning.

Stunned, he turned to seek support from his powerful companion, but Kakombe had vanished. The senior warrior was nowhere to be seen. Convulsively clutching the ebony spear, Oak stumbled backward until he felt the unyielding bulk of a tree against his spine. His throat had gone dry and his legs trembled. He was alone against them, all alone this time with no help in view. They'd been sniffing after him for years and now their time had finally come. They were going to get him. There was no escape for him here, not in this dark, alien place. And there were so *many* of them! Somehow he hadn't thought that when they finally came for him there would be so many.

His worst nightmare was a populous one.

26

In the forefront marched the whey-faced men in their white robes. Bloody crosses stained their cowls and breasts. Several of them held small burning crosses out in front of them, as though Oak were a vampire they sought to exorcise. The flames did not bother them because there was no meat on their bones. White skeleton hands reached out from skeleton arms that disappeared into the sleeves of white sheets. Beneath the cowls eyeless skulls grinned out at him.

He pushed away from the tree and tried to run, only to find the way blocked by a couple of hirsute, bent shapes. Their eyes were wild in anticipation of destruction. Two held guns and the third a cluster of dynamite on which the fuse was rapidly burning down. Oak retreated and nearly backed into a cluster of men and women clad in neat red, white, and blue uniforms. On each chest was sewn a black swastika.

They were closing in on him; all the extremists and murderers and political and religious fanatics, all the would-be usurpers and führers and emperors. He knew them all intimately. They were ready to kill and destroy because they didn't like the way the government interpreted the law, *their* law. They were ready to beat and maim because they were offended by their neighbor's skin color, or his beliefs, or the country his grandparents had emigrated from. They were all there, all the bigots and fanatics and throwbacks he'd helped to crush or humiliate with the truth or put behind bars. Dead minds, dead bodies, they'd come for him at last.

It didn't matter that he'd done what he'd done to uphold the right and protect the helpless. There was no right in this place, no truth or justice, and the only law was the law of the maniacally insane. Half faces, half skulls, all of them grinning at him while they mouthed empty slogans and curses and most of all, one name: *his* name. He couldn't hide his identity here, couldn't hide beneath a cleverly constructed false persona. Because this was *his* nightmare. One that wouldn't end until they'd torn the flesh from his bones to get at the soft, pulsating soul buried within.

There was no retreat. He lowered the spear and searched for an opening, even a tiny gap where he might have a chance to dart through before they descended on him. One of the white-robed figures came too close and he slashed sideways with the spear. The long blade sliced through sheet and bone but just like the real bigot the nightmarish form was a shade of, there was neither blood nor dampness, no real juice at all. The figure collapsed and Oak saw that it had no backbone.

A cry halfway between a whistle and a yelp split the air as Kakombe fell on them from behind, swinging the ebony spear in wide arcs. Phantom neo-nazis splintered under the force of the senior warrior's attack. Soulless fundamentalists burned in the hellfire they had reserved for all who did not agree with them.

Oak struck out with his own weapon, cutting a path to his friend. His nightmare tried to close in around him. A lesser man, one without Oak's experience and determination, would have gone down in the grasp of those clutching, groping fingers. A giggling mouthless horror wrapped long arms around his waist. He cut it away. Then a strong arm was pulling, then pushing him back into the woods and he was running, running hard and sucking in the thick, cloying air as though it blew straight off the clean, salty Atlantic. Each stride away from the nightmare seemed to add strength to his legs.

Only when they finally stopped deep in the forest did he realize how weak he really was. He had to sit because he could no longer stand. As he lay on his back staring up at the purple sky he realized it wasn't the skeletal hands or flames or ghostly weapons which had threatened him. It had been the presence of so much unadulterated evil, so much mindless hatred. It had been sucking the life out of him and he hadn't even realized it at the time.

But it didn't seem to have affected Kakombe.

"Not my nightmare." Viewed from the ground, the warrior resembled one of the tall trees more than he did a man. "The ilmeet have very strange dreams. It meant nothing to me, but I saw it would be best to attack it from behind. So I waited and then fell on the nightmare from a tree." He wore the satisfied look of someone who had finally managed to pay off a long-standing debt.

"Something struck at me from out of a tree and I thought it a good opportunity to return the favor."

Oak sat up, put his arms around his knees. "Damn good thing you did."

"Who were all of those people, anyway? Some looked like spirits, but stranger spirits than I thought even the ilmeet believed in. They were all dead."

"A lot of them don't look or act all that much different when they're alive." He extended his right hand and let Kakombe pull him to his feet. "Okay, I'm lost. Which way now, tracker?"

The senior warrior studied the wall of decaying vegetation, finally pointed. He took a step in the chosen direction, only to be restrained by Oak.

"Hang on. Didn't you hear that?"

"Hear what? If there was anything to hear, my friend, I would hear it before you. My ears are trained to forest sounds and yours are not. Come, we must—"

He broke off, listened hard. Had he missed the sound the first time? There was no mistaking it now. It was uncertain at first, but as they listened it grew deep and penetrating.

Oak could feel the Maasai's muscles quiver in the arm he'd grabbed as he wondered what kind of noise could frighten a giant like Kakombe. At the same time he realized how often during the past few days he'd come to rely on the warrior's common sense and strength.

The sound grew louder, until even Oak knew what it must be. Then he fell backward as something huge and yellow erupted from the trees on their left. Both men reacted instinctively, Oak reaching for the pistol that was not riding in its shoulder holster beneath his left arm, Kakombe dropping to one knee as he dug the butt of his spear into the ground.

Oak heard the senior warrior grunt as he absorbed the full weight of the lioness on the spear. By the time he rolled over and came up clutching his own weapon, man and beast were lying together on the ground. The dead animal had his companion pinned.

He laid his own spear aside and moved to help Kakombe. The warrior's ebony spear had pierced the still twitching body completely, the blade penetrating the heart to emerge between the shoulder blades. Together they heaved the tawny bulk to one side. Then it was Oak's turn to give the Maasai a hand up.

Breathing hard, Kakombe brushed dirt and mud from his left shoulder and the three parallel bloody gashes long claws had gouged in the skin. He stared at the dead lioness for a long time. Then he grabbed the butt end of his spear and tugged hard. It slid out smoothly. As the tip of the blade emerged from the broad chest, Oak felt a rush of cold air as the corpse exploded, knocking both men backward. Yellow-white fur struck him in the face. As he picked it out of his eyes and nostrils he saw that nothing remained of the muscular feline body; no bones, no blood or flesh. Only tufts of fur sifting down through the lavender light like yellow snow.

Come to think of it, even when Kakombe's spear had penetrated the powerful body there had been no blood. He recovered his own weapon, joined the warrior in staring at the place where the lioness had fallen.

Kakombe lifted his eyes from the spot to survey the encircling forest. Oak listened with him to the rising chorus of coughs and grunts. They heard also the distinctive mournful cry peculiar to lions, a sad and yet somehow still threatening sound.

The senior warrior wore an expression of calm resignation as he indicated a break in the vegetation. "Go that way, my friend. Find Merry. My fate is decided now, but yours and hers need not be. I will stay here and take them as they come. When I am dead they will occupy themselves with my body. That should give you time enough to go around." He smiled sadly. "I am sorry I will not have the chance to see which of us she would have chosen."

Oak's eyes darted from bush to tree, seeking stalking leonine outlines. "What the hell are you talking about? If we fight 'em back to back maybe we can hold them off. Spear them and they blow up, and these aren't your ordinary everyday spears. If we kill a couple more maybe that will discourage the rest. It doesn't sound like there are that many out there." The last he added to boost his own courage as much as Kakombe's.

"This pride will not be discouraged. I know where they come from and who they come for. They want me, friend Oak, and they will keep coming for me until I am theirs. Because this is the pride of the lion I slew."

Oak looked at him in surprise. "I thought you were kidding about that. Olkeloki told us lion hunting has been banned by both governments."

"That is so. It is a fortunate junior warrior who has the chance to prove his manhood in the old way. But we are still allowed to protect ourselves and our cattle from attack." He had turned away and Oak had to walk around him in order to see his face. What he saw there shocked him almost as much as had the attack by the ethereal big cat.

The senior warrior, the Alaunoni, was ashamed.

"Tell me what this is all about, Kakombe. I won't tell anyone else. You've got my word on that. I'm not Maasai anyway."

Both men continued to watch the trees as a reluctant Kakombe explained.

"Whether one seeks out a lion illegally to prove himself or slays one in the course of defending a herd does not matter. It is the killing that is important, the demonstration of bravery that identifies one as a true warrior according to ancient Maasai tradition. It is valued all the more nowadays because the opportunity arises so rarely.

"This happened many years ago. I was barely a junior warrior, helping to keep watch over my uncle's herd, when I heard the moan of a lion in pain. I should have gone immediately to the engang for help, but I did not. Instead I followed the sound. This was my first offense, for a herder does not leave his cattle unless he has no choice.

"I did not have to walk far to find him. It was near the water hole. The lion was an old male, very big, but he had been caught by the leg in a trap poachers had set to take eland. Close to him lay a dead impala which had been killed by another trap. Only the chance at such an easy meal had drawn such an old, wise male so close to the village. Now he had trapped himself alongside his chosen prey.

"All I could see when I looked at him was the glory that would accrue to me and my clan. I saw myself wearing the warrior's headdress which is fashioned from the lion's mane. So I killed him. He was still dangerous and he fought hard, but I had three spears with me. Trapped by the leg like that, he didn't have a chance." The senior warrior's sides were shaking now and tears were running down his cheeks. "I will never forget the way he looked at me."

He took a deep, unsteady breath. "When he was dead I released his leg and threw the trap far out into the water. Then I cut the leg several times with my knife to make it look as though the injury had been caused by a spear. Returning to the village I boasted of what I had done. The senior warriors and elders did not believe until they saw the corpse. I was awarded the tail and the mane as a sign of my prowess. Everyone acclaimed me a great warrior and hunter. To my surprise I soon found that the more they praised me, the smaller I felt. But I did not have the courage to admit to the deception. To this day I have told no one about this. Now, I have told you.

"That night no one slept in the village because of the lions. They moaned and cried until dawn and then they went away. I lay awake like everyone else, frightened in my bed—I, the great warrior! When I asked the village elder about it he told me the cries came from the dead lion's pride, his harem of females. They had stayed one night to mourn his death."

The moaning was loud on two sides now. They could advance or retreat, but Oak suspected the moment they broke and ran the lionesses would close in on them.

"The next day I went back to the water hole to make sure no sign of the trap remained. I happened to look up at a kopje, a pile of big boulders, which stood on the far side of the water. There were six females, all mature and healthy. Some sat on the rocks, others lay sprawled across the stones. They did not look at me but at the deep part of the water hole, where I had thrown the trap. I knew they were the wives of the old male I'd killed. They had not gone away like the elder said they would.

"I was too fascinated to move. Finally they looked up from the water, one by one, until all six were staring at me. There is no feeling on earth like that, friend Oak. Lions have two distinct stares. One is of disinterest. The other is the one they use when they are stalking prey. It is as cold as the stare of a snake and as single-minded as that of a machine.

"We stayed like that for a long time, myself and the six. Then they got up in ones and twos and wandered away. I never saw them again, but I never stopped looking for them, either." He gripped his spear and turned a slow circle, watching the trees. "Now they have come for me, with as many of their sisters as will be necessary. I must stand and meet them. At least this time it will be a fair fight."

"Listen to me, you crazy African! There's no such thing as a fair fight between a man without a gun and a lion, and I don't give a damn what Maasai tradition says. All the advantage is with the lion. So maybe one time the odds evened out a little. That lion, any lion, would've jumped you if you'd been bent over weaponless and taking a drink from that water hole. Besides, you said that lion was old and caught in a trap. If you'd gone off and left him he would've died there anyway; from infection, from starvation, or at the hands of the poachers who'd set the traps in the first place. Even if you'd been able to free him, with his age and the addition of a crippled leg a younger male would've taken his pride away from him anyway. Hell, he was probably thanking you for the quick death. To me it sounds like it was a mercy killing straight down the line."

"I should have tried to free him, yes. Then we could have met on even terms. But killing him while he was trapped like that was wrong. That is the way the ilmeet kill, with their high-powered rifles and telescopic sights. That is not hunting, not a fair fight. One might as well drop bombs from a plane."

Even as he finished, another one charged them. It exploded out of the brush on their right, where it had crawled while Kakombe had been talking. Oak saw massive white teeth coming straight for his throat.

This time two spears pierced the attacker. She blew up before she struck the ground, filling the air with drifting fur and the rapidly dissipating odor Oak would remember forever after as Essence of Cat.

"These aren't real lions. They're just air, fur, and stink. They're ghost lions, Kakombe. They can't be your pride. This is *your* nightmare, your old fears coming back to haunt you. The real lionesses, if they're even still alive, are back in the real world. None of my old enemies were real and neither are yours."

"Spirits they may be, but they can still kill. Go on, Joshua. Go after Merry and I will hold them here until I die."

"Like hell you will. You're feeling guilty for nothing. When you put that crippled old lion out of his misery you were doing him a favor. Not to mention protecting your people. Don't crippled lions become man-eaters?"

Kakombe seemed to hesitate. "Sometimes."

The bushes on their left began rustling. There was no more time for talk. Individuals having twice failed to bring down the prey, the lion spirits had decided on a shift in tactics. Four, a dozen, at least twenty of the powerful, lean bodies were stalking the two men. As they walked, their massive heads swayed from side to side in time to the secret lion music. Oak thought he could hear the *pad-pad* of heavy paws. A cloud of fur floated above them, as if they were moulting. The effect made the relentlessly advancing pride look like it was on fire.

They were not roaring now, not even moaning. Save for the tread of dozens of paws they made no sound at all. Even his pistol would be useless against so many, Oak knew. You'd need a full-size machine gun at least, or . . .

He had to fumble through both pockets before his fingers closed around the cigarette lighter. The lighter which his buddies at the Bureau had given him on his birthday and which he'd been too polite to refuse. It was a handsome thing, gold-plated, smooth and slick and sophisticated. Charles Boyer or Louis Jourdan might have used it to light a cigarette for Bette Davis. Oak found it handy to have around on camping trips and at barbecues. How well was it made? Well enough so that all the butane hadn't evaporated?

He flipped it open and flicked the switch. The result was an inch-long flame that burned steadily in the unwholesome light. By rotating the tiny, hidden wheel he was able to coax a tongue of fire nearly a foot long from the lighter. At that rate of consumption the butane would give out quickly.

Would the diseased vegetation burn? He passed the flame over the grass and fungi underfoot. Most of it felt greasy rather than wet.

It caught slowly at first. The fire that leaped upward was blue and indigo instead of red-orange. Bitter cold came from the vicinity of the intensifying blaze as he built a wall of flame between himself and the advancing lionesses while Kakombe guarded his back. His nose wrinkled at the aroma that rose from the burning vegetation: it smelled like rotting flesh. Where the indigo-blue blaze touched, it left behind grass and brush that had been frozen solid.

He'd gauged the slight breeze correctly; it blew the fire toward the lionesses and away from him and Kakombe. Fascinated, he touched a tall reed that had been kissed by the blue flame and quickly drew back his burned finger. The skin had frozen on contact while the reed crumbled like powder. It was the cold of absolute zero.

Frustrated by the indigo-blue barrier one of the lionesses took a run and leaped. Kakombe raised his spear but the apparition never cleared the flames. As they struck her she exploded, showering the retreating Oak and senior warrior with blue and yellow ice crystals.

Kakombe slowed and Oak grabbed his arm, trying to pull him along. It was like trying to pull a bus. The warrior was staring back toward the wall of flame. On the other side the lionesses snarled and spat, nipping at one another in their frustration.

"Come on, man, move it! You want to stay here and wait for the fire to die down?"

"But they came for me," he mumbled dazedly, "to revenge the old one I killed."

"If the old boy were here he'd be grateful. Use your head!"

"It is . . . destined." A hopeful Oak thought it sounded reluctant.

"Nothing's destined, damnit, except we're all going to die if you don't move your ass."

Kakombe blinked at him. "Maybe—yes. Maybe it is time for entomito ilmoran tooengejek." He replaced his trancelike look with a wide grin. "That means it is time to save the warriors with their feet." He increased his stride rapidly. Oak had to strain to keep up with him, but he didn't mind. He didn't mind a bit.

Behind them the lionesses roared furiously at having been defeated by the simple magic of an ilmeet.

27

The disappointed moaning of the lions had long since faded behind them when Kakombe bent low and called a halt. He wore a look of uncertainty.

"I hear roaring again, ahead of us this time."

Oak frowned. "Another pack, or could the others have circled around in front of us already? I don't hear anything."

The warrior led them cautiously forward, whispering as he walked. "It does not sound like the roar of a lion. It seems I should recognize it, and yet I do not. The shriek of a leopard is higher and this is not the sort of country favored by cheetahs. It could almost be a herd of hippo."

Oak conjured up an image of a herd of the big, lazy animals clustered along the shore of a river. "That's no problem, then."

"Speak only of what you know, my friend. Hippos kill more people each year in Africa than any other animal. Ignorant ilmeet think that because they look fat and friendly, they can approach closely and even pet them. Hippos are fat, but they are anything but friendly, and their teeth put a lion's to shame." He was straining to hear. "Certainly there are more than one of whatever they are."

As they moved through the sickly woods Oak picked up the sound too. Rumbles and growls, sometimes sharp and distinct, other times overlapping. He listened until he was positive.

"I know what it is." Kakombe glanced over at him in surprise.

"Those aren't animals roaring. They're motorcycles; big ones. Probably a lot bigger than you're used to seeing, which is why you didn't recognize the sound right away."

When the noise had increased to the point where they knew they were very near, they dropped and proceeded on hands and knees. They crawled beneath a series of bushes whose leaves had been eaten away by some kind of rust-colored spiderwort and almost fell over a sharp incline. The roar of the big cycles was almost deafening now.

Merry had been staked out in the center of the depression below. Straps secured her hands and wrists to pins buried in the ground. Her clothing was in tatters. The bikers were riding around her like so many movie Indians circling the proverbial settlers' wagon. Occasionally one of them would break from the circle and rush straight at her only to turn sharply at the last instant, his rear wheel showering her pinioned form with fresh dirt.

The cycles were all Harleys, of course, most of them chopped too radically for any human being to ride in comfort. Which didn't matter because the only human in the depression happened to be Merry. The demons and gargoyles atop the bikes looked like they had descended en masse from the battlements of Notre Dame Cathedral.

There were banshees with twisted, leering faces; homunculi with bat wings for ears and long forked tongues. Some had no noses and others glared out at the world through pupils that were vertical instead of round. All wore standard outlaw biker attire: denim jackets cut off at the shoulder and emblazoned with swastikas and death's heads, vests with fur-lined armholes, heavily scuffed boots decorated with hobnails and spikes. Some went hatless, others boasted Nazi helmets and leather caps. Heavy chains dangled from belts and shoulders.

One bowlegged yellow-faced parody of humanity abandoned his chopper to paw at Merry's body. His cackling companions chased him off with their bikes. One of them ran over her right leg and Oak heard her scream. He had to bite his lip until he tasted blood to keep from calling out to her. If he and Kakombe went charging wildly down the slope, Merry's nightmare would finish them as surely as it threatened to ruin her.

One swarthy demon took a run at Merry. His bike hit a rock and he flew one way, his machine another, much to the amusement of the others.

Suddenly Oak felt something stronger than fear for himself or concern for Merry: embarrassment. This was her nightmare. He felt like an intruder, a Peeping Tom spying on her deepest emotions.

"We've got to get her out of there," he rasped at Kakombe. "The next time one of those things rides over her she could lose an arm or a couple of ribs." He started to rise. Kakombe held him back.

"Now it is my turn to say use your head, my friend. There are too many. I see no guns, but there are many knives, not to mention claws and teeth."

"So what do we do? I'd rather take a chance than lie here and watch them cut her up."

Kakombe looked thoughtful. When he spoke again he sounded almost mischievous. "Do you think you can run as fast as a Maasai moran?"

"Depends on the circumstances. I'm faster than I look."

"Suppose you are being chased and are running for your life?"

Oak nodded. "Yeah, I think that would help me maintain a pretty fair pace. What've you got in mind?"

Kakombe turned. "We must return to an earlier place, an earlier nightmare. We must go back to where we were."

"Back?" Oak's expression reflected his confusion. "You mean the lions? The fire will be dying down. What if they're still around there?"

"That is what I am counting on."

Oak grasped what the senior warrior had in mind. It just didn't strike him as very promising. "Are you sure you want to try this? This is your nightmare we're returning to. The last thing most people want to do once they've shaken a bad dream is live it over again."

"It's the only way, my friend. Yes, it frightens me, but I cannot think of anything else to do. And we have no time." He gestured back toward the depression. Several of the demonic bikers were parking their machines. Those who had already dismounted were fighting and joking among themselves while pointing toward the helpless Merry.

Probably there was a better way, but Oak didn't manage to think of it as he followed Kakombe back into the woods, retracing their earlier headlong flight. Finding the place was easy; a broad swath of jungle had been reduced to icy powder. Indigo-blue flames flickered here and there, isolated cold hot spots. The air above the burn was arctic.

There was despair in the giant's voice. "They've gone."

"No, over there!" Oak pointed with the tip of his spear toward a still standing clump of high grass. Tawny outlines were visible within. He started jumping up and down and yelling. "Hey, you, lions! Over here! Come on and eat me if you can!"

This is without question the craziest thing I have ever done in my life, he thought. But he kept bouncing around and screaming. Next to him Kakombe was doing likewise, making loud whooping noises and whistling shrilly.

The heads of the two lionesses lifted simultaneously. The instant they settled on the source of the disturbance the curiosity in their eyes was replaced by a look as cold as the flames that still licked at the vegetation surrounding them. As they rolled onto their feet Oak saw other yellow shadows beginning to emerge from the woods behind them. One particular lioness was staring straight at him, her gaze shifting neither to right nor left as she advanced, like a bombardier locking on to her target.

Something rapped him hard on the shoulder: Kakombe's hand. The giant had begun to back up. Oak joined him, keeping his spear ready. As soon as the standing vegetation had closed in between them and the pride, they turned and took off.

Just pretend you're back in school running the 400, he told himself. Don't look back for the other runners and you won't lose your nerve. Nobody thought you were fast back then until you showed 'em otherwise, just like nobody thought you were smart until you proved it in class.

So if you're so smart, why are you doing this?

Kakombe ran alongside him, his huge strides eating up the ground like those of a giraffe. Oak knew the giant could outdistance him, was glad he chose not to. They would fight together, they would run together, and they would bring this off together. He prayed.

They slipped through brush and around trees. In the denser growth Oak had the advantage. Kakombe simply bulled his way through obstacles, but every time he had to run over something it took a little out of him.

Out of him, Oak thought. His own heart was beating against his chest, trying to force its way to freedom. His throat was dry and his lungs threatened to burst. A rawness was growing in his throat but he didn't slow down, nothing to it, just keep lifting those knees and planting those feet and hope that Kakombe doesn't take a wrong turn because if he did they'd run out of steam and vanish beneath a wave of big cats.

It was eerily quiet in the woods with the only sound the painful panting of the two running men. The pursuing lions made no noise. They were conserving their energy for the forthcoming kill. Only occasionally was the silence broken by the sound of brush being smashed down and heavy masses striking the ground.

They leaped together over the edge of the slope, arms windmilling to maintain their balance, and actually picked up speed as they half ran, half fell downhill. So sudden was their arrival and so intent were the demons on their amusement that the two men were in among the cloud of dust before anyone noticed their presence. One gargoyle whose belly hung down over his belt was just about to bestow his attentions on Merry when Oak slammed the butt end of his spear into its mouth. Splintered teeth and blood went flying. The obese monstrosity staggered backward and dragged two of its companions down into the dirt with it.

Merry tried to say something but her throat was gagged by dust and tears. All she could do was sob and try to choke out a few words as Oak slashed at her restraints with Nafasi's wondrous razor-edged knife while Kakombe stood prepared to fend off any assailants. Most of the demons were so drunk and occupied with their choppers they still hadn't noticed the intruders in their midst.

She was scratched and bruised over every inch of her body, but Oak didn't see anything that looked like a crippling injury. The serious wounds she'd suffered were mostly mental.

"You'll never get away," she finally managed to gasp. "There are too many of them. They'll kill you and me and Kakombe too."

"Maybe not," he snapped as his eyes hunted for a way out.

A green-visaged little horror with pointed ears, snaggle teeth, and the legend "Born to Haunt" stitched into the back of his frayed denim shirt intruded on the senior warrior's space. Kakombe's blade sliced through the demon's torso and lopped off the right arm at the elbow. Green blood spurted and the ghastly amputee launched into a wild, shrieking dance, splattering the noisome ichor over everything in sight.

This finally attracted the attention of the other bikers. They turned their machines inward preparatory to charging the interlopers. Kakombe readied himself and Oak planted his feet between the demonic horde and Merry. Engines raced hellishly.

The mechanical rumble was overwhelmed by an earth-shaking roar that shook most of the Out Of as thirty or more powerful muscular shapes poured over the slope above in a single leonine wave that smashed into the unwary demons with all the force of a fully loaded eighteen-wheeler going ninety per. Arms and legs, horns and heads went flying in all directions as the pride took out its accumulated frustrations and anger on the stunned demons. One bucket of banshee blood spewed across Merry's face. At any other time she might have reacted by shrieking till her lungs burst. Now she was all screamed out.

Oak cut the last of her restraints, got an arm under her, and helped her to her feet. She tried to take a step, stumbled.

"Come on, Merry, try!"

She doubled over and grabbed at her thighs. "Josh, I've got a cramp. I've been tied for so long—it hurts!"

He refused to let her stop. "One leg in front of the other. That's it. Use your brain first. Foot out, leg down, come on—move!"

It was hard to make himself heard over the squeals and shrieks of the demons and the roaring of the lions. Kakombe stayed close to fend off any of the bikers who might venture close, but there was little work for his spear. The demons weren't interested in them. They were starting to scatter in panic as one nightmare preyed upon the other.

Oak watched as one scrawny gargoyle tried to claw its way up a steep slope. A lioness grabbed its leg in her mouth and dragged it,

wailing and screaming, back down into the depression. As soon as she
got him to the bottom she freed the leg, put both paws on the demon's
chest, and clamped her huge jaws around his throat. It didn't take long
for him to suffocate. The last Oak saw she was carrying the dead demon
off in her mouth, the body dragging limply along the ground, the head
lolling free.

"It's getting better, Josh. I can feel the muscles loosening up and
I'm starting to get some feeling back." He removed his arm and let her
walk by herself. By the time they reached the top of the low bluff she
was jogging a little.

"They grow 'em tough in the North Woods," Oak said as he smiled
encouragingly at her. She grinned weakly at him through the grime and
trailing hair that covered her face. She was exhausted and hurting, but
she didn't ask to stop and rest. Not with hell only a few yards behind.

The woods closed in around them, muffling the circus of carnage
that was taking place back in the depression. Both men kept their eyes
open for any stray lionesses whose fury hadn't been sufficiently sated
by the taste of gargoyle flesh. With each step away from her tormentors
Merry gained confidence and strength. Eventually she'd recovered
enough to explain what had happened to her as they jogged back toward
the river.

"About ten years ago I got stuck in a small town south of Tacoma.
I was just out of high school. I was having breakfast in this little coffee
shop when a whole gang of real bikers pulled up outside. Not movie
types; the kind who trade runaway girls around and sell dope outside
junior highs. They were all laughing and joking when they came in. The
one old waitress and I were the only women in the place. They ordered
coffee and rolls and stuff and kept looking at me and whispering. I was
too scared to get up and leave because I would've had to walk right
past them.

"But nothing happened. Just a lot of leers and comments. Nobody
spoke to me and nobody tried to touch me. Aren't nightmares always
worse than the realities they're based on?"

Oak recalled his own. "Not always."

It had been a while since they'd heard a distant shriek or muted
roar. Goddamn, he thought excitedly, we may actually get out of this.

Sure. Out of it into what? They were still trapped in the Out Of.

Olkeloki had better be about finished making his magic, Oak
mused, because he was ready to take the car and burn rubber racing
back the way they'd come. At that moment he'd have traded his whole
pension for a glimpse of pure blue sky.

Merry was still rambling. "I thought I'd forgotten that. I guess there
are things the mind stores away in secret places and only drags out
when you're least expecting them."

"Yeah. Did we get there in time? It *looked* like we got there in time."

"Just in time, I think, though I was so out of it when you two showed up I don't know if I would've felt anything. I'm sure it would've been worse than the airplane, though. God, I feel like I'll never be clean again!"

If it hadn't been for Kakombe they would have burst tired and sweaty out into the clearing where they'd left the four-wheeler parked. And if they'd done that, everything they'd accomplished up to that point, everything they'd battled and overcome to reach Ruaha—penetrating into the Out Of, fighting off nightmares—all would have been lost, and the rest of the world with them.

Maasai senses were functioning at peak efficiency. Kakombe heard in time and ordered them to drop where they were standing. They lay motionless for a long moment. Then he gestured for them to continue crawling forward.

The little Suzuki rested where they'd left it. Mbatian Olkeloki stood nearby, looking calm and composed.

A dozen gleeful shetani were dancing a circle around him.

28

While Oak and Kakombe had been occupied trying
to rescue Merry, the shetani had found and trapped the one person in
all the world who represented a threat to their plans. They formed the
circle with their bodies and linked arms. From time to time two of them
would drop those attenuated limbs and mockingly invite Olkeloki to
walk out of the circle. He stood motionless among the celebrating
horrors, ignoring their taunts.

Fifteen feet in front of the four-wheeler Olkeloki had built a rock
cairn. Atop it rested a single clay pot. Indecipherable inscriptions
decorated its sides and within the singular vessel a small fire burned
steadily. The cairn stood in the center of the inscribed circle the old
man had been working on when Oak and Kakombe had gone after
Merry.

At first Oak was surprised they hadn't destroyed the cairn, scattering the carefully placed stones and shattering the firepot. Then he
saw that from their point of view this was better, this taunting and
teasing of the human who dared pursue them to their sanctuary.

Kakombe gestured for them to rise and attack, but Oak shook his
head no. The senior warrior whispered excitedly. "Remember how it
was on the slopes of Ol Doinyo Lengai. We will charge them again and
they will flee."

"Maybe they will—and maybe they'll turn and tear us to shreds.

This is their world, not ours, and there's no platoon of laibon to back you up this time. There are only two of us." Kakombe stared back at him, then nodded ruefully. A wild charge was the last resort of the tactically ignorant.

Most of the shetani were human-sized or smaller, but there was one giant that stood a good ten feet high standing off to the side watching the rancid dance. Its knuckles dragged the ground and its lower jaw flapped loosely beneath the upper. Vacant, bulging eyes looked down on the ring of its prancing, cavorting cousins. Oak did not envision it fleeing in panic from a couple of puny, spear-wielding humans.

"This time we use a little ilmeet strategy. You know what a diversion is for?"

Kakombe sneered at him. "Ilmeet think they invented everything."

"I stand corrected. See if you can slip around behind them, and stay away from that big one. Merry and I will try to get to the car. As soon as you've found a spot you like, start trying to draw their attention. Maybe you can get them after you."

The Alaunoni considered this. "I have a better idea. Why do you not sneak around to draw their attention while Merry and I run to the car?"

"Because you're better in the woods than I am and I'm better behind a wheel than you are."

Kakombe reluctantly agreed. "I see what you have in mind. It is a good plan, but one that must work the first time because we will not live to try it a second."

The two men shook hands. Then Oak and Merry watched as the warrior disappeared into the thick brush surrounding them. Taking her hand, Oak headed in the opposite direction, keeping low.

"I'm glad Kakombe thinks this is a good plan," he whispered to her, "because I'm not so sure. But it was all I could think of."

"Of course it's a good plan, Josh. It'll work. It has to work. We have to get those creatures away from Olkeloki so he can do whatever it is he plans to do." She tried to pull away from his grasp. "Hey, take it easy. I'm not going to fall behind."

"Sorry." He released her fingers. As he did so he took a long look at her. Her skin was filthy. What remained of her makeup had been smeared all over her face, which was scratched and bruised. Dried blood stuck to her upper lip and there was a large black and blue lump on her forehead where one of the demons had struck her. Her hair resembled the branches of a thornbush. Sweat poured from her temples down her neck, staining what was left of her blouse.

Oak wore the look of someone who'd just found a ruby the size of a hen's egg in his mailbox.

She made a face at him. "What's wrong with you? What are you staring at?"

"You. You're beautiful."

"And you're a damn liar, but I think you're beautiful too."

"I love you, Merry."

"I love you back. Wonder when that happened?" She grinned delightedly at him. "We'll talk about it later."

"There may not be a later. If there's one thing I can't stand it's leaving either my office or my life in a mess. I think Kakombe loves you too."

"I know, but I'm into a different lifestyle. You think he'd take a steady city job and settle down in Seattle?"

"Unlikely."

She nodded. "That's what I think. We'll have to name our first boy after him. Kakombe Oak. Won't that turn heads in school?"

"Hey, what's this about kids? I don't remember proposing."

"Foregone conclusion. Hell of a time to start arguing."

"I wasn't arguing, I was just—You realize we may both be dead in a few minutes?"

"Then it's good to get the important things out of the way." This time she took *his* hand.

They'd almost reached the shore of the sand river. "Funny how life sneaks up on you when you're not paying attention to it," he whispered to her. They were still holding hands. "I came along to watch out for you. Didn't think it would turn into a permanent gig."

"Tough. You'd better get used to the idea. Just like you'd better get used to the idea of living in the north woods. I'm not moving to an eastern city."

"What happens if I don't like your hometown?"

"Oh, you'll like it. It's peaceful and quiet and green. You'd be surprised how fast you can get used to stuff like that."

"Maybe you're right, but let's hold off picking out the furniture and wallpaper until we see if we can get out of here without having our hearts ripped out."

A bloodcurdling whoop rose from the woods directly opposite the circle of shetani. The dancing slowed. A fist-sized rock flew out of the trees to strike one of the man-sized apparitions in the back of what passed for its head. It staggered, then angrily put the bite on its unoffending neighbor. The two fought wildly for a moment until they were separated by a third. The lot of them began gibbering at one another.

Kakombe appeared on the edge of the clearing. Several of the arguing shetani noticed him. As soon as he had their attention, the senior warrior bent over and pulled up his toga, wiggling his backside at them with insulting abandon.

"Come then!" he yelled through his legs. "Come and see how a Maasai can run!" He dropped his toga and dashed back into the woods.

A chilling ululation poured from inhuman throats as the shetani rushed after him. As they ran and hopped and stumbled into the trees, the ten-foot-tall giant lumbered forward to gently but firmly enfold Olkeloki in its arms and hold him in place.

Run fast, tall brother, run fast, Oak thought solemnly. "Let's go," he told Merry.

Keeping low, they headed for the car. The giant shetani continued to stare blankly into the forest. It was almost too easy. Oak opened the door quietly and peered inside. The key was still in the ignition. Sliding into the front seat, he reached down to start the engine. As he did so he happened to glance into the rear-view mirror just in time to duck away from the sharp claws that were clutching at his throat. They tore harmlessly into his shirt as he fell on his side and rolled.

Staring over the back of the seat at him was a grotesque, lopsided shetani face. It, or rather she, wore Merry's spare blouse. Long thin breasts pushed pendulously against the fabric. Merry's only necklace hung slack from the narrow neck. Two earrings dangled from one rabbitlike ear and the rest hung from the drooping nose. The shetani had been going through Merry's backpack when Oak had slipped into the car and she'd just missed tearing out his jugular.

He lay paralyzed by the ghastly sight. Then those claws reached for him again and he was shocked into action. They dug into the seat where his head had been resting an instant earlier, penetrating deeply into the thick, tough upholstery. Jerking and bouncing like something out of a cartoon, the female shetani struggled to pull her claws free.

Oak's right hand was on the floor. He contacted something hard: the inside tool box. Shoving back the lid, he grabbed the first thing his fingers touched. As the shetani fought to free itself he brought the wrench up in a sweeping arc against the pinned arms. Both shattered under the force of the blow.

Letting out a scream of pain, the shetani yanked back both useless limbs. Thick, tarry goo that smelled like the residue from the bottom of an old cesspool dripped from both cracked joints. It scrabbled over the seat back, straining to reach him with its gaping mouth. Sharp teeth gleamed darkly, coming close. Filled with disgust and terror, he brought the wrench around sharply. More black syrup spattered and the horrible creature slumped down behind the seat.

Breathing in long, hard swallows he leaned into the back and flailed away at the voiceless monstrosity until he'd hammered it to a pulp, filling the four-wheeler with loud cracks and damp thuds as the wrench slammed again and again into the now unrecognizable body. Even after he'd pounded it into immobility, the glaring red-orange eyes continued to stare malignly up into his own. Only when he was positive it was dead and the glow had gone from its eyes did he force himself to reach back and grab it with his bare hands.

Ignoring the black goo that oozed over his fingers, he threw the battered corpse out of the car. One of the legs continued to twitch in a grotesque parody of life long after the body had struck the ground.

The door on the passenger side opened and he raised the wrench again, lowered it when he saw it was Merry. Her eyes bugged out and one hand went to her mouth.

"Jesus, what have you got all over you? I saw you throw that thing out. Is that what their blood is like?"

"I don't know what it is," he replied grimly. "Maybe they run on 10-40 oil."

She found a rag and started trying to wipe it off his arms. "My God it stinks."

"Wait till you see your backpack." He turned the key. The sound of the four-cylinder engine turning over cleanly was like the voice of a heavenly choir. Putting the Suzuki in gear, he tromped the accelerator and sent it barreling toward the towering shetani that held Olkeloki.

The monster held its ground as long as possible. At the last instant it flung the old man aside and swung at the oncoming car with both fists. The heavy blow dented the roof of the four-wheel but did not break through. Blessed are the steel-makers of the rising sun, Oak thought wildly.

The car slammed into the giant's left leg, slid sideways as if they'd struck a tree. When it came to a halt Oak found his nose was bleeding from striking the wheel. Gritting his teeth, he worked the gear shift and sent them roaring at it a second time. Out the side window he could see Olkeloki limping toward the rock cairn and its still-smoking clay pot.

This time when they hit the leg it was the shetani that fell backward.

It lay on the ground supporting itself on one arm while swinging the other wildly in the direction of the agile little car. Merry was watching the forest, but there was still no sign of the shetani who had been dancing around Olkeloki. Kakombe must be leading them a hell of a chase, she thought. It occurred to her they might never see the tall Maasai again.

Oak brought the four-wheeler around and ran over the fallen shetani's midsection. It struck weakly at them and the blow missed badly. When Oak drove over its head it stopped fighting, though individual body parts continued to jerk convulsively like the spring of a clock that refused to run down.

His breathing and heart slowed as he pulled up alongside Olkeloki. The old man ignored the car as he made repeated passes over the smoking pot with his open palms. He spoke without looking around.

"It is good to see you again, Joshua Oak. And you, Merry Sharrow. Alas, my preparations were interrupted, you saw by what. All is not yet in readiness. Join me."

Reluctant to abandon the comparative safety of the car, Oak and Merry nevertheless climbed out and approached the cairn. They weren't going anywhere without Kakombe anyway, Oak told himself.

Olkeloki chanted something in a language older than Maasai. The smoke rising from the clay pot thickened. Then he turned to Oak and extended a hand.

"We are nearly done. Now the triangle is ready to be completed." He was having a hard time standing, Oak noted. A tear showed in the blue fabric of his toga and there was a flash of red beneath. "The seal lacks only the final ingredients."

Oak anxiously scanned the forest for signs of the senior warrior. "What ingredients? I'm not carrying anything."

"The most important three, of course. The points of the triangle. Why did you think I insisted you come with me, Joshua Oak? Because of your strength and cunning? Because of your good looks? Why do you think you were made known to me?" His voice had changed somehow, Oak thought. Not for the first time it struck him that Mbatian Olkeloki was something more than a man and something less than a deity.

Hell, maybe he *was* almost eight hundred years old.

"Give me your eye, Joshua Oak. The false eye you have made part of you, the eye of glass you showed me that night when we sat and talked together on the banks of the Great Ruaha. It is imbued with all you have seen, with the knowledge of all the days you have struggled to help your fellow man. With the brilliance of day, for only the right sort of light can seal in the Out Of." He uncurled his fingers.

Without hesitating, Oak reached up and carefully removed his right eye. Hadn't the old man said once that Oak would be on his right when he needed him? He felt the cool air swirl into the vacant socket and wondered what Merry must be thinking, how she must be reacting inside. He would improvise a patch to cover the cavity as soon as he could and he had replacement eyes back home.

"I don't know what the hell you're talking about, old man, but here."

At that moment Mbatian Oldoinyo Olkeloki looked Oak straight in the eye. Once before he'd looked at him like that. Once before, back on E Street, after the riot. Had looked into Oak's right eye, just as Oak had imagined looking back out of it. He'd known, Oak suddenly realized. Way back then, he'd known!

As Oak looked on speechlessly the old man took the glass orb and rubbed it between his palms, murmuring softly to himself with his eyes closed. Then he dropped it into the smoking pot. Oak heard it shatter when it struck bottom and winced instinctively.

But if the old man's first request had been unexpected, it was nothing compared to the second. He turned slowly to face Merry. She was staring at Oak and the vacant socket in his face. That was understandable. There'd been no reason for him to mention the prosthesis previously.

Just as there'd been no reason for her to mention hers to him. As he stood and gaped dumbly at her she lifted her right hand and calmly plucked her beautiful left eyeball out of her head.

She handed it wordlessly to Olkeloki. "He knew," she whispered, not to Oak but he heard anyway, "he knew about my eye, and he knew about yours. I saw a shetani on the road. It disguised itself to look like a dog but I saw it as it really was. It tried to run me off the pavement, tried to kill me." She turned to face him. "Because it knew I had something, Josh. Just as Mbatian knew. It tried to stop me but it didn't." She looked back at the old man. "And then," she murmured in wonder and amazement, "I decided to go to Washington."

The old man just smiled at her. He must have repeated the rubbing chant and dropped the second orb atop the first, but Oak didn't see him do it. He was too busy staring at Merry, the man with the good left eye gazing silently at the woman with the good right one and neither of them knowing whether to laugh or cry.

"Thank you, Merry Sharrow," Olkeloki was saying softly, "for your false eye, the eye of glass that I saw as I lay in the street outside your chief's house. It is imbued with all you have seen, with all the knowledge of all the nights you have struggled to help your fellow man. With the knowledge of the dark where you have chosen to live, for only the right sort of light can seal in the Out Of."

Merry ignored him. She was talking to Oak, answered the question that did not need to be asked. "I was five years old. We were vacationing in the Cascades. I tripped and fell facedown on a log with a broken branch sticking out of it. That's all there was to it. I know how to use the muscles that surround the glass so well that people can't tell it from my real eye, but I still think it's one of the reasons I've always been so shy." Her voice rose slightly. "But *you*—you never . . ."

"No, I never told you. Just like you didn't tell me." Then a new thought made him turn from her to Olkeloki. "Wait a minute—there are *three* points to a triangle."

The old man nodded. "One has come from you, Joshua Oak, and the second from Merry Sharrow. Only the last remains to be added." So saying, he reached quickly upward with his fingers extended.

"No!" Both of the old man's eyes were real—he was sure of it. But even as he lunged at the laibon he knew he couldn't reach him in time.

Mbatian Oldoinyo Olkeloki's fingers did not touch his good right eye. They did not touch his good left eye. Instead they passed between and slightly above. As Oak and Merry stared, those long, limber digits penetrated an inch, two inches, a full three deep into the old man's forehead.

When he withdrew them they were cradling a third eye. The third eye that is more rumored than real, the extra eye that some people are thought to possess but which is never seen. He held it easily in his hand and as Oak stared at it he swore it winked back at him, for all that it had no eyelid.

Chanting softly, the old man rubbed it between his palms. Then he stepped forward and with great dignity deposited it in the smoking clay vesicle. This time there was no echo of breaking glass. Oak found himself unable to turn away and barely able to breathe.

Something was coming out of the pot.

The smoke gave way to pure white radiance, and then to a milky, opalescent glow. The air shimmered around it as it intensified and strengthened and finally became too bright to look at directly. It faded a little and Oak found he could squint at it through slitted eye. A Lilliputian thermonuclear bomb had gone off inside the pot, producing a minuscule mushroom cloud only a few inches across. Undoubtedly it was something else entirely, but he was using the only frame of reference he had.

The cloud expanded and filled with laser-intense color: blue and purple, green and red, orange and yellow and gold. And something else, a hue so distinct and unique Oak had no word for it. It paralyzed him with its beauty. He and Merry might have stood there staring forever had Olkeloki not taken them gently by the hand to guide them back into the four-wheeler.

"Look away now, my friends. It is time to leave before it concludes itself."

Merry spoke as though she'd been drugged. "B-e-f-o-r-e w-h-a-t h-a-p-p-e-n-s?" Oak was struggling with the ignition.

"Paasai Leleshwa."

She was about to ask him what it meant when movement in the trees caught her attention. "Look! It's Kakombe!"

That snapped Oak out of his haze. An eerie resonating hiss was

coming from the glowing clay pot, which somehow had not yet disintegrated under the impact of all that brightness. Olkeloki didn't have
to tell him not to look at it; he could feel the heat on the side of his
face and knew it didn't come from the shrunken sun overhead.

Kakombe had burst free of the woods and was racing toward them,
waving his ebony spear over his head. The sweat was pouring off him
in streams.

Flooding out of the forest behind him were more shetani than even
Olkeloki could imagine.

There were big shetani and small shetani, lanky gangling shetani
and squat muscular shetani. The grossly fat waddled forward among
columns of the anorexic, the top-heavy strode shoulder to shoulder
alongside the faceless. They covered the earth like a blanket, crushing
bushes, grass, trees, and anything else in their path. This was the horror
of the Out Of in all its relentless power. There was no end to it. Oak
tried not to stare but couldn't help himself. The tide of terror held its
own hypnotic fascination.

There must have been a million of them, and every one was after
Kakombe.

He let out a yell, one of those high-pitched Maasai war whoops,
and it galvanized Oak into action. Olkeloki piled into the back seat
next to Merry. As soon as the old man's feet left the ground Oak
slammed the car in gear and shot forward, the open door banging like
a cymbal against the jamb. He swung around sharply until they were
racing parallel to the sprinting senior warrior. The big trees were going
down under the shetani now as the Spirits of the Earth lumbered out
of the twilight. The ground shook under their weight. Dozens of smaller
shetani, chittering and gesticulating, rode atop each narrow-bladed skull
or dangled from those shovellike jaws.

No hope of fighting back anymore. All they could do was run and
hope the four-wheeler didn't give out on them. Kakombe grabbed hold
of the swinging door, timed his jump, and leaped into the seat next to
Oak even as his ilmeet brother rammed the accelerator pedal into the
floor. Sand and dirt flew in the faces of the nearest shetani, blinding
them as Oak swerved out of the path of the onrushing wave and headed
for the river.

Clutching the back of her seat to steady herself, Merry turned on
her knees to stare out the back window. Her gaze was caught by a tower
of intense colored light which was reaching for the sky like a tornado
straining to break free. The tide of shetani parted to spill around the
smooth-sided spire that was climbing heavenward from the belly of
Olkeloki's little clay pot, those in back running over and trampling the
ones up front.

Merry bounced off the ceiling once as Oak sent them careening wildly down the steep bank. As soon as they hit the sand he wrenched the wheel hard right. Swerving and sliding and picking up speed, they began to retrace their path back downriver.

"How far?" Oak asked Olkeloki. He had to yell in order to make himself heard over the stentorian hiss of the spire of light, which by now had climbed higher than the tallest tree, and over the hysterical babble of the shetani horde.

"Not far." The old man had joined Merry in looking out the back window. Now he spun and squinted forward. "It *cannot* be far. We do not have much time. I did not get the chance to thank all of you for rescuing me."

"Save it until the job's finished." In the rear-view mirror he saw the shetani spill into the sand river. Dozens were crushed by the weight of their fellows. Thousands more came skittering and running in mad pursuit of the fleeing car.

And something huge, something that dwarfed even the Spirits of the Earth, was coming after them under the sand.

He forced himself to focus on the river ahead. If they struck a hidden rock or concealed log now it would be fatal. Where the hell was the weakness, the tear in the fabric? The sand river seemed to stretch on to infinity, heat shimmering above the granular horizon. Some of the shetani were starting to gain on them, including the gargantuan unseen shape that was tunneling its way beneath the sand.

Abruptly the way was blocked. There was something in front of them. It was part shetani and part real and part something else, and it stood directly athwart the old tire tracks Oak was following. Even if he'd had the inclination to try to go around it, he didn't have the time. It had emerged from beneath the sand directly in their path.

It was at least as big as the four-wheeler. Massive paws sought purchase in the bed of the river. The magnificent black mane seemed fashioned from smoke. The wind whipped at it, tearing off bits and pieces and making its owner appear as though he were on fire. Eyes that were red-rimmed coals glared at them. When it roared Oak could feel the sand shift beneath the wheels and when it snarled it showed fangs the length of the blood-stained wrench bouncing on the floor of the car. The sound chilled his blood and turned his muscles to jelly, but somehow he held on to the wheel.

Muscles went taut beneath titanic shoulders. Oak heard a weak voice whisper behind him: Mbatian Olkeloki.

"Keep going. Do not stop now, do not turn away, or we are finished."

The blockading figure loomed larger and larger, until it blotted out the sky and sun and sand river altogether. Oak's last words were, "The son of a bitch is as big as a house!"

Then it leaped at them, its mane blotting out the horizon, claws reaching for the hood, jaws agape. A long black tongue licked out to wipe away the windshield. The glass went without a sound, not so much shattered as vacuumed away. Oak threw up his hands to protect his face. As he did so an impossibly bright light filled his eye all the way back to his brain.

The last voice he heard was Olkeloki's sighing, "Ahhh—Paasai Leleshwa," and then, "This is *my* lion . . ."

29

Oak awoke to the sight of flames, but contrary to his first thoughts it wasn't the world that was on fire. He tried to sit up, decided it would be better just to lie still for a few moments. No endless wave of giggling, taunting shetani was trampling him underfoot. No drooling half-faced abomination was chewing on his feet.

Furthermore, the flames were a reassuring red-orange instead of indigo-blue. They gave off warmth instead of cold. Smoke rose into a pale-blue sky and the sun shining down was an old friend newly won.

Eventually he decided to try sitting up. It worked, but it cost him. It felt like unseen thugs had worked him over from head to toe while he'd lain unconscious. Every muscle, every tendon and ligament in his body had been pounded like taffy, until the ache was something solid he felt he could spit out if only he knew how. His bones had been kneaded like dough.

The fire he'd seen was rising from the corpse of the four-wheeler. It lay twenty yards away in the middle of the sand river, its windshield gone, the frame bent and broken, a blackened, burned-out hulk the same color as its tires. Oak knew exactly how it felt. Those of their supplies that hadn't been cremated lay scattered all over the river. What had happened? He tried to remember.

The lion. The great black-maned lion. Olkeloki's lion, the old man had claimed. And the light, a wonderful, incomparably bright light the color of—the shade of—he was damned if he could remember. Olkeloki had called it something in Maasai.

No fanged colossus bestrode the sand now, and the only light was the gentle light of the real sun. He was alone on the riverbank with only the smoking Suzuki, bits and pieces of their personal possessions, and Africa for company. No shetani. Where were the shetani? In the Out Of.

Whatever that crazy, wonderful old man had done had worked.

Rising painfully, he brushed dirt from his pants. A long groove in the sand led from the burning skeleton of the four-wheeler to where he was standing. It occurred to him that his body was the missile which had cut the groove. Something had thrown him out of the car with tremendous and yet carefully controlled violence, to fetch up against the riverbank. Several small bushes had further cushioned the impact.

There was something near his left foot. Ignoring the protests of his back, he bent to pick it up. It was a tan polyurethane bottle with a white cap and a familiar legend.

SOLARCANE SUNSCREEN

Too tired to laugh, he tossed it into the shrubbery. A couple of young male impala were pacing the far bank, nibbling at the fresh green grass that grew in the shade of the trees. Healthy grass, healthy trees. He wanted to kiss the one standing next to him. As he stared, one of the impala raised its delicate doelike head to give him the once-over before returning to its grazing. The burning four-wheeler they ignored. Oak watched them until they disappeared into the forest.

There ought to be a wake for the car, he mused. It had carried them in safety to places its builders had never dreamed of. Its death meant a long, hot walk back to the river camp.

Better look for the others. Could he walk? He put one leg in front of the other without falling down. Not bad. He tried it again, steadying himself by holding on to a low-hanging branch that reached out over the river. The branch was already occupied by an agama, a bright turquoise blue and red lizard a foot long. It bobbed its head at him a few times before whirling to vanish back among the leaves. Its proper prey consisted of insects, not people.

He was debating whether to try sliding down the sandy bank when the bushes off to his right began to rustle as something big came toward him. All he could do was watch its approach, be it lion, leopard, shetani, or some other toothy antagonist. He was too tired to run and too weak to put up any resistance.

"We made it," Merry said as she saw him. He almost collapsed with relief. "We got through and the shetani didn't. Hey, you look terrible."

"Then I look exactly the way I feel." Kakombe was right behind her. He carried the shaft of Nafasi's miraculous spear. Oak wondered what had happened to the blade. His own knife and spear were probably contributing to the blaze in the four-wheeler.

She sat down on a fallen log. "I feel like I've swum to Vancouver and back." One hand kept brushing her hair out of her eyes. It kept falling back. "Ever have the feeling you've been dead and buried and just dug up by a pack of dogs?"

Oak looked out at their immolated vehicle. "Anybody seen Olkeloki?"

"We were hoping to find him with you." Merry followed his gaze. "Maybe—maybe he didn't make it through."

Kakombe made a face, spat out a bloody fragment of tooth. "The laibon said it was his lion."

"Yeah. I heard him say that too." To his great surprise, Oak found he was starting to choke up. An unaccustomed tenseness threatened to force tears from his eyes. He hadn't cried even when his father had died a few years back. "He always said everyone had their lion. I guess the size of the lion matches the size of the individual."

Merry sniffed. "I don't see any shetani."

"It is done," Kakombe said with finality. "The laibon did what had to be done. Paasai Leleshwa. He was the wisest among the Maasai. He will be missed in council."

Oak held back his own tears while Merry shed hers. Kakombe looked down at her disapprovingly. "The laibon would not have liked for you to cry over him."

"How the hell do you know?" Angrily she got to her feet, glared up at him as she wiped at her eye. She barely came up to his ribs. "My tears are between me and whoever I'm bawling about." Turning away from him, she walked over to Oak and sobbed into his chest.

When he looked up he found Kakombe staring at him. Their eyes locked for an instant. That was enough, just a look. An important matter had been settled without a word. Kakombe nodded imperceptibly, a thin smile on his face, and then turned away to gaze out across the sand river.

"It does not matter," he murmured to no one in particular. "It would not have worked anyway. Most ilmeet women cannot stand the smell of cattle."

Oak joined the senior warrior in surveying the sand. "I guess we ought to see if there's anything worth salvaging besides ourselves. Be nice to find an intact canteen or calabash."

"Yes," Kakombe agreed. He pointed downriver. "Dry it may appear, but we will find a place where the elephants have dug down to water. We will follow the sand river until it rejoins the flowing Ruaha, then follow the water back to the camp."

Most of the wreck had cooled enough to hunt through, but they found neither calabash nor canteen, and the big water cans that had been strapped to the roof rack were so much shrapnel. They did stumble over Merry's backpack. There wasn't much inside, the contents having been extracted by the rampaging female shetani who had tried to rip Oak's throat out.

Half buried in the sand was a case of engine oil. The box had burned away, but the cans were miraculously intact. Kakombe used his Nafasi knife to punch holes in the top of each can and they let the oil drain out into the sand. Each can would hold half a quart of water, if they could find any. Against Kakombe's protests Oak shouldered the torn but still serviceable backpack. They put the cans inside, along with a few other useful and still unbroken items, and started hiking.

The first elephant well lay only a few hundred yards from the burning car, around a bend in the river. Someone was already drinking from the tepid pool. Mbatian Olkeloki looked up and grinned at them.

Merry ran forward and threw her arms around the old man, nearly knocking him down. She was sobbing all over again, but this time the tears were tears of joy. He tried to disengage himself.

"Please, Merry Sharrow, I am happy to see you too, but I am very tired and cannot support the both of us." She stepped away from him.

"Sorry. It's just that I was . . ." She let the sentence fade. Then her expression changed. Tentatively she reached out and touched the old man's forehead. The skin was taut and cool to the touch and her fingers didn't sink in at all. He smiled at her.

"It will be difficult now to see what the signs and stars portend, but at least there will be something to see."

"I saw you do that," Oak told him, "but I still don't believe it." He stood straight while Kakombe removed the oil cans from the pack and set to washing them out.

"Why not? Everyone possesses that additional perception you perceived as a third eye, my friend. But few people can access it mentally, fewer still physically."

"You knew." Oak stared at him, feeling like a total fool. "You must have known from the beginning that I had only a good left eye and Merry only a good right one. Why didn't you say something? Why didn't you ever mention it?"

"Think now, Joshua Oak. If we had stood together, you and I, in your home city of Washington, D.C., and I had said that in addition to wanting you to accompany me to Africa I was going to need your artificial eye to complete a certain magical Maasai spell, what would your reaction have been? I do not think you would have been more encouraged to help me."

"The lion," Merry said. "What about the lion?"

The old man laughed out loud. Watching him, Oak knew he couldn't be more than eighty years old. Probably not that much. Anything else was nonsense, pure nonsense.

"I expect I made a mistake, Merry Sharrow. I guess that was not my lion after all. If he had been, I would not be here sharing this delicious dirty water with you now. Are you ready, senior warrior?"

Kakombe placed the last of the water cans in Oak's pack and nodded.

"Then come, my friends. This has been a memorable day's work well done, and we have a long walk ahead of us." He took a step forward.

A thin black arm exploded from the sand just to the right of the water hole and the fingers locked tight around Merry's ankle. She let out a high-pitched scream as Oak grabbed her around the waist. The arm retracted, pulling her down into the sand. Then they both fell backward, Merry on top of him.

As they lay there panting hard, Kakombe bent over and yanked the arm out of the ground. No dark fluid oozed from the cut. The limb had been severed and cauterized as cleanly as if by a surgical laser.

"The last of the nightmare." He took the amputated arm from Kakombe and examined it with interest while Oak helped Merry to her feet. "Sometimes a few tiny places are difficult to seal. That is how other shetani slip through into our world one at a time. But this one was only wide enough to let in an arm, and it closed quickly. Paasai Leleshwa." He shrugged.

"What is that, anyway?" Oak asked him.

"It has no literal translation from the Maasai. 'The indescribable color' is the nearest I can come."

"What about all the shetani already in our world?" Merry wanted to know. "Aren't they going to cause trouble?"

"I think not. At least, no more than they ever have. Most of them will scatter and hide, many will perish. It is like the seals who live under the polar ice. The narrower their air holes become, the closer they stay to them. With Paasai Leleshwa we have sealed the shetani's principal air hole. We have interdicted that which refreshes their souls." He held out the severed arm. "Will you have it? It was reaching for you."

She took a step backward. "Are you kidding?" Olkeloki turned and offered it to Oak. "Friend Joshua?"

"Thanks, but it clashes with my decor."

"I will take it, laibon." Olkeloki handed it to the senior warrior, who tucked it into a fold on his torn toga.

"Think that water will last all the way back to the river?" Merry indicated the bulges the water cans made in the remnants of her backpack.

"If not we shall find another water hole. I am more concerned about food. We must have the strength to reach the water." He scanned the near bank. "Perhaps we can find some nuts and fruits."

"Nuts and fruits," she repeated. "God, I could eat a whole impala by myself. Horns and all."

"I would look for a baobab pod to crack," said Kakombe, "but it is late in the season and I fear the baboons have eaten all."

Half an hour later they had to stop to drink. At his rate, Oak thought, they'd have to find another water hole soon. He was lowering one of the cans from his lips when he heard the faint rumble. It came from downriver. As they stood and stared a Land Rover with an extended cab came bouncing around the next bend, heading straight toward them. He tensed, wondering if the friends of the two unlucky poachers had come looking for them. Then he relaxed so much he sat down in the sand.

It was Axel Wolf with a load of tourists from camp.

The Land Rover squealed to a stop a few yards away. Wolf came over to stare at them, shoving his hat back off his forehead. "Now what the bloody hell happened to you people?"

"Had an accident." Oak gestured back upriver. "Rolled her. Must've hit a rock. The tank blew."

"Looks like the lot of you nearly went with it." He was eyeing Oak shrewdly. "Funny, but you didn't strike me as the reckless driver type." Oak favored him with a bland smile.

"How about a lift?"

"We're pretty full up." Wolf indicated the gaggle of sightseers who by now had piled out of the big four-wheeler. "I guess the lady and the old man can ride inside, but you and the moran will have to ride on top."

"No problem."

"The tsetses'll come for you as soon as we start moving. I'll drive as fast as I can but you're still going to get bit."

"For some reason I don't think a few tsetse bites will bother us." He raised his oil can. "Cheers."

"Look, Sherry. Isn't he handsome?"

Oak struggled back to his feet. The women weren't looking in his direction, however. All eyes were on Kakombe. The woman who'd spoken wore shorts which did nothing to flatter her pear-shaped lower body. Her friend was clad in white-hunter-style khakis complete with fake bush hat. She approached Oak, flinched when she got a look at his face.

"What happened to your eye?"

"It's an old injury. Don't let it bother you." He could see that it did but wasn't in the mood to coddle anyone.

She spoke without getting any closer to him than absolutely necessary. "Does he speak English?" She nodded toward Kakombe. "Do you think he'd mind if we took his picture?"

"I'm sure he'll be delighted. But watch out for his spear."

She giggled. Another woman joined them. It was Oak's considered opinion that sequined sunglasses didn't go with safari outfits. He watched as they clustered around the senior warrior, who looked at Olkeloki and muttered darkly in Maasai. The old man replied with what sounded to Oak's ears like a terse lecture. Occasionally the women would glance back at Oak and look away quickly when they saw him returning their stare. Cameras began to click. Kakombe muttered again.

"What did he say?" the first woman asked the laibon.

"He says that you may take all the photos you wish." The old man walked over to whisper to Oak. "What he really wanted to know was if he could boot the big white lady in the backside. He says he has never met such impolite women, not even in America. I told him such an action would complicate our situation unnecessarily, besides which it would be unbecoming for an Alaunoni. We have had enough complications to last us a while."

"Except one." Merry stepped between them, her one good eye darting from Oak to Olkeloki. "Can you marry us? You can perform marriages, I'll bet."

Olkeloki was clearly taken aback. "It is one of a laibon's pleasanter duties, that is true, but would you not prefer to be wedded according to the customs of your own country?"

"We can take care of that later. How about it, Josh?"

He drained the last of the oily water from the can and tossed the empty container aside. "I still don't recall proposing."

"You'd better say yes, and fast." She indicated her belt. "I still have my knife."

"Since I have no choice . . ." He took her hand in his.

"How strange." The women had finished photographing Kakombe, to the senior warrior's great relief. Now they were staring at the trio standing close together in the sand river. The one in the safari hat leaned close to whisper to her companion. "They're each missing an eye. I wonder what happened?"

Her friend peered over the rim of her sequined sunshades. "Maybe they're part of some African cult."

"Look at the way they're holding hands," said the third woman. "Whatever they're doing, you can tell they're in love."

The first woman shrugged, turned a slow circle. "That much I can understand. Can you imagine a more beautiful, peaceful place?"

Epilogue the First

Arkady Dorovskoy dismissed the general and turned to gaze out the window toward St. Basil's. From his office he could see over the Kremlin wall into the city beyond. Things had been quiet for several weeks. No more nerve-wracking incidents, no more sabotage—if sabotage it had been, and not something as yet unexplained. That unprecedented phone connection, for example. He was sure he'd heard a third voice whispering over the line. He shrugged. Impossible, absurd. Not that it mattered. All that mattered was that everyone could breathe again.

There were agricultural difficulties in Kazakhstan, but there were always agricultural difficulties in Kazakhstan. Nothing to blame on outside forces. More problematic was the secret computer network that had been set up by students at the universities in Pskov and Kiev.

We need a good Russian word for "hacker," he told himself solemnly. In order to catch up with the West in computer technology, students and technicians were going to have to be allowed a certain amount of freedom. Tightly monitored, of course.

It didn't matter. Nothing could upset him now. Not with the worst crisis of his administration defused. There would be plenty of time to deal with ordinary, mundane problems. A few extremists in the Politburo were still demanding some kind of reprisals against the Americans, who steadfastly continued to maintain their innocence. Dorovskoy had taken care of that promptly. *No solid evidence indicating complicity, no reprisals.* Let the fanatics chew on that for a while.

To hell with agriculture. What he needed, what Moscow needed, was a little color. Take that dull gray building over there: why not paint a few rainbows on the old stone. Hardly worth a directive, but maybe it was time for a few changes. *These last few days have made all of us more aware of our own mortality. We make the best vanilla ice cream in the world. Why can't we brighten up this ancient city?*

Feeling much better about the state of the world and himself, the Premier left the window and went back to work.

Epilogue the Second

Disgusted with himself, the President of the United States undid his tie and set about redoing it. If he couldn't fix a lousy tie, how the hell was he going to push that education bill through Congress?

He was looking forward to the celebration on the Potomac tonight. There would be fireworks and music and maybe if the Secret Service didn't think they were all booby-trapped he could buy himself a hot dog. For the first time in weeks everyone would be able to relax.

Kennedy had the Cuban missiles, I had this, he thought. Geary and the rest of the hard-liners in the cabinet were feeling pretty good about themselves, convinced they'd broken a complex Soviet espionage and sabotage network by not backing down on their threats. Weaver knew better. When the moment of crisis had finally come, both sides had turned away out of mutual respect for each other—and out of mutual fear. Sources now hinted that the Soviet hierarchy was half convinced a third party had been responsible for all the trouble. That jibed neatly with the CIA's own most recent reports. Working together, sooner or later the two governments would discover who was responsible. Initial suggestions pointed to the Albanians. That made sense to both sides. Everyone knew the Albanians were crazier than Stalinist bedbugs.

All that mattered was that the flash point had never been reached.

Cooperation in hunting down the cause held out the promise of cooperation in other areas, Geary and his clique of rabid anti-reds notwithstanding. Meanwhile he could get back to the business of running the country. That education bill promised to be a real barn burner up on the Hill. Not to mention the matter of renewed price supports for Midwest grain.

We sell the Egyptians surplus wheat by underwriting Kansas exports, and that enables the Egyptians to lower the price of *their* wheat on the world market, thus forcing us to increase price supports for our farmers so they can continue to compete—against themselves. Hell of a world. Whoever called economics a science deserved to be horsewhipped. You might as well put a witch doctor or something in charge of the Federal Reserve.

"Paul?" He glanced to his left, having almost mastered the stubborn tie. Jennine stood in the entrance to the dressing room. His wife looked ravishing, which didn't surprise him. She'd been ravishing on the day he'd met her, and despite the pressures of Washington life she'd managed to stay that way ever since. Every hostess in the city envied the First Lady.

"I'll be finished here in a second," he told her.

"Could you give me a hand with something first, sugar?"

He sighed and turned away from the mirror, leaving the tie triumphant for at least another minute. "What is it? Button trouble?" He followed her into the bedroom.

"No. It's probably nothing." She smiled apologetically. "Don't worry. Colonel Sherwood will get us to the stands in time for you to make your speech."

Every time she smiled at him like that it took him back twenty years. "Then what's up?"

"Well, I'm not sure, Paul." She sounded a touch less than her usual completely confident self. "Like I said, it's probably nothing. I'm just being silly." She knelt and lifted the handwoven cotten spread. "But I could've sworn I saw something moving under the bed."

The author wishes to thank the following people:

Rashidi of Morogoro, for his insights.

The manager of the Ngorngoro Hotel, who gave us extra blankets.

The Ugandan students, who should be running Kampala, at least.

Kalalumbe, for the cocoa, conversation, and Cape buffalo filets.

Thomas Nafasi of Lindi, Tanzania, for his extraordinary sculpture.

The foxes of Ruaha.

The lionesses of Ngorngoro, who got up and formed a picket line for us.

All the people of East Africa: black, brown, white, and in-between, but most especially the Maasai and in particular the Maasai of Mayer's Ranch Manyatta. I hope their Alaunoni enjoys his Frisbee.